EVERYBODY'S SOMEBODY

BERYL KINGSTON

ENDEAVOURINK

AN ENDEAVOUR INK PAPERBACK

This paperback edition published in 2017
by Endeavour Ink

Endeavour Ink is an imprint of Endeavour Press Ltd
Endeavour Press, 85-87 Borough High Street,
London, SE1 1NH

ISBN 978-1-911445-45-6

Typeset in Garamond 11.5/15.5 pt by
Palimpsest Book Production Ltd, Falkirk, Stirlingshire

Printed and bound in Great Britain by
Clays Ltd, St Ives plc

www.endeavourpress.com

WITHDRAWN

Beryl Kingston was born in Tooting in 1931 and was evacuated during the war. She studied at King's College London, qualified as a teacher and headed an English department. She has been a published author since 1980 and is a self-confessed 'political animal', taking part in street demonstrations and protests. She was also a beauty queen in 1947!

PRAISE FOR BERYL KINGSTON:

'A new novel by the warm and observant Beryl Kingston is not to be missed. Each one is special' – Elizabeth Buchan, bestselling author of *The New Mrs Clifton*

'Beryl Kingston understands how to weave dialogue, character, theme and a thumping love affair into unity' – *Sunday Times*

'Warm-hearted . . . bags of energy bringing a host of lovable people to life' – *Mail on Sunday*

'Beryl Kingston writes with such a lovely light-handed touch it is impossible not to warm to her novels' – *Historical Novel Society*

'Travel through the early twentieth century and see history unfold through the fierce and caring eyes of a woman in love' – Emily Murdoch, historical romance author of the *Conquered Hearts and Seasons of Love* series

Table of Contents

Prologue

It was very quiet in the gallery, so quiet that the class instinctively tiptoed into the room, glancing up at the vaulted roof and gazing at the great works lining the walls, too awed to speak. Some of them had never been to a national art gallery before, even though they were eighteen and studying painting and sculpture; others had visited local art shows but had never faced anything on this scale. For this was a place built to daunt and impress. Silence swirled about the elaborate moulding in the high ceiling, was absorbed by the richness of the red flock wallpaper, drifted reverently over the great works of art. Even the attendant was caught up in the stillness, sitting motionless on his uncomfortable chair beside the door, unsmiling as a statue.

When their tutor spoke, her voice brayed into the silence like a trumpet call. 'Now this,' she said, stopping beside a very large canvas, 'is one of Gerard de Silva's most famous works. Gather round.'

They shuffled into an obedient circle, feeling embarrassed by the noise she was making, and gazed at the painting.

The tutor moved into her spiel. 'You will observe,' she said in her lecturing voice, 'the technique de Silva used in the painting of the face and hands. We were talking about it yesterday. Anyone?'

The group shuffled and most of them looked at the floor to avoid her gaze, but one boy offered an answer, tentatively.

'The puddle of paint?'

'The puddle of paint,' the tutor said, with satisfaction. 'If you look closely you will see where the first 'skin', as he called it, has been applied. Note the highlights of blue and green. Note also that the portrait is almost entirely composed of a pale, sandy brown and cream, which gives unity. Always important in portraiture.'

Her class looked up at her, feeling more at ease now that the first question had been asked and answered, and one of the girls ventured a question of her own. It took some doing because she was excessively shy, with a trick of keeping her head down and avoiding eye contact.

'Who is the sitter?' she said. 'He looks familiar.'

'As well he should, Tiffany,' the tutor said, smiling at her. 'It's Lawrence of Arabia, the great T E Lawrence who drove the Turks out of Arabia in 1918, so, as you will understand, a palette of sand yellow and cream is particularly appropriate. Now we move on.'

'Who's the woman in red?' Tiffany whispered to her best friend, who was another West Indian called Jasmine.

Jasmine gazed round the room. There was nobody else there, except them and the statuesque attendant, and certainly not a woman in red.

'On the wall. Bit further along,' Tiffany whispered.

There wasn't time to say anything more because the tutor was walking towards the next two canvases.

'Now here,' she said, standing between two painted figures, 'we have two contrasting portraits, which we will examine in detail. The seated gentleman to my right was a very great man. His name was Sir Anthony Eden and he was Prime Minister from 1955. You will note the quiet confidence of his expression, beautifully observed, and the way the highlights used for his dark hair are echoed in that elegant moustache. A picture that radiates calm and assuredness. The man on my left is Keir Hardie, who was a rabid left-winger and very obviously working class. Observe the rough cloth of his coat and how well it has been depicted. Note the frayed edge here and the unkempt nature of his beard, a certain wildness in the eye, sepia and purple highlights. His use of colour is truly admirable, as you will agree. Examine the difference in the brush strokes.'

Her class duly examined the difference, making copious notes to prove how hard they were working, while she gazed at their bent heads with happy satisfaction. Finally, feeling she had given them sufficient time for note taking, she sounded her trumpet and called them to order. 'Any questions?'

The two girls had been gazing across the room at the woman in red. 'Who is the sitter in that portrait?' Jasmine asked.

'One of his models, I dare say,' the tutor told her, vaguely. 'He kept several models over the years. An interesting portrait, however, because of his use of such a dominant colour. We will examine it, if you like. It is a good example of his technique. You will note that this model has a strong, dark hair colour to offset the richness of all that red. Again the puddle of paint. Any comments?'

Tiffany lifted her head to ask a question of her own, as that seemed to be permissible. 'Is the sitter named?' she asked. 'She's got a very strong face.'

The tutor consulted her catalogue. 'It's called *Rosie in Autumn*,' she said, 'but there doesn't seem to be anything else about her. Nobody of consequence anyway. He probably picked her because of her hair and her colouring. You will observe that the basic palette here is alizarin, vermilion, ochre and bronze. The fire is the most dominant element in the picture – apart from the standing figure of course. You will observe that there are highlights of red and ochre in the mirror here, the fire irons, those glass ornaments, and here in the skin tones of the model. All in all, it's a bit loud for our modern taste but skilfully done nevertheless. See if you can analyse the mixture that would have been used in this puddle of paint.'

Her students examined the highlights and made notes, all except for Tiffany who was looking at the expression on the model's face and glancing at the rows of huge portraits to her left. 'There's three more of her a bit further along,' she whispered to Jasmine.

The tutor was looking at her watch. Her pupils seemed to have stopped making notes and she didn't want them to lose interest or they'd start chatting and horsing around. Some of the boys were rather too prone to horseplay. Raging hormones of course, but inappropriate in a public place, especially now there were other visitors arriving. 'It is half past three,' she said, in her loudest voice. 'I will give you an hour's free time to examine whatever other portraits you might like to see. You may explore the other galleries if you wish. There are some of de Silva's lesser works in the adjoining gallery, townscapes and so forth, and the gypsies he painted for chocolate boxes. Heaven only knows what he thought he was doing to take on such a commission when he was such a fabulous portrait painter. But there you are, there's no accounting for artistic temperament. Anyway, you might like to look at them while you're here. One hour mind. Make sure you are all back here at half past four.' Then she gave them her stern smile and set them loose.

The wild horses were off like a shot, charging away from her control, of course. But the girls were drifting slowly.

She noticed that her two, nice, quiet West Indian girls were heading for the three companion portraits to *Autumn*, and smiled her approval. Time for a cup of tea, she thought, and headed for the café.

'Well it's obviously her,' Tiffany said. 'Even if he doesn't say so.' The three great canvases were labelled '*Spring '23*', '*Summer '26*' and '*Winter '28*'. 'She's very pretty. I like that coat.'

They were standing in front of *Winter*, which was a study of their model, bright-eyed and red-cheeked with cold, skating on a frozen lake with two little girls beside her. She was taking long confident strides and seemed to be smiling to herself and she was wearing a long sky-blue coat with white fur cuffs and collar and a huge fur hat.

Jasmine said she preferred *Spring*, which showed their model in a garden full of daffodils and jonquils holding a trug overflowing with flowers on her arm and wearing a straw hat and a long gentle-looking dress in some creamy material, patterned all over with tiny red, white and yellow flowers.

But it was *Summer* that was the most interesting, for this time he'd painted her on a beach in a bathing suit, sitting on a breakwater, dabbling her feet in a rock pool and smiling at a group of small, suntanned children who were building a sandcastle beside her.

'I'll bet those two in the yellow cossies are hers,' Jasmine said. 'They're dressed the same and the bigger one's just like her. All that dark hair.'

'She looks happy,' Tiffany said, gazing at her. 'And sort of confident, as if she's enjoying herself. Strong. Happy in her skin.'

'Ah, but don't forget she's *nobody of consequence*,' Jasmine said, imitating the tutor's sneering voice. 'We're supposed to be admiring the portraits of the great.'

'I don't care if she had "*consequence*" or not,' Tiffany said. 'She looks strong. And if you think about it, she must have been somebody. Everybody's somebody. I'd like to have met her.'

Chapter One

'Oh, when's he comin', Ma?' the child asked, drumming her fingertips against the window sill. 'He should ha' been here long since. I been packed an' ready for *ages*. What's he doin'?' She leant out of the open window, standing on tiptoe and craning her neck to look as far along the lane as she could, her face burnished by the early morning sun, her tangle of thick dark hair falling across her cheek. 'Oh come on, Pa!'

Her mother sighed. She was churning butter in the scullery and was hot and sticky with sweat. 'He'll be here presently,' she said, pushing the damp hair out of her eyes. 'You just got to have a bit a' patience, tha's all. You can't rush them ol' cows.'

But she was wasting her breath. It was no good suggesting patience to her Rosie. She was the most headstrong, impatient child she'd ever known in her life and so unlike her brother and sisters there'd been times when she'd found herself wondering how on earth she'd ever come to breed such a child and had thought darkly about changelings and fairy children swapped in the cradle. It wasn't to be wondered at when all was said an' done. For a start off, she didn't even look the same as the other three. They were pale-skinned, brown-haired, gentle children, round-faced and wide-eyed with soft mouths and stocky bodies like hers and John's. Biddable children. Rosie had always been a child apart, a child who went her own way, not biddable at all. You only had to glance at her to see that, with all that unruly hair and those bold brown eyes and that determined chin. Look at her now, twelve years old yesterday and itching to be off to Arundel to start work. It wasn't natural. She'd seen girls a-plenty going off to work during her thirty-four years in Binderton and they'd all been worried sick about it, poor little things, pale-faced and withdrawn, even weepy, some of them, not wanting to leave their mothers. Never raring to go, never hanging out the window with impatience, never eager.

'He's here!' Rosie shouted, jumping away from the window. 'He's comin'!'

Maggie Goodison sighed. 'Put your bonnet on,' she said. Then she set the churn aside, left her stool and ambled to the backdoor to fetch the others. 'Your sister's goin',' she called. 'Leave the hoeing, Tommy. You can do that later on. Come an' kiss her goodbye.'

They came in at once in their obedient way, young Tess with Baby Edie sitting astride her hip, Tommy wiping his hands on his breeches and shaking his hair out of his eyes, all of them blinking as their eyes accommodated to the darkness indoors after the blaze of sunlight in the vegetable patch. Rosie swooped across the room at once to throw her arms round them and kiss them and the baby held out her arms calling to her big sister, 'Ro-Ro! Ro-Ro!' and was seized and kissed and tossed in the air until she squealed. Then Tommy and Tess kissed her and said, 'Come back soon,' while their mother stood apart feeling rather left out of it. And in the middle of all the noise, their father strode through the door in his white smock coat and his old straw hat, bringing the smell of the cowshed with him, filling the room with his comfortable bulky presence and grinning all over his face. 'Ready for the off?' he called to Rosie.

'Ready an' waitin',' Rosie said and she picked up her canvas bag and skipped towards him, swinging it in her hand. 'You been *ages*, Pa.'

'Don't I get no kiss goodbye then?' Maggie said.

Rosie looked momentarily smitten. Then she rushed to her mother and flung her arms about her neck. 'Course you do, Ma,' she said, kissing her lovingly.

'Now mind you do everything they say,' Maggie told her, holding her by the shoulders and looking at her earnestly. 'An' don't go answerin' back. The gentry don't like answerin' back. Just say, "Yes sir," and, "No sir." An' mind your P's and Q's. An' don't forget to curtsey. Are you listenin' to me?'

Rosie shook her shoulders free. 'It's all right, Ma,' she said. 'I shan't forget.'

'Yes, well, I know you,' Maggie said and sighed.

Rosie kissed her again. 'Don't look so sad,' she said. 'I'll be all right, truly I will. I got my pencil and paper what you gave me yesterday, an' my new jersey what you knitted, an' my bonnet – see? – an' I shall see you again ever so soon. Be back 'fore you knows it.'

Then she was off, running light-footed out of the door. The rest of them trooped after her and stood in a subdued little group beside the cottage to watch as she climbed into the cart and turned to wave at them and blow kisses. Then their father clicked to his mare and their journey began. Tess held her mother's hand for comfort as they watched the cart joggle away.

'She'll come back soon, Ma,' she said.

'She'll come back the fourth Sunday in Lent,' Maggie told her dourly as the cart disappeared round the bend.

Tess's face fell. 'That's a long time,' she said. 'That's months.'

'Yes,' Maggie said shortly. 'It is. But it's no good sayin'. There's nothing we can do about it.' Then she straightened her spine and took a deep breath. 'We must get on,' she said. 'It's no good standin' around. There's work to be done. Butter don't make itself.'

*

Out in the fields, the grey mare plodded steadily eastward, flicking her ears against the flies. The path they were taking ran between familiar fields of new green corn, the farm sat in its hollow to the left of them, the River Lavant trickled past them on their right, its waters polished white by the sunlight, the long familiar hill of the Trundel rose before them, blue-green against the clear sky. But Rosie didn't notice any of it. Although she wouldn't have wanted her father to know it, she was feeling too anxious.

'Will it take long to get there?' she asked.

'Seven miles takes a bit a' time,' her father said. 'You'll see it up ahead presently. Huge great place it is. Up on a hill. Mind you write to us. There's a good gel. We'll be wantin' to know how you gets along.'

Rosie said, 'Yes, Pa.' But she was thinking what a waste of time it would be to send letters to him when he couldn't read. Ma would do her best because she'd had a bit of schooling but even she found it hard to make out the words. They'd probably have to get Tommy to read it out loud to them and he wouldn't be much good at it either because he thought learning was useless and said so frequently. 'I mean for to say our Rosie, you don't need to read an' write an' that to look after the cows.'

The miles plodded past; now and then the mare flicked her ears; once, a skylark rose from the young corn and trilled into the sky; once her Pa farted lengthily. There was no sign of the castle. Only the dusty track, the blue sky and the long low slope of the downs.

And then suddenly and without any warning at all there was a very loud and very alarming noise behind them. Her father reined in the mare at once and turned to see what it was.

It was the most extraordinary thing they'd ever seen in their lives, a beautiful bright red carriage travelling along the track towards them making a loud chugging chuffing noise and *with no horses pulling it*. Neither of them could believe their eyes but there it was, large as life, twice as bright and getting closer to them with every second. It made Rosie think of the stagecoach she'd seen in Lavant two years ago. It was the same sort of shape and the same sort of colour only cleaner and brighter and it had the same huge white wheels, only they were cleaner and brighter too. But there the similarities ended. It wasn't just that there were no horses. There was no coachman, no whip, no lantern on a pole, no horn, nothing at the front of it at all, just two big brass lanterns sticking out like great round eyes. And there weren't crowds of people inside the thing either, all squashed up close together, just one grand lady in a fine blue coat and a huge hat tied in place by a long scarf and, beside her, a gentlemen in a tweed suit and a deerstalker hat, looking serious. They were sitting on a high-backed settee, upholstered in black leather, and the gentleman was holding onto another big wheel which rose out of the floor towards him. It was such an amazing apparition that for once in her life, Rosie Goodison was too astonished to speak. She just watched with her mouth open as the car swerved to avoid them (how did it do that?) and then chugged cheerfully alongside. The lady smiled and waved her gloved hand as if she was stirring the air, the gentlemen gave a brief nod, the car coughed and then they were past and heading off along the empty track.

'Oh Pa!' Rosie said. 'Tha's the most mar . . .'

But at that point, the mare, who'd been shivering her flanks and showing the whites of her eyes in terror, suddenly took off and galloped full tilt along the track with John pulling on the reins with all his strength, as the cart rocked and threw him about, and calling to her to calm her, 'Whoa, my beauty! Whoa there! Whoa!' It took several dangerous minutes before she stopped and then it was only because the rear wheel of the cart had racketed into the ditch.

John jumped down at once and ran to her head to stroke her and calm her and Rosie climbed down after him, her heart beating most uncomfortably. What a thing to happen! Poor old Snowy! And she'd been going along so steadily too. 'Is she all right, Pa?' she asked.

'She'll do,' John said, rubbing the mare's nose. 'Won't you, old gel?'

Rosie stood beside him as the mare blew and shivered and wondered how they would get the cart back on the track again. It was horribly lopsided.

'She'll be all right presently,' her father said. 'Then you can hold her head while I get that wheel out. Lead her when I call "walk on".'

It took considerable heaving and straining and, by the end of it, John was blowing almost as hard as the mare but the cart was upright on the path and their obedient animal walked as soon as she was told.

'Dratted contraption!' John said as he took up the reins. 'They ought to be ashamed a' theirselves. Climb aboard, our Rosie.'

Rosie climbed and settled beside him as their rural silence eased back upon them. His face was so stormy and bad-tempered she felt she had to say something to soothe him, the way her mother would have done. 'No harm done though Pa,' she encouraged. That wonderful red carriage had been so breathtaking she didn't like to hear it being described as a contraption. 'We're all right now, ent we?'

'That's as mebbe,' her father growled. 'Could ha' been serious though. They wasn't to know. Roaring about like that. Takin' up all the road. Nasty noisy thing. 'Tweren't nat'rul.'

'I thought it were lovely,' Rosie said. 'All that colour an' all, an' those great wheels. Like a stagecoach. An' did you see the seats? They was lovely. You think how comfy they'd be. When I'm grown up, I'm going to ride about in a carriage just like that.'

'Don't talk daft, gel,' her father said. 'They won't let you.'

'Who won't?'

'The people what owns 'em. That's who. Rich people.'

'They might. Or I might be rich mesself by then.'

Her father looked at her eager face and smiled pityingly. 'That ent the way the world goes, gel,' he said. 'The rich stays rich and the poor does the best we can.'

16

'That ent fair,' Rosie said passionately and she made up her mind that things would be different for her or she'd want to know the reason why.

'Soon be there now,' her father said.

And sure enough, after another twenty minutes or so, they rounded a bend in the lane and there it was rising above the trees, Arundel Castle, even more huge and impressive than she'd imagined it, its crenelated stone walls and rounded tower, honey coloured in the spring sunshine. It was so big and so splendid, it made Rosie feel small and insignificant.

'Oh Pa!' she said.

'You'll be fine there, our Rosie,' he said, feeling he ought to comfort her. 'They'll look after you.'

But she sat quietly beside him and didn't speak, which worried him because it was unlike her to be quiet, and the mare took them steadily on, past a row of cottages like their own and across a bridge over a wide green river until they came to a halt under the walls of the castle. There was a very grand door to their right, with a round tower on either side it.

'That ent the one we're to use,' John said. 'Tradesmen's entrance is up the hill. We'll tether her down here. No need to wear her out wi' climbin'. Tha's a mortal steep hill.'

He tethered the mare to one of the posts that lined the road, and Rosie stroked her nose and said goodbye to her. Then she took her bag out of the cart and she and her father toiled up the hill together. It was a very long hill and very steep, with grand shops on either side of it and lots of grand people coming and going and a huge inn halfway up and a baker's shop with its windows full of loaves and pastries that were a temptation even to look at, although they didn't stop to look, naturally, but just climbed on, further and further up, until her calves were aching with effort. And at last they reached the top of the hill and another part of the castle wall where there was another grand gate so large and tall that she felt daunted all over again. But her father was pulling the bell and the door was opening and a porter in a very grand uniform was standing in front of them asking what their business was and it was time for her to walk into the castle and start her new life.

'Ah yes,' the porter said, when he'd been told who she was, 'I been expecting you. If you'll just follow me I'll show you the way.' And he stood aside to let her through the gate.

Whatever else, she wasn't going to let her father see she was afraid. That wouldn't have done at all. She'd made up her mind a long time ago, when she saw Milly crying and clinging to her mother, that when the time came for her to go into service, she would go boldly and without carrying on. She straightened her shoulders and stuck out her chin, found a bright smile for her father and kissed him goodbye as if she hadn't a care in the world, even though her heart was beating much too hard. Then she followed the porter.

They walked along a neat gravel path that curved through a bewilderment of shrubs and bushes until they reached the castle walls and a short flight of stone steps that lead them into a small dark hall, with high stone walls and stone flags under their feet.

'Wait there,' the porter said and walked up another flight of stairs and disappeared.

Rosie stood in the stony silence with her bag at her feet and waited obediently, feeling overawed and a bit too aware that she was only twelve years old and had no experience of the world beyond Binderton at all. It seemed a very long time before the porter's boots appeared on the stairs again and he rejoined her, followed by a portly lady in a fashionable dress of lavender silk, with puffed sleeves like the posh ladies were wearing in the town and a white cap, frilled and beribboned and stiff with starch. She had a very stern face and she looked down at Rosie for a long time before she said, 'Rosemary Goodison.'

Rosie didn't know whether she was supposed to curtsey or not so she just nodded and said, 'Yes, ma'am.'

'Follow me,' the lady said and led the way up another flight of stairs into a long, dark corridor. The walls were decorated by deer's heads, nailed to wooden plaques and hung as though they were three dimensional pictures. They had such soft faces and such reproachful eyes that Rosie felt quite sorry for them but she was brisked past before she could take a really good look.

'It is nearly time for the staff luncheon,' the lady said, turning in at the next door. 'You will eat here – I daresay you're hungry after your journey – and then one of the maids will take you up to the nursery, where you will be given your uniform and your duties will be explained to you.'

It was a very long room with high windows on one side of it and an enormous table set in the middle. Two servants in grey cotton dresses and starched white caps and aprons were busy laying the table, one from each end, working steadily from chair to chair with long baskets full of cutlery over their arms. One of them looked up and smiled. So Rosie smiled back. And just as the girl set her last knife, fork and spoon on the tablecloth, all three doors were opened and the rest of the servants streamed into the room. There were so many of them that Rosie wondered where they would all sit and they were all in uniforms of one kind or another and looked very smart. Watching them, she was acutely aware that her own clothes were horribly patched and faded and felt out of place among so much clean linen and so many white aprons. But there wasn't time to think about it because an obviously important man had walked in and was taking his place at the head of the table and he'd no sooner arrived before the kitchen maids carried in two huge pies that were so hot they were steaming visibly and set one at each end of the table. Seconds later everybody in the room was standing behind a chair. Rosie looked round in a bit of a panic, uncertain what to do, saw a chair that had no one standing behind it and ran to fill the space. Mr Importance nodded, put his hands together and said a ponderous grace, then there was a loud scraping of chairs as they all sat down and he and the housekeeper, who had taken her position at the other end of the table began to cut the pie. Rabbit, Rosie thought and waited happily for her portion of it.

It was a sumptuous pie and must have contained several rabbits because everybody got a joint and a good helping of sliced potato topped with chopped parsley and plenty of vegetables and gravy. Rosie ate every mouthful that was put on her plate, pie crust, chopped carrots, peas, onions, capers, ham, rabbit, gravy and all. And that wasn't the end of the feast for when the plates had been cleared, the kitchen maids carried them out and returned with two enormous roly-poly puddings, oozing treacle. Pa was right, she thought, surreptitiously licking her spoon so as not to waste a drop. Hadn't he said she'd eat well?

When the meal was over the important man rose, nodded at them all and left, which seemed to be the sign for everybody to get back to their work. Rosie went to stand by the window out of the way of all those moving bodies, noticing that the housekeeper was talking to a pale girl in a blue uniform and a ruffled cap and apron. That must be the one who's going to take me up to the nursery, she thought, and, as the conversation was obviously going on for a bit longer, she looked out of the window so as not to be seen staring.

There was a courtyard below her, with a neat green lawn circled by wide gravel paths and there, right underneath the window, was the red carriage, fairly gleaming in the sunshine and looking even grander than it had done when it was in the lane. She was staring at it when she became aware that the pale girl was standing beside her.

'I'm Maisie,' the girl said. 'Mrs Tenbury says to take you to the nursery.'

'Thank 'ee kindly,' Rosie said, being careful to be polite.

Maisie grinned. 'I'm the other nursemaid,' she said. 'It's not a bad life, all in all. The grub's good. We've only got the one baby to look after at the moment but there's another one coming in a week or two so we'll be run off our feet then, what with nappies an' all. I 'spect that's why you been hired. What's your name?'

Rosie told her and, because she couldn't resist it, took a last sneaking look at the red carriage.

'That's a motor car,' Maisie said. 'Bet you never seen one a' them before.'

'I seen that one on the road this very morning,' Rosie told her. 'It drove past us.'

'Fancy,' Maisie said. 'Come on. I got to take you up to the nursery.'

*

John Goodison was tired when he finally got back to Binderton but he gave Snowy a good rub down and put her in the field before he went in for his dinner.

'I thought you was never coming,' Maggie said, lifting a covered plate from the oven. 'I kep' it hot for you.'

'It was a fair ol' journey,' John said, taking up his knife and fork. 'You got any pickle?'

The pickle was produced and then Maggie asked the question she'd been holding back until he was settled at the table. 'Did she go off all right?'

'Right as rain,' her husband said. 'Not a peep out of her. You know our Rosie. She don't worry about nothin'.'

Chapter Two

After all those forbidding stone walls and those long dreary corridors, the nursery made a pleasant change to Rosie Goodison. It was up on the third floor and full of light, with a pretty wallpaper brightening the walls, a carpet gentling the floor and long white curtains to soften the windows. All the furniture was painted white too, nursery table, high-backed chairs, dresser, toy box and all, except for a rocking horse that was standing in the corner looking so lifelike it wouldn't have surprised her if it had kicked up its heels and galloped out of the room.

There was a discontented-looking young woman sitting at the table, wearing the same blue and white uniform as Maisie and jabbing a spoonful of bread and milk at a baby girl, who was turning her head away from it and scowling.

'You took your time,' the young woman said, glaring at

Maisie. 'I thought you was never coming back. Is this the new 'un?'

Maisie introduced them, briefly. 'Rosie, Janet.' And Janet grunted and turned her attention to the little girl, jabbing the spoon at her again. 'Eat it, when I tell you, you naughty little thing,' she said.

The baby stood up for herself. 'Shan't!' she said. 'Don' like it.' Her face was dark with distress under her lace cap and she was squirming in her high chair.

'What's her name?' Rosie said.

Janet scowled at the child. 'Disobedience,' she said. 'I never knew such a child.'

But Maisie introduced her properly. 'She's Rachel,' she said. 'Aren't you Rachel? I don't think she likes it, Janet.'

'She'll do as she's told,' Janet said, scowling worse than ever. 'If I say she's to eat it, she's to eat it.'

The baby turned down her mouth ready to battle on but at that moment a kitchen maid arrived carrying a tray covered by a table napkin. 'Brought yer dinner,' she said to Janet and looked at the dish of congealing bread and milk. 'She finished with that?'

'Yes,' Rosie said firmly. 'It's gone cold.'

Janet was uncovering her meal. 'And whose fault's that?' she said. 'Rabbit pie is it?'

Rosie handed the remains of the cold bread and milk to the kitchen maid, lifted the baby out of her chair and set her on the floor. 'What does she do now?' she asked Maisie.

'Rides on the horse sometimes,' Maisie said. 'Plays with her bricks. She likes her bricks. Only I'm supposed to be showing you your uniform.'

Rosie could see the bricks from where she stood, all neatly packed in a little box. She bent down and took the baby's hand, very gently the way she'd done with the babies at home. This part of the job was going to be easy. 'Shall we build a little house?' she said.

The baby nodded so they took her and her bricks into the next room and made a quick escape, leaving Janet to stuff her face with pie.

It was another white room with two beds, a small china chamber pot, a washstand with a basin, jug, and soap dish, and standing on either side of the fireplace, a neat white cot and a crib, hung about with embroidered muslin.

'This is where we sleep,' Maisie said, when she'd shut the door behind them. 'That's Baby's cot an' that's the crib for the new baby what's coming an' this is your bed and that's mine. Janet's got a room of her own. We could take it turn an' turn about to look after baby in the night if you like. She's good most a' the time but she gets restless sometimes.'

Rosie sat on the carpet with Rachel and took the bricks out of their box. 'How old is she?'

'Three in June.'

'No wonder she don't like bread an' milk,' Rosie said. 'Our babies was eating all sorts by the time they was three. We'll have to smuggle her in some roly-poly. She'd like that. We'll see if Hoity-toity leaves any.'

The name made Maisie laugh. 'You'd better not let her hear you if you're goin' to call her that,' she warned. 'She's got a sharp tongue on her.'

'I seen that,' Rosie said, grinning. 'Like a razor. It's a wonder she don't cut her mouth to shreds.' Then she turned her attention to the more important things about this new life. 'When do they pay us, Maisie? They told Ma it was £8 a year.'

'Quarterly,' Maisie told her. 'At the end of the month. Next time's the end a' June. An' we gets a half day off every week starting at three o'clock. I 'spect Mrs Tenbury'll tell what day you got when she sees you tomorrow. We takes that turn an' turn about too, like going to the hall for our dinner. It'll be Hoity-toity's turn to go down tomorrow an' we shall be up here.'

'Good,' Rosie said. 'Then we'll give our Rachel some pie or whatever it is and see how she likes it. That'll be good won't it Rachel?'

Maisie giggled. 'I'd better show you your uniform,' she said, 'bein' that's what I'm s'posed to be doin'.'

It was folded up in the clothes press and was exactly the same as Maisie's, a pale blue cotton dress, a white cotton apron with ruffles round the bib and a ruffled cap. She even had a new pair of shoes and some garters, as well as several pairs of woollen stockings and a collection of bodices and drawers. 'I shall be quite the lady in all this,' she said, when she was dressed.

That afternoon they took their baby for a toddle through

the gardens, where she picked the head off a tulip and fell in the vegetable patch twice, once by accident and once deliberately, and enjoyed both tumbles very much, especially when Rosie picked her up and tickled her and told her she was a bad lot.

Maisie was lost in admiration. 'You're ever so good with her,' she said, as they walked back towards the castle.

Being admired raised Rosie's spirits, which was just as well because, although she hadn't said anything, she'd been feeling rather down after Hoity-toity's disapproval. 'I'm used to babies,' she said. 'I looked after my brother and sisters.' That wasn't strictly true, because she'd only been three when Tommy was a baby, but she'd looked after Tess and Edie every day. 'It comes natural when you do it a lot.'

'You know what to say,' Maisie said, rather mournfully. 'An' how to pick her up an' get her to do things. You've got a real knack for it. I wish I could do it.'

'Didn't you have no brothers and sisters then?'

'They was all older than me,' Maisie explained. 'I mean I never looked after them or nothing. They're all out at work now. I was the baby.'

They'd reached the steps. 'Oh well, that accounts,' Rosie said, picking Rachel up and carrying her into the castle. 'Tell you what, watch what I do and do the same. It's easy when you know how. I done the same as my Ma. Now then Rachel, can you manage these ol' stairs d'you think? I'll hold your hand.'

Which she did, leading the child on until they were

standing in the long corridor, where the gentle deer still gazed in soft-eyed reproach above their heads.

There was a strong smell of baking wafting towards them from the other end of the corridor. Maisie sniffed it happily. 'Sponge cake for tea,' she said.

That was a surprise to Rosie. 'Tea?' she said.

'They brings us tea in the afternoons,' Maisie explained. 'Pot a' tea, milk an' sugar, bread an' butter, cake. All laid out lovely. It's our treat.'

'Um,' Rosie said, thinking about it. 'Does Rachel get any?'

'She has a cup a' warm milk. They make it ever so nice for her.'

'But not cake?'

'No. Janet says she's not to have cake.'

Rosie snorted. 'Ho, does she!' she said. 'We'll see about that.'

Her face looked so determined that Maisie was alarmed. 'Don't say I told you,' she began. 'I mean for to say . . .'

But Rosie had settled Rachel on her hip again and was walking towards the kitchen. She'd been secretly afraid of Janet's sharp tongue and this was a chance to fight back.

'You can't go in there,' Maisie warned, trailing after her. 'We're not allowed. Mr Rossi don't like it. He's ever so fierce. Oh Rosie, please don't!'

She was wasting her breath because Rosie was already opening the kitchen door and walking through it. It was a nasty moment for poor Maisie because she knew she would have to follow her, otherwise Janet would give her what for. But it took several seconds of fluttering hesitation before she could pluck up enough courage to walk in.

They were in an enormous room that seemed to be full of women in grey dresses and cream-coloured caps and aprons, and men entirely in white, all rushing about doing things. There were three huge ovens on one wall, with a row of kettles steaming on the hobs in front of them and in the middle of the room a long table where a group of women were cutting up bread and arranging little cakes on paper doylies and setting out cups and saucers on pretty trays. And standing at the far end of the table, watching over them, was a man in a dazzling white apron and a floppy white hat. He had such an air of authority about him that Rosie knew at once that he had to be Mr Rossi. She settled the baby on her hip, lifted her head, stuck out her chin and walked towards him.

The noise in the kitchen shushed to silence as she walked and Mr Rossi's face looked more thunderous with every step she took. It was making her heart jump to look at him, for he really was a stern-looking man with all that thick dark hair curling out from under his hat and those sharp brown eyes and that great black moustache curving above his mouth like the wings of some fierce bird. But she'd started this now and she had to go on with it. She couldn't back down. She walked until they were an arm's length away from one another and the kitchen was completely quiet.

'What-a this?' he said, glaring at her. 'Who this person? You don' hear what I say? I don' allow other staff in my kitchen. I make-a my point quite clear. No other staff!'

Rosie planted her feet firmly in the flagstones and stood boldly in front of him, 'If you please Mr Rossi, sir,' she said, keeping her voice steady with an effort. 'I'm Rosie Goodison from the nursery, sir. I come to ask you please, if you will send up some cake for Rachel today, what she'd like very much.' And she looked down at the baby, who smiled up at her rapturously.

'Cake is it?' he said. 'You think I bother my 'ead with cake?'

'Yes sir. If you please sir.'

He looked at her for such a long time that she was afraid he would see that she was shaking. But when he spoke again it was in a gentler voice. 'What you sayin', eh? Don' she get no cake when I send it?'

Rosie heard Maisie drawing in her breath and flashed a quick eye message at her that she was to keep quiet. Then she turned back to Mr Rossi and tried to be diplomatic. 'Not always, Mr Rossi sir,' she said. 'But if you was to send up a plate special for her, she would then.'

He put a finger over his red lips and stroked his moustache, pondering. His staff were completely still and silent, watching him and waiting. Rosie's heart was beating so violently it was hurting her. The kettles bubbled and boiled and tossed their lids in the air and were ignored.

Eventually he looked up and beamed. 'Missis Taylor,'

31

he said, looking at one of the women at the table, 'please to put out liddle plate for liddle cake for the liddle milady.' Then he turned and beamed at Rosie. 'How that do, eh?'

Rosie was so relieved she felt sick but she managed to control her feelings and dropped him a curtsey and said, 'Thank 'ee kindly, Mr Rossi.'

At which he beamed again and Rosie noticed with relief that his face was quite transformed now that his mouth was lifted and his eyes were smiling. 'Qui' right,' he said, winking at her. 'All-aways feed bambini good.'

And that seemed to be that. The two girls carried their baby out of the room and headed for the stairs and the nursery. Halfway up the first flight Rosie burst into tears.

Maisie was most upset. She took the baby and sat her on the step beside them and then she put her arms round her new friend and cuddled her. 'Please don't cry,' she begged. 'Not when it's all over an' you done so well.' But Rosie had to weep away the fear that had followed her up the stairs like something from a nightmare and it took her a long time to do it.

'We won't tell Janet what we done,' Maisie said, when they were climbing back to the nursery again. 'She don't need to know till she has to.'

'She'll know when the cake arrives,' Rosie said.

After so much unexpected excitement and such torrential weeping, to be back in the quiet of the nursery felt almost like a homecoming. Janet was sitting by the window, letting out a seam in one of Rachel's pinafores and looking sour. 'I thought you was the tea,' she said. 'You been a long time.'

'We went a bit further today,' Maisie said. 'It was ever so nice out.' Then she turned to the baby. 'Let's wash those little hands, shall we. We shall have tea presently.'

Tea and a newly washed baby arrived in the day nursery together.

To Rosie's relief, the moment was delicately handled. 'There's a little plate with a little cake on it for the baby,' the kitchen maid said. 'Nice soft sponge. Mr Rossi said to tell you he thought she might like to try it.'

Janet thanked her. What else could she do? But when the maid had left them, she was quick to amend her gratitude. 'Well, we shall have to see, wont we,' she said. 'She might not like it at all.'

She was quite cross when Rachel ate up every last crumb. 'We shall have to watch you,' she said to her, 'or you'll get greedy.'

But Rachel was drinking her warm milk and didn't pay any attention to her.

*

Later that night, when Rachel had been put to bed and Rosie had sung one of her mother's lullabies to settle her, and they'd had supper and tidied the nursery and were finally off duty, Rosie lay on her back in her unfamiliar bed and gave herself up to the homesickness she'd been pushing away from her all through the day. She yearned to be back in Binderton and missed her mother with an ache that was so strong and painful that the tears began to roll out of her eyes again. No matter how well she did in this job of hers, she didn't want to be doing it, not if the truth be told. She wanted to be back at home with Ma and Pa and the littl'uns. But it would be ten months before she could see them all again and ten months felt like a very long time. Oh a very, very long time. It was going to be a job to keep cheerful all the time. But she'd do it because she'd made up her mind to it.

The next day their midday meal arrived on a rather larger tray than they expected and when they lifted the linen cover, what they found made them both grin. Mr Rossi had done them proud. As well as two ample portions of cottage pie and vegetables for them, there was a third dish for the baby with a portion of mashed potato and pie and lots of gravy, and as well as two plates full of spotted dick and custard there was another smaller dish containing a little pink blancmange with a note beside it, '*To tempt the little milady's appetite*.'

'My stars!' Maisie said. 'D'you think he's done it deliberate?'

Rosie had no doubt. 'Yes,' she said. 'Course he has. He knew what we was telling him. He's a clever man.'

'D'you think she'll eat it?' Maisie said. 'It's a big portion.'

'I 'spect so,' Rosie said, noticing that the baby was licking her lips. 'Put her in her high chair an' we'll try her. Come on little milady. Come an' see what our nice Mr Rossi's sent for you.'

The little milady ate everything that was set before her, using her spoon more or less accurately and her fingers when the spoon was too cumbersome and smiling at them rapturously all the time.

'Well I never!' Maisie said. 'Who'd ha' thought it?'

'I would,' Rosie said. 'Well I did, didn't I?' And she grinned at their triumphant baby. 'Look at the state of you,' she said, affectionately. 'Your face is all over blancmange. I'll have to take a flannel to you.'

Unfortunately she was out of the room getting the flannel when Janet came back from her dinner and Janet was *not* pleased at what she found. 'Now what's she been eatin'?' she said crossly. 'It's not cottage pie surely to goodness. Whatever were you thinkin' of? An' what's all that pink stuff on her face? Where's her bread an' milk?'

'It's blancmange,' Maisie said, answering the question that seemed least likely to lead to a row. 'Mr Rossi sent it up special.'

'What he'd got no business doing,' Janet scowled. 'She's supposed to have bread and milk. Mrs Tenbury said so.'

Rosie had come back with her damp flannel in the middle of the conversation. 'When was that?' she said. 'Put your little face up Rachel.'

'When I came here,' Janet said. 'She was most partic'lar about it.'

'But that would ha' been months ago,' Rosie said, reasonably. 'You can't keep babies on slops for ever. They needs more nourishment when they gets older. Don't you poppet?'

'Well don't blame me if she gets the bellyache,' Janet said.

'There's no sign of it yet,' Rosie said, happily. It was so good to get the better of Hoity-toity. High time somebody did.

'How would you know?' Janet persisted.

'Well it's obvious. She'd cry.'

At that, Janet flounced out of the room in a temper. 'Oh you're so clever!' she said. 'Well we'll just see what Mrs Tenbury has to say, that's all. That dreadful cake was bad enough but this beggars belief.' And she was gone.

Maisie put her hands to her mouth in distress. 'She's going to make trouble,' she said. 'I seen that look afore, many and many's the time. What are we going to do, our Rosie?'

Outside their window the lawn was bright with sunshine and the sky was summertime blue. 'Well I don't know about you,' Rosie said, 'but I'm going to take Baby for a nice walk in the fresh air. You'd like that wouldn't you Rachel? Let's get our hats, shall we.'

So they walked in the gardens again, and Maisie did her best not to worry and failed, and Rachel fell in the flower-beds and rolled about on the lawn and covered her pinafore with grass stains and squealed with delight when Rosie told her she was a terrible bad lot and they didn't get back until it was nearly teatime.

The day nursery was very quiet and Janet was sitting by the window again with her sewing in her hands. She looked up when they were all in the room and put her work aside and stood up. Her face was so full of importance that Rosie could feel her heart sinking. I'm for it now, she thought, and stood quite still ready for the blow that was sure to come.

But Janet had something else to tell them. 'Mrs Tenbury's with milady,' she said, 'They've sent for the nurse. We're to make up the crib. The footman will be coming for it presently. They've just sent up to tell me. Look sharp. I'd like to see it done before tea.'

Maisie and Rosie took Rachel into the night nursery at once to find the sheets and blankets for the crib. How quickly things change in this place, Rosie thought. We came creeping up those stairs thinking we were going to be scolded and now this.

'D'you think it's the baby coming?' Maisie whispered.

'Sounds like it, if they've sent for the nurse.'

They spread the little sheet over the mattress. 'Do you think she saw Mrs Tenbury?'

'I shouldn't think so,' Rosie whispered, 'or she'd've said. Where'd you put the little bedspread?'

They'd only just finished the job when the footman appeared and carried the crib away. And after that the tea arrived. It was a subdued meal although Rachel ate her cake very happily and drank her warm milk and allowed the two girls to take her off to lullabies and bed as good as gold.

Then they waited. Supper time came. And they waited. The nursery clock struck ten. And they waited. Eventually, when it was nearly midnight, Janet announced that she was 'for her bed' and left them. So the two girls went to bed too.

Rosie had been trying to remember how long her mother had taken to birth young Edie. She had a hazy idea that she'd gone to bed in the morning and the baby had come in the afternoon but it had been a long time ago. 'We shall hear in the morning,' she said, as they settled to sleep.

But the morning brought no news and the day went quietly on. It wasn't until they gathered for their supper that they heard anything at all and then Mrs Tenbury stood up at the foot of the table and held up her hand for quiet.

'I'm sure you will all be pleased to know that milady has been safely delivered of a son. He will be the sixteenth Duke of Norfolk and is to be called Bernard Marmaduke.'

There was a ripple of careful applause around the table and Mrs Tenbury inclined her head towards it, smiling right and left. 'I am sure you will all want me to convey your congratulations to the duke and milady. It is a happy day for the family.'

'We shall see some changes now,' the second footman said to Rosie. 'You mark my words.'

Chapter Three

Change arrived in Arundel castle four days later in the cheerfully stout and rather flat-footed person of Sister Mary Castleton. Within twenty-four hours the dining table was buzzing with news of her. The second footman said she was 'a good egg', the kitchen maids said she'd come down to the kitchen with milady's tray and she was lovely and the lady's maid told them she'd done wonders with the new baby.

'I wonder if she'll come an' see *us*,' Maisie said as she and Rosie climbed back to the nursery.

'Bound to,' Rosie said, 'being we looks after baby Rachel. I mean that's her job, ent it. Looking after the babies. I expect they'll send this new one up to us an' all, when he's a bit older. They don' seem to look after their own children these ol' dukes.' She'd been in the castle for over a week and wasn't impressed by the fact that neither duke nor duchess had come near the nursery once.

In fact the much-talked-of Sister Castleton arrived there three days later. Unfortunately she chose a very inopportune moment for her visit because Janet and Rosie were in the middle of furious argument about a dish of steak and kidney pudding, which Mr Rossi had sent up for 'the little milady's dinner' and which Rosie had happily fed to her while her adversary was in the staff dining room and safely out of the way. Both of them were shouting and red-faced with anger.

'You had no business feeding her such a thing,' Janet was roaring. 'You could ha' made her sick.'

And Rosie was roaring back, 'She wasn't sick. Look at her. She loved it. She ate every last mouthful.'

Poor Maisie had retreated into a corner with the baby and was watching them anxiously, wishing they'd stop. When she realised who was walking into the room it gave her such a shock she turned pale.

But Sister Castleton's entrance was serene. 'Is this our other baby?' she said, sailing towards Maisie and Rachel. 'It's little Rachel isn't it?'

Maisie dropped a curtsey and said, 'Yes ma'am' and Janet and Rosie stopped in mid roar with their mouths open, looking foolish. All three of them watched as Sister Castleton drew up the nursing chair and sat in it so that she and the baby were eye to eye. 'I can see you're a good girl Rachel,' she said. 'Is that your rocking horse?'

Rachel was too cautious about this new arrival to do anything more than nod and cling to Maisie's skirt.

'He's a beautiful horse,' Sister Castleton said. 'I expect you like riding him, don't you?' And when the child nodded again, 'Would you like to ride him now? I could lift you on if you like and push him for you.'

At which Rachel actually held up her arms to be lifted and Sister stood up and carried her to the horse and settled her in the saddle. Then she rocked her very gently while she turned her equally gentle attention to the others.

'She's a good weight,' she said, smiling round at them. 'I can see you feed her well. Lovely round face and nice plump arms. Just as she should be. No wonder Lady Howard is so pleased with you. And which one of you let out the seams on this pinafore? That's very neat.'

Janet and Maisie were very surprised to hear that the duchess was pleased with them because she'd never said as much when she visited and Janet was happy to confess that she was the needlewoman and blushed when she was praised again.

'How they do like being rocked,' Sister Castleton observed. 'Our new baby loves it. In fact between you and me, it's the only thing that will settle him at the moment, poor little lamb, wrapping him up all nice and warm in his shawl and putting him in his crib and rocking him. He found being born quite a trial. How do you settle this little one for the night?'

'We give her cuddles,' Maisie volunteered, 'and Rosie sings her lullabies. She likes lullabies.'

'I'm sure she does,' Sister Castleton said, beaming at

Rosie. 'We all like singing, don't we? That's a sort of rocking too. And you take her for walks too, don't you? I've seen you from milady's window and thought how pretty you looked out in the fresh air.' She went on pushing the horse very gently and Rachel patted its mane and smiled at her and got a beaming smile in return and the three girls watched them both. It had suddenly become very peaceful in their pretty white room.

'I went down to the kitchens yesterday to see them about a little matter of Lady Howard's present diet,' Sister Castleton said in her quiet way. 'They were so helpful. But I don't need to tell you that because I'm sure you know it already. We are very lucky in our kitchen staff.' Then she changed tack – slightly but alarmingly. 'The steak and kidney pudding they gave us today was delicious. Don't you think so?'

Rosie and Janet stiffened with distress, both thinking the same thing. She'd heard what they were shouting when she came in and now they were going to be scolded for it. She was smiling at them and didn't look cross and seemed to be waiting for an answer but that only made things worse because neither of them knew what to say. Their thoughts were too complicated by anxiety to put into words. In the end Rosie swallowed her panic and spoke up. 'Mr Rossi sent up a little plateful for Rachel,' she said, hoping it was the right thing. 'She liked it ever so much. She ate every mouthful.'

Sister Castleton smiled approval. 'I'm sure she did,' she

said. 'It was beautifully cooked. So tender. And of course highly nutritious. But then Mr Rossi has children of his own so he knows how to tempt them.' She smiled encouragingly at Janet. 'You don't look sure about it, Janet.'

'I wouldn't want to upset her digestion,' Janet said, defending herself. 'I mean she's very little. Mrs Tenbury said I was to feed her bread and milk.'

'Weaning these little ones is a delicate business,' Sister Castleton observed. 'The trouble is, all our babies are different and they all grow at their own pace. Sometimes it's very hard to tell when they're ready for solid food. It's a matter of trial and error really, isn't it? But you seem to be doing very well at it, tempting her with little portions and watching to see if she enjoys it and if she would like more. Isn't that so?' The two girls nodded and were relieved to be able to agree with her. Perhaps they weren't going to be scolded after all. 'In fact,' the sister went on, 'if I were to be asked my opinion I would say you're very good at it. And of course you've got the sense to ask for advice if you're not sure about anything.' More nodding.

'Get down,' Rachel said, holding out her arms. And then added, remembering her manners. 'Please!'

Sister Castleton lifted her down and gave her a kiss. 'Now you must show me the room where your little brother is going to sleep,' she said. 'He'll be here in a day or two and we must make sure everything is ready for him.' She looked at Janet. 'There are five rooms in the suite I believe.

I must be quick about it because it wouldn't do to leave the little man for too long.'

Janet led the way and the rooms were inspected. Then the sister thanked them and told them everything was in order and left them with a final smile. They were glowing at the praise she'd given them and missed her as soon as she was out of the door. 'Isn't she lovely!' Maisie said. 'I mean for to say . . . Lovely. When she smiles like that it makes you feel all warm and lovely. It was like the sun coming out.'

When I'm grown up I'm going to be just like her, Rosie thought. Putting people right and making them feel good at the same time. It's very clever. I shall watch her and see how she does it. I wonder when she'll come and see us again.

Sister Sunshine was back in the nursery a few days later and baby Bernard came with her. He was very small and very pale but he had a footman to carry his crib and two maids struggling with a basket full of his clothes. He was a mere ten days old. Rosie was horrified.

'He'll starve,' she said to Maisie when Sister Sunshine had carried him into his nursery, followed by his puffing retinue. 'Poor little thing. Never mind baskets and cribs, what will they do when he cries to be fed?'

They were to discover that almost at once when another maid arrived carrying a square basket full of extraordinary things, several bottles shaped like bananas, a dish full of rubber things that looked very peculiar, two kettles, two jugs, a small one made of glass and a large one of blue china, a long spoon, a scoop and a little spatula, and a tin with a blue-and-white label that said '*Cow and Gate Dried Pure English Milk*'. They stood in a circle round the table where she'd put it, with Maisie holding Rachel's hand, and examined the curious things for some time.

'How can you have dry milk?' Janet asked. 'Milk's wet. We all know that.'

They couldn't explain it but that's what it said on the tin.

'Now,' Sister Sunshine said, coming up behind them, 'if one of you will fill one of these kettles for me, we'll make up a nice little bottle ready for baby when he wakes. There's a nice fire in his nursery. It shouldn't take long.'

So Maisie entertained Rachel with her bricks and Rosie took the kettle into the baby's nursery where there was a sink with a tap above it and set it on the trivet in front of the fire and then they waited to see what would happen next. It wasn't long before the baby began to cry, '*A-la, a-la, a-la.*'

'He wants his titty,' Rosie said knowledgeably.

'He does,' Sister Sunshine agreed, turning to the basket of curiosities. 'Watch closely and I'll show you what we're going to do about it.'

They watched as she opened the tin and measured out a scoopful of milk-coloured powder into the blue jug, poured a measure of boiling water on top of it, stirred them together with the long spoon and poured the resulting mixture into one of the banana bottles, finishing off by fixing a rubber plug on one end and a rubber teat on the other. The baby went on crying the whole time, '*A-la, a-la.*' Poor little thing.

'Now,' Sister Sunshine said, standing up with the bottle in her hand, 'all I've got to do is to cool it down under the tap until it's the right temperature and then we're ready.'

It seemed to take her a very long time and the baby cried more and more pathetically all the while. But at last she took the bottle away from the running tap and shook a few drops of milk out onto her forearm. 'Perfect,' she said. 'Hold it for me Rosie and I'll go and get him.'

The baby was lifted out of his crib and settled on her lap before the fire. By that time he was hiccupping with distress and when Sister eased the teat towards his mouth and gave it a little shake so that a few drops of milk fell out onto his lips, he turned his head away from it and began to whimper.

'This may take some time,' Sister said. 'We'll get there in the end, won't we, my little man, but we might be better if we were on our own.'

They took the hint at once and went to get on with their work in the day nursery. But Rosie was brooding and thinking dark thoughts as she worked. That poor baby should have been fed and comforted the minute he cried, the way Ma had fed and comforted young Edie. It wasn't kind or natural to make him wait. She's not much of a mother that ol' duchess, she thought an' someone should tell her so. But when Lady Howard came into the nursery two days later to check on her children, she was so grand that Rosie was speechless at the sight of her. She was dressed in the most elaborate dressing gown Rosie had ever seen, all pale blue silk and lace, her hair was piled up on her head in such a complication of curls that Rosie wondered if it was a wig and she spoke in such a drawling voice it was quite hard to understand what she was saying. Not that she had anything to say to her nursemaids. She spoke directly to Sister Sunshine and didn't even look at them, although they bobbed curtseys to greet her. Rosie felt aggrieved to be so carelessly ignored and was quite glad that the illustrious lady didn't stay for long. Just time enough to satisfy herself that her son was gradually learning to take his bottle and that her daughter was 'doing nicely' and then she swept out of the room, leaving her perfume behind her.

Nobody's going to tell that one anything, Rosie thought, glaring at the door. She wouldn't listen, leave alone hear. Pa was right. If you're a servant you ent allowed to have an opinion. You just have to say, '*Yes, me Lord,*' an', '*Yes, me Lady,*' an' do as you're told. And that's not natural. We're humans same as she is.

But at least they had their dear Sister Sunshine to look after them all and she was doing it wonderfully. As soon as she discovered that Rosie had been out on her own on her first afternoon off and hadn't enjoyed it very much, she arranged for her day to be changed so that she could go out at the same time as Maisie, 'and leave your work behind and just have a bit of fun together, which you've earned.' It changed the colour of her week.

It took the two of them a little while to work out what they were going to do about Rosie's lack of money. Maisie said at once that she'd pay for things until Rosie got her wages but Rosie was adamant that she would only borrow money if she could pay back every penny and insisted that they keep accounts in a little notebook. So it was agreed and on their first afternoon they went to the Post Office and bought a pen and a bottle of ink and four stamps and a little pocket notebook for their accounts. Then, having satisfied Rosie's conscience, they explored the town.

There were so many shops to see and exclaim over and so many grand ladies in their fine clothes drifting in and out of them that it was four o'clock before they realised how hungry they were and how much they needed tea.

'I know just the place,' Maisie said. 'It's my favourite.' And she turned into one of the side streets, where there were lots of general stores selling jams and biscuits and walked until she reached a little tea shop. It was a little low room, a step down from the street, with dark oak beams striping the ceiling and an oak shelf all along the walls where there were blue plates and jugs, and tables and chairs everywhere they looked – most of them noisily occupied – and even a clock, 'so's we can keep an eye on the time an' not be late.' Rosie was very taken with it. They found themselves a seat in the chimney corner and ordered tea and sticky buns.

'What a day we've had,' Rosie said, taking her pencil out of her pinafore pocket and making a note of her share of the tea.

'An' we can do it again next week,' Maisie said, licking the end of her finger so that she could pick up the last crumbs of her sticky bun.

'What a lot I shall have to tell Ma,' Rosie said happily.

Her letter ran to two tightly written, excited pages and was posted the next day, so it was rather a disappointment when a week passed without an answer. And an even bigger one when the answer finally arrived. It was put beside her plate at breakfast time but she didn't open it until she was back in the nursery because she wanted to enjoy it privately. It was written on half a sheet of notepaper in her mother's painstaking handwriting and very brief. '*Dear Rosie*,' it said. '*Thank you for yours. I am glad to see you are goin on orl right. we are well. Your loving Ma.*' And that was all.

Tears filled Rosie's throat and tumbled out of her eyes. She had to run into the night nursery or she'd have been weeping in front of the others. I sent her that lovely long letter, she mourned, as she sat on her bed reading the note again, and I told her everything I could and this is all she can send me back. It made her feel as if she'd been forgotten. But no matter how sad and angry she felt there was a day to get on with and work to be done. She dried her eyes and squared her shoulders and got on with it.

It was over a week before she could bring herself to write another letter home and this time she wrote to Tommy. At least he knew how to read and could write a bit more than Ma if he stirred his stumps enough to do it.

The stumps were stirred the very next day. '*Dear Rosie,*' Tommy wrote. '*Got yours this morning. what larks your having We got a good crop of apples coming along Ma says to tell you we will save some for you when you come what she'll store away. One of Pas ol cows was took sick but she is better now. Tess say to send you her love. We are orl well. Charlie and me been fishing Chichester way an I cort a eel. Didden half riggel. youd ha laffed. Your loving brother Tommy.*'

She wrote back to him that evening and from then on they kept up a cheerful if rather disjointed correspondence through the summer, the autumn and the winter. It was still a long way to Mothering Sunday but the days passed and she intended to enjoy whatever pleasures came her way. Sister Sunshine left them; the new baby grew plump, sat up, crawled and began to gabble towards speech; the old one continued on her serious way; Rosie and Maisie took tea in their favourite shop every week, and once they'd saved up enough money from their wages and found that the castle dressmaker would run things up for them cheaply, they bought material to make new clothes for themselves, in Maisie's case a pretty blouse with puffed sleeves, in Rosie's a red skirt that swirled when she swung her hips. They wore their new finery at Christmas dinner and were much admired. But it was still a long way to Mothering Sunday.

January passed quietly: Maisie celebrated her fourteenth birthday and woke up to find the world was white with snow: Spring arrived cautiously: and at long, long, achingly yearned-for last, it was the twenty-first of March and Mothering Sunday and they were standing in line to be given a simnel cake and a little bunch of violets to take home to their mothers.

It seemed to Rosie that it took a very long time to travel home although in fact it was a quicker journey than the one she and her father had undertaken all those months ago, because this time she travelled on a train, from Arundel to Chichester and from Chichester to a little stop called Lavant which was just across the fields from the church of St Mary's at East Lavant where she'd always gone with her parents.

It was such a joy to walk through those familiar wooden gates under that familiar lantern and stroll through a crowd of her neighbours along the winding path to the church door. I've come home, she thought. This is how things ought to be. And then, with a rapturous lift of her heart, she saw Ma and Pa and Tommy and the little 'uns, waiting for her in the sunshine. She ran towards them with her hands full of gifts and Ma caught her up in her arms and hugged her tight until they were both crying and Pa gave his gruff, embarrassed cough and kissed her cheek.

Then they were all inside their familiar church with the great east window, blue and white and full of sunshine, smiling down upon them and the organ pipes rising before them like golden reeds. Oh it's so good to be home, she thought, as she settled in her familiar pew between her parents. And so good to be sitting round the same old table in the cottage and talking in almost the same old way. It was a very short visit but she savoured every moment of it, Sunday dinner, village gossip, simnel cake and all. She even enjoyed the walk to the station to catch her train back to Arundel because they all came with her.

'See you next year,' they called as she leant out of the window to wave goodbye.

She blew kisses at them until they were out of sight. Oh yes, yes, she thought, I will see you next year. It was all right. She still had her family.

Maggie Goodison was very quiet on the walk back to Binderton. John gave Edie a piggyback all the way home and joggled her and made her laugh and Tommy and Tess skipped along behind them telling one another what a lark it had been to see their Rosie but Maggie was torn with misery. It had been such a short visit. They'd hardly had time to say anything to one another and there was so much that needed to be said. There's this baby coming, she thought, rubbing her swollen belly, and it'll be seven months old before she sees it. And she's grown so tall I hardly knew her. What a weary world we live in. It wasn't like her to give in to misery but when that hateful train had gone steaming off to Chichester in its nasty heartless way she felt so lost she wanted to cry.

Had she known it, Rosie was feeling equally tearful now

that she was on her own and the hateful train was joggling her back to work. It was much worse leaving them this time. Another year away from Ma an' the littl'uns, she thought. Another year cleaning nappies an' coaxing babies to eat, an' bathing them, an' sewing their clothes an' picking up their toys. It felt like an eternity.

Chapter Four

Rosie's second year at work passed slowly. May arrived and she passed her thirteenth birthday and didn't mention it. Rachel grew taller, Bernard crawled about and was sick in the toy box. But at least she had regular letters from home, usually from Tommy or Tess but sometimes from her mother. She answered them all on the day they arrived. Until July, when Tess wrote to tell her they'd got a new baby brother and they were going to call him John and wasn't it lovely.

It took her a while to digest the news and think what to say in answer to it. Her first instinctive reaction was to feel sorry for poor Ma. Babies meant such a lot of work and she'd already had four of them. That ought to have been enough, she thought, surely to goodness. I can't think why she wanted another one. I shan't want any babies at all when I get married. I've had quite enough of them, nasty, smelly, little things. But she could hardly write and tell her mother that. In the end she simply said she was glad to hear the news and she hoped Ma was well, and was looking forward to seeing her new brother in the spring. It wasn't strictly true but it was the right thing to say.

The year continued. A second Christmas was celebrated. She and Maisie had to let out the seams in their clothes because they were growing so fast. Lady Howard made occasional visits to the nursery to see her children. And eventually her second Mothering Sunday came round and she was walking across the fields to see her new brother.

He was so like Tommy it made her laugh out loud. He had the same round face, the same shock of brown hair, the same blue eyes, even the same chuckle.

'Why Ma,' she said. 'They're like peas in a pod.'

'It's a good pattern,' Tommy said cheerfully, 'so she used it again, didn'tcher Ma?' He'd grown taller since Rosie saw him last and said he was looking forward to starting work.

'We got him took on at Langford farm,' Pa said. 'He'll do orl right there, won't you son, ploughing an' all. He'll be startin' come harvest time, what's a good time to start.'

'I got some material for you,' Ma said. 'I thought it might make a warm jacket. It's a lovely colour, sort a' russet with red flecks in. Come an' see. That blouse is nice. Did you get it with your wages?'

Rosie spent rather longer at home that day because she'd arranged to catch the last train back and she made the most of every minute, cuddling the baby, which pleased Ma, letting Edie sit next to her all through dinner which pleased them all and entertaining them with tales from the castle.

'It's ever so lovely having you home, our Rosie,' Tess said as they walked to the station in the half light of a gathering dusk. 'I wish you could come home every Sunday.'

'So do I,' Rosie told her, giving her a hug, 'but that ent the way the world works. Hope you gets on all right with your job, our Tommy. Write an' tell me.'

He wrote to her once a week as soon as he'd started work and his letters were cheerful and spoke warmly of the two other boys he was working with who he said were '*good sorts*'. But by November a new tone was beginning to creep in. '*You get teased sommink cronic by the men,*' he wrote. '*My hands are all over blisters wot you woudden believe.*'

'*It ent the best of worlds being at work,*' she wrote back. '*We just got to get on with it, that's all. At least you get home of a Sunday, which is more than I do.*' And she was thinking, you don't have to put up with the mucky business of 'being a woman'.

Janet had enlightened her about that one afternoon just before his letter came.

'Have you been having pains in your belly?' she asked.

'No,' Rosie said, feeling aggrieved to be asked. 'My belly's fine, thank you very much.'

'It won't be fine for long,' Janet warned. 'Not now you're fourteen. First you'll have pains and then you'll find blood on your bloomers.'

Rosie was horrified. 'I shan't,' she said.

'You will,' Janet said. 'It happens to all of us. Anyway I've brought you a clout just to show you.' And she pulled a piece of heavy towelling out of her apron pocket and a pad of cotton wool and a long strip of white tape. 'Watch how it's done. Then you'll be ready for it.'

Rosie watched obediently but her thoughts were seething. It seemed such a horrible thing to have to put up with, month and after month and being told she'd have to wash the clouts and burn the cotton wool on the fire sounded like just two more objectionable chores.

*

'I'm going to treat myself to a hat to match my jacket,' she said to Maisie as they set off for town that Thursday. 'I think I've earned it.'

'What a good idea,' Maisie said, tucking her hand in Rosie's arm. 'I shall an' all.'

'Quite right,' Rosie said. 'If we've got to bleed like stuck pigs once a month at least we can look stylish while we're a-doin' of it.'

Maisie was shocked and impressed. 'You do say some dreadful things, our Rosie,' she said, admiring her.

*

The hats were a great success. They wore them to church on the rare Sundays when they were both allowed out to attend and they were a splendid finishing touch to their outfits when they walked to town on Thursdays. And Rosie wore hers with her bunch of violets tucked into the brim when she went home on her third Mothering Sunday. But they didn't make the chores any easier. Nor did the news that they were given in September. Their rarely seen employer was expecting yet another baby.

'That'll be three of 'em,' Rosie grumbled. 'When's she going to stop? It's babies everywhere you look, on an' on an' on.'

'Rachel'll be out of the nursery soon,' Janet said. 'They're hiring a governess for her.'

'I'd rather have our Rachel to look after than another new baby,' Rosie said. 'At least she don't make horrible messes for us to clear up.'

But the baby was coming and on her fourth Mothering Sunday she told her mother all about it. 'Any minute now,' she said knowledgeably. 'She looks like a barrel for all her fine clothes.'

'We can't help looking like barrels,' Maggie said. 'It happens to all of us. It'll happen to you one day. You'll sing a different tune then.'

Rosie made a grimace but she was nearly sixteen now so she didn't argue. She just made a silent promise to herself. Ma can say what she likes, she thought, but I'm not going to spend my life having babies. Not if I can help it.

Tommy looked across the table and winked at her. It was the first time she'd ever seen him do such a thing and it made him look as if he was a conspirator. Does he think things too and not say them, she wondered. She wished they could have a bit of time on their own together so that she could ask him. But the spotted dick was being served and baby John was waving his spoon and the meal was pushing them away from their thoughts.

It wasn't until they were all walking back to the station in their now customary way that she found the moment she wanted.

'You know when we was sitting at the table,' she began.

'Yep.'

'You looked as if you was thinking.'

'I does a lot a' thinking. Private like.'

'What about?'

He shrugged his shoulders. 'Work.'

'You don't like it,' she said, with a rush of fellow-feeling.

'Not much. I'm tryin' to find somethin' else fer mesself. Onny don' say nothin' to Ma. She don't know.'

'I'd like to do that an' all,' she said. 'I don't like my work neither.' But there was no time to say anything else, much though she wanted to, because the little station was just ahead of them and she would soon have to say goodbye.

'I'll write to you,' she called as the train chuffed away. She was waving to them all but was looking at Tommy.

And he winked at her again. It made her feel warm all the way back to Arundel.

*

The Howard's third baby was born on March 25th, eight days later and Sister Sunshine came back to the castle again for the confinement. The staff were given the news at supper and told that it was a girl and that she was to be called Katherine Mary and they all applauded politely. But Rosie didn't care what she was going to be called. She was another baby – that was all there was to it – and her coming meant more nappies and more sick-sour clothes and endless bottles and more broken nights. I really will have to start looking for another job, she thought, as she crawled wearily into bed after the new baby's first day in the nursery. If Tommy can find something else, I should too.

But that was easier thought than done. There was so much work in the nursery now, with a new and very demanding baby, young Bernard who was a toddler and very upset to be displaced by the newcomer, and Rachel who was nearly seven and being taught by a governess every day and needed the comfort of her favourite fairy stories at bedtime. And Tommy's letters were rather intermittent. He was asking around for any possible vacancies and meant to find one. *'I means to keep on going till I gets what I wants,'* he told her.

But it was taking him a very long time. It wasn't until the autumn that he finally wrote in great excitement to tell her he was going to work as a gardener at Binderton House. *'What do you think to that our Rosie? parrently, the old feller what lives there is a clergyman of some sort what is always out an about soemwheres being religus an wants someone for to tend his vegetable patch an' such like. I will write again when I'm settled in. Wot larks!'*

His next letter bubbled with excitement. '*I like it here,*' he wrote. '*The clergyman leaves orders what I carries out and the old lady comes out for to see what I done what she seems for to like. She is a nice old biddy. Wooden say boo to a goose. Once she knows wat I'm doing she lets me be to get on with it. I won't say it ent hard work but I likes it. I gets home at night and the grubs good and its easier than milking them ol cows and plowing.*'

Rosie envied him. Lucky thing. But she wrote back to tell him how glad she was he'd found somewhere he liked, adding, '*I only wish it was me.*'

'*I will see if I can find soemthink for to suit for you,*' he promised in his next letter. He wasn't sure how he could do it but he'd keep his ears open. You never knew when something might turn up.

It turned up when he was deadheading the roses in the front garden one May morning. The sun was warm on the nape of his neck and he was working slowly because the clergyman was out, when his gentle peace was suddenly broken in a very noisy way. He looked up, startled, to see one of them terrible motor car things fairly roaring up the gravel path towards him.

There was a grand lady sitting in the back in a grand black coat and an enormous hat and it was being driven by a man in a peaked hat and a coat made of beige Holland with brown cuffs and collar. He brought his machine to a halt and climbed out of it to open the door for the lady.

'Binderton House ma'am,' he said.

'Ring the bell,' she said.

Well, well, well, Tommy thought. What's a grand lady like that doing visiting Binderton House? The missus never said nothing about no lady coming. And he stood quite still, secateurs in hand, to see what would happen next.

The bell was rung and the lady stepped delicately out of the car and walked in a stately way towards the door. Tommy's mouth fell open at the sight of her for she looked even more impressive out of the car than she'd done in it. She was dressed entirely in cream, black and scarlet and now he could see that it wasn't a coat she was wearing but a flowing black cape that looked as though it was made of velvet and was lined in scarlet silk. The suit beneath it was the colour of cream and had swirling patterns of black braid all over the front of it and she wore cream-coloured gloves to match it and her hat was black velvet with scarlet ribbons and a topknot of huge black feathers. Even her shoes were black and red too. She was a wonder to behold and she stood on the doorstep as though she knew it. When the door was opened, the housemaid took one look at her and dropped a curtsey.

'Lady Eden,' the vision said. 'You are expecting me.' And the maid curtseyed again and ushered her in.

As soon as she was gone, the driver took off his cap and his gauntlets and tossed them into the car, fished a packet of cigarettes from his pocket, leant against the side of the car and lit up. He looked a friendly sort of chap without his cap so Tommy ambled across to talk to him.

'Come far?' he said.

The driver blew smoke from his nose like a dragon. It was very impressive. 'London.'

'Tha's a mortal long way.'

'She wants ter take a cottage for her boys,' the driver said. 'Fer the summer when they ain't at Eton. 'Tween you an' me, I reckon it's to get 'em out the way of her ol' man.'

'Oh?'

'He's a proper tartar, he is,' the driver said. 'Flies off the handle like you wouldn't believe. Hollerin' an' roarin' fer the least little thing. I'll give you a fer-instance. He only allows blue flowers to grow in his garden. Blue or grey. An' one year a lot a' red ones come up an' you'd ha' thought it was the end a' the world. He roared an' screamed summink chronic. Had 'em all dug up. Pretty they was too.'

Tommy grimaced. 'So she's puttin' 'em out a' harms' way.'

'That's about the size of it. She wants 'em here by half term.'

'When's that?'

'Week after next.'

Tommy's mind was working at speed. 'That's a rush. 'Specially if she's got to get servants an' all.'

'Oh the old lady'll do that,' the driver said.

'What ol' lady?'

'Her at the house. The one my lady's come ter see.'

Tommy's mouth was hanging open. It was heaven sent. Rosie could run a cottage easy as pie an' he could fix it for her. The idea swelled in his head until it was quite uncomfortable but he'd made up his mind. I'll do it the minute that lady's gone, he thought.

He had to wait for a very long time before the vision reappeared and was driven away. But as soon as she was out of sight he put down his secateurs and ran to the kitchen door to find the missus.

'I got just the one fer you, mum, if you're looking fer a housekeeper,' he said, blue eyes earnest.

She was so surprised she barely knew how to answer him. 'Oh yes,' she said vaguely.

He was hot with good intentions and pressed on without noticing her vagueness. 'My big sister, mum. She works at Arundel Castle an' she's been wantin' to come back here fer ages. She'd be just the ticket. Shall I write an' tell her?'

'Well . . . yes . . .' she dithered. 'I suppose you could.'

The letter was written that afternoon. He knew he had no business leaving his work but it had to be done. He ran all the way home, wrote his letter as quickly as he could and posted it on his way back. Now it was up to Rosie.

She arrived on Thursday afternoon, wearing her new hat, her best jacket and her most determined expression. By the time she got back to the castle the job was hers, starting in a week's time.

Maisie was impressed. 'Housekeeper!' she said. 'My stars! That's a step up. You'll see some changes now.'

'Yes,' Rosie said. 'I hope I do.' And she grinned. 'Whatever it's like it'll be better than non-stop nappies an' cleaning up sick.'

Chapter Five

Rosie's new job began at eight o'clock the next Saturday morning with a blaze of sunshine and the roar of a car. She went out of the cottage at once to welcome her new employer and watched as she emerged in full elegance from her great car and was followed by her sons, who weren't the two little boys she was expecting but two languid young men who weren't very much younger than she was and were dressed in the most extraordinary uniform – black top hats, black jackets, waistcoats, striped trousers – and with a peculiar white collar to set it all off. They mean to be noticed she thought.

'Ah yes,' Lady Eden said, when Rosie curtseyed to her. 'Miss Goodison isn't it. Take their hats.' And she swept into the house.

Rosie took the top hats and hung them up on the hall stand. Then she watched as the lady climbed the stairs, trailing her gloved hand along the banister to check for dust. The boys' bedrooms were inspected and approved of, the sitting room nodded at, the boys kissed perfunctorily, 'Goodbye Anthony, goodbye Nicholas,' and then she was gone.

The very grown-up boys sprawled in their easy chairs and the older one ordered coffee which Rosie made and served to them. That Anthony is seventeen if he's a day, she thought. What's he still doing at school?

She was to learn a lot about the differences between her life and theirs in the days that followed. Early the next morning, two brand-new bicycles were delivered and propped against the back wall, ready for their use but they didn't get up until the morning was half over and then they lounged around the cottage in slippers and silk dressing gowns, smoking cigarettes and reading a newspaper called *The Times*, which had been delivered to them all the way from Chichester. In the afternoon they got dressed in white trousers, cotton shirts and cravats and cycled off to go sailing. They were horribly lazy, leaving their dirty clothes on the floor for her to pick up and clean, their dirty coffee cups for her to collect, their discarded newspapers all over the room. They had opinions about everything and were quite sure they were right in everything they said.

She came into their sitting room on Friday to clear their coffee cups and found them in the middle of a languid conversation that made her feel quite cross.

'It's so presumptuous,' Nicholas was drawling. 'The man's

a pleb. What does he know about government? Have you read this?' He quoted from the paper he was holding.

"*If today there is a kindlier social atmosphere it is mainly because of twenty-one years' work of the ILP.*" What rot!'

'They don't know any better,' Anthony told him. 'One can't expect intelligence from the working classes. I'm off to get dressed. We said we'd meet old Pongo at one and it's nearly that now. Come on.'

They trailed out of the room without giving Rosie a glance. They're so superior, she thought angrily, so arrogantly sure of themselves. And because she was cross, she picked up the paper and read it at the page Nicholas had left open. It was an account of a speech someone called Keir Hardie had made at some meeting or other and it was a revelation.

*

'*I shall not weary you by repeating the tale of how public opinion has changed during those twenty-one years,*' he'd said. '*But, as an example, I may recall the fact that in those days it was tenaciously upheld by the public authorities, here and elsewhere, that it was an offence against laws of nature and ruinous to the state for public authorities to provide food for starving children, or independent aid for the aged poor. Even safety regulations in mines and factories were taboo. They interfered with the "freedom of the individual". As for such proposals as an eight-hour day, a minimum wage, the right to work, and municipal houses, any serious mention of such classed a man as a fool.*' (And wasn't that exactly what that silly little boy had just said?) *'That was the political, social and religious element in which our party saw the light. If today there is a kindlier social atmosphere it is mainly because of twenty-one years' work of the ILP.*

'The warming influence of Socialism is beginning to liberate people, frozen and hemmed in by a cold, callous greed. We see it in the growing altruism of trade unionism. We see it, perhaps, most of all in the awakening of women. Who that has ever known woman as mother or wife has not felt the dormant powers which, under the emotions of life, or at the stern call of duty are even now momentarily revealed? And who is there who can even dimly forecast the powers that lie latent in the patient drudging woman, which a freer life would bring forth? Woman, even more than the working class, is the great unknown quantity of the race.'

He's right, she thought. I don't know who he is but I understand exactly what he's saying. It's what I've been thinking ever since I been at work. He's right about working people toiling unceasingly and how greedy the nobs are and he's right about women. We *are 'the great unknown quantity'*. It was as if someone had switched on a light in her mind. I'm one of the patient drudging women, she thought, and I'd certainly like a freer life. She took out the page, folded it carefully and put it in the pocket of her apron.

Anthony and Nicholas lounged around at the cottage for the next nine days while Rosie waited on them hand and foot, brought up their warm water in the mornings, learned how to cook them meals on their impressive gas oven, cleaned up after them, read their newspapers when they were out sailing and spent a lot of time thinking. On their second Sunday evening they changed into their Eton uniform and their important car arrived to drive them back to their prestigious school. Rosie stood on the doorstep to wave them goodbye.

'Toodle-pip!' Nicholas called to her. 'Back on Friday. Get us a chicken for our dinner will you.'

Then they were gone.

Rosie was glad to see the back of them. Her five work-free days beckoned to her like sunshine. I shall have time for all sorts of things now, she thought. I can visit Ma an' the littl'uns. Wash my hair. Have a bit of a rest. Read that speech again maybe. She went to see her mother as soon as she'd cleaned the cottage the next morning and that afternoon she washed her unruly hair and sat in the garden to dry it in the sunshine while she read Keir Hardie's speech with careful attention. By the end of the week she'd read it so often she knew it by heart.

*

It was a beautiful summer. The warm days followed one after the other with barely a cloud in the sky and by the middle of June a good harvest was plainly well on its way. John Goodison said it was the best growing season they'd ever had. 'Even better'n last year's, an' that's sayin' something.'

The two Eden boys spent most of their time out of doors in the sunshine, either lolling about in deck chairs, reading their papers and drinking lemonade, or out on their bicycles. They were easy enough for Rosie to look after now she'd got into a routine, although she found their conversations incomprehensible for they talked about themselves and their friends and another world that was totally foreign to her. Anthony had been to watch his older brother play in the Subaltern's Cup, whatever that was, at Hurlingham, wherever that was, and he and Nicholas told one another that they were going to join the Twelfth Lancers too because they were a fine body of men. In their third week, Anthony went to a camp of some kind with the Eton College OTC and came back talking about war.

'There's one coming,' he told his brother, looking very pleased with himself. 'There's no doubt about that. Ranger says the Russians are mobilising.'

'Oh well, that's likely then,' Nicholas drawled, as if he knew all about it. 'Shall you join the army?'

'Naturally,' his brother said. 'I wouldn't want to miss the show for all the world. The adjutant says it's unlikely because the City would never allow it. But I'm not so sure.'

'If you go, I shall,' Nicolas said. 'It'll be a lark.'

Behind them in their peaceful garden, the flint walls were richly coloured in the sunshine, the rose bushes heavy with flowers and a blackbird was singing his fluent summer song from the topmost branch of the apple tree. Rosie picked up their dirty coffee cups and their smelly ashtrays and carried them into the kitchen. How can they sit there talking about war and what a lark it is on a day like this? she thought. They're like silly little boys. She remembered Tommy pointing a broom handle at the gooseberry bushes when he was about six and shouting Bang! Bang! You're dead! And now here he is tending the gardens and as happy as Larry. Well I hope these two will grow up half as good. Although as she frothed up the soap to wash the cups, she very much doubted it. They were a breed apart.

But they were right about the war. On June 28th Anthony's newspaper had a big black headline saying '*Hapsburg Heir Assassinated in Balkans*'. He was very excited by it and read the article avidly.

'There you are!' he said to Nicholas. 'The war will start now. It's bound to. We can't allow some fanatical Serb to shoot the Archduke Ferdinand. Read that.'

Nicholas read with mounting excitement, growing pinker by the second and Rosie put their breakfast on the warming plates as slowly as she could so that she could watch them. 'I say!' he said when he set the paper aside. 'Now the fur *will* fly. Killed by a single bullet they say. And his wife too. Imagine that. Have we got kidneys Miss Goodison? I could rather fancy a kidney this morning.'

'Kidneys, bacon, tomatoes, poached eggs,' Rosie reported, pointing to each serving dish in turn. 'I'll just get your coffee.'

They were in the middle of an excited discussion when she got back, about how they could leave school for a month or two and get a commission in the army.

'You are much too young,' Anthony was saying, 'and

that's all there is to it. You'll have to wait until you've turned sixteen.'

'It could all be over by then,' Nicholas complained. 'I'll bet I could get into the Royal Navy. They'd take me.'

'Not at fourteen they wouldn't,' Anthony said. 'Unless you want to be a midshipman.' Then he turned to Rosie. 'Ah. Is that the coffee?'

So she had to put the coffee pot down and leave them to their talk even though she was itching to know what they would say next. There couldn't really be a war. Could there? I'll get hold of that paper the minute they go out and see what it's all about, she promised herself. Which she did.

It didn't enlighten her at all, although it gave her all sorts of details about the assassination. There was even a picture of the murdered man, sitting in his carriage with a hat like an upturned coal scuttle on his head and a plump wife sitting beside him with her lap full of flowers. They said his name was Archduke Franz Ferdinand and that he was the heir to the Austro–Hungarian empire, whatever that was, and that the man who'd shot him was nineteen years old and a Serb, whatever that was, and he'd done it because he wanted to take *revenge for the suppression of the Serbian people*', and that it had happened at a place called Sarajevo which as far as she could make out was the capital of Bosnia, wherever that was. But there was nothing anywhere in the paper to tell her why England should be going to war because of it. Why should we? If some young man kills some old archduke on the other side of the world, that's their affair and they should deal with it. Anyway she had a kitchen floor to scrub.

The newspapers became steadily more hot and excitable. The kaiser had 'reaffirmed his alliance' with Austria, the Serbs were mobilising, the Royal Navy was on 'standby', the Tsar had ordered the mobilisation of over a million troops, and at the end of July they fizzed with the news that Austria had sent an ultimatum to Serbia which she couldn't possibly accept without 'impairing her sovereignty'. Rosie didn't have the faintest idea what they were talking about and wished they'd write in English but Anthony and Nicholas were sure that war was only a matter of days away. And it was.

On August 4th the headlines announced that Britain had declared war against Germany and there were pictures of ardent young men marching along in the streets of London, waving their boaters and cheering. She couldn't make any sense of it at all. But it had triggered a mood of frantic excitement and the recruiting sergeants were out in force all over the place, determined to take advantage of it. One splendid specimen turned up in East Lavant with a very loud pipe band to announce his presence and call the young men of the surrounding villages to arms. And the young men were duly called and left their farms and their families to hear what he was going to say.

He took up his position beside St Mary's church at East Lavant, right in front of the school they'd all attended when they were little and they gathered around him open-mouthed and wondering in the easy sunshine. He was an impressive vision in a bright red coat and the biggest, blackest boots that Tommy Goodison had ever seen.

'I come 'ere,' he said in a very loud voice, 'I come 'ere young feller-me-lads, for to hoffer you the chance of a lifetime. That's what I come 'ere for to hoffer. The chance of a lifetime. All you got for to do is to sign this 'ere form an' the harmy'll make 'eroes of you 'fore you can blink an eye. 'Eroes, I ain't a-kiddin' of yer. 'Eroes. Don't you make no mistake about it.'

The local feller-me-lads stood in their subdued semicircle before him and listened enraptured. Tommy couldn't make much sense of the harangue but he was bewitched by the sergeant's red cheeks and pouter-pigeon chest and listened avidly, gradually imbibing the notion that he was being offered a job that would make a man of him or 'an 'ero' and that all he had to do to acquire such an admirable status was sign 'this 'ere piece a' paper what I'm a-holding in my 'and.'

'What d'you think Charlie?' he whispered to his friend. 'Shall we do it?'

Charlie was smaller and slower witted than Tommy Goodison, so he looked upon him as an older brother and admired him very much. 'Will *you* do it, our Tommy?' he said.

'I think I might,' Tommy said. The excitement of entertaining such an idea was making his cheeks almost as red as the recruiting sergeant's. 'I mean to say, Charlie, it 'ud be a good life. See the world, good grub, be an 'ero. Hush up. He's off again.'

'So what d'yer say boys?' the sergeant boomed. 'Are you comin' with us or what? You'd better make yer minds up sharpish 'cause I'm a-tellin' yer it'll all be over by Christmas. All you got ter do is ter walk into this 'ere recruitin' hoffice – wot used to be your school so they been a-telling me, an' what more fittin' place? – this 'ere recruiting hoffice an' take the shilling. It's as simple as that.'

'Shall we do it, our Tommy?' Charlie asked again.

Some of their friends were already walking to the school door and forming a queue. Their eager movement made up Tommy's mind for him. 'Yes,' he said, walking after them. 'Let's.'

'Let's 'ave a cheer fer our brave boys,' the sergeant said, beaming round at the crowd. ''Ip, 'ip, pip!'

Their neighbours cheered them into the building. They were swollen with the pride of being so special.

*

Back in the cottage the two Eden brothers were sitting in their dining room, sulking. They'd had a letter from their mother that morning and they were not pleased.

'It's so ridiculous,' Nicholas said, crossly. 'It's not as if we're asking to leave school or anything silly like that. We just want a term's leave that's all, to serve our country in her hour of need.'

'The one thing you have to accept,' Anthony explained, as much to himself as his brother, 'is that the Mater's word is law. If she says we're not allowed to go, we're not allowed to go. I can't see the sense in it either but we don't have an option.'

Nicholas threw his table napkin onto his plate and scowled hideously. 'I wish you weren't being so deucedly calm about it,' he complained. 'It's deucedly unfair.'

'Yes,' Anthony agreed. 'It is. But she can't stop us for ever. If it goes on past Christmas I shall make enquiries about a commission and if it's still going on when I leave school, I shall volunteer without telling her.'

'That's years,' Nicholas said. 'It'll never go on for years. We need to enlist now or we shall miss it. Why can't she see reason?'

Anthony changed the subject. 'I'm off to Bosham,' he said. 'Spot of sailin'. Are you up for it?'

Nicholas rolled his eyes. 'Well at least she can't stop us doing that,' he said.

Rosie watched them cycle off from the open kitchen window. She'd overheard most of their conversation and been amused by it. It pleased her to think that these two arrogant young men could be put down by their mother. It showed there was still some justice in the world. She was picking up the tray ready to clear away after their lunch when she became aware of a shadow in the window and turned her head to see her own mother looking in at her.

'Your brother's gone for a soldier,' she said. 'Mrs Taylor's just come an' told me. Him an' Charlie both.' Her eyes were shining and her face was flushed with excitement.

It's a fever, Rosie thought, all this silly talk of war. She didn't know whether to be cross with her brother for being so foolish or sorry for her mother for being caught up in the nonsense. But she swallowed her feelings and managed not to say anything that would upset her.

'Come in for a minute,' she said, feeling pleased with herself for being so calm, 'an' I'll make us some tea.'

*

War fever grew all through the rest of the summer. Charlie and Tommy got their orders within five days of joining up and went off to some camp or other on a train packed with young men all looking pleased with themselves and waving goodbye to the relations who'd come to see them go.

'He'll be all right, won't he, our Rosie?' Maggie said as they walked back to Binderton. It had upset her to see him go, proud though she was of him. 'I give him a rabbit's foot to keep him safe.'

'Yes, course,' Rosie said. 'He'll enjoy it. You'll see.'

And sure enough he wrote to them four days later to tell them that the grub was good and that they were '*larning*' him to fire rifles '*wot is easy*' and that he was living under canvas '*wot is good sport*'. They wrote back at once to tell him to look after himself because they couldn't think of anything else to say and then there was a long pause when they heard nothing.

The newspapers, on the other hand, were yelling the news at them every day in huge alarming headlines. On the day war was declared, they reported that the German army had invaded Belgium and two days later they spread the news that Austria had declared war on Russia, and that Serbia had declared war on Germany.

'So it's spreading,' Anthony said, giving the paper a satisfied shake.

His brother nodded. 'We knew it would,' he said. 'If only the Mater would let us go. She must see the need now, surely to goodness with all this going on. Shall we try writing to her again?'

But Anthony thought not, even when the reports from France grew steadily more alarming. Liege was captured on the sixteenth and the French army was retreating, which Nicholas thought was 'a damned bad show'. But he cheered up the next day when the papers were full of the news that the British Expeditionary Army had landed in France.

'Not before time,' he said. 'It's no good running away. You have to stand up to the Hun. Show a bit of steel. We shall see some changes now.'

What they saw was a British defeat at a place called Mons. The word defeat was skilfully avoided but it was obvious what had happened because the British army were said to have 'fallen back to defensive positions' and what was that but a retreat?

'What's the matter with them?' Nicholas said, passionately. 'Why don't they stand and fight? That's the way to deal with the Hun. I thought everybody knew that.'

But it was soon admitted that the Germans had actually captured Mons and, not long after that, news came through that they'd captured Rheims, Ghent, Bruges and Lille as well, and were advancing towards Paris. There seemed to be no end to the defeats the French and English armies were suffering, huge though they were. But when the German army reached the River Marne at the end of the summer their run of conquests was brought to a halt and they were driven back.

'Thank God for that,' Nicholas said. 'Now what will happen?'

'Now,' Anthony sighed, 'we will pay Miss Goodison off and return the keys to our reverent neighbour and go back to school.'

Rosie was quite prepared to be told that her stint as a housekeeper was over. After all, she'd known all along that it was only for the summer but she was surprised by Anthony's kindness when he handed over her last wages.

'It has occurred to me,' he said rather stiffly, 'that you might require another job, Miss Goodison. That being so I have made some enquiries on your behalf and I can tell you that the RAC Club in Pall Mall is looking for staff. Waitresses I believe. Should you be interested, I have written their address for you on this card and this (handing her an envelope) is a reference in case you need one. You will see

I have addressed it *to whom it may concern* so that it will be suitable on other occasions.'

She took the card and the envelope and thanked him with real gratitude and when he and Nicholas had climbed into their car to be chauffeured away to school, she took the reference out of the envelope and read it to see what he'd said. It was short and quite flattering.

To whom it may concern,

Rosemary Goodison has worked for me and my brother in Binderton for quite some time and would have continued to do so, had it not been for the present war with Germany, in which I am called to serve. I thoroughly recommend her to any future employer. Her work is thorough, conscientious and reliable.

Yours truly,

Anthony Eden Esq.

Well fancy that, she thought, smiling at her description, and here's me thinking he barely noticed me. Then she looked at the address of the club and discovered that it was in London, and that gave her pause. But only for a few seconds. She stuck her chin in the air, squared her shoulders and made up her mind. London might be the capital and a very big city but it'ud be an adventure to work there. She'd soon find her way round.

The next morning, having given the cottage a thorough good clean, she packed her belongings in her battered old bag and went round to say goodbye to her mother. She found her sitting at the kitchen table with a stricken expression on her face and a letter in her hand.

'He's gone to France,' she said to Rosie. 'This come this morning.'

'That makes two of us,' Rosie said cheerfully. 'I'm off to London. I come to say goodbye.'

'And just when I thought you were both settled down so nicely,' her mother sighed, looking at the letter. 'It's a weary world.'

'Yes,' Rosie agreed. 'But it's the only one we've got. Cheer up. I'll write to you as soon as I get there an' I'll be home again soon. Now I must go or I shall miss the train.'

'Look after yourself,' Maggie said, managing a smile.

'You know me,' Rosie said and bent to kiss her. She looked worn this morning. Worn and swollen about the belly. Not another baby, she thought, poor old thing. Hasn't she had enough? But there wasn't time for any more talk and certainly not for that sort of question. London was waiting.

It seemed a very long journey from Chichester to London but she'd found herself a corner seat by the window and watched the countryside as they passed. Arundel, looking romantic, the snaking curves of the river, fields and fields and fields, here a horse and cart plodding along a narrow road, there a solitary ancient house crouched among the trees, and at last she was travelling past long rows of houses and across a wide river full of boats and barges that had to be the Thames and she knew she'd arrived in the capital.

Even though she'd prepared herself to be in a big city, she hadn't imagined it would be quite so overwhelming.

The station was an enormous vault full of trains, steam and noise and hundreds of people rushing about so quickly, it made her head spin to look at them, and when she'd found her way out of it, she was in another huge place, a cobbled roadway full of buses, some horse-drawn, some motor-driven standing in line one behind the other or pulling away so crammed with passengers that the horses were sweating and straining under their weight. There were crowds of people here too, rushing and pushing, and none of them were looking at one another. As far as she could see, there was only one person not on the move and that was a boy in a cloth cap who was standing on the edge of the pavement selling newspapers and calling his wares, 'Star, News, Stannard!' People were dropping coins into his palm and snatching a paper as they passed, as if he was some sort of machine. It was very odd.

But gawping at crowds wasn't going to find this Pall Mall place. She squared her shoulders and lifted her chin and set out on her search.

It was extremely difficult even though she asked the way at every street corner. The first lady she stopped told her to follow 'that road over there until you come to Buckingham Palace where the king lives'. And added vaguely, 'Then you just go on from there.' The second directed her to Green Park, which was a most complicated place with so many paths to follow that she was confused and stood still under the trees for a long time trying to get her bearings until an elegant couple strolled past her and she dared to ask them for directions. This time she was in luck. The gentleman took a notebook out of his pocket with a little pencil attached to it tore out a page and drew her a map, with all the streets labelled and arrows to point her in the right direction. And with the map clutched in her hand, she found the RAC Club.

It was a very grand building, made of stone and with huge curved windows that shone in the sunshine and a flag flying above the front door. She had arrived.

Chapter Six

Tommy Goodison didn't think much of France. He didn't say anything about it to Ma because he thought it might upset her. He'd written to her twice since he arrived and tried to keep his letters cheerful, telling her everything was ticketty-boo and he couldn't wait to get stuck into the Hun and that sort of thing. But really it was boring out there in the wilds and they were sleeping in tents, which was all very well when the sun shone but foul when it rained and there was mud underfoot. He and Charlie told one another they'd be glad when the train came and they could get on with the war. They'd been hanging around waiting for the blessed thing for eight days and there was no sign of it coming.

For the first two days he was actually quite glad to be able to do nothing but drill and fatigues. It had been a rough crossing and he'd been as sick as a dog all the way over and had needed time to get over it. But by the third day he was ready for action and got the fidgets having to stay where he was.

'If this is what war's like I don't think much of it,' he said to Charlie, as they tucked into their bully-beef, 'stuck out here, hangin' around wi' nothin' to do 'cept drill all on an' on. I thought it was gonna be exciting, firing guns and everything.'

'Per'aps that ol' train'll come tomorrow,' Charlie said. 'You never know. Here's our corp coming. Ask him. He might know what's holdin' it up.'

'Search me,' the corporal said, taking his first mouthful. 'Blamed thing's broken down I shouldn't wonder. Or the Bosch have blown up the line. It's the sort a' thing they do. We'll soon have it running again. Don't you worry.'

As he seemed in an affable mood Charlie asked him where they were going.

'Wipers,' the corporal said. 'Over Belgium way. There's a fine ol' scrap goin' on up there. Can't let the beggars take Wipers, you see, on account of, if they do, they'll take Calais an' Dunkirk an' Boulogne an' all. What we got ter keep open being that's the way our supplies come in an' you can't live without supplies.'

'Wipers,' Tommy said, considering it. 'They got some rum sort a' names round here.' He felt easier knowing where they were going, especially if it was going to be a fine ol' scrap. That would be something to tell Ma. I wonder how they are, he thought, ol' Ma an' Rosie. He didn't exactly miss them, that wouldn't be manly but he thought of them a lot, especially at night, when he couldn't get to sleep and tossed and turned and rolled from side to side, holding his rabbit's foot for luck. There was too much to think about, that was the trouble. If he was honest, he didn't really know how he'd manage if it came to hand-to-hand fighting and he had to stick a bayonet into another man's guts. He'd seen plenty of animals killed but that was for food. This would be different. It'ud be him or me, I suppose, he thought, but that was no comfort. Our Rosie'ud know the answer, he thought. And he yearned to see her and talk to her.

*

Rosie was enjoying her new life at the RAC Club. She was working long hours, but it was in the most luxurious place she'd ever seen. To wait at table in a sumptuous restaurant was a regular daily wonder, with soft carpets under her feet, the most elaborately patterned ceiling above her head, snow-white cloths on every table with silver cutlery at every place setting and patterned glasses polished and gleaming and enormous chandeliers above the tables fairly burning with electric light.

It was a rich man's club. There was no doubt about that. They arrived in enormous cars and dined in splendid clothes and smoked cigars and drank port or champagne, neither of which she'd even heard of until she came there. But what was most impressive about them was that they actually looked at her when she was taking their order and thanked her when she brought it to their table. At first she thought they were smiling at all the waitresses but after a few days she realised that they weren't looking at 'a waitress' they were looking at *her* and they were looking with admiration. It was a revelation. It meant she was worth looking at, even pretty, and that was something that hadn't occurred to her. It was wonderful to feel admired. Or it was until the artists arrived. Then she wasn't quite so sure about it.

They appeared one smoky October evening when the London parks prickled with bonfires and approaching trams glowed ruby red through a smokescreen of autumn dusk. Their arrival caused a palpable stir in the quiet restaurant room. They seemed to know everybody there and were greeted and waved at as they walked towards their seats, moving slowly as if they were royalty and waving their cigars at their friends. They had full dark beards and magnificent heads of hair and were dressed in the showiest clothes, velvet jackets and soft white shirts and huge cravats, one purple and the other scarlet, held in place with jewelled pins, and they didn't sit at their chosen table, they took possession of it. Rosie couldn't wait to take their order. She walked towards the table, notebook in hand, and the younger of the two looked straight at her and smiled. His admiration was so open and bold it made her blush.

'It's Helen of Troy, bigod,' he said, holding out his hand to her, 'or I'm a Dutchman. And where did they find *you*, you delectable creature?'

She was shocked because waitresses didn't shake hands with the guests and there was an awkward pause before she managed to stammer, 'I've come to take your order, sir.'

That made him worse. 'Have you indeed?' he said, making eyes at her. 'What shall we order her to do, Augustus? D'you think she would dance on the table for us? Or pose *au naturel*?'

'For pity's sake, Gerry,' the older one said. 'You're embarrassing her. They won't allow you to go to France if you carry on like this.'

'Don't you believe it, old fruit,' Gerry said, grinning at him. 'They'll let us both go, beards and all. And I'll tell you why. They'll do it because they want this show of theirs recorded. They want accuracy, which they will certainly get from me and they might even get from you too, now and then, if the mood takes you.'

Augustus grimaced at his teasing and turned to Rosie, smiling at her kindly. 'You must forgive my friend,' he said to her. 'He's a little under the weather. Do you have the Dover sole tonight?'

Rosie took their orders in a daze. Then she strode off to the kitchen, trying to look as if she didn't care but itching to find out who they were.

'They're artists,' the *maître d'* said, curling his lip with disdain, 'so we have to make allowances for them. I hope they're not troubling you.'

'Oh no,' Rosie hastened to reassure him. 'Nothing like that. I was just wonderin' who they was.'

'The older one is Augustus John,' the *maître d'* told her. 'Quite a famous man by all accounts. I've not seen any of his paintings, of course, but he has a good reputation. The young one is called de Silva so I should imagine he's foreign. Let me know if you have any problems with them.' And he swept back to his domain.

'You wanna watch out fer the younger one,' one of the other young waitresses said. 'He pinched my bum the last time he was here.'

'If he tries that trick with me,' Rosie told her, 'he'll get more than he bargains for.'

But she was intrigued by him no matter what he'd done. He was wonderfully handsome. They both were, with those dark eyes and those beautiful beards framing their faces and their lips so red and moist and that bold way of looking right at you as if they could see through you. Artists she thought. That'll be something to write home about.

*

'Look at that,' Charlie said to Tommy. 'That'll be something to write home about.'

The train had arrived that morning, at last, and had taken the brigade to Wipers – which turned out to be spelt Ypres according to the sign on the station – and now they were marching through a sizeable town in a long khaki column, heading north-east towards the battlefield and singing to keep their spirits up. At that moment they were passing a long, impressive building with so many tall windows you couldn't count them and a huge tower at one end with a spire at each corner. Their corporal said it was the cloth hall but it wasn't the building that had caught Charlie's eye. Standing on the cobbles a few yards away from them was a motorised delivery van labelled '*Waring and Gillow, Oxford Street, London*'. The sight of it was so warming and reassuring that they gave it a cheer as they passed and the driver got out and waved his cap at them.

'There you are,' Charlie said. 'It's an omen.'

Tommy said he hoped so. It was giving him the collywobbles to be so near the battlefield. Not that there was anything he could do about it except trudge on and keep singing. But he couldn't help wondering what it would be like.

It was a huge, rather muddy plain, striped with trenches, some just a scoop out of the ground, others that looked deeper and more permanent. There was a sloping hillside immediately in front of them and away to their left a ridge of land covered in trees. 'That's where the Bosch are,' their corporal said, 'so keep your eyes skinned. Now get yourselves dug in.'

They dug in diligently along with the rest of the brigade. The line of trenches seemed to go on for miles on either side of them. 'No sign of the Hun,' Tommy said as he straightened his back. It was rather an anti-climax to be digging trenches.

And then everything changed so suddenly and dramatically he didn't have time to take it in. There was a roar of artillery fire and voices yelling at them to take cover but shells were already exploding right in front of them, showering the trench with mud and shrapnel, and when he peered through the sudden smoke, he saw that the hillside was covered in marching men, all in grey-green uniforms, all carrying rifles and all walking straight towards them. All carrying rifles! Jesus!

'Bloody hell fire!' Charlie said. 'There's hundreds of the beggars.'

The corp was bellowing orders. 'Take aim! Fire!' and they obeyed without thinking, aiming at the figures advancing towards them as shells screamed over their heads. 'Fire! Fire!' Tommy could see grey figures falling, writhing in the mud, and he knew he was killing them but he felt no pity. There wasn't time to feel anything. There was just an overpowering need to drive them back before they could reach the trench. 'Fire!' They were falling, one after the other, and yet they still came on. The noise of explosions had grown so loud it was deafening and there was so much mud being flung in the air and such clouds of thick smoke swirling around them it was almost impossible to see what was happening. Surely they can't keep on advancing?

Whistles shrilled all along the line and he recognised the signal to advance and climbed out of the trenches along with everyone else and walked forward jerkily, like a mechanical toy, firing as he went and heading straight for the grey-green figures. Whatever was to happen would happen and there was nothing he could do about it. Then someone was cheering and he looked up to see who it was and saw that the grey-green enemy were stopping, turning, running away. If this is what it's like to be in a battle he thought, it's wonderful. Quick, inevitable, unstoppable.

But while the thought was still in his head, there was a flash of extreme light and something struck him in the chest with such burning force that he couldn't breathe. He was briefly aware that he was falling. Then the blackness took him.

*

Rosie got the letter first thing in the morning when she walked into the kitchens ready for her early morning duty. She didn't recognise the handwriting on the envelope. It wasn't Ma's or Tess's and it was disquieting to have a letter from someone else. She opened it quickly to find out who it was. '*Dear Rosie,*' it said. '*I am ritting for to tell you your Ma had the telegram yesterday for to tell her your Tommy has been killed wot I am very sorry to say. She say to tell you she is in a bad way or she wuld hev writ herself. Milly Enders (mrs)*'

The shock of hearing such dreadful news made her tremble so violently that she had to find a stool and sit down. It couldn't be true, she thought wildly. Not Tommy. He's strong and full of life. It couldn't be him. Someone must have made a mistake.

She became aware that the long pinstriped legs of the *maître d'* were standing right beside her and she looked up at him thinking she would have to find the words to explain why she was sitting down but his face was so full of sympathy she burst into tears.

'What is it?' he said. 'Can I help in any way?'

She held the letter out to him mutely and he took it and read it and pursed his lips. 'You will want to travel as soon as possible,' he said. 'Leave it to me. I will see what can be arranged.'

Somebody gave her a cup of tea and a waitress rubbed her hands and presently the *maître d'* came back to tell her that he'd changed her shift and she could catch the eleven o'clock train from Victoria that morning.

It was unreal to be sitting in a train. Unreal to be going home. Even when she was walking across the fields on her way to Binderton and could see the cottages in the distance, it was still unreal, as if it was happening in a dream. She couldn't think what on earth she could say to poor Ma.

The cottage was unnaturally quiet. Tess and Edie and Johnnie were sitting together on the old sofa, looking unwashed and pale and tear-stained.

'I *am* glad you've come our Rosie,' Tess said. 'She's upstairs. Mrs Taylor's with her.' She was clutching a soaking wet rag in her lap and her face was strained with grief.

Rosie climbed the stairs slowly, still struggling to think of something to say, but as soon as she walked into the bedroom she knew there was no need for words at all. She sat on the edge of the bed and put her arms round her poor stricken mother and rocked her as if she were a child.

'First our Tommy and now the baby,' Maggie mourned.

'It ent fair, our Rosie. It just ent fair. What did our Tommy ever do to deserve this? An' young Charlie an' all. An' he only went because of our Tommy. It ent fair.'

'I'll be here for as long as you need me, Ma,' Rosie promised. The *maître d'* would understand.

She stayed for more than a week, running the house, cooking the meals, washing the dirty sheets and her siblings' clothes and doing her best to comfort Ma and Pa, while Tess and Edie helped her whenever they could and wept on her shoulder whenever they couldn't. The baby was buried in its pathetic white coffin early on Sunday morning and that evening, feeling she'd done all she could for the moment, Rosie said goodbye to her shattered family and caught the train to London. She felt as if she'd been away for a lifetime.

*

It was a little easier to be back in the familiar surroundings of the club, doing her usual work in her usual way. Grief terrorised her dreams and kept her wakeful in the small hours but at least there was a pattern to the days. It was only her half days off that presented a problem and that was because she didn't know what to do with them. She drifted through the London streets, week after week, cocooned in grief and disbelief, discovering well-known landmarks without being moved by any of them. In Trafalgar Square she gazed at the height of the column and walked round the plinth from one stone lion to the next and drifted away. She traversed the length of the Mall in a shower of rain, and circled the monument to the old queen and thought how stern and disagreeable she looked and drifted away from that too. Tommy was dead and nothing was real, nothing had substance, there was no meaning to anything.

Which was how she found herself in the middle of a demonstration without realising where she was.

She'd gone out one chilly October afternoon with a vague idea that she would take a look at the Charing Cross and was standing gazing vacantly at the elaborate stone tracery of it rising in front of Charing Cross station when she was jostled by a passer-by and looked round to find herself surrounded by a group of women all marching towards Trafalgar Square. They were a fierce-looking bunch in well-worn clothes, tatty hats and down-at-heel boots and they were carrying a huge banner that read *'Human suffrage and no infringement of popular liberties'* which didn't make much sense to her.

But then she became aware that there was a sizeable crowd of people standing on the pavement on both sides of the road, most of them women and all of them clapping and cheering and calling out to the marchers. 'Votes for women!', 'God bless you!', 'Keep up the fight!' and, 'Good old Sylvia.' And she realised that these marching women must be the suffragettes she'd been reading about in the papers and she looked at them again with greater understanding. One of the marchers, who was a most determined-looking young woman, was moving from side to side of the column so that she could shake hands with their supporters. They seemed very fond of her and clung to her hands. And then, as if in answer to some hidden signal, the marchers began to run and the crowd on the pavement ran with them and there was a headlong rush into Trafalgar Square with Rosie carried along in the middle of it, willy-nilly. Within seconds they reached the nearest plinth and began to climb up on it so that it was lined with women all waving to the crowd gathered and gathering below them. And the determined-looking one began to make a speech.

Rosie couldn't hear a word of it because there was such a din in the square, women shouting and cheering, motor buses and cars making their horrid roaring noises and sounding their horns and a group of red-faced men standing just north of the plinth shaking their fists and bellowing abuse. Their voices were so loud and angry she could hear everything *they* said. 'Shut yer face!' they roared, 'Trollop!', 'Slag!', 'Stinkin' whore!' She watched them closely, ready to run if they got out of hand. They were hurling screwed up balls of paper at the platform. They came flying over the back of the nearest lion and burst into colour when they landed. The women on the platform were daubed with crude patches of red and yellow. That's paint, Rosie thought and looked round wildly to see if she could push her way out of the crowd. The girl standing next to her had the same idea.

'Stone me!' she said. 'They're throwin' paint at us. How dare they!' And was struck on the side of the face by a missile full of red ochre. It stained her pale cheeks and fell into her hair and onto the collar of her jacket. 'Oh fer cryin' out loud!'

'Don't rub it,' Rosie said. 'It'll brush off. Stand still an' I'll do it for you.' She took her handkerchief out of her pocket and began to brush the powder away, flicking it delicately. She was concentrating so hard she didn't notice the approach of the young man until his face was within inches of her own. Then she looked up to find that she was staring at a lion. Such a mane he had, escaping from underneath his cap and falling over his forehead, and such a broad nose and such eyes, almost as tawny as a real lion's would have been but full of tender concern.

'I can't leave you fer a second, our kid,' he said, putting a large hand on the girl's shoulder. 'Now what you been up to?'

She waved a vague hand at the crowd by the plinth. 'It ain't me, our Jim,' she said. 'It's that lot over there. I never done nothink.' And she appealed to Rosie. 'Did I?'

He'd seen the yobs and the balls of paper and taken it all in before she could reply. 'Leave it to me,' he said to the girl. 'I'll soon 'ave *them* sorted out.' And was gone, padding through the crowd in a leonine way, moving remarkably neatly and quickly for such a big man.

'He will an' all,' the girl said, admiringly.

He picked his prey very neatly too, seizing the biggest

of the bullies by the throat and pushing him backwards against the plinth. There was a brief struggle. Another man tried to intervene and was punched to the pavement, a third shouted obscenities and threw a couple of punches that didn't land and then it was over and the lion was walking back to them, rubbing his knuckles and looking pleased with himself.

'That's seen 'em off,' he said. 'Good job I come here. Time fer tea, our Kitty.' And he gave Rosie a grin. 'You an' all, if you like.'

She followed them obediently. After all, if you get an invitation from the king of beasts, you don't say no.

He took them to the Strand to a teashop called the Lyons Corner House, which seemed marvellously appropriate, and they were served tea and buns by a waitress in a black dress and an elaborate white cap with black ribbon threaded through it and sat at a long table with lots of other people who were all very friendly. By the time she'd drunk two cups of tea and eaten half her bun, Rosie had discovered that Kitty *was* a suffragette and a very ardent one and that she worked 'in munitions' and that the lion was her brother and a docker.

'What's 'ard grind I can tell yer,' he said to Rosie and grinned at his sister. 'Not that she'll let me get a word in edgeways now she's on about her suffragettes.'

'Who was the woman what spoke?' Rosie asked.

'That's Sylvia Pankhurst,' Kitty said. 'Ain't she marvellous! She'll get the vote for us if anyone will. I never see such a fighter. She says they should give the vote to everyone what's serving in this war, soldiers, sailors, munition workers. Everyone. If you're good enough to go out an' risk gettin' killed, you're good enough to get the vote.'

Killed, Rosie thought. Oh dear God. Killed. The word clawed at her, tearing her chest with an onrush of grief, filling her throat. She put her face in her hands and wept with anguish.

Kitty was most upset. 'What've I said?' she asked, looking at her brother. 'I didn't mean . . . This is awful Jim.'

He put his arm round this poor weeping girl and silenced his sister with a quick shake of his head. 'Someone you knew?' he asked.

There was so much sympathy and kindness in his voice that Rosie told him. 'My brother.' And that made her cry even more.

'Cry all you want,' he said, looking at her bent head with an aching pity. 'We'll look after yer.'

She cried until there were no more tears. Then she felt a bit ashamed of herself, weeping like that in a public place, and looked up at him ready to apologise.

'Don't say nothink,' he told her. 'There ain't no need. 'Appens to all of us.' And when she'd wiped her eyes, he stopped cuddling her and finished his tea. 'Tell yer what,' he said. 'Seems ter me you could do with a bit a' cheerin' up. How'd yer like to come to the music 'all?'

'What's that?'

'What's that?' he echoed in feigned disbelief. 'D'you mean

ter say you never been to 'alls? Well stone me. We must put that ter rights. Don't yer think so Kitty. What yer doin' tonight?'

'Well nothing much,' Rosie admitted. 'I usually just go back to the club.'

'Then that's settled,' he said, standing up. 'Come on. We'll jest be in time fer the first 'ouse. It's jest what you need.'

Put like that, how could she refuse?

Chapter Seven

Despite its tear-stained start, that evening was one of the best that Rosie had ever spent in her life. Everything about it was perfect from her first open-mouthed sight of the amazing hall, all red and gold and blazing with gaslight, to the last triumphant song of a riotous evening. She sat between her two new friends, happy and safe among the hundreds in the hall and there wasn't a toff in sight. All the men wore the same sort of clothes as Jim: cloth claps, work-worn jackets and ragged trousers, with bits of coloured cloth tied in a variety of knots around their throats, and they talked in the same London accent, sharp and quick. The women were dressed to the nines in feathery hats, embroidered blouses and their best skirts and jackets, which might be patched and darned but were being worn with determined style. Wafts of their cheap perfume mingled with the usual London smell of unwashed clothes and dust and sweat, and there was a feeling of happy excitement, even before the curtains opened.

And when they did, what treats were in store. First came a master of ceremonies, very grand in evening dress and smoking a big cigar, who introduced a succession of turns in the most extravagant language she'd ever heard – a magician in a spangled cloak who pulled eggs out of his mouth and his ears, several comedians, one with a dog that jumped along on its hind legs to rapturous applause, and lots of singers dressed in dazzling costumes. They all spoke with London accents too and sang about their lives, mocking the situation they were in and the way they were dealing with it.

One man sang about his *pretty little gardin* and what a wonderful view it had, finishing with some gently ironic words that the audience were obviously waiting for. *'Wiv a ladder an' some glasses, you could see the 'Ackney Marshes, if it wasn't fer the 'ouses in between'*. They clapped him for so long he had to sing it again and this time they all joined in.

'Good?' Jim said to Rosie, when the singer finally waved his hat at them and left the stage.

'Wonderful,' she told him and it wasn't an exaggeration.

'You wait till the last act,' he said grinning at her. 'We got a real treat then.'

'What is it?' she asked.

'It ain't a what,' Kitty told her. 'It's a who. It's Marie Lloyd. Whatcher think a' that? Marie Lloyd. Come 'ere special.'

Rosie said, 'Oh,' because she was obviously expected to

say something and then added. 'Who is she?' because Kitty was waiting for her to say more.

Kitty was so shocked her eyebrows disappeared into her tawny fringe. 'Who is she?' she repeated. 'Ain'tcher never heard a' Marie Lloyd? Well stone me! She's only the best thing on the 'alls.'

But there the conversation had to stop. The master of ceremonies was on his feet, flicking the ash from his cigar and beaming. 'And now, Ladies and Gentleman, I give you the moment you've all been waiting for. I give you, the one and only, artfully, artistically amazing, musically masterful, mistress of sweet and saucy songs, our terpsichorean temptress, our own, our very own, Miss Marie Lloyd.'

The applause sang in Rosie's ears like the roar of the sea. They were stamping their feet, whistling, cheering. And a short dark-haired woman with huge dark eyes strode out onto the stage, holding out her arms to them as if she was going to hug them all. She was wearing a very tight gown over a very tight corset, pretty shoes and a flamboyant hat topped with ostrich feathers that dipped and trembled as she moved and she had a wonderfully cheeky expression on her face. Rosie liked her at once and when she started her first song her voice was so strong and extraordinary that she forgot about everything else – the war, Tommy's death, her poor Ma, even her grief – and just gave herself up to the joy and shock of what she heard.

It had a catchy chorus that sounded almost innocent. '*I always hold in havin' it if you fancy it. If you fancy it, that's understood. An' suppose it makes you fat, I don't worry over that, a little of what you fancy does you good.'* But the verses hinted at pleasures that Rosie wasn't at all sure should even be talked about leave alone sung about on a public stage and that was amazing and scandalous. She could feel her cheeks growing hot at the ideas this Marie Lloyd was putting into her head. How could she be so bold? But wasn't it wonderful that she could?

By the end of the evening, she cheered her new heroine so long and so loudly that her throat was sore.

'Pie an' mash an' a pint,' Jim said, taking her by the elbow.

'Yes, please,' she said. It was just what she needed. But when her belly was full and her throat washed smooth with beer she began to feel guilty. She'd taken so much that evening and not offered to pay a penny. 'Could I pay for the beer?' she said when the second round arrived.

He grinned at her. 'My treat,' he said. 'Like I told yer, I'm flush. What time you got to be back?'

She glanced at the clock on the wall and was horrified to see that she'd only got half an hour left. Where had the time gone?

'Don't worry,' he said, when she told him. 'I'll get you there in plenty a' time. Sup up.'

She tried to protest that she could make her own way back but there was no arguing with him. 'Can't have you wanderin' about the streets a' London on yer own this time a' night,' he said. 'I'm takin' you home an' that's that.'

They talked about the music hall all the way back to Pall Mall. Rosie was enjoying it so much, it seemed no time at all before they were standing in front of the servants' entrance at the club. Then she realised that this amazing evening was nearly over and felt quite cast down.

But Jim had a surprise for her that lifted her spirits at once. 'There y'are,' he said. 'Home safe an' sound. Same time next week?'

She was pleased to find that she could recover from her surprise quickly enough to find an answer. 'All right,' she said, 'but only if I can pay my way.'

'Quarter past seven at the tram stop,' he said, gave her a grin and walked away.

She couldn't linger to watch him go because she was afraid of being late in and she knew she was cutting it fine, but later that night, when she was on her own in her narrow bed and couldn't get to sleep for thinking, she turned the whole evening over and over in her mind and wondered. Are we walking out? she thought. She could see why he'd invited her to the halls in the first place. It was because she'd been so upset and he was being kind and trying to cheer her up. But to ask her out a second time felt different. Was it different?

It was a disappointment to her that it turned out to be exactly the same. He and Kitty met her at the tram stop, they all went to the music hall and were happily entertained, they ate pie and mash afterwards, all of which he paid for, and then he took her home and said, 'Same time next week?' just before he left her. All exactly the same. She tried to be sensible about it even though she was disappointed, telling herself that they'd hardly known one another any time at all and that he was a good friend and she ought to be satisfied with that. But she wasn't satisfied and that night she dreamed of him, yet again, and this time he was kissing her the way she'd seen poor Charlie kissing that girl Millie, mouth against mouth and with his arms right round her. She woke in confusion, feeling ashamed of herself to be even thinking such things. It was downright immodest. She would have been surprised and encouraged if she'd known that her handsome lion had been dreaming very similar dreams.

Jim Jackson had always been a stolid sort of boy, getting on with his work, looking after his Ma when his father died, running errands when he was twelve, heading off to the docks when he was fourteen and old enough, always making the most of things. Now he was a bit taken aback by the strength of his dreams. He'd lusted after quite a few girls since he started at the docks, all of them pretty or saucy and none of them attainable but this one was different and had been since that first evening, when he'd put his arms round her without thinking and had hardly been able to think of anything else ever since. His dreams were wildly erotic and, as he told himself in the morning in his sensible way, wildly unlikely. But being sensible about them didn't stop them returning night after night. Sometimes, when he was walking home from the docks and his back was aching with the effort he'd been making, he thought of her most tenderly and wished he could be walking home to a place of his own where she would be waiting for him. And then he wondered whether dreams ever came true and hoped that they did. She came to the halls with him every week now and that was a start, wasn't it? We'll see how we go along next Thursday.

But that morning Rosie had a postcard from Edie that changed both their plans.

'*Do you think you culd come and see us again,*' it said, '*onny its Ma. She is in a weird state a mind and dose so want to see you. We are well enuf being it is so cold. I hope you are well enuf too. Your ever loving sister, Edie.*'

She wrote back that afternoon to say she would ask for some time off and promised she would be with them as soon as she could manage it. And the next day she consulted with the *maître d'* and arranged to swap shifts so that she could have two days off instead of one and could be with them the Thursday after next. Taking action so quickly made her feel proper and virtuous. But her virtue didn't protect her from her disturbing dreams. They continued and got progressively more daring so that when her next night at the halls arrived and she was sitting next to big Jim in the gallery and so close that they were arm against arm, she felt suddenly shy. Good job he can't see what's going on in my head, she thought. But he'd brought a paper bag full of humbugs and, not having x-ray vision, was more concerned with sharing them round between every act.

It was very cold when they emerged from the warm cocoon of the hall, so cold that it made her shiver, and the street lights had acquired a fuzzy halo.

'There's a fog comin',' he said, smiling at her. 'You need a pair a' gloves. Put yer 'and in my pocket. That'll warm yer.'

It also meant that they had to walk very close together. Closer than they'd been since that first evening, when he'd put his arms round her. So close she could smell his jacket. It made her quite breathless. 'You been working with coal,' she said.

'All day,' he said. 'Wears you out coal does. Wears you out, breaks yer back an' makes yer stink.'

'I don't mind the smell of coal,' she told him. 'Makes me think of fires.'

They'd arrived in Pall Mall so she had to take her hand out of his pocket. The loss of his warmth made her shiver. 'You're still cold,' he said and took both her hands in his and chafed them. 'Why, you're like ice.'

To have her hands held was so pleasant she just stood still and enjoyed it. 'You need a pair a' gloves,' he said.

'Yes,' she said.

He went on chafing her hands while she grew steadily more breathless and the fog gathered around them like a veil. 'Get inside quick,' he said at last, 'or you'll be late. Same time next week?'

It was dreadful to have to tell him she was going back home and couldn't manage it. 'It's my Ma you see,' she explained. 'She's in a state.'

He was disappointed but tried not to show it. 'I 'spect she is,' he said seriously. 'Losin' her son an' everythin'.' But he was thinking how close and pretty she was and wishing he could kiss her.

'Yes,' she agreed sadly. Oh how close and handsome he was. If only he'd put his arms round her the way he did before.

But he was turning, moving away. 'Look after yerself,' he said. And then he was striding into the fog, growing less substantial by the second, dissolving before her eyes.

If only he could've kissed me, she thought as she climbed the stairs to her bedroom. Just once. The way he does in my dreams. But then she felt ashamed of herself for being silly. Life ent like a dream, she thought ruefully. Life's for real an' you got to get on with it.

*

The journey to Binderton was bitterly cold and far too full of anxious thoughts to be comfortable and her walk through the fields was wind-battered, slippery and difficult because the footpaths were full of frozen puddles and ridged with recent wear. But when she saw Edie standing at the cottage window looking out for her she forgot about the weather because she looked so upset and was biting her nails, which was always a bad sign.

'I *am* so glad you've come our Rosie,' she said, pulling her into the warmth of the cottage. 'I been at my wits' end with her. She does the housework an' everything same as usual but she will keep all on about how he's not dead. It's awful.'

The room had been swept clean and tided and there was a good fire burning in the hearth but there was no sign of their mother.

'Where is she?' Rosie asked.

'Out in the garden,' Edie sighed. 'I can't get her to come in. I've tried but . . .' She shrugged her shoulders. 'Go out an' you'll see what I mean.'

Their mother was digging up the vegetable garden. She was wearing her boots and her gardening hat and an old blanket wrapped around her oldest clothes like a shawl and she looked formidably determined.

When she saw Rosie, she straightened her back and rested on her spade and looked at her with such an odd expression on her face that Rosie was quite chilled by it. 'Hello Rosie,' she said. 'You got a day off then? I'll just get this done, ready for our Tommy. He'll want to plant it out when he gets home. Won't take me a minute, and then we can have some bread and cheese.'

Rosie was torn with pity for her. She's lost her memory poor old thing, she thought. 'Oh Ma,' she said. 'He ent comin' home. He's gone. You got the telegram. Don't you remember?'

She couldn't have said anything worse. Her mother's vague expression changed into the darkest fury she'd had ever seen. 'Don't you start all on,' she shouted. 'You're as bad as Edie an' the others. I won't have it. He ent dead. I won't have it. They got it wrong. You'll see. He's comin' home. I give him that rabbit's foot. An' you can just shut up about it. D'you hear me? I'm sick to death, hearing all this rubbish. I don't want a peep out of you.'

Rosie was so upset she didn't know what to say or do. She stood in front of her furious mother with the wind stinging her face and whipping her skirt against her legs and struggled to keep herself under control. 'I'll go an' put the kettle on shall I?' she said at last. 'Make a nice cup a' tea.'

'Tea!' her mother screamed. 'I don't want tea. What good's tea? Oh go away for pity's sake an' stop keepin' on at me! You're no earthly good to anyone. I can't waste my time on bloody stupid tea. I got to get this dug over 'fore it's dark. He's coming home. Don't you understand? We got to have everything ready for him.' And she jabbed the spade into the hard ground as if she was stabbing it.

Rosie fled. What else could she do? And when she reached the kitchen door she burst into tears. Edie led her to the sofa and sat her down and made her tea, her face drawn with concern.

'How long's she been like this?' Rosie asked when the tea had soothed her a little.

'Months,' Edie said.

'What does Pa say?'

'He don't say nothing,' Edie told her sadly. 'He's given up. Well you'll see when he comes in. He still keeps us fed but, apart from that, he's just sort a' quiet.'

Quiet and much smaller than she'd seen him the last time as if he was shrinking into himself. He kissed her lovingly and said he was glad to see her and praised the pie that she and Edie had made that afternoon. 'You make a good pastry our Rosie.' But she noticed that he was watching Ma all through the meal and the watch was anxious. It was an unnaturally quiet meal. Edie hardly said anything and Johnnie ate quietly too, sitting as close to his protective big sister as he could, and Ma didn't say a single word until the dishes were being cleared. Then she stood up and announced that she was off to her bed and left them. And as soon as she'd gone, Pa began to cry.

'What are we to do with her, our Rosie?' he asked.

'I don't know,' Rosie said honestly. 'We can't change what she thinks. I mean, she's wrong. We all know that. But she seems stuck in it.' And, as she felt she ought to hold out some hope for them, she added. 'I'll see what I can find out.'

'How long you stayin', our Rosie?' Johnnie said.

'Just 'til tomorrow morning,' Rosie told him. 'But I'll come back as soon as I can. I promise.'

She was touched by how grateful they were to her. It made her feel ashamed because there was so little she could do to help them.

*

Life back in London went on its predictable way. Rosie did her work, sent postcards to Edie and read the newspapers that the wealthy guests left lying about in the lounge, even though the news from the Front was always bad. There was yet another battle at that dreadful Ypres place. The fighting there seemed to have been going on for ever. From time to time, when she could bear to, she read the casualty lists in the *Times* and was horrified by the numbers being killed. It's thousands and thousands, she thought. If they go on like this there won't be any young men left. Why don't they stop it? It was quite a relief to set out for the halls on Thursday evening.

Jim and Kitty were waiting by the stop as they usually did and Kitty was pink with excitement.

'Guess what I seen while you been away,' she said as they walked towards the Star. And when Rosie looked a question at her. 'I seen a *woman* conductor on one a' the trams. Up the Embankment. Imagine that. Our Sylvia was right. There's women working all over the place. It ain't jest munitions. They'll 'ave ter give us the vote now. We're having a meeting about it on Sat'day at the Central Hall. Why don'tcher come? It'll be ever so good. Keir Hardie'll be there.'

The name gave Rosie quite a shock. 'Keir Hardie?' she said. 'The politician one?'

'That's 'im,' Kitty said. 'He's wonderful. Backed us from the beginning. Took in our petition. Spoke up fer us at our meetings. An' such a speaker! You wait till you hear 'im. You will come, won'tcher?'

'I will if I can get the time off,' Rosie said, and was rewarded with a hug.

And oh it *was* good to be back in the old Star, in all that red and gold warmth with the gaslights so gentle and people singing and enjoying themselves and being normal. And humbugs to chew and fish and chips afterwards because Jim said they needed warming up before their walk home. That was true enough because it was trying to snow and the air was so cold it hurt their lungs. This time, instead of just telling her to put her hand in his pocket, he plucked up courage and put an arm round her shoulders and held her quite close as they walked along the icy pavements, saying, 'Can't 'ave you tumbling.' It was worrying him a bit that, after all the fun in the Star, she was being so quiet. Eventually he asked her a question.

'Did it go off all right, your trip to the country?'

'No,' she admitted sadly. And because his face was full of concern and she thought she knew him well enough to confide in him, she told him what had happened and how very odd her mother was being. 'I can't understand it,' she said. 'She was always so sensible and now she's like a wild thing.'

He thought about it for quite a long time before he answered. 'Could be grief,' he said at last. 'You ain't yourself when you're grievin'. As I know. I done some stupid things when my ol' man died. Kicked out at things. Tore things up. I don't know how my poor Ma ever stood it an' that's a fact. Wasn't like me at all. I mean I aint the sort to fly off the 'andle.'

'No,' she said. 'I can see that.' And ventured a question. 'Were you very young?'

'Nine,' he said. 'Goin' on ten.'

She was full of sympathy for him. 'That's awful,' she said.

'It was,' he told her. 'End a' the world.' He was lost in the aching memory of it. 'It was 'orrible death. He was crushed, yer see. Down in the 'old.'

She could see it clearly even though she'd never been near the docks. Crushed. Down in the hold. It was dreadful. 'Oh Jim,' she said, turning towards him, 'that's dreadful.' And without thinking whether she should do it or not, she put up her free hand to touch his face.

The touch broke his careful control. He pulled her into his arms and held her, kissing her hair and her forehead, trying not to tremble. Her mouth was so close he could feel the flutter of her breath. She was such a darling that to kiss her was the most natural thing in the world. He didn't need words or explanations. And although their first kiss was shy and rather awkward, by the time they'd kissed for the fifth time they weren't just breathless, they were triumphant. They had taken love's bait and everything was changed.

At last, she had to disengage herself and leave him.

'See you Sat'day,' he said.

She'd forgotten about her promise to Kitty. 'If I can wangle it,' she said.

'I'll pick you up at quarter to seven,' he said.

And did. So they went to her first political meeting together and for the first time in her life she felt the power of a large group of people all working for the same admirable ends. It was even more of a revelation to her than her first trip to the Star had been. For these were people who meant business, who were going to change things. And Keir Hardie was exactly as she knew he would be, strong, outspoken and full of compassion.

'We are very close to gaining the right to vote that we've all been striving for all these long and difficult years,' he told them in his rolling Scottish voice. 'There are now so many women at work in every part of the country that your presence is too obvious and your value too undeniable for even your most hard-bitten opponents to ignore you. Gone are the days when half our population was hidden away in their homes and powerless. Today, as well as making the munitions our troops depend upon, women are driving trams and trains, delivering coal, teaching our children, running our post offices, nursing the sick and the wounded in ever greater and greater numbers. You are a strong army, as numerous as the army in the field, and your day of victory is close and coming closer.'

He was cheered until the huge crowded hall roared with sound. Kitty was in tears and Rosie was so moved by it all that she could barely breathe.

'Glad you came,' Jim asked as he walked her back to the tram stop.

'I wouldn't've missed it for the world,' she said. 'You're right Kitty. He's wonderful.'

Chapter Eight

London was changing day by day and because her brain was fired by Keir Hardie's speech, Rosie was now acutely aware of it. She noticed something new every time she emerged from the cocooned world of the club, here a woman in a Holland overall and a mop cap climbing up a tall ladder to clean windows, there a woman tram conductor in her smart and now familiar uniform, women delivering bread and milk, a woman driving a van and smiling at all the passers-by, two nurses in long dark-blue capes and white caps, pushing the wheelchairs of two wounded soldiers under the denuded trees in Green Park. There seemed to be more wounded soldiers out on the streets every day too, all very noticeable in their bright blue uniforms and their blood-red ties. And still the killing and maiming went on. All that silly talk about what a 'good show' it was going to be and how it would be over by Christmas, Rosie thought, remembering the Eden boys and their fatuous conversations, and look at us now. One terrible casualty list after another. I'll bet Keir Hardie didn't think it would be over by Christmas. He's got more sense in his little finger than all the swells put together. If I ever get the vote I shan't waste it voting for any a' the swells, I shall vote for Keir Hardie.

But she didn't get the chance to vote for her hero, because in September the papers reported his death, far away in a place called Glasgow. Kitty was terribly upset and said she didn't know what they'd do without him.

It was bad news for Rosie too, because she'd admired him very much, but she was selfishly happy because she and Jim were walking out and wrote to one another every day and saw one another every week. And on top of that, they were going to the special Christmas show at the Star all on their own because Kitty was off somewhere else with her friends from the munitions. Jim was very excited about it and kept saying it was going to be 'somethin' really special', and so it was.

The master of ceremonies strode onstage, puffing his usual cigar but dressed in a full Father Christmas costume, long red coat, fur trimmed hood, white beard, black boots and all, and the performing dog made his entrance with a red pixie hat on his head and when he was applauded, took umbrage and scratched it off and killed it like a rat, leaping about the stage with it in his mouth, growling and snarling and giving it a thorough shaking. All the songs were old favourites so the choruses were sung by everybody in the hall and there was such a happy atmosphere of idiocy, beer and well-being that they emerged at the end of it as if they were tipsy.

'Pie an' mash?' Rosie said hopefully.

But Jim was standing still in the middle of the surging crowd, pulling something out of his pocket. It was a small parcel wrapped in brown paper.

'Let's 'ave one a' them cold 'ands,' he said to her. And when she held out her hand, he put the parcel onto her palm. 'To keep you warm,' he said. 'Merry Christmas.'

It was a pair of brown leather gloves with fleecy linings. 'Oh Jim,' she said. 'They're lovely. Thank you ever so much. Can I put them on now?'

'That's what they're for,' he said laughing at her and watched as she slid her cold hands inside the sturdy leather and flexed her fingers, smiling at him with the pleasure of it. He was so pleased with the success of his gift that he took her face in his hands and kissed her full on the mouth, right out there in front of all the people streaming out of the hall.

There was a chorus of cheers and whistles and cat-calls and one man called out, 'Don't eat her Jim!'

'She's my gel,' Jim said, grinning at him.

'I should 'ope so an' all,' the man said, punching his shoulder.

They were surrounded by a group of grinning men, all chiyicking and teasing. 'When you gonna make an 'onest women of 'er, our Jim?' one asked.

'Soon as she'll 'ave me,' Jim told him and made a joke of it. 'Not right this minute though. We needs our pie an' mash first.' And he put his arm round her and began to walk her away.

That was almost a proposal, she thought, and she was suddenly so full of happy excitement that she could feel her throat constricting. First a Christmas present and now this. She couldn't wait to get to St James's Park and the privacy they both needed. They ate their supper in a dream, holding hands whenever they could, and ran to catch the tram. And oh! it was wonderful to be on their own at last, in the grassy darkness of the park, away from street lights and crowds, with the stars white and unwinking above their kissing heads and the silence so intense they could hear it hissing.

'I shall love you fer ever an' ever an' ever,' Jim said, holding her face between his rough, gentle hands. 'I'd do *anythin'* fer you.'

'There's only one thing I want you to do for me,' she told him seriously, 'and that's not to do something.' That puzzled him so she went on quickly. 'What I mean to say is don't go joining up. Bad enough for Tommy to do it. I don't want you killed an' all.'

'Don't worry,' he told her seriously. 'I'm not a mug. My mate Sid had a letter from his son. He got a French woman to post it for him private like so's it didn't get censored. Told him exactly what it's like out there. He let me read it. That would a' made my mind up, never mind nothin' else.'

'Good,' she said trenchantly. 'I'm glad to hear it. If they want to fight their stupid war let them. Just don't you go gettin' involved in it.'

He laughed at her. 'I promise,' he said.

But he was reckoning without the government's power to control their lives. Just over a year later, they passed a bill that, although very few realised it at the time, would prove to be a death sentence for millions of men.

Jim and Rosie saw the news of it on a newsvendor's placard as they climbed down from the tram late one Thursday night, ready to start their walk to St James's Park. '*Conscription*' it said in letters a foot high.

The sight of it made Rosie feel afraid. 'What's that?' she asked.

'Wait there,' Jim said, 'an' I'll nip an' get a paper an' see.'

They read it together under the light of the nearest street lamp. '*The government has introduced a bill making it compulsory for all single men between the ages of eighteen and forty-one to join the armed forces. Every British male subject who on 15 August 1915 was ordinarily resident in Great Britain and who has attained the age of 19 but is not yet 41 and all those who on 2 November 1915 were unmarried or a widower without dependent children, unless he meets certain exceptions or has met the age of forty-one before the appointed date, is deemed to have enlisted for general service with the colours or in the reserve and is forthwith transferred to the reserve. He will now come under the controls specified in the Army Act.*'

'Well that's it,' Jim said bitterly. 'They can't get enough men to volunteer. They been floodin' us with posters but it don't do 'em no good 'cos we ain't mugs, not now we know what's goin' on out there. So they're goin' to call us all up whether we wants to go or not. If you're over nineteen you've had it. An' I shall be twenty-one come February.'

Rosie was so horrified that the government could do such an appalling thing that for a moment she didn't know what to say. Then she was shaken with fear that he would be sent away from her and killed like poor Tommy and even the thought of it turned her fear to anger. 'That ent right!' she cried. 'Oh they're such fools. Why don't they work out how to stop this stupid war instead a' sending more men out to be killed? That's just stupid an' wasteful an' cruel. Ent they killed enough already? Tell 'em you won't go. They can't make you.'

He looked at her furious face, chin in the air, brown eyes blazing and sighed because he knew he couldn't do what she was suggesting. 'They can,' he said. 'They're the government. They can do what they bleedin' like. They've already done it. They're not askin' us if we *wants* to go, Rosie. They're tellin' us we're goin'. We're in the reserve already.'

She was too busy planning his escape to pay attention to what he was saying. 'We'll run away,' she said. 'That's what we'll do. We'll go to Binderton an' you can hide there an' live in the cottage. Pa wouldn't mind. You could work on the farm or somethin'. You mustn't let them tell you what to do. They got no right. No right at all. I'll write to Edie an' tell her we're coming. You'll be safe there.'

'You're not listenin' to me,' he said angrily. He was caught up in a terrible creeping fear, knowing what he would have to face out there in those God-awful trenches, and it was making him furious, the way fear always did.

She was afraid and angry too. 'I'm not having you sent into the army, Jim, and that's flat. You'll be killed as sure as fate. I'll write to Edie the minute I get in. The sooner you get out of harm's way the better.'

His anger erupted before he could control it, the way it did when he was in the middle of a brawl. 'I'm *in* the army,' he yelled. 'Don't you understand? "*Forthwith in the reserve*" means I'm *in* the army. I was in the army the moment they passed this sodding law. In the army and subject to army law.'

'It's a law, that's all,' she said, her chin up and her face stormy. 'Just a law. Ignore it. You don't have to do what they say. I keep tellin' you. Just run away to Binderton an' keep right out their way. If you go to France you'll be killed.'

He couldn't understand why she was being so pig-headed. It was so stupid to say ignore it. Didn't she understand how dangerous that was? Over the past few months he'd heard some terrible stories about what was happening at the Front. He knew what army law could do. 'Ok. I run away,' he said mockingly. 'That's a wonderful idea. I don't think. An' what then? D'you know what then? Well I'll tell you. If you run away they send the military police after you an' they put you on trial as a deserter an' they find you guilty an' then they take you outside an' put you up against a wall an' shoot you dead. How'd you like that to happen?'

She was so appalled she denied it at once, her face fierce in the moonlight. 'They don't. They couldn't. You don't kill people on your own side.'

'They do. It's happening all the time out there, onny the papers don't tell you.'

It was more than she could bear to hear. 'Don't speak to me!' she yelled and swept off at a furious speed, running into the private darkness of the park as if she were being pursued by devils.

For the first time in his life Jim was too off balance to know what to do. He stood completely still and thoroughly uncertain and watched as her flying figure melted into the darkness and was gone. He was buffeted by powerful emotions, all of them strong and some of them shameful, fear, fury and a dreadful, puzzled anger at the way his Rosie was behaving. How could she be so stupid? Why didn't she understand? Why couldn't she just stop and listen to him for a moment? He felt she'd rejected him by running off and now he didn't know what to do. In the end he sloped off to the nearest pub and bought himself a pint of consolation. It didn't console him in the least, and nor did the second nor the third. After that, there was nothing left for him except to trail home feeling aggrieved and miserable, with a fine old headache gathering.

It was a relief to find that the living room was empty and quiet and the fire had died down to ashes. Kitty must have turned in, and just as well because he couldn't have faced having to tell her what had happened. He couldn't even face it himself. Loving his Rosie, and knowing she loved him and that, as soon as they could afford somewhere to rent, they would marry and live together, had become part of the fabric of his life, almost the reason for being alive at all, and now it had all been spoilt and he didn't know what he could do about it. He pulled out his truckle bed, tugged off his boots, tossed them under a chair and spread himself out on the mattress still fully clothed. He was so tired he couldn't think straight.

*

Rosie didn't stop running until she reached the club and by then she was so out of breath she had to stand still and recover a little before she could climb the stairs to her bedroom. But once there, she threw herself on the bed and wept with abandon. It was too awful to be borne, too awful to think about, too awful, awful, awful. Why wouldn't he listen to her? She could hide him away as easy as pie and they'd never find him. All he had to do was agree to it and she'd see to everything else. But no. He was going to let them put him in their rotten army and send him to France where he'd be killed as sure as fate. She couldn't bear it. It was just awful, awful, awful.

She must have cried herself to sleep because she woke in total darkness, feeling stiff, cold and very uncomfortable just as Big Ben was striking two. She got up, feeling it was time to be sensible, changed into her nightgown and went to bed properly, pulling the blankets right up under her chin and snuggling down to get warm. Then because her conscience was beginning to trouble her and she couldn't sleep, she tried to get her thoughts in order. It had been horrid of him to shout at her like that but then he was the one who'd been told he'd got to go into the army and that was enough to make anyone shout. Did they really kill the men who ran away? She couldn't bear the thought of such an awful thing but he wouldn't have said it if it hadn't been true. He might have a temper on him but he always told the truth. It was stupid of me to run off and leave him. I should've stayed where I was and argued it out, even if he *did* shout. And now we've had a row and heaven knows what that's going to do to us. I must write to him, she decided, and say I'm sorry for running away. I'll do it first thing when there's light enough. On which faintly comforting thought she fell asleep for the second time.

She wrote her letter before she went down to start work and posted it as soon as she was free to slip out for a minute. Then there was nothing she could do but wait and get on with her day.

Jim's day was peculiarly difficult. He'd managed to get taken on quite quickly but he had such a banging hangover he knew he was working too slowly to satisfy the gaffer and that made him clumsy as well as slow. He'd come home feeling bruised and miserable to find Kitty waiting with her hat and coat on, ready to go out to get fish and chips.

'You 'ad a right skinful last night, didn'tcher?' she said cheerfully. 'Look at the state of yer. I got the fire goin' all nice an' warm fer us. Kettle's on the 'ob. You can make the tea while I'm gone, can't you. Oh, an' you got a letter by the clock.' And she was off.

He was across the room in two strides to pick up his letter. If she'd written to him things couldn't be so bad, could they? He tore the envelope open and pulled out the letter with shaking fingers. The first words on it were such a relief he had to sit down.

'*My darling Jim,*' she'd written. '*I am so sorry I ran off like that. I shouldn't have done it. I been thinking about it ever since. I love you. Rosie.*'

He rushed to the dresser drawer to find a postcard, pushing the contents about much too roughly in his excitement, found a rather battered one and answered her at once. '*Sweetheart, I will see you on Thursday. Same place, same time, Jim.*'

It was in the post before Kitty arrived with their supper.

And oh what a wonderful thing it was to sit side by side in the warmth of the Star that Thursday and stroll into the private darkness of the park to kiss and kiss again and be forgiven. At one point, Rosie tried to tell him how sorry she was but he put a finger over her mouth to stop her.

'Don't let's talk about it, Rosie,' he said. 'What's coming'll come no matter what we do. Let's just enjoy ourselves while we got the time, eh?'

So they tried to forget their quarrel and enjoyed as much

time together as they could, acutely aware of how precious it was and how soon it could come to an end. His call-up papers arrived eleven weeks later at the daffodil end of March, together with a chit for the train to take him to Salisbury. Their lovely, easy courtship was over.

Chapter Nine

Jim spent the next six weeks on Salisbury Plain, mostly in unseasonably cold and rainy weather, learning how to be a soldier. He wrote to Rosie and Kitty every evening, even when he was aching with fatigue, partly because he knew they'd want to know what he was doing, but mostly because it was comforting to think of them as he wrote and it made him feel close to them. '*I got a uniform and a number and had a haircut, what you wont like.*'; '*The grubs pretty good. We eat it out of tins.*'; '*They learnt us to fire a rifle so now we have target practice.*'; '*It is very cold and muddy and the trenches are full of water.*'; '*We are getting used to artillery fire now what is very loud. The gunners practise every day and a right old row it is.*'

They wrote back to him every day too because they missed him every bit as much as he was missing them. It was a wonderful relief when he wrote to tell them he was coming home for two days on embarkation leave. Rosie swapped her next two evenings off so as to be with him and she and Kitty put money aside from their next pay packets so as to have enough for their outings.

It shocked them to see how much he'd changed. Neither of them liked his uniform although they pretended to admire it and they both secretly thought that he didn't look like their Jim anymore with all his lovely mane of hair shaved back to stubble but they were careful not to tell him that either. They just hugged him and sat on either side of him at the Star and held on to his arms every moment they could and kissed him goodbye most lovingly when they all went off together to catch his train. Neither of them cried until the train was out of sight and they were sure he couldn't see them. Then they put their arms round each other and sobbed their hearts out.

'It ent fair,' Rosie said angrily. 'Takin' him off like that when he never wanted to go. It shouldn't be allowed. Oh! If I was a politician there'd be some changes.'

'We can't do nothin' about it,' Kitty said resignedly.

'I'll do somethin' about it, one a' these days,' Rosie said fiercely, 'you see if I don't.'

'We'll 'ave to get the vote first,' Kitty told her, sadly. 'Can't do much wivout a vote an' that's a fact. Trouble is, I can't see us gettin' it now Keir Hardie's gone. I do so wish 'e 'adn't gone.'

She looked so downcast that Rosie yearned with pity for her. She set her anger aside and gave her a hug. 'Come an' have a pint,' she said.

But it took more than one pint to shift their misery and the next morning Rosie had to face work with a pounding headache. Serves you right! she scolded herself. You should've had more sense. But no amount of scolding could cure the headache nor stop her worrying about her Jim. She'd never been a particularly religious person but at that moment she sent up a prayer and meant every word of it. *Please God don't let him be killed.*

*

Jim wrote her a postcard as soon as his journey was over. His battalion was at a base camp in Picardy a few miles from the front line, but as they'd had strict instructions not to give anyone any details about where they were and warned that everything would be '*took out by the censor*' if they didn't do as they were told, he just said he'd arrived, that the crossing had been '*a bit rough*' and that the grub was '*pretty good considering*'. The next day they were given breakfast and set off to march to the front line, wearing their tin hats and carrying their rifles, respirators and all their kit, which got heavier with every step they took.

They sang music hall songs as they marched, the way they'd been taught to do on Salisbury Plain. It seemed cruelly unsuitable to Jim to be singing '*Pack up yer troubles in yer ol' kit bag an' smile, smile, smile*', when they could all be walking to their deaths but at least the song had a good strong rhythm that helped them to keep up a steady pace and after a while he gave up thinking about whether it was unsuitable or not and just plodded on, putting one foot after another, bellowing with the rest.

They arrived at the rear trenches in the middle of the afternoon and then they had to slog their way through the maze of trenches until they reached the front line, where they were shown their posts by a burly sergeant with a loud voice, a dry sense of humour and an irrepressibly cheerful grin. When he'd satisfied himself that they all knew what they were going to be doing in the front line, he led them to another trench and showed them the bunks where they would sleep *'if you ever gets the chance what I very much doubt'* and the latrines *'what you're to use at your convenience so to speak and don't let me catch none of you piddling nowhere else'*. Jim liked him at once although, from the stink in the trenches, it was obvious that a lot of men were piddling wherever they could. Then they were led back to the front line and shown the positions they were to take on the fire step when stand-to was called, and warned not to put their heads above the parapet *'unless you wants it shot off, what Jerry'll be only too happy to oblige'*. And after all that, they were given their duties. Jim and another new recruit called Fred were told to pump out the trench and lay down new duckboards where they were needed. Others were sent to dig new latrines and cover up the old ones, or to repair the sandbags, which were sagging and evil-smelling. And they were all advised to kill any slugs or stag beetles they found crawling up the sides of the trenches and give any rats they found a good thumping with their shovels.

'They're as big as bleedin' cats,' the sergeant warned, 'an' there's thousands of the beggars. They'll bite yer face off as soon as look at you, so watch out for yerselves.'

'An' a merry Christmas to you too Sarge,' Fred said.

That made them all roar with much needed laughter.

'All right! All right!' the sergeant said, grinning at them. 'Now let's be 'avin' yer, you dozy lot. We aint got all day.'

Jim and Fred worked hard that afternoon. Pumping out the trench was a foul, smelly job and by the time it was done their boots were clogged with mud, their puttees were more slime than cloth and Fred said they were like 'a couple a' mudlarks, strike me if we ain't'.

'*Strike me*' made Jim laugh. 'What part a' London *you* from then?' he grinned, leaning on his shovel.

'The Borough,' Fred told him. 'My ol' man's got a stall in Borough Market. Feigenbaum, fruit an' veg. I was workin' wiv 'im 'fore I got called up fer this lot.'

'Is that your name then?' Jim asked. 'Feigenbaum?'

'Bit of a monicker,' Fred said and explained. 'It's Jewish. My grandfather come to Whitechapel in the eighties to get away from the pogroms.'

'An' now you're in the Borough,' Jim said. 'So we're neighbours. I live in Southwark.'

'Near the ol' Star,' Fred said.

'Just up the road.'

'I used to go there a lot. Seen Marie Lloyd there once. Lovely she was.'

Jim was instantly back in the Star with Rosie sitting warm and close beside him. 'Me an' all.'

'I was a boxer once wiv her daughter,' Fred said.

Jim was intrigued, 'Whose daughter?'

'Marie Lloyd's. She runs the boxing in the Surrey Chapel up Blackfriars Road. She's the promoter like. Great lady. She's on the 'alls an' all. Bella Burge. Bella a' Blackfriars. You might ha' seen her.'

'So you was a boxer,' Jim said, resting on his shovel. 'Don't surprise me. I reckoned you was on account a' that hooter.'

Fred touched his broken nose, ruefully. 'Yep,' he said. 'Took a right hook I done. More fool me. You should ha' seen the shiners what went with it.'

'Takin' 'oliday are we?' the sergeant said, coming up behind them.

'No Sarge,' Fred said. 'Just breavin'.'

'Well leave orf breaving an' fix them duckboards,' the sergeant said. 'It'll be stand-to directly an' I wants 'em good an' ready by then.'

They grinned at him and took up their shovels. If he wanted it done by stand-to, it would be done. He was a good old bloke. It was tiring to be on the go all the time but, after six weeks on Salisbury Plain, reassuringly familiar. Stand-to, when it came was something new, nerve-racking and different. Commands were given briskly – fix bayonets, take position, keep yer eyes skinned – then they were left to stand on the fire step and watch the muddy wreckage in no-man's-land for any sign of movement from the German trenches. Dusk was the time when an attack was most likely and it was their job to watch out for it. When it was finally dark, they were given the order to stand down and the supply wagons began to arrive but that seemed to be the signal for the Germans to start shelling. The noise was so sudden and overwhelming that there was an outburst of terrified swearing all along the trench and within seconds two shells had exploded to their left and they could hear shouts and screams, so they knew some of their mates had been injured.

'Bloody hell fire!' Jim roared, as another shell shrilled overhead, and the sergeant stormed along the trench shouting at them to keep their bleedin' heads down. 'How long's this gonna go on, Sarge?'

'We 'ave a bit of a truce when it's grub-time,' the sergeant shouted back, 'as a general rule. But I shouldn't bank on it if I was you.'

The shelling went on until the supplies had all been delivered and the wagons had left. Then it stopped as suddenly as it had begun. Jim and Fred pulled off their helmets and wiped the sweat from their heads, looking at one another rather sheepishly.

'Gaw deary me,' Fred said. 'Look at the state a' this trench. It's shot to buggery.'

Jim took a hard look at it. It was full of mud, ancient rags and debris, broken planks, chunks of shrapnel still red hot, a trail of rusty barbed wire. And one section of the wall had fallen in and was blocking the walkway.

'Well I tell yer what,' he said, 'the grub had better be good after all this.'

It was the usual Irish stew served up in the usual mess tins, and they ate it by candlelight perched on the broken planks. But after that, the evening perked up no end because the mail arrived and Rosie's letter was so warm and loving, he felt almost normal again just reading it and took out his pencil and paper at once to answer her. Not that there was very much he could say, given it would all be read by the censor with his rotten blue pencil, but he told her he was well and that the grub wasn't bad and signed it with a long line of kisses. Even when the sergeant arrived to chivvy them all into working parties to clean up the trenches and take their turn on the night watches, he fell to willingly although he was tired to his bones.

He was still tired when the orderly officer arrived next morning to bully them awake. It was an hour before dawn and hideously cold but his orders were clear. They were to get their boots on smartish and look lively for stand-to. Then it was fix bayonets and they were up on the fire step again, peering into the darkness just as they'd done the previous evening, stamping their feet to keep warm and complaining to one another. Day broke far too slowly, staining the sky a lurid green and orange and revealing the filthy mess they were standing in. And just as they were beginning to hope it would get a bit warmer now the sun was up, there was a sudden rattle of machine gun fire from the German trenches followed by a deafening volley of artillery. They were instantly alert and afraid and peered through the mist that was rising from the miasma of no-man's-land, ready to give the alarm at the first sight of advancing troops. But none appeared and after a few seconds the sergeant bustled along the trench giving orders.

'Morning hate!' he called. 'Let 'em have it boys! Fire at will!'

They did as they were told, although they felt baffled to be asked to fire at the mist, but after a few minutes they got into the swing of it and were soon firing like maniacs. When the German guns finally fell silent they were wild with excitement, as if they'd won a victory. And then as if that weren't treat enough, they were all given a tot of rum. It made a cheerful start to the day.

After that they were back to their routine chores, taking it in turn to clean their rifles and stand guard, eating breakfast in the early light, being inspected by the company commander, hunting rats, picking the lice that had suddenly appeared to plague them, from the seams of their clothes, toiling to clear the filth in the trenches again and again. It was an incessant, daily drudgery. They were quite glad when their first fortnight in the front line came to an end and they could pick up all their equipment – shovels, respirators, backpacks, rifles and all – and trudge back to the rear trenches, where they handed over their filthy uniforms to be washed, slept on a bunk instead of the cold earth and were out of the stink and squalor for a couple of weeks and away from the fear, which was always there, every hour of the waking day, dragging at their guts, waiting and inevitable but kept private. It was no good talking about it. They all knew that. The horror would come sooner or later, when some fool general thought it was time for another push and then they'd be for it and there was nothing they could do about it. In the meantime there were orders to be obeyed, jobs to be done, a steady supply of grub, and letters to write and receive. Thank God for the postmen!

The horror came at the beginning of July. It opened with an artillery barrage that was so massive and went on for such a long time they were deafened by it and none of them were in any doubt that there was going to be a major assault. On the fourth of July, they were woken before dawn in the usual way and given a rather larger tot of rum than they were used to, which alerted Jim and Fred although, apart from making a grimace at one another, they were careful not to say anything. Then the changes began. They were ordered up on the fire step as usual but this time they were wearing their full battle kit, respirators, ammunition, water bottle, grenades and first-aid pack. And as the sun came up, the bombardment decreased and they all knew it would only be a matter of minutes before they were sent over the top.

Jim was more afraid than he had ever been in his life. His heart was beating so hard it was painful. It filled his chest and rose into his throat, tightening it so that he could barely breathe. He couldn't speak. He couldn't think. Swallowing was difficult, any movement impossible. He stood on the fire step, stiff as a mechanical toy, rifle at the ready, waiting and knowing that it was death he was waiting for. He was so taut that, when the whistles began to shrill, the sound made him jump. Then they were all on the move, scrambling over the parapet, struggling through the coils of barbed wire, walking forward into the smoke, crossing the stinking mire of no-man's-land, as the guns roared, shells screamed overhead and the enemy machine guns stuttered and rattled and spat red fire. Jim walked blindly, obeying orders in the way he'd been taught, but noticing everything as though his senses had been sharpened. The land in front of them wasn't flat as he'd imagined but rose in a gradual slope where the German trenches were, slightly above them and with a clear line of fire. We're open targets he thought, trudging forward, one foot after the other, as men screamed and fell all round him and lay in the mud crying and groaning and the machine guns went on spitting out their lethal fire. He was walking right behind a tall soldier who seemed to be firing his rifle with every step, steadily and stolidly. But then things happened at such speed there wasn't time to take them in.

A shell fell so close to them that they were covered in gobbets of mud and Jim could feel a piece of shrapnel falling hot and heavy on his tin hat. The tall soldier toppled backwards and fell towards him knocking him off his feet so that they were both falling. They landed in a shell hole full of muddy water and, for a few seconds, Jim struggled to stand and found he couldn't do it. Then he must have passed out because the next thing he knew he was waking to the sound of a duck quacking and lay on his back looking up into the smoke of the battle wondering what a duck was doing out there in that hellhole. It took him some time to work out that the sound was coming from the tall soldier who was lying virtually on top of him and was extremely heavy. They were both soaked in blood and Jim had no feeling in his feet. He knew he ought to get up and go on marching but he didn't have the energy to do it and, although he scrabbled in the mud to try and find something to grip to give him some leverage, he couldn't do that either. He lay on his back listening to the soldier's terrible breathing until he gave one last long choking sound and stopped. He's dead, Jim thought, poor sod, and he made another effort to struggle out from underneath him, pushing against the sides of the shell hole until he was more or less sitting up and then hauling the body to one side until he could ease out from underneath it. The smoke had cleared a little by that time although the sound of gunfire and the screams and groans were still going on. He had to pull his legs from under the soldier's body using both hands because by that time he had no feeling in the lower part of his body at all but at least his arms and legs were in one piece, although they were slimy with blood. But the soldier was mutilated. His face was just a mass of torn flesh, his belly was a huge gaping hole and his guts had fallen out and lay in the mud beside him in grey, bloodstained coils.

Jim was so shocked at the sight of him it made him

shake but, oddly, he felt no pity for the man. That should have shamed him but he didn't feel any shame either. The poor devil was gone. There was nothing he could do to help him. And he was left in the shell hole and would have to get up and go on with the attack even though he felt so tired all he really wanted to do was to lie down and go to sleep. He struggled to one knee and peered out over the rim of the hole. The rest of the battalion had moved a long way since he fell. He could see their moving bodies in the far distance, but there were other bodies too, hundreds and hundreds of them, lying in distorted positions everywhere he looked, limbs missing and faces blackened. It had been a massacre. A total, bloody massacre. And beyond all those obscene deaths were others that were even more horrific. The men in the front line had reached the enemy barbed wire and been caught up in it and shot to pieces where they struggled. Some were still hanging by the arms, some kneeling as if they were praying, but all of them were shattered and dead. It was a horror like nothing he had ever known or could possibly have imagined.

He slid back into the shell hole and tried to breathe normally. Then he passed out again.

*

When he came to for the second time, it was dark and there was a soldier leaning over the shell hole looking at him.

'Two more here, Corp,' the soldier called.

Another voice answered him, sounding quite close. 'Dead or alive?'

'Dead,' the soldier said.

Jim struggled to form words, swallowed, gasped and managed to croak. 'No. No. I ain't dead.'

'Correction,' the soldier said. 'One dead. One wounded.' Then he turned his head back to his casualty. 'Come on, then,' he said. 'Let's be 'avin' yer.'

They hauled him out of the slime, gave him a fag and asked if he could walk. When he said he thought so, they slung his arms round their shoulders and set off. He managed three steps before his legs gave way and he sank to his knees in the mud in an agony of frustration.

The corporal was calling for a stretcher and one seemed to have arrived, although he couldn't be sure because he was finding it hard to focus his eyes. He was lifted up and lowered onto the canvas and then four of them were carrying him through the squelch of the mud and the noise of the incessant shellfire towards the British trenches. Then he was in a wagon, sitting on benches with a lot of other wounded men, and he knew there were horses straining and blowing as they pulled it along.

After that he was too confused to be able to pay any attention to anything except the difficult business of sitting upright and the fact that there was a horrible painful pounding in his head and he knew from the smell that was rising from him with every jolt that he must have shit himself on that nightmare advance. He was relieved when they arrived at the casualty clearing station and he was eased out of the wagon by two more orderlies and half walked, half dragged into a dugout, which was crowded with wounded men. There was an overpowering smell of blood and shit. But there were also long rows of camp beds and he was able to lie down.

A uniformed doctor was inching along the packed rows examining his newly arrived patients one after the other with an orderly in attendance. He shone a torch into Jim's eyes and then asked, 'How many fingers am I holding up?' but it was difficult to answer because the fingers wouldn't stay in focus.

The doctor spoke to the orderly. 'No physical injuries,' he said. 'Probable concussion.' Then he turned to talk to Jim again. 'I'm sending you to a CCS,' he said. And moved on to the next soldier.

Another stretcher, another crowded wagon, another journey as the wagon walls swam in and out of focus and his nose was clogged with the smell of his own foul shit and the men around him groaned and cursed. And then they seemed to have arrived at a hospital of some sort. There were nurses waiting for them, clean and pretty in their white aprons and their white caps ready to lead them, gradually and carefully, into a tent full of beds. Oh the bliss of lying on a bed. The two nurses who were looking after him were gentle and thorough and set to work at once to strip off his blood-soaked uniform and examine him for wounds, gentling his shamefaced apologies aside.

'Not to worry,' one said. 'Most of our patients come in like this. Soon have you clean again. You'll feel better then.'

She was right. It was such a relief to be lying down in a clean bed wearing clean clothes – although the things they called pyjamas were a novelty to him. He managed to smile, for the first time since he'd gone over the top and the nurse smiled back.

'Better now?' she asked.

'I reckon I've died an' gone to heaven,' he said.

Chapter Ten

Rosie saw the headlines in *The Times* the following morning as she was serving breakfast at the RAC Club. Most of the people at the table had brought a copy in with them and they were all reading avidly. '*Great British Offensive*,' it said. '*Attack on 20-mile front. German trenches occupied. Our casualties not heavy.*' It made Rosie's heart constrict most painfully. Jim would've been in that, she thought. Bound to have been. *Oh please, please God don't let him be killed.*

It took all her self-control to take orders, serve the meals and keep smiling but she managed it and, when they'd all gorged themselves full in their rich, idle way, she loitered by the kitchen door until the room was empty, and darted in to retrieve one of the papers that had been left behind and hid it behind a curtain, working quickly before the others arrived to clear the tables and lay them again ready for lunch. The minute the tables were set she retrieved the paper and took it off to the kitchen where she read it attentively. Underneath the headlines were the words '*Official Statement*', so it had to be true, didn't it? If they said our casualties weren't heavy, there was some hope. *Oh please, please, please God don't let him be killed.*

As the day toiled on, she wondered whether she ought to write to him to find out how he was but thought better of it. If he was fighting he wouldn't have time for writing. She'd have to wait until he wrote to her. Oh she did so hope it would be soon.

A card came four days later, to her heart-juddering relief, and such a pretty one, embroidered all over with pansies and green ribbons and inscribed, '*To my sweetheart*'. He'd written a short message on the reverse side. '*I have been in action. I am ok. One of the chaps sewed this card and I bought it off him.*'

She took it with her when she went to meet Kitty at the Star on Thursday and Kitty was squeaking with delight because she'd had one too.

'An' all in Suffragette colours,' she said, taking it out of her pocket and passing it to Rosie. 'Ain't he jest the best bruvver you ever 'eard of?'

Rosie agreed that he was, but the sight of two embroidered cards worried her. A single card might have been embroidered in the trenches but two were most unlikely. And if he was buying them somewhere else, then where was he? Had he been injured and wasn't admitting it? If only they didn't have those stupid silly censors blue-pencilling everything out, he could tell her everything she wanted to know. As it was, she couldn't even write and ask him because they'd probably censor that too. High time they got this stupid war over an' done with, she thought fiercely. Then the curtain went up so she settled down to enjoy the show and tried to put her thoughts aside. They came back to torment her in the middle of the night, of course, but even then she did her best to be sensible. He would write again. She could depend on him to write.

The next letter arrived on Saturday to say he was at rest behind the lines and everything was ticketty-boo. She was so relieved she wrote back to him at once to thank him for the lovely card and to tell him how glad she was that he wasn't hurt. It didn't matter where he was as long as he wasn't injured. But the fear growled in her belly whenever she wasn't working and no matter how hard she tried to be sensible it wouldn't go away.

*

Jim stayed in the field hospital until the doctor was sure he could see properly, then he was sent to the rear trenches for the usual fortnight's rest. It was a sobering return. There were so few men there that he knew or could recognise. But when he was standing in line for his grub, mess tin in hand, he was suddenly thumped between the shoulder blades and, when he turned to see who it was, he found himself staring into the grinning face of Fred Feigenbaum.

'Thought you'd gone an' all,' he said.

'Not me!' Jim told him happily. 'Charmed life me.'

'Me an' all.'

They were so pleased to find one another again they spent the next five minutes punching each other's arms and backs and only stopped when the men behind them shouted that they were holding up the queue. But what Jim found out when they were settled on the benches eating their grub was dispiriting in the extreme. He knew there'd been hundreds of casualties. He'd seen them with his own eyes but to be told that there were only about a hundred of his own battalion left alive made his heart shrink with horror and pity.

'Took 'em three days to clear the bodies, poor sods,' Fred said bitterly. 'An' then we was sent over the top again. Bleedin' ridiculous. They brought in another battalion fer reinforcements. Didn't make a happorth a' difference. That bleedin' Haig should come down and try a bit of action fer hisself, instead a' sitting in a bleedin' castle miles away. Then we'd see some changes.'

'It's a stalemate,' another soldier said. 'Anyone can see *that*. We should pack it in an' all go home. We're never gonna get anywhere this way, keepin' all on an' on.'

That provoked a growl of agreement all along the table and, in the middle of it, a familiar voice spoke above the growl. 'Might a' know'd it'ud be you two,' it said. And there was their sergeant grinning down at them, mess tin in hand. 'Shift yer bums.'

They made room for him at once and slapped him on

the back, sergeant or no, because they were so pleased to see him still alive.

'Heard you was wounded,' he said to Jim, as he spooned his first mouthful into his face. 'Bli! This is hot.'

'Had it warmed up for you, special, Sarge,' Fred told him. Oh it *was* good to see him again, with his cap on sideways the way they remembered and his grin as friendly as ever and those blunt, tobacco-stained fingers clutching his spoon.

'So what they got planned fer us this time?' Jim asked.

'You got three weeks lolling around like the great lazy lumps you are,' the sergeant told them, 'what you'd better make the most of, let me tell yer, then we're off to another section.'

'Where's that then?' Fred wanted to know, 'or ain'tcher 'lowed ter say.'

'Got it in one, private. Not that you'd be none the wiser if I did on account of no one's ever 'eard of it.'

*

That night Jim composed the longest letter he'd ever written to his Rosie, telling her he was well but missed her more than he could say, that he'd got a bit of leave from the front line and wished he could spend it at home with her, that the grub was good but he wished he could be back with her eating their pie an' mash, '*What woulden I give for some fish and chips*' and signing it by writing her name in crosses for kisses.

Her answer came by return of post and from then on they wrote to one another every day, sending their love to one another and signing off with kisses. His final letter at the end of his three-week rest, was to tell her it might be a day or two before he could write again '*on account of we're on the march again*' and ended with her name and surname in an elaborate pattern of kisses, yearning to see her with every mark he made.

She understood the message at once. 'They're sending him back to those horrible trenches,' she told Kitty, when they met up that evening. It upset her so much her eyes were brimming with tears. 'God rot the lot of 'em. Why can't they stop it?'

Kitty put her arms round her neck and kissed her. 'Don't take on our Rosie,' she said. 'He'll be orl right. You'll see. Come up the pub an' get yerself warm. Your 'ands are like ice.'

'We don't even know where he is,' Rosie wept. 'He could be anywhere.'

*

He was in a narrow and extremely uncomfortable trench, looking out over a total wasteland towards a village the sergeant said was called Courcelette, 'if you ever 'eard such a damn silly name. I seen plenty a corsets in my time but never a one of 'em was a town.' It was hilly territory and had originally been wooded but now the trees had all been blown to bits and there were only blackened stumps sticking out of the mud like rotten teeth and the long slopes were gouged with trenches, as far as they could see, one line behind the other.

'They seen some action here,' Jim said.

Fred sucked his teeth. 'An' now they're gonna see some more,' he said. 'You got a gasper?'

Jim took his battered packet of Wills from his tunic pocket and lit up for them both. 'When d'you reckon it'll be?' he asked as he handed Fred's one over.

'Don't ask me, mate,' Fred said, bitterly. 'We're just the poor bloody infantry. Yes sir, no sir. That's us. I'll tell you somethin' though. It'll be the same bleedin' shambles as all the others.'

But he was wrong. This time it was different although it began with the usual routines, early rise, tot of rum as the barrage continued, inspections, breakfast, stand-to. But then they were suddenly warned to keep their heads down and seconds later a huge engine roared above them, and an enormous machine dipped towards the trench, juddered, righted itself and rolled straight across the gap. It was made of metal, painted khaki and instead of wheels it had long rollers that turned slowly, churning up the mud but moving inexorably forward toward the German lines. They had never seen anything like it in the whole of their lives. Even a motor bus seemed puny compared to a machine so large and powerful and dominating.

'Cor, strike me blind,' Fred said, gazing at it. 'What the hell is that?'

'It's armour plated whatever it is,' Jim said watching it. The German machine guns were firing straight at it and it didn't seem to have taken a single hit.

But there was no time for speculation. No time for thought. Whistles were blowing, they were scrambling over the parapet plunging through the gap the machine had torn in the barbed wire, marching out into no-man's-land. Jim had a brief impression that there were a dozen of the things all round him, maybe even fourteen, then he ran to get behind the nearest protective flank as quickly as he could. The sky was full of whizz-bangs, the stink of foul mud, cordite, shit and rotting flesh was as foetid as ever, but at last there was a safe place to run to. Even when the fight grew bloody, shells were exploding all round him and men were falling and screaming, the sound of those engines was a steadying roar that made him feel confident. He walked behind his one, following the track it was making and after a while he thought he could hear cheering and Fred appeared out of the smoke to shout, 'We're through! We've broken through!' He shouted back at him to keep his bleedin' head down, but the message made him feel triumphant, as if it was possible to win this war after all. It was a momentary feeling because the pulse of their attack was beating hard. There were orders to obey, a clear trail to follow through the German barbed wire, now flattened and neutered by the ponderous weight of the new vehicles, and then they were jumping down into the German trenches and the only Germans there were dead ones. All the others had gone. And it was time to dig in.

In the days that followed, the Germans counter-attacked and they had to fall back again which they did without taking too many casualties. Then it was a long battle to and fro among the decaying dead and the putrid filth of no-man's-land until their uniforms were more mud than cloth and they were so dumb with fatigue they hardly knew where they were or even noticed the loss of their mates. And then the whole thing petered out and they were back in control of the German trenches and not long after that they were allowed to trudge back to their own lines for a few days' rest.

'It's the third bleedin' Christmas of the war,' Fred said lugubriously. 'All that rot about how it was only gonna last fer six months an' look where we are.'

'Reckon we should be owed some leave,' Jim said. 'I've a good mind to ask the sergeant.'

He was surprised to find that leave was not only owing to them but was going to be granted.

'We shall be there in the new year,' he said to Fred. But the words were empty in his mouth and he didn't believe them. It wasn't until he stepped off the train at London Bridge and saw Rosie standing on the platform waiting for him that he finally realised that good things could happen to him again. He ran to pull her into his arms and stood on the platform kissing her hungrily and publicly for a very long time.

'Oh Rosie!' he said when he finally paused for breath, 'this is just . . . you don't know how . . .' But there were no words to tell her how he was feeling.

Not that either of them needed words. What they felt was clear on their faces.

'I got time off,' Rosie said, linking her arm in his and leading him out of the station. 'They been ever so good. Nearly a week. Kitty'll be home in an hour or two. She said to tell you. What d'you fancy to eat?'

He was so happy to be back home with her he felt as though his chest was bursting. 'Anythink 'ud be nectar,' he said.

They lived on kisses and nectar for the next ten days, walked in the park, cold though it was, ate well and went to the Star and the pictures in the evenings. Once, he told her about Fred and what a good mate he was; on another occasion, he told her about the tanks and how they might be the thing to end the war, 'if they can make enough of 'em' and Kitty told him they were making shells as hard as ever they could. 'They turn yer yeller,' she said, which was true, because her face looked decidedly jaundiced, 'but it's got ter be done.' And he kissed her and said she was 'one a' the best'. But for most of his leave they simply enjoyed themselves and put the war out of their minds. By the time he went to London Bridge to catch his train back to France, they'd spent every penny they'd saved.

Their last kiss was more anguish than pleasure.

'Come back soon,' Rosie begged, as the train began to pull away.

His face was so bleak it made her want to weep. 'Soon as ever they'll let me,' he promised, hanging out of the window. 'An' if I live through this lot, we'll get married the day it's over.' And he just had time to snatch one last kiss before the train picked up speed and she had to jump off the step and let him go.

She waved until his face was just a pale blur, his waving hand small and white as a petal. Then she wept with distress. If only they'd stop this horrible war, she thought. It's gone on far too long and there's been far too much suffering.

But there was worse to come and some of it was to hit East London.

*

Rosie was hard at work on that particular evening. The restaurant was full of regulars, many of them army officers, and many of whom she knew. She'd noticed Anthony Eden as soon as she walked into the room. He'd grown a neat moustache and looked slightly older but there was no doubt who he was, sitting there so confidently among his fellow officers.

'That's Captain Eden,' one of the new waitresses told her. 'Ain't 'e good looking.'

'I know,' Rosie said feeling superior. 'He comes in a lot. I was his housekeeper before I come here.'

The waitress was very impressed. 'Never!' she said.

Rosie gave her the correct London answer. 'Straight up,' she said and walked off to take her first order.

There were two familiar faces sitting at that table too so she greeted them both by name. 'Good evening Mr John. Good evening Mr de Silva.'

The two artists looked up and smiled. 'It's our Rosie, bigod,' de Silva said, sparkling at her. 'And as gorgeous as ever. Have you missed me?'

She decided to sauce him. She was in the right mood to sauce somebody and he was asking for it. 'Have you been away then, sir?'

'Have I been away?' he said, holding up his hands in mock horror. 'How can you ask such a thing, pretty though you are? I've been in France, serving king and country.'

Rosie looked at his luxurious beard and his curly hair and thought of Jim's poor shaven head and the terrible bleak look he'd had on his face the last time she saw him and she was suddenly full of anger. But she held onto her control and simply asked, 'Are you ready to order sir?'

He picked up the menu and began to study it and Rosie stood and waited for him while the buzz of conversation in the restaurant rose and fell in soft waves of polite sound. And then without any warning, the comfortable air was shattered by the noise of an enormous explosion. Several of the diners jumped to their feet, looking startled, some called, 'Good God! What was that?' as the roar of the explosion reverberated round the room and made the chandeliers chime like bells. The officers and the two artists were impressively calm.

'That was an explosion,' Augustus John explained to the table behind him. 'Pretty big one. Munitions I should think.'

'Let's nip out and see what we can see,' de Silva said.

It's excited him, Rosie thought, noticing the flush on his cheeks, and the thought made him drop even lower in her estimation. That was a terrible explosion, she thought. It'll have killed people and injured them. Then it occurred to her that if it was a munitions factory it could be the one Kitty worked in and that thought frightened her so much she had to put one hand on the table to steady herself. She noticed that the *maître d'* was walking from table to table smiling and reassuring the guests and that people were calming but her heart was racing with alarm.

De Silva came back in a matter of minutes to report that the sky was red and 'full of sparks', that he'd made a sketch of it and that the taxi driver reckoned it was the Silvertown munition works. And that made her relax a little.

The newspapers the following morning proved him right. It *had* been the munition factory at Silvertown. Sixty-nine workers had been killed and there were *'many more'* casualties. Rosie read the paper in a mixture of shamed relief and anguished horror. There's no end to the terrible things war does to us, she thought. It's as wrong and vile as anything can be. Why doesn't somebody stop it?

But nobody did. In April, the papers were full of the news that the Americans had declared war and were sending troops to France *'with all speed'*. The diners in the club told one another that this could make all the difference. 'Fresh blood,' they said, without seeming to understand the irony of the words they'd chosen. Rosie winced to hear them and thought of all those men coming over to Europe to be shot to pieces.

'It just goes on an' on,' she said to Kitty, when they were in the Star next day.

'Keep yer pecker up!' Kitty advised. 'It don't do to think about it too much, our Rosie. Jest keep on keepin' on.'

But that was easier said than done. There seemed to be one 'push' after another all through the year, and each one kept her tense with fear that Jim would be hurt. He wrote to her as soon as he could, to tell her he was all right, but that only reassured her until news of the next battle. And there didn't seem to be any sign of them letting him home on leave again. In June, the first convoy of American troops arrived in France and were christened *doughboys* by the British, which Rosie thought was a very peculiar thing to call them. In August a third battle began at Ypres but that didn't worry her so much because she knew Jim wasn't anywhere near it. Christmas came and went, the weather was bad and there was a lull in the fighting. But then they were into the fourth year of the war and they were still no nearer the end of it.

'I think it'll go on until every single soldier's dead,' Rosie said gloomily to Kitty.

Kitty tried to comfort her. 'No they won't,' Kitty said. 'Something'll happen. You'll see.'

What happened was an act of Parliament that neither of them expected. It was passed on February 6th and reported in the papers the next morning. Women over thirty who *'occupied premises of a yearly value of not less than £5'* were to be given the vote.

Kitty saw it at work and brought it to the Star that evening to show to Rosie.

'We been passin' it round all day,' she said. 'Whatcher think a' that? Our Sylvia said they'd have ter do it.'

Rosie read it thoughtfully. 'It's only for middle-aged women though,' she said. 'Not for us.'

'It's fer women,' Kitty told her happily. 'That's the important thing. It's the thin end a' the wedge. They'll 'ave to give it to all of us in the end.'

The encouraging news carried them through the chills of the winter but then April began and there was another news item that brought a terrible and familiar fear. General Sir Douglas Haig had decided that there would be yet another push. His speech was reported in the papers and it made Rosie so angry she didn't know what to do with herself. *'Every position must be held to the last man,'* he'd said. *'There must be no retirement. With our backs to the wall and believing in the justice of our cause, each one of us must fight on to the end.'*

'Vile, monstrous, stupid, old imbecile,' she raged. 'I don't notice *his* stinking back to the wall. Oh no! He's skulking in some great, big, comfortable house somewhere safe keepin' out the way. It's the poor devils in the trenches what are going to fight to the last man. Our Jim. That's who'll cop it. How can he be so cruel?'

But Haig was the general and when he gave an order it had to be obeyed.

*

Over in France a gentle summer was under way. The sky above the wreckage of the battlefields was peacefully blue, birds sang joyously in the trees behind the long embattled lines, the distant fields were lush with green corn, the distant roads dusty and untroubled, the sun shone like a blessing. But the men waiting in their stinking trenches hardly noticed it. They were taut with the dread of what was to come.

'They must start soon,' Jim said irritably, climbing onto the parapet for his next turn on watch. 'What are they waiting for?' The tanks were already in line, the artillery was ready, the ammo had been delivered.

'Don't wish it on us mate,' Fred said, following him. 'They can wait for ever far as I'm concerned. I'm in no rush.'

It began two days later with the usual preliminary barrage but this time it was louder and longer than anything they'd ever heard. It went on for six days non-stop and the noise was shattering. Then on the seventh day it died down and the signal was given for them to attack. Jim walked through the filth of no-man's-land surrounded by tanks. There were hundreds of them heading towards the German trenches in their implacable ponderous way, rolling straight across, heading out towards the next line. Shells exploded all round him, the machine guns fired incessantly, men were dropping everywhere he looked, being blown apart before his eyes. But he trudged on, keeping in the shelter of the nearest tank, through the enemy trench and out the other side, pushing the Germans back. At last.

The attack went on until the next line of trenches had been captured. He and Fred were light-headed with relief. The first push was over and they'd come through. Imagine that. They were so tired they slept where they stood but they were alive. The next morning they were ordered to attack again. There was a second line of trenches to be taken, their artillery had moved into new positions and were already firing, they had tanks to support them. It was possible.

That day, it seemed to Jim that the Germans were fighting more desperately. The machine-gunners still had their range and were killing at will, there were men dropping in their hundreds but they were still advancing, dodging behind the tanks, firing when they could.

Then things went wrong. The tank they'd been following was hit by a shell and skidded to a halt.

'Find another one,' Jim yelled to Fred and followed where his mate ran. It was murderously hot and there were shells exploding and men being killed to right and left. And then suddenly there was an explosion immediately in front of them and the air was full of mud and shrapnel and there was a burning pain in his thigh.

'Oh shit!' he cried. 'Shit! Shit!' Then he was falling and the darkness took him.

Chapter Eleven

'Anything?' Kitty asked. She'd been waiting for Rosie at the tram stop for quite a while, her sallow face wrinkled with anxiety and her brown eyes strained.

Rosie gave her a hug, took her arm and began to walk towards the Star. 'No,' she said. 'Nothing yet. I'd've written if there had been, you know that, Kitty.'

The street was so warm in the evening sun that the shop blinds were still down and as usual at that time of day it was full of people, either heading home or off to the pub; dockers and stevedores weary in their work-stained clothes, women in black with shopping bags over their arms returning with their last-minute bargains from the Borough Market, boys in cloth caps and down-at-heel boots running errands, skinny girls with toddlers on their hips trailing after their mothers.

'It's seventeen days,' Kitty mourned.

'I know.'

'That's a dreadful long time.'

Rosie was monosyllabic with distress. 'Yes.'

'Ain't there someone we could write an' ask?' Kitty said and her voice was desperate, 'We can't just wait like this.'

'I've thought an' thought,' Rosie told her. 'Truly I have Kitty, an' I can't think of anyone. We ent had the telegram. That's one thing.'

Kitty stopped walking and turned to face her. 'I can't bear it, our Rosie,' she wailed. 'He could be dead, or lyin' out there in the mud, all shot to bits, or anythin'. They ought to tell us. It ain't right ter keep us hangin' on an' on an' on like this.' Tears rolled out of her eyes and down her cheeks but she was too fraught to notice them.

Rosie had been holding onto her own self-control all through the long seventeen days and the sight of Kitty's tears pushed her into an outburst of frightened weeping. They stood clinging to one another in the crowded street until the first fit had eased and the passers-by gentled around them eyeing them with pity. Grief was too universal now to be mocked or commented on but one or two of the older women touched them gently as they passed in unspoken sympathy.

'Don't let's go to the Star,' Kitty said, when she was calmer. 'I can't face all that larkin' about. Not tonight. Let's go back to my place, eh?'

So that's what they did and the peaceful room comforted them a little. When they finally kissed goodbye, Rosie said.

'It'll come soon, Kitty. It's bound to.' But they were both so down that neither of them believed it.

*

It came three days later and it wasn't the much-feared telegram, nor a postcard in Jim's bold hand but a letter in an envelope postmarked '*Tooting SW*' and addressed in unfamiliar writing. Rosie's hands were shaking so much that she tore the envelope in half as she opened it.

It was an official letter written on notepaper with a printed address across the top of it. *Church Lane Military Hospital, Church Lane, Tooting, SW London.*

'*Dear Miss Goodison,*' it said.

'*I am writing this letter at the request of Private Jim Jackson, who is a patient at this hospital in Ward 24. He asks me to tell you that he has been wounded and is not able to write to you in person but he wants you to know that he is now recovering and hopes you will be able to visit him. Our visiting hours are at the head of this letter.*

With kind regards,

Nurse M Aitcheson.'

Rosie was sick with relief. He wasn't dead. Oh thank God. Thank God. But then her common sense returned and she wondered how badly he'd been wounded and wished Nurse Aitcheson had told her more. It must have been bad if he can't write, she thought. I'll send a postcard to Kitty and then I'll arrange time off so that I can go and see him. She was full of unstoppable energy. Now that she

164

knew where he was and that he was alive, anything was possible.

*

It took two trams to get to Tooting and felt like a very long journey but the conductress on the second tram told her where to get off and pointed her in the right direction. 'That's Church Lane up there,' she said. 'Go past the church and it's just a bit further up the road. Huge place. You can't miss it. Good luck!'

She was right. Rosie could see the building rising above its surrounding wall as she approached it and when she'd walked through the gate, past a sign that read '*Tooting Military Hospital*', and followed a short, straight driveway up to the front entrance, she saw at once that it was a very big hospital. It was three stories high for a start and had so many windows she couldn't count them. The entrance was very grand, surrounded by four white pillars which supported a balcony like the one at Buckingham Palace and there was a huge clock tower rising importantly above the chimneys. It gave her hope just to see it. They'll look after him in a place like this, she thought. Bound to.

Finding the ward was easy too. A uniformed porter standing behind the reception desk just inside the door, told her all she had to do was follow the signs. 'You'll find it's all pretty straightforward.' It was finding Jim that was the difficult bit. Ward twenty-four was crowded with beds so close to each other that there was barely room for a chair and a small locker between them and every one was occupied by a gaunt-looking man with a shaven head either lying flat on his back asleep or propped up on pillows with the bedclothes tightly tucked around his legs. They looked like grotesque dolls and most of them smelt so sour that even passing them made her retch. But none of them was Jim. She walked from one end of the ward to the other and back again, checking every bed but there was no sign of him. In the end she gave up searching and went to ask the nurse who was sitting at a desk at the far end of the ward, keeping watch.

She looked up and smiled as Rosie approached and said, 'Can I help you?' in such a kind voice that Rosie took heart.

'I'm looking for Jim Jackson,' she said, 'but I don't think he's here.'

'You must be Rosie,' the nurse said, smiling again. 'He *is* here. Let me show you.' And she stood up and led the way to a bed in the middle of the ward, where a gaunt man was lying on his back asleep with his mouth open. 'Jim!' the nurse said, giving his arm a little shake. 'Wake up. Your Rosie's here.'

No, Rosie thought. That's not Jim. It can't be. But then the man opened his eyes and looked her and they were Jim's lovely tawny eyes in that haggard face, gazing at her with such pain that she wanted to scream and howl at the sight of him. She sat down heavily on the hospital chair, took his limp hand and made a huge effort to speak to him, but she had to swallow three times before she could get a word out. 'Hello our Jim,' she said, huskily.

To her horror, he turned his head away from her and began to cry.

'What's the matter with him?' she whispered to the nurse.

'He's had dysentery,' the nurse said. 'Still has it, to be truthful. It's not as bad as it was when he came in but it's bad enough. It makes them very weak. He's lucky to be alive.'

'A nurse wrote to me,' Rosie told her. 'She said he'd been wounded.'

'That was me,' Nurse Aitcheson told her. 'And yes he *was* wounded. His right thigh was full of shrapnel when he came in and rather seriously infected. He had a long struggle with that too but the infection's clearing now. He's a very brave man.'

'Yes,' Rosie said. 'He always was.' She lifted his hand and held it to her face and kissed it. 'My poor Jim.'

'See if you can coax him to drink some water,' Nurse Aitcheson said. 'Dysentery dries them out. That's his drinking cup.' She nodded her head at a cup with a spout like a miniature teapot that was standing on the locker. Then she left them to it and went off to attend to another patient who was groaning.

Rosie stayed on the ward until the bell rang to mark the end of the visiting hour. She managed to persuade him to drink some water and held his hand while he slept and kissed him on the two occasions when he woke and looked at her. When she left him she felt as bleak as he looked and she cried all the way home. Her poor, poor Jim to be lying there in that dreadful smell all day looking like a skeleton and feeling so weak. But when she reached Southwark she gathered her strength and her determination, put her chin in the air and went off to tell Kitty what she'd found and to plan how they could take it in turns to visit him.

'You go on your afternoon off an' I'll go on mine,' she said. 'That way he'll get two visits a week an' we can keep an eye on him.'

'Is he very bad?' Kitty asked mournfully.

I can't protect her, Rosie thought, sadly. She's got to know or it'll give her a shock like it did to me. So she told her, not in too much detail, but just enough to alert her. Kitty wept piteously despite her caution. And then they sat with their arms round each other, while Rosie tried to comfort her. 'We'll soon have him out a' there, don't you worry,' she said. 'Then we can feed him up an' get him well again.'

*

The two young women visited the hospital every week from then on and every single visit was difficult. Sometimes Jim seemed a little better and was sitting up. He didn't say very much but at least he seemed to be listening to them. But at other times he was lying down and weepy and listless and could barely answer them when they said hello. It worried them terribly.

'I shall ask someone if there's anything we can do for him,' Rosie said when she and Kitty went to the Star on

Thursday evening. 'We can't let him go on an' on like this. I've hardly had a word out of him this afternoon.'

Kitty sighed. 'But who's there to ask?' she said. 'I mean for to say, the nurses are ever so nice but they don't seem to know much, do they? I mean they only say coax him to drink his water an' a fat lot a' good that is, the state he's in.'

'I been thinking on the way home,' Rosie said. 'I think I ought to try an' find a sister. There's bound to be one somewhere about an' she'll be bound to know.'

Kitty was too down to be convinced. 'She might not,' she said.

'Oh she will,' Rosie reassured her. 'I worked with a sister once an' she knew everything there was to know. Lovely she was. I shall find the sister first thing I do, I promise, the minute I get there.'

*

It was a cold depressing journey, for autumn had denuded all the trees and a fog had been gathering since mid-morning. The dampness of it was chill to her lungs and tasted of soot and sulphur but Rosie wasn't going to let a bit of cold deter her. She pulled her muffler over her mouth and walked up Church Lane as quickly as she could so as to keep warm, passing the now ghostly church and peering through the murk to make sure she didn't miss the entrance. The hospital loomed before her like a castle from a fairy story – oh if only it was and she could find her fairy godmother – and then she was through the half-open door and in the foggy entrance hall and following signs she could barely see. I must get him out of here, she thought as she walked between the clammy walls of the corridor. It's worse than ever today. He should be back at home all nice an' snug, by a nice coal fire. I could build it halfway up the chimney and put a blanket over his knees and make him really warm and give him a jug of beer and tempt him with something tasty to whet his appetite.

She reached the ward full of determined plans and there, to her great delight, was a plump lady in the familiar dark blue uniform of a ward sister bending over one of the patients, talking softly to him and holding a cup to his lips. Rosie walked into the ward on hopeful feet and waited at the foot of the bed until the sister stood up and straightened her back. Then she stepped forward to make herself known. And found herself looking into the gentle, reassuring face of Sister Sunshine.

They recognised one another in the same instant, Sister Castleton with surprise and pleasure, Rosie with a rush of relief.

'Rosie, my dear girl,' Sister Castleton said, all smiles. 'How good to see you.' But then she saw the expression on Rosie's face and moved into practical concern. 'Ah!' she said. 'Come into my office and tell me all about it.'

It was a small office at the end of the ward but a very warm one. There was a gas fire popping with exertion in one wall with two easy chairs drawn up beside it and a pair of good thick curtains to shut out the fog.

'You have a young man here,' Sister said when they were both comfortably seated.

'Jim Jackson,' Rosie told her.

'Ah yes. And you're worried about him, naturally. You know he's had an infected wound, don't you? And dysentery?' They were only just questions and when Rosie nodded, she went on. 'The wound is healing. Rather slowly but it *is* healing. But I'm afraid the effects of the dysentery are lingering. It's a horrible disease. It drains them of water and energy.'

'Yes,' Rosie said, sadly. 'We seen that, me an' his sister.'

'But?' Sister prompted.

Rosie thought about it for a few seconds and decided to confide the worst of her worries. 'When I first met him,' she said, 'he was like a lion, a great strong feller with lots a' thick hair. Determined sort a' man, if you know what I mean. The sort that 'ud stand up for you through thick an' thin.' She could see him so clearly charging through the crowd to tackle the roughs that afternoon in Trafalgar Square. 'Now he's so low I can't recognise him. He's hardly the same man. I know I shouldn't say this because it sounds so terrible, but it's almost as if he's lost the will to live.'

'We've got forty men with dysentery in this hospital,' Sister said. 'Two wards full and most of them are depressed, to some extent, if that's any comfort to you. It's pitiful to see. I think they've seen too many horrors.'

'I sit by that bed,' Rosie said sadly, 'and I wonder if it's still him. I want to help him, to make him feel better about things, to smile maybe, and I don't know how to do it.'

Sister Castleton leant forward and patted her hand. 'It's very hard,' she said. 'What did he enjoy before he got called up?'

Rosie thought about it. 'Fish an' chips,' she said, 'going to the pictures or the Star, walking in the park. That was the best thing for both of us.'

'Perhaps you could remind him how good it was,' Sister suggested. And when Rosie looked doubtful, 'Try remembering aloud. When he wakes, tell him you've been thinking about all the good times.'

But when Jim woke that afternoon he was thinking about Fred Feigenbaum and it was making him agitated. 'I ain't had a letter from him,' he said. 'Not since I come in. They'd have give it to me if I had.'

'Have you written to him?' Rosie asked.

He sighed. 'Ain't got the energy.'

'That nice nurse'ud write it for you if you asked her.'

He shook the idea away irritably, like a horse trying to rid himself of flies. 'What's the good?' he said. 'He'd never get it in that bleedin' place.'

Rosie was trying to remember what he'd told her about Fred in those first postcards. 'Don't his father work in the Borough Market?' she asked.

'Well yes,' Jim said dourly, 'but I can't see what good that is. I can hardly go lookin' for him stuck in 'ere like this.'

'No,' Rosie said. 'You can't. But *I* can. All you got to do is tell me his name and what he sells an' I'll find him for you.'

She went to the market as soon as she got back to the Borough High Street and was rather daunted by what she found. It was a huge, impressive, confusing place, with a high glass ceiling curving many feet above her head and trains passing noisily just below it, behind an elaborately carved tracery of green cast iron. It was lit by naphtha flares and jostling with shoppers, with so many stallholders calling their wares to entice them, it made her feel quite dizzy. And to complicate matters even further there were several pathways leading off in various directions, strewn with sawdust and littered with empty crates, tufts of straw, crumpled orange wrappers and trails of blood and fish scales. She walked down the first path wondering how on earth she was going to find one man in all that. There was a stall selling fruit and vegetables just ahead of her but the name above the stall wasn't Feigenbaum.

She waited until the stallholder had finished serving all the women who were standing in front of his stall and then stepped up to ask for directions, as boldly as she could and speaking loudly so that he could hear her above the noise.

'Ol' Manny?' he said. 'Yeh! I know him. Good bloke. He'll cost yer though. My stuff's cheaper.'

'I'm not buying,' Rosie explained. 'I got a message for him.'

He grinned at her. 'Oh well if that's the case, I'll tell yer,' he said. 'Turn off to the right. Four stalls down, left-hand side.'

After that it was easy because she liked Mr Feigenbaum from the moment she saw him, stooping beside the stall, in his long black coat and his little skullcap, gently putting a pile of speckled apples into the battered basket of a grubby-looking girl in down-at-heel boots and a coat that was far too big for her. There was a tenderness about him that made her think of Pa. When the little girl had handed over her pennies and he'd patted her tousled hair, she stepped forward and greeted him by name. 'Mr Feigenbaum?' It was only just a question.

'I am Mr Feigenbaum,' he said, smiling at her. 'Vhat I can do for you?'

'I've come with a message for your son Fred,' she told him. 'It's from Jim Jackson. He's his friend. From the trenches.' But then she faltered because the moment she'd spoken Fred's name, Mr Feigenbuam's face had changed in the most terrible way. It was as if it was folding in on itself, creasing and crumpling. Then he began to rock, backwards and forwards and she saw he was weeping and knew what had happened. 'Oh Mr Feigenbaum,' she said. 'I'm so sorry.'

Mr Feigenbaum was speaking in fits and starts. 'Such a good boy,' he wept. 'The best of sons. I should live to see – this day. To be killed – so young – and so strong. All the vorld to me he was. All the vorld. He was going to – vork with me – in the market. Now – vhat vill I do?'

Rosie held his hand and rubbed his arm and said, 'I know, I know,' and wished she hadn't spoken to him so carelessly. Eventually he calmed and wiped his eyes on a huge check handkerchief and was able to speak normally again. 'You must forgive me my grief,' he said.

'It's all right, Mr Feigenbaum,' she said. 'My brother was killed. I know how it is.'

'You too,' he said sadly, shaking his head. 'Vhat vaste. You vill tell your Jim, maybe?'

'Not yet,' she decided. 'He ent well enough. I'll tell him when he's better.'

And then, as more customers had arrived and were waiting patiently, they parted.

*

It was hard to find things to talk to Jim about. She did so want to cheer him but nothing she said had any effect. He *did* say it was a good thing when she reported that Fred was all right but after that he just sighed no matter what topic she chose. Remembering their walks did nothing for him, he wasn't interested in the latest pictures or the good turns at the Star, and even the news that the Germans were asking for an armistice only provoked a sigh and the bitter comment that he'd believe *that* when he saw it.

A fortnight later the papers were full of the news that an armistice had been signed and that bonfires were being lit all over the country, but he only said, 'Not before time,' and went on staring gloomily into space. She decided it was time for her to take action or he'd go on sitting there feeling miserable for ever.

'Right,' she said, briskly. 'The war's over. Now we can get married.'

'You don't want to marry me,' he told her sadly. 'I'm

just a bleedin' wreck. They made me walk this morning. Give me a crutch, they did. Six steps an' I fell over. I wouldn't even get up the aisle.'

'Yes you will,' she said, sticking out her chin. 'I'm goin' to organise it. The minute they say you can leave here I shall take you down to Binderton an' feed you up an' sit you in the sunshine an' make you better. An' then I shall call the banns an' find us a flat an' get it all clean an' lovely ready for us, an' then you can come to my church and say, "I do," like you promised.'

That actually made him smile. 'I'm a lost cause Rosie,' he sighed. 'You can't cure me.'

'No you ent,' she said forcefully. 'An' it's no good sayin' *can't* to me on account of I'm goin' to do it. You just watch me. I shall go down to Binderton next Thursday an' get started. You'll have to do without me for once but Kitty'll come same as always.' They were ringing the bell to mark the end of visiting hour so she stood up, put on her hat and stooped to kiss him. 'I'll have a lot to tell you next time I come,' she promised.

Which was true, although not quite in the way she foresaw.

Chapter Twelve

The train to Chichester was rather slow that Thursday afternoon and there was a lot of grumbling in Rosie's carriage, which was full of people, all bundled up in their warmest clothes and eager to get to their destinations. A slow train didn't bother Rosie. She was too busy making plans. By the time she was walking across the frozen fields to the cottage, she had everything sorted out in her mind. I'll see the family first an' cheer Ma up – she'll like to know I'm goin' to get married – an' then I'll go to St Mary's an' see Father Alfred an' fix the wedding. She was smiling as she lifted the latch and walked into the cottage.

There was no one in the room, nor in the kitchen, which was odd, nor upstairs as far as she could hear, although there was someone coughing somewhere. She was just wondering where they could all have got to, when Edie appeared on the stairs and came tiptoeing down. She was wearing a scarf over her nose and mouth and her eyes looked so fraught that Rosie was alarmed.

'What's up?' she said, looking up at her.

'Oh I'm so glad you've come, our Rosie,' Edie said, pushing the scarf down under her chin. 'I been at me wits' end. Mrs Taylor come in. She's been ever so good onny she said I was to wear a mask for the infection, an' I ent got one but then she said a scarf would do. Oh it *is* good to see you. Did you get my card? I onny sent it this morning. I been at me wits' end.'

She was so distressed that Rosie ran to hug her. 'Is it Ma?' she asked.

Edie nodded. 'She's ever so bad. It onny come on yesterday. She went to Chichester Tuesday an' she was all right then. I mean she would go. She said she'd got to get some cloth to make a shirt for Tommy. An' then yesterday morning . . . I been up all night with her. She's ever so bad.'

'Come on,' Rosie said, heading for the stairs. 'Let's have a look at her.'

Edie climbed after her, worrying, 'You got to wear a scarf our Rosie. Mrs Taylor said.'

But Rosie was already in the bedroom and scarves were the last thing in her mind because she could see how seriously ill her mother was. She was turned on her side, struggling to breathe and coughing up a dreadful blood-streaked phlegm, and her face was streaked with sweat and an ominous shade of grey-blue. The room smelt very bad, of sweat and piddle and something else that Rosie couldn't quite place. 'Where's Pa?' she said.

'Diggin' ditches.'

'Go an' find him. Tell him he's to go for the doctor.'

Edie was alarmed. 'We can't afford doctors, our Rosie,' she said. 'I mean for to say not with the rent an' all, an' me not earnin'.'

'Just go!' Rosie said shortly. 'I'll pay him. An' be quick about it.'

'She's wet the bed,' Edie said, sniffing the air.

'Yes,' Rosie said, 'she has. I'll see to it.'

'I'll have to get a towel to mop up the worst,' Edie said. 'We put the rubber sheet under her but it needs a good wipe.'

'I'll do it,' Rosie said. 'Just go!' And as soon as her sister had left her, she went to the linen cupboard to find clean sheets and set about making her mother more comfortable.

It was a back-breaking job, because although Maggie had lost a lot of weight she was still very heavy to lift and pulling the wet sheets out from under her took a lot of effort. But eventually the bed was clean again and Rosie could fetch a bowl of warm water, a towel and a cake of soap and wash her patient down, stopping whenever a coughing fit began and cleaning her poor mouth when it was ended. And as she worked, she was remembering the newspaper headlines that had been screaming at her for weeks, only she'd been too concerned about Jim to pay much attention to them. '*Spanish Flu. Hundreds ill.*'; '*Spanish flu. London Telegraph Office crippled. 700 workers taken ill.'; 'Death toll rises.'* She was exhausted and anguished by the time Edie and Pa returned but she did her best not to show it.

'We been to the doctor's our Rosie,' her father reported. 'He said he'd be here presently. An' we told young Johnnie. He says he'll come directly, onny he's got to see Bert first. Is there anythin' we can do?'

But there wasn't anything any of them could do except watch and wait. At about half past three, Johnnie walked in and at four o'clock Tess arrived from Petworth in a dog cart, her eyes popping with anxiety. 'I just got your card Edie. Is she very bad?' Edie made tea for them all and they went on waiting, taking it in turns to sit with their mother, with scarves over their mouths and watching the clock. It was half past six before the doctor put in his appearance, looking very grand in his black suit and his yellow waistcoat and his fine white shirt. He took his half guinea before going upstairs and once there, he didn't take long to make his diagnosis and come down again.

'I'm afraid your mother has the Spanish flu,' he said. 'There is very little I can do for her. Keep her clean and warm. If she can drink water offer it to her.'

'Should we give her aspirins?' Rosie asked.

'There would be no point,' the doctor said. 'And in any case I doubt whether she would be able to swallow them. Her throat is too congested. We have no cure for this disease, I'm sorry to say. We just have to let it run its course. Good evening.'

With which he touched his hat and left them. They watched from the window as he drove smoothly away in his big black car. Edie, Johnnie and Tess were crying, Pa was biting his lip and Rosie felt deserted.

'Can you stay here, our Rosie?' Tess asked her.

'Yes,' Rosie said firmly. 'I can. I'll write to the *maître d'* and ask him.'

*

She stayed for the next three days, cooking for her family, washing all the dirty linen and doing what little she could to care for her mother, living in a nightmare. On the first day she sent a letter to Jim and another to Kitty to tell them what was going on and they both sent loving messages back by return of post, but for the rest of the time she lived in abeyance, doing things automatically and always aware that there was worse to come.

It came at two in the morning on Sunday, when Tess shook her awake to tell her that their mother was 'breathing funny'. Rosie had never heard a death rattle before but she knew what it was as soon as she heard it. 'Go an' wake the others,' she said to Tess.

'Is it the end?' Tess asked, her face very pale in the candlelight.

'Yes,' Rosie said. 'Make haste an' tell them to wrap up warm.'

They kept watch for the next two hours, huddled together on the chairs they'd brought up from the living room and saying very little. The wonder of it was that their mother could breathe at all, but she struggled on, occasionally stopping for several seconds before making yet another shuddering effort. And after what seemed an interminable time, her long struggle suddenly stopped and she was still and peaceful. The three kids cried most terribly and Rosie hugged them all in turn and rubbed their backs and told them she loved them. And at six o'clock, as it was still dark and very cold, Pa went back to bed and the rest of them huddled together in Edie's bed, where they talked until the sun came up. And after breakfast she had to go back to London.

'I'd stay longer,' she said to her father, as she washed the dishes, 'only it's Christmas comin' an' it's very busy Christmas time, an' we're short staffed.'

'No, no, 'course you must go,' her father said. 'I mean to say work's work. You got to go to work. We'll be orl right. Mrs Taylor'll come in an' lay her out an' such. I'll have to burn that old mattress. It's soaked right through, never mind the rubber sheet.'

He looked so crumpled and woebegone that Rosie stopped the washing-up and turned to hug him, soapy hands notwithstanding. 'Oh Pa!' she said. 'This is so awful.'

He put his arm round her shoulders and kissed the top of her head. 'Truth is we lost her when our Tommy died,' he said. 'She weren't never the same after that. Fine woman she was afore that. Salt a' the earth. But after we got the telegram, she sort a' became someone else.'

'I know,' Rosie said, still hugging him. It was true. She had a sudden vivid memory of her mother down on her knees scrubbing the kitchen floor and wiping the sweat from her forehead, her hands red from the soda. The image made her yearn with loss. Poor, poor Ma, she thought. You worked so hard and suffered so much. And poor Pa. 'I wish I didn't have to leave you with all this to see to,' she said.

He was steadfastly under control. 'We'll be orl right,' he said. 'You go.'

So she kissed them all and went, even though she was ashamed to be leaving them when she knew they needed her. And grief walked with her across the fields, freezing her into a state of such aching emptiness that nothing she saw seemed right or as she expected it to be. The hedges loomed over her, goblin-black and foreboding, like creatures from a nightmare, the frozen grass was the colour of steel and sharp as knives, the downs brooded on the wintry horizon, as distant and uncaring as whales. It's a terrible, ugly, cruel world, she thought, and death is everywhere, first Tommy and then Fred Feigenbaum and all the millions of other poor devils the papers keep talking about, and now Ma. She wept as she walked, feeling totally bereft.

It wasn't until she was on the train and heading for Victoria that she began to feel even marginally better and then the fog in her brain began to clear and she remembered why she'd gone to Binderton in the first place and realised that she hadn't done anything she'd planned to do and,

Everybody's Somebody

worse than that, she'd bargained away her next two days off and wouldn't be able to visit her poor Jim for another fortnight. I'll see if I can nip out for an hour or two to see Kitty, she decided. She'll have visited him again by now and she can tell me how he is. I'll drop her a card.

It was a cold walk back to the RAC Club but, now that she'd started to think her life back into a little more order, she felt a bit better. She wrote her postcard to Kitty as soon as she finished work that evening and took it out to the postbox at once. And Kitty wrote back the next day to say she'd be in all evening and to promise '*all the news then*'.

She was in and she had a good fire going and the kettle on the hob and two mugs and a tin of condensed milk ready and waiting on the table. She pulled Rosie into the room as soon as she knocked, kissing her most lovingly and once she'd tucked the draught excluder back into place below the door, settled her in Jim's chair by the fire with a rug over her knees and made a pot of tea. 'How'd'yer get on then?' she asked, as she poured. 'How's yer Ma?'

This was the moment Rosie had been dreading. She took a deep breath and told her quickly before she could be overcome by tears. And when Kitty's face wrinkled into concern and sympathy and she was afraid she would cry just for looking at her, she turned the conversation in a new direction by asking how Jim was.

'Orl right,' Kitty said. 'I seen him twice last week. Still a bit down. You 'ave to aspect that, don'tcher? But I tell you summink good. Leastways, I think it's good. He asked when you was coming to see him.'

'*That*,' Rosie said approvingly, spooning the condensed milk into her tea, 'is a step in the right direction. I can't do it this Thursday, tell him, nor the next, on account of me taking time off an' it bein' Christmas an' all, but I'll come the week after.'

'Not ter worry,' Kitty said, dipping her spoon into the tin. 'You'll visit when you can. He'll understand. You can't do no more'n that, can yer? We can go together.' And when Rosie looked a question at her. 'I been laid off. Munitions is closing. Don't need shells no more. Which is good in one way an' bad in another, if you takes my meanin'. I'm orl right. I got another job. Starts termorrer.'

'What sort a' job?'

'Postwoman. Won't last though that's the trouble. When the men start comin' home they'll want their jobs back, a' course, an' then I'll be out on me ear again. But it'll tide me over fer the time bein'.'

There was nothing Rosie could say to that, so she changed the subject again. 'You make a good cuppa,' she said.

'Wan' another?'

'If I drink too much,' Rosie warned, 'I shall need a wee.' She wasn't sure whether this house had a WC and thought it a bit unlikely and she didn't want to go out in the backyard if she could avoid it.

'Drink what yer like,' Kitty said. 'I got a jerry in the other room.'

So they emptied the teapot between them. Then Rosie watched as Kitty tidied up. First she poured the remains of the hot water from the kettle into an enamel bowl and washed the mugs, spoon and teapot, and put them away in a cupboard, then she emptied the dirty water into a covered bucket that stood under the table and then she did something rather odd. She picked up the condensed milk tin and lowered it into another larger tin with a lid before she put it away on the top shelf of the cupboard.

'I likes ter keep it all neat an' clean an' have everythink tidied away,' she explained, 'on account a' the black beetles.'

'Beetles?' Rosie asked. 'Do they eat condensed milk?'

'This lot do,' Kitty said, making a grimace. 'They eat anythink, 'orrible things. They ain't beetles really. That's jest what we calls 'em. You'd call 'em cockroaches.'

Rosie's heart contracted with revulsion and pity. 'Ah!' she said, understanding. She knew they waged an unceasing war against vermin in the kitchens, traps and a cat for the mice, Keating's Powder for what the chef called 'livestock'. Everything had to be scoured and cleaned every day. He was most particular about it.

'I keeps 'em down as best I can,' Kitty said, 'but the best way is to keep everythink locked away where they can't get at it. Let 'em go hungry, 'orrible things. I wish I could do that to the bedbugs an' all. They're worse. Ain't so bad at the moment. Not like they are come the summer. They breed in the heat, d'yer see, that's the trouble. No sooner d'you get rid a' one lot than you got another.'

And my Jim's been living in that ever since I've known him, Rosie thought. And she made up her mind that the first thing she would do, once she'd arranged the wedding, would be to find a proper place for all three of them to live, where they had water on tap and a WC and no vermin. She wasn't sure how she'd set about it, but she was determined to do it.

*

It was nearly three weeks before she and Kitty could get to Tooting again to visit their wounded soldier and by that time Rosie had been down to Binderton for her mother's funeral, and had managed to get through it somehow or other, but only with a lot of weeping, and Kitty had started work as a postwoman and said she felt quite a swell in her uniform. They found him in a different ward, which was encouraging, dressed in the familiar bright blue uniform of a wounded soldier, white shirt, red tie and all, and sitting in a chair, looking quite pleased with himself. He seemed clean and smelt freshly washed and was a much better colour.

'This is my fourth day,' he told them. 'They're learnin' me to walk better. I'll show you presently. Then I'm to go to the seaside to be convalesced. Whatcher think a' that? An' if everythin' goes to plan, they'll sign me off an' I can come home.'

They both told him it was wonderful news and Kitty said he was a 'giddy marvel'. Then he reached behind his chair and produced a wooden crutch and after a bit of a struggle stood up and began to walk along the ward. It upset them both to see how slow he was and how painful it looked but they praised him fulsomely.

'We shall 'ave you runnin' about in no time,' Kitty told him.

He grinned at her almost happily. 'You watch me,' he said. And the other men in the ward cheered him and grinned at him.

'I'll call the banns then shall I?' Rosie said, grinning at him.

He looked at her sheepishly. 'If you think I'm worth it.'

She stamped her foot in exasperation, frowning at him. 'Don't keep on sayin' silly things,' she said. 'Do you want me to or don't you?'

He looked at her, tawny eyes anxious in his thin face. 'You know I do,' he said. 'I jest don' want you to regret it, that's all. I'm not much cop when all's said an' done. Not now.'

She was so touched by his concern, she rose from her chair and rushed to throw her arms round him and kiss him, as his fellow patients cheered and whistled. 'I shall start getting it organised first thing,' she promised.

And did. It took her every spare minute for the next two weeks, but she was able to report on her progress each time she went to visit. 'I've written to Father Alfred,' she said on her first visit, 'an' he's agreed to it an' sent us this leaflet to tell us all about it.' And on her second visit she told him she'd arranged for the banns to be called at St George's Church in the Borough as well and that she and Kitty were planning a trip to Petticoat Lane to choose a frock 'or some such'.

By that time Jim had good news of his own. 'They're sendin' me ter this convalescent place day after termorrer,' he said, beaming at them in quite his old way. 'I'll be home in no time at this rate. You'll come an' see me there, won'tcher?'

'Try an' stop us,' Rosie said, grinning at him and then at Kitty. 'We shall have to put a jerk on with that dress,' she said to Kitty.

'We'll go Sunday,' Kitty said, rubbing her hands. 'I ain't 'alf looking forward to it, our Rosie.'

It was an extraordinary outing. Rosie had never been in a street so crammed full of people nor heard so many voices all shouting at once, nor seen so many stalls in such a narrow space, nor smelt so many old clothes, piled in tousled heaps on every stall and hanging from every available hook and rail, dolefully flapping their sleeves in the rush of air as the crowds pushed from place to place and giving off a strong smell of sweat and long dried dirt so pungent that it made her eyes water. We'll never find *anything* in all this, she thought, gazing round her, never mind a wedding dress. But Kitty had another opinion.

'Come on,' she ordered. 'Foller me. An' keep yer 'ands on yer purse or they'll nick it soon as look at yer. I know jest the place.' And she was off, dodging through the crowds as if she was dancing.

Rosie followed her, keeping one hand in the pocket of her coat so that she could keep her purse safe and trying to avoid being trodden on. At first she tried saying, ''Scuse me!' but that was no good at all and, after a few minutes, she was pushing and shoving with the rest. They arrived at a shop draped with clothes and presided over by a small plump man in a Jewish coat and a black yarmulke embroidered in gold thread. He threw up his hands in delight when he saw Kitty and greeted her by name. 'Pretty Kitty Jackson, as I live an' breathe. Vhat I can do for you, my darlink?'

Kitty explained what she wanted and within seconds he had pulled four possible dresses from his rails and held them out for inspection, extolling the virtues of each one. 'Nice bit a' schmutter,' he said, offering a blue velvet dress with a long stain down the front of it, 'or you could try this one,' showing a yellowing white lace. 'That'ud wash up lovely.' Then a pink skirt, 'Just your colour darlin',' and finally a faded grey dress with a dilapidated collar. But Rosie grimaced and shook her head at all of them.

'Well thank you very much, Mr Levy,' Kitty said. 'But they ain't quite the thing we 'ad in mind. I think we'll go on looking.' And when Mr Levy gave a rueful grimace they were off into the throng again and pushing their way to another shop.

This one was run by a tall man with a horribly tangled

grey beard and kind eyes, which lit up when he heard what they were looking for.

'Now ain't you the lucky ones,' he said. 'I got just the thing. Come in yesterday. Vait there, my darlinks.' And he disappeared into the dark cavern of his shop and reappeared with an elegant cream-coloured suit hanging over his arm as if it had fainted. He hung it on the nearest rail, pushing the other clothes aside to make room for it and smoothed the sleeves and the skirt with a reverent hand. 'Vhat you think of that, eh?' he asked, looking from one to the other.

Rosie made her mind up at once. It was just the thing, it looked so soft and so stylish, with all those little buttons running straight down the coat and straight down the skirt and all covered in the same pretty silk. But before she could say she wanted it, Kitty started to bargain.

'It's good cloth,' she said nodding her head from side to side. 'I'll give yer that. All depends how much yer want for it.'

'For you darlink, two quid an' cheap at the price.'

Kitty made a grimace. 'Oh do me a favour, Mr Segal,' she said. 'Twenty bob more like.'

Mr Segal spread his hands before her placatingly. 'For you darlink, thirty shillin',' he offered. 'Can't drop it no further'n that or there'll be no margin.'

Another sideways nod of the head and a pause for thought. 'Twenty-five.'

Again the hands were spread. 'Oy, oy. You drive hard bargain. I tell you vhat I do. Call it twenty-eight an' I throw in a pair of shoes for free. Vhat could be fairer?' And the shoes were produced from a dark chest of drawers just inside the door and held out for Rosie's inspection. They were the prettiest shoes she'd ever seen and matched the suit to perfection. There was no doubt in her mind at all that she would buy the entire outfit. And she did.

'Won't you have a lot ter tell our Jim,' Kitty said, as she and Rosie went home on the tram with their parcels. 'When you goin'?'

'Thursday,' Rosie told her. 'I can get to Angmering on the train an' then I shall have to walk. I don't think it's far.'

It was actually rather further than she expected and took her thirty-five minutes but happy anticipation made her quick and when she finally reached the convalescent home it was such a splendid place, all red brick and huge windows under a grey tiled roof, that she was cheered by the sight of it and set off across the lawn to find her darling, singing Marie Lloyd's happy song, '*The boy I love is up in the gallery. The boy I love is lookin' down at me.*'

And there he was, taking a walk with another soldier, both on crutches and both laughing. To see him walking out there in the open air was wonderful enough but to hear that easy laugh made her heart lift with pleasure.

'Whatcher think a' this, our Rosie?' he said, as she ran towards him. 'We're comin' on like a house afire, ain't we Jesse? They reckon they're gonna discharge us in a week or two, if we can run down to the beach an' back.'

'Run?' Jesse said, squinting at him.

Jim grinned. 'Well hobble then,' he said. 'All we got ter do is get as far as that ol' beach an' back an' we shall be free men, with a month's paid leave an' all. We're gonna live like lords.'

You won't live like a lord in two rooms full of bugs and cockroaches, Rosie thought, but she didn't say anything. 'Guess what I've bought,' she said, falling in alongside them as they started to walk again.

He looked a question at her, his eyes teasing. 'Well go on then. Spill the beans. What've yer bought?'

'My wedding dress.' What a marvellous thing to be able to tell him.

'Oh well then,' he said, pretending to sigh. 'I s'pose I shall 'ave ter marry you now.'

It was so good to be teased. It felt so normal after all those awful weeks watching him grow thinner by the day and looking so ill and downhearted. 'The banns've been called,' she said. 'We can fix a date as soon as you get home.'

He laughed again, grinning at his friend. 'She don't give me no option,' he said and took her arm. So they walked across the lawn together, heading towards the beach. Everything about the afternoon was easy, it was Spring, they were into 1920, the sun warm on their heads, wall-flowers scenting the air around them, sparrows chirruping in the hedges, the rippling sea calm and peacock green, the sky full of innocent clouds, the grass soft under her feet, his hand warm and alive on her arm.

Chapter Thirteen

Ex-Private Jim Jackson was so happy to be back in Parish Street he couldn't stop grinning. He had to admit it was a bit of a job getting up the stairs, which were a lot steeper than the ones he'd got used to at the convalescent home, but once he was inside his room and breathing in the familiar smell of home he was quite himself again.

'This is the life!' he said, sinking into the comfort of his lovely old battered chair. 'In me own clothes, in me own 'ome, wiv no bleedin' guns an' no gas an' no stink an' no rats an' four weeks' pay. Think a' that, Kitty. Holiday wiv pay. I shall live the life a' Reilly.'

'I got sausage an' bacon an' fried bread fer yer supper,' Kitty told him happily. Oh it *was* good to have him home. 'I'll get the fire goin' shall I?'

'Real grub!' Jim said rapturously. And he leant back in his chair and sighed with satisfaction at the thought.

For the next few days he spent his time and his holiday pay down the pub looking up old friends, getting tiddly and catching up on the local news. But it was Thursday evening he was waiting for and that seemed a long time coming. He came back from the pub early that afternoon, lit a fire, boiled up a kettle and took it off into the bedroom to give himself a thorough good wash. If he and Rosie were going to finish the evening in the park he didn't want to smell. Since that stinking dysentery he'd been very particular about how he smelt. And then it was off to the Star and he had his two best girls on either side of him, holding onto his arms and singing and he was so happy he felt as though his chest was going to burst.

It was such a good night. The comedians were on top form and they sang all the old songs and the performing dog was so badly behaved he made their sides ache with laughing at him. Then it was time for pie an' mash and a quick half. And then it was time for kisses in the park.

'Oh Rosie! Rosie! Rosie!' he groaned when they'd reached their protective oak tree and he'd kissed her at last. 'You don't know . . .'

'I do,' she said. 'It's like it for me an' all.' And she held his face between her strong warm hands and kissed him lovingly, again and again. Above their heads the oak leaves shushed and whispered and the distant moon looked down on them with its lopsided face and touched them with magic, making their eyes shine and edging their darkened faces with silver. The world and its incessant traffic were a distant murmur a long way away. They kissed until they were both taut with longing, aching to go further than kisses, sweet though they were, and oblivious to the time. Big Ben struck eleven and they barely heard it, he because he was nuzzling into her neck, she because she was enjoying it so much and never wanted him to stop.

'In three weeks' time,' she said dreamily, 'we shall be married. Think a' that.'

'I never think a' nothin' else,' he told her, stroking her cheek with his thumb.

'It's all fixed,' she told him. 'All I got to do is find us somewhere to live.'

'You'll come an' live wiv me an' Kitty, won't yer?' he said. It was only just a question because he was so sure of the answer.

She was instantly alert. She knew how glad he was to be home, he'd hardly talked about anything else all evening, but she couldn't live in a bug hutch. 'We planned to rent a flat,' she said, as reasonably as she could.

'Yeh, I know,' he said easily, 'but people like us don't live in flats. Not really.'

'I don't see why not,' she said. 'Why shouldn't we go for somethin' better?'

"Cause we can't afford it,' he said, still speaking easily because he was drowsy with kisses. 'You'll never find nothin' nowhere near what we could afford.'

'I ent found it yet,' she said. 'I'll grant you that. But I'm goin' to. I've made up my mind. I been looking for weeks. I'll find it in the end.'

'Well we'll see,' he said. She couldn't do it. He knew that, but there was no harm in her trying. It was a flash in the pan. That was all. A daft idea. 'Now we'd better be gettin' you back or you'll be late in.'

By the time he got home to Parish Street, he'd forgotten all about it so when he got a postcard from her on Tuesday morning it came as quite a surprise.

'*Darling Jim,*' it said. '*Meet me by the newsagent's in Newcomen Street at 10 o'clock. I think I have found just the place. Your ever-loving Rosie.*'

He was feeling so much easier that morning he went to meet her. Nothing'll come of it, he thought, as he limped along the pavements in the sunshine, but I'll go an' see it, just to please her. She can't help getting ideas above her station. That's what comes a' working in that club with all them toffs.

He saw her before she caught sight of him. She was standing on a street corner looking very pretty in her tawny jacket, her red skirt and her best straw hat. He was seized by two strong, conflicting emotions. The first was lust which was usual, the second was sorrow because she was going to be so disappointed when she found out they couldn't afford these rooms she'd found. Then she was running towards him, her face bright.

'Come on,' she said, grabbing him by the hand. 'Just wait till you see this.' And without giving him a chance to answer she pulled him into the corner shop. He had a vague impression of rows of newspapers on a wide counter, shelves full of fags and jars of sweets, but he didn't get a chance to say anything or even to take it all in because she was beaming at the man behind the counter and saying, 'All right to go up, Mr Rogers?' and the man was beaming back and lifting the flap on the counter to let them in. Through a door, up a flight of stairs to the first floor, then along a short corridor and up two more flights to the third.

'I've brought you up here first on account a' the stairs,' she explained. 'There'll be fewer of them going down. There ent much to see up here so we can get this bit over quite quick.'

Two doors, one in front of them, the other to the left, two rooms, both empty, the walls plastered and painted cream, brown lino on the floor, a fireplace in each one. The larger of the two overlooked the street, the smaller one looked out on a backyard and the roof of a two-storey building set at right angles to the shop. 'This 'ud be our room,' Rosie said as they stood in the larger room, 'an' the other one'ud be Kitty's. Now come an' see the rest.'

Down the stairs and into a room immediately below 'their' bedroom, same size, same cream walls, same lino, larger fireplace. Out onto the landing again. Rosie standing with her hand on the doorknob of the smaller room and a devilish expression in her face. 'Take a look at this!' she said and led him into the room.

It was the same size as the back bedroom and overlooked

the same backyard but there the similarity ended. There was large cupboard filling the corner beside the fireplace, a butler sink with two taps on the opposite wall with a cylindrical contraption attached to the wall above it, which she said was a geyser for hot water, and, standing beside the sink, what looked like an iron cupboard, with a pipe running up one side and a very solid handle to the door and the words '*A & R Main*' embossed below the door. He was intrigued despite his misgivings.

'What's that?' he said,

'*That*,' Rosie said happily, 'is a cooker. I used one a' them when I was keeping house for that Anthony Eden feller. Cooks by gas, what there's a meter for out in the hall. That's the pipe that brings up the gas and that's how you turn it on and this is the oven where you can cook roasts an' pies an' all sorts and these things on top are gas jets for cooking, so's we can have vegetables and cook chips and make soups. What d'you think a' that?' She was glowing with such excitement he was caught up in it too, and said it was amazing, even though he knew they couldn't afford such a thing.

She rushed at him and gave him a quick, happy kiss, holding his face between her hands. 'An' that ent the end of it,' she said. 'Wait till you see the rest.'

Out to the landing again and on into another part of the house. Two doors right and left facing one another. She opened the right-hand one with a flourish. 'Take a look at that. We got our own WC. Think a' that. No more carrying stinking jerries down to the yard and scrubbing 'em out after. You just pull the handle and it's all gone. And this,' opening the left hand door, 'is the coal-hole, what'll hold all the coal we want. And this,' leading him towards a third door straight ahead of them, 'this is the best a' the lot.'

He followed her through the door into a small rectangular room, with a window giving out to the yard, a washbasin with two taps, a copper for the laundry and an enamelled bath tub all clean and white with another one of those geyser things set in the wall above it. His jaw fell open before he could prevent it.

'What d'you think?' she asked. 'Ent it just the best ever?'

He took a breath to steady himself. 'It's a palace,' he said. 'I'll grant you that. A palace But what's the rent? That's gonna be the problem.'

She told him straight, chin up and face determined. 'Seven and six a week.' And when his face darkened, 'An' don't say it can't be done. There's three of us working an', if we all chip in, that's only 'alf a crown a week. We could afford that.'

'Oh come on, Rosie,' he said, 'that's ridiculous. Seven and six is a hell of a lot a' money. A hell of a lot. If we spend all that on rent, what would we live on? An' how would we furnish the place? We couldn't live in empty rooms. An' what if one of us got the sack? We'd never be able to manage between two of us. Be reasonable.'

But she'd found her dream house and there was no such

thing as reason. 'You can leave the furniture to me,' she said. 'I been savin' up my wages ever since they sent you to that hospital. I reckon I got enough put by. Me an' Kitty are going shopping on Thursday to find the best bargains. She's swapped her shift.'

Now he was too furious to hold himself in control. He felt that she and Kitty were ganging up against him, going shopping as if it was all signed and settled. *He* was the breadwinner for Christ's sake. If anyone was goin' to make this sort a' decision, it should be him. Not them. 'You an' Kitty?'

'We been talking about it ever since I start looking,' she told him. 'She's all for it. I told her as soon as I saw the advertisement. She'd ha' come this morning an' seen it for herself if she could ha' swapped another shift, only she couldn't, because she's done it already, so's we can go out Thursday. Oh come on Jim. We could afford half a crown. Think how good it'ud be to live here, with our own cooker an' as much hot water as we want an' a WC an' a bath an' a copper an' no black beetles an' no stinking bedbugs. Well worth half a crown.'

He was shouting now. 'You're not listening,' he roared. '*We can't afford it.* Don't you understand? It's out of our range. We can't afford it.'

She knew she would have to fight him. 'Yes, we can,' she shouted back, 'if we make up our minds to it. Or d'you want to go on living with bedbugs for the rest of your life?'

'We all have ter put up with bedbugs,' he said dismissively. 'It's a fact a' life if you live in London.'

'No we don't,' she said. 'You'll never have to put up with 'em ever again if we live here.'

She looked so ravishingly pretty and so determined with that chin stuck in the air that he lusted for her despite his anger. And that irritated him and made the anger worse. 'We can't afford it,' he said, furiously. 'We can't. An' that's all there is to it. We can't.'

She was blazing at him. 'We can! We can!'

He turned on his heel and headed for the stairs, taking them quickly even though it hurt him. She was calling after him, 'Jim. Please!' but he was too angry to stay with her another minute. Through the shop, a brief nod at the shopkeeper and then he was out in the street and limping home. How could she be so bloody stupid? She just rushes off like a bull at a gate. Why don't she ever stop to think?

She was thinking at that moment and thinking hard. She couldn't let this flat go. It was the best place she'd ever seen and just right for them. She simply couldn't understand why Jim couldn't see it too. It was so silly. He can be very stubborn when he likes, she thought. But she could be stubborn too. She'd got the money in her purse. Three weeks' rent in advance. It was all there. All she had to do was hand it over. It would make him cross but she couldn't help that. She couldn't let a place as good as this go to someone else. He'd come round to it in the end. He'd have to, once she'd settled it. And having made up her mind, she went downstairs to settle it, there and then.

Mr Rogers took her money and smiled at her and said she wouldn't regret it. He could guarantee it. And when Rosie said she'd like to move in on Thursday fortnight, he agreed to it at once, before attending to his next customer, and said he'd have the rent book ready for her the next time she came in.

There's a lot to be done, she thought, as she walked rapidly along the road towards the Borough High Street. And she began to make a list in her head of all the things that would have to be bought for a start. But even as she was thinking, she knew that what she was really doing was deferring the moment when she would have to tell Jim that she'd taken the flat. I'll wait till I've seen Kitty on Thursday, she decided. She might have some ideas. And then she had to run because she could see her tram coming.

*

Kitty turned up to inspect the flat on Thursday afternoon, wearing a flower in her hat and a happy expression. She looked so completely and contentedly herself that Rosie had hopes that Jim had told her about the flat and had accepted that they'd rent it. They went upstairs at once and Rosie led her from room to room and watched as she squealed with amazement at all the modern things she was seeing and sniffed the air with a rapturous smile on her face. When they were back in the kitchen, she said, 'I never smelt nowhere as clean as this in all me life.'

'Didn't Jim tell you what it was like then?' Rosie asked.

'No,' Kitty said, looking out of the window at the yard below her. 'He jest said he'd seen a flat an' then he wen' out ter the pub. I ain't seen much of him since, ter tell yer the truth, except fer mealtimes. But he's took it ain't he? That's the great thing.'

'Ah!' Rosie said. Then she paused, uncertain how to go on. 'The thing is, he ent exactly taken the flat.' And when Kitty looked puzzled. 'What I mean to say is, it's taken but it was me that took it. What I mean to say is, I paid for it.'

'You ain't told 'im, 'ave yer?' Kitty understood. And when Rosie shook her head. 'Oh my dear life! Whatcher gonna do now?'

Rosie didn't know the answer to that, so she said the first thing that came into her head. 'I'm going to get it furnished and ready for us to move in,' she said. 'And it'll need to be at bargain prices.'

Kitty grinned at her. 'Better get cracking then,' she said. 'We'll go to Clapham Junction to Arding an' 'Obbs. That's a good place. Lots a' bargains there.'

'We'll start with the beds,' Rosie said, when they reached the store.

'Well you'll only need one,' Kitty said. 'I can bring me own.'

'No,' Rosie said. 'You can't.'

That was a surprise to Kitty. Why not?' she said.

'On account a' the bugs,' Rosie told her. 'They live in wooden furniture. An' mattresses a' course. That's how they get carried from place to place. Filthy things.' So they bought two new brass bedsteads, one double and one single, and two brand-new flock mattresses and three goose feather pillows, and all the sheets and blankets and pillow cases they needed to cover them and arranged to have them delivered before the next Thursday.

Kitty was most impressed. 'You ain't 'alf saved up a lot a' money, our Rosie,' she said, as Rosie opened up her purse yet again.

'Well at least we'll sleep easy,' Rosie said. 'Let's go an' see what their china's like, shall we.' She was full of excitement now that she was spending her money. It was almost as if she was rich. But when the shopping was over and she went back to the club, she still hadn't said anything to Jim. There was a postcard waiting for her telling her he'd got a new pair of trousers for the wedding and she sat down at once and answered it saying she was glad to hear it. But she couldn't bring herself to say anything else. I'll wait till everything's ready at the flat, she thought, and I'll tell him then.

By the following Thursday everything *was* ready. The beds were up and made, the china in the kitchen cupboard, the kettle on the cooker; there was coal in the coal-hole and spare linen in the linen cupboard, they had a table and three chairs; she'd even run up two pairs of lace curtains on the sewing machine in the laundry room at the club and hung them in the rooms at the front of the flat. But she still hadn't told Jim. By Friday afternoon, she'd seen the *maître d'* and asked for his permission to be a day worker instead of living in and although his consent had been rather grudging, it was given and her new life was arranged. And she still hadn't told Jim. But by then it was Friday evening and she was on the train and on her way to Binderton and tomorrow was her wedding day and it was a bit too late. I'll tell him when the wedding's over, she decided. There wasn't any other time.

*

Her sisters were waiting for her at the window and they pulled her into the cottage at once to tell her they'd got a nice hotpot all ready for her and that the roses were all coming along lovely for her bouquet. 'We'll pick 'em first thing tomorrow morning,' Tess said, 'while the dew's on 'em. An' Pa's got his suit ready. We hung it up didden we Edie? Everything's organised.'

And so it seemed to be. Rosie ate what she could of the hotpot, slept soundly all night, rather to her surprise, and woke to sunshine, birdsong and a newly cut bouquet of pink and yellow roses, carefully laid out on the dressing table. Then the day slid out of her control and became a kaleidoscope of fleeting emotions and vague impressions; missing Ma and Tommy, feeling weepy; her sisters dressing her and gazing at her in awe, telling her she looked '*real lovely'*; her father offering his arm to her as if she were royalty as she climbed out of the cart; the sudden peace of the church, with the organ pipes shining gold in the sunshine and the familiar pattern of the tiles under her feet; Jim standing without his stick, waiting for her and looking ill at ease, Father Alfred smiling encouragement as they exchanged their vows; stumbling over the words *'Till death us do part'* because that was too awful to think about and Jim leaning towards her and whispering, *'Well it won't now.'* Dear, dear Jim. It *was* going to be all right, wasn't it? But she still hadn't told him.

Then they were all on their way back to Binderton, she and Jim sitting side by side in Pa's cart, and everybody else in procession. She caught a brief glimpse of Kitty and Tess and Edie, walking arm in arm and looking very grand in their rose-trimmed hats, and then they were back in the cottage and it was full of trestle tables set with meat pies and fruit pies and jellies and custards in a variety of teacups and she thought what a lot of work had gone into cooking such a feast and stammered her thanks. But she was swamped by smiling faces and urged to *'sit 'ee down and try some of Mrs Taylor's pie'* and soon they were all eating and drinking apple cider and Pa was making a speech, in which he called her *'the best a' gels, damn me if she ent'*, and there was so much going on she couldn't take it all in. Presently, old Mr Boniface struggled to his feet and reached across to the dresser to get his fiddle and, at that, they all stood up and the chairs and tables were carried out into the garden, dirty dishes and all, and space was made for them to dance. And she discovered that Jim couldn't dance for toffee nuts and had to show him where to put his feet – to chirruping applause.

It was growing dark by the time Pa went off to get the mare so that he could take them to the station. They changed into their ordinary clothes while he was gone and Rosie went out into the darkening garden to retrieve her bouquet. But when she went to find Kitty, she said she was staying where she was.

'It's all arranged,' she said, hugging her new sister-in-law. 'Me an' Tess thought it'ud ne nicer for you an' Jim to have a bit a' time on yer own. Get things sorted out like, what you'll 'ave ter do now, won'tcher. I'll come back termorrer. Don't worry about yer things. I'll bring 'em.'

So they travelled to London without her, feeling a bit self-conscious and in no mood for tricky conversations, especially in front of the strangers who were sitting in front of them, eyeing the bouquet and exchanging knowing looks. But the conversation rushed up to bite them as soon as they arrived at Victoria station because, naturally enough, Jim headed off to catch the tram to Tooley Street. He was walking so quickly that Rosie had to pull on his arm to stop him.

'No,' she said. 'Not that way.'

He was in a cheerful mood and teased, 'Whatcher mean, not that way? I thought we was goin' home.'

She planted her feet firmly on the pavement and faced

him squarely. 'We are,' she said. 'Only not to Parish Street. We're going to the flat. The one I found for us in Newcomen Street. That's our home now.'

He was so surprised that for a few exasperated minutes he didn't know what to say and stood there glowering at her. 'You don't mean that,' he said, eventually, although he could see she did. 'Oh come on, Rosie. I thought we'd dealt with all that silly nonsense long since.'

'It ent silly nonsense,' she told him, staying calm with an effort because the expression on his face was making her feel guilty. 'I paid three weeks' rent in advance, if you want to know, an' it's ours. It's all clean an' furnished an' ready for us. You can say what you like but we're not going back to those awful rooms with all those awful bedbugs an' cockroaches an' everything.'

'You never give up, do you?' he said, glaring at her. 'You just go yer own way and damn the consequences. What'll happen if we can't afford it? What'll we do then? Have you thought a' that? No course, you ain't. You never think a' nothink.'

She was trembling but she still stood her ground. 'Don't!' she said. 'Please don't.'

He ran his hands through his hair and scowled quite terribly.

'It's late,' she said. 'Let's sleep on it.'

It *was* late. She was right about that. It was late and they were both tired. 'All right then,' he said. 'We'll go back to this flat a' yours, if that's what you want, an' we'll think about it in the morning. I can't say fairer than that.' And he headed off for the tram to the Borough. He didn't hold her hand or offer her his arm and didn't seem to notice when she ran to catch up with him and walked beside him.

It was a silent journey to Newcomen Street and a silent arrival in the empty shop. The key clicked as she opened the shop door and she was so tense the little sound made her jump. But he didn't speak to her. And when they'd walked through the shop and up the stairs to the flat, he just kept on going until they were in the bedroom.

He was frowning so terribly she took her nightdress out of the cupboard as quietly as she could and tiptoed downstairs to put it on in the bathroom, taking her lovely bouquet with her so that she could put it in water. She heard him come down to the WC while she was brushing the rose petals out of her hair. Then she too went to the WC and followed him upstairs.

He was already in bed, wearing his shirt instead of a nightshirt and with his eyes closed as if he was asleep. When she crept into the bed beside him, he turned his back on her. It was the saddest wedding night she could possibly have imagined and she didn't get to sleep for a very long time.

Chapter Fourteen

When Rosie woke the next morning it took her a few seconds to work out where she was. She knew she'd slept late, the light told her that, and she knew it was Sunday, because the bells were ringing, but the rest of her brain was taking its time to catch up with her body. Then she realised with a frisson of shock that there was somebody coming up the stairs and she scrambled out of bed at once and went to see who it was. It was quite a relief to discover that it was Kitty, who was standing in front of the fireplace, taking off her hat. She'd put Rosie's old bag and Ma's old basket on the table and was arranging her clock and her row of knick-knacks on the mantelpiece.

'Morning, slug-a-bed,' she said, grinning at Rosie's tousled head. 'I brought yer things for you an' Jim, look, an' Tess sent you the last a' the pie an' some lettuce all fresh from the garden an' a jar a' Mrs Taylor's pickle. She thought we might like it fer dinner. Go an' get dressed an' wake his nibs up an' I'll set the table. Your landlord's in the shop selling the Sundays so we might get a copy. Whatcher think? I don't suppose you got any beer 'ave yer?'

Rosie went back upstairs wishing Kitty hadn't come home so soon and feeling guilty to be thinking such a thing. But if she'd stayed in Binderton just a little bit longer, and she and Jim could have been on their own, she could have tried to talk to him about their miserable first night and explain why she simply *had* to rent this flat, and that wasn't possible with his sister in the room. So she gave him a shake to wake him, told him Kitty had arrived and then just got on with the day and let it carry her along.

Jim was in a dour sort of mood when he finally joined them in the kitchen but he went downstairs to buy a *Sunday Pictorial* and out to get some beer when Kitty hinted that that was what she wanted. Then they made a leisurely meal out of the leavings and talked about the wedding and managed to keep everything on a more or less even keel. And when they'd finished eating, they left the dishes to soak in the sink and took a walk along Borough High Street to London Bridge. The Thames was sparkling with sunshine and instead of its usual muddy fawn was sky blue and olive green. They stood in the middle of the bridge and watched the barges and the great cargo ships coming and going and Jim cheered up a bit and said he was looking forward to getting back to work.

'Time I brought in a bit a' cash,' he said. 'Can't be idle

all me life. 'Specially now we've got this great rent ter pay. At least there's a lot a' new ships in. That's a good sign.'

'Will you go tomorrow?' Rosie asked.

He nodded, watching the riverside. It would be better once he was back at work. He wouldn't feel such a kept boy then.

Rosie was thinking along the same lines. Going back to work would perk him up and it might make him feel better about the flat. It might even be better for us tonight. We've had a good day.

It was a faint hope. That night, he kissed her, once but without any passion, and then turned on his side and settled to sleep. Well if that's the way he's going on, she thought, it's just as well we're all back to work tomorrow. He needs something different to pull him out of this or he'll just get worse and worse. I don't want him going back to where he was in that awful hospital.

She worried about him all next day, while she took orders and served meals and cleared tables and remembered to smile. It felt like a very long day and as she rode home on the tram that evening, she knew it had taken the spirit out of her, because she felt weary and not like her usual energetic self at all.

Kitty was already home and had the kettle on ready to boil but there was no sign of Jim.

'He can't still be at work,' she said. 'Surely to goodness. It's gettin' dark. I'll bet he's gone up the boozer.'

'We'll give him another half hour,' Rosie said, feeling

cross, 'an' then we'll cook our supper an' if he's not back, we'll eat ours an' keep his warm for him.'

But they'd eaten theirs and washed the dishes and set the kitchen to rights and he still wasn't back. It was closing time before he put in an appearance and then he was so drunk he couldn't see straight and had a job to stand upright.

'What sort a' time d'you call this?' Kitty said, heading for the cooker and attacking at once.

He sat on his chair at the table, wearily and as if he didn't know where the edges of it were. 'Don't start, Kit,' he said but he didn't look at either of them.

His face was so drawn and haggard that Rosie knew something bad had happened. 'What is it, Jim?' she said. 'What's up?'

'Wha's up?' he said angrily. 'Wha's up. I got no job. Tha's wha's up. Said I was a cripple, fer Chrissake. Don't hire cripples, they said. I knew it was mishtake ter take this place. Now what'll we do? We'll 'ave ter move out. I got no money. I'm finished. I should ha' died in the bleedin' trenches wiv all the others.'

She pulled up her chair and sat facing him, reaching across the space between them to hold his hands, which she did even though he tried to shake her off. 'You're *not* finished,' she said. 'There's other jobs. You'll find something.'

'I'm a cripple,' he said, dropping his head and refusing to look at her. 'Finished. On the scrapheap. A cripple an' a bleedin' kept boy. Who's gonna hire a cripple? Tell me that.'

She knew what she had to say to him, in a flash, like sunlight. 'I can tell you one man who would,' she said. 'He wouldn't call you a cripple neither.'

He was too down to entertain the hope she was offering. 'You ain't listenin',' he said. 'Finished. On the bleedin' scrapheap.'

'No you ent,' Rosie said, giving his hands a little shake, 'an' I'll tell you for why. Mr Feigenbaum'll have you like a shot. He wouldn't call you a cripple. He's a good man.'

'Feigenbaum?' Jim said thickly. 'Fred's dad?'

'That's the one.'

'He won't want me,' Jim told her, scowling. 'He's got Fred.'

Rosie caught her breath because her flash of sunlight had turned into a bayonet. It was time to tell him the truth and she had to do it, even though she knew it would upset him. 'Listen to me, Jim,' she said, holding his hands firmly. 'I got somethin' to tell you.'

He listened, grudgingly, and she was aware that Kitty was listening too from her post by the cooker. 'Fred was killed,' she said. 'I didn't like to tell you before, when you was so down, but you need to know it now.'

'Killed?' he said, looking at her for the first time since he came in. His face was haggard with emotion. He was drunk and ashamed and pushed so far down by this hideous, unending, dragging despair that he couldn't make sense of anything and now she'd given him this terrible grief on top of everything else. 'He can't be.'

'He is,' she said sadly. 'I'm sorry, Jim, but that's a fact. Mr Feigenbaum told me himself.'

He was crying, although he didn't seem to be aware of it, tears rolling down his cheeks and spilling onto their hands. 'Poor sod!' he said. 'Poor bleedin' sod. He was a good bloke, our Rosie. Never oughter've died.'

'No,' she said. 'None of 'em should. So you can see why I suggested his pa, can't you? He'll need someone to help him now. Someone who knew his Fred.'

He didn't answer so she pressed on. 'So you'll go an' see him tomorrow, won'tcher?'

'I need a piddle,' he said, struggling to his feet. They watched as he stumbled to the door and went through it, closing it behind him with elaborate and inaccurate caution.

Kitty was looking cross. 'What sort of answer was that?' she asked.

Rosie defended him as well as she could. 'I think it was to give himself a bit a' time to think,' she said.

'Will he go to this Mr Feigenbaum's then?'

Rosie wasn't at all sure. 'Let's hope so,' she said.

They could hear Jim stumbling up the stairs, muttering to himself as he went.

'Time to turn in,' Kitty said. 'I don't know about you but I've had a day an' a half an' there's nothin' more to do here.'

'I'll just set the breakfast things,' Rosie said. 'Then I'll be up.' There was no point in rushing. If she was any judge, Jim would be asleep by the time she got upstairs. As he was.

I know I promised for better or worse, she thought, as she lay down beside him and pulled the covers under her chin, but I never thought the worse bit would come first. Oh God, if you're out there, can we have a bit of better stuff tomorrow?

*

Jim was the first one up the next morning, heading off to the bathroom to wash and dress as if it was an ordinary day. And as soon as they'd finished breakfast and Rosie and Kitty were clearing the table, he put on his cap and said, 'I'm off then, since I got to.'

He was gone so quickly, they didn't even have time to wish him luck.

'Now what?' Kitty said.

'Now,' Rosie told her, 'we wait.'

It was another long day but when she and Kitty got home, Jim was already back and sitting in his chair, reading the *Evening Standard*. 'You're right about Mr Feigenbaum,' he said to Rosie. "E's a good chap. Took me on fer a week's trial. Started this mornin'.'

Both his women gave an audible sigh of relief.

'I'm not sayin' it'll work mind you,' Jim said. 'But I'll give it a try. Can't say fairer than that.'

*

217

By the end of that first week it was obvious to all three of them that Jim was going to be kept on and that he was doing his best to cope in his new line of work, although he was still very down. Now, Rosie thought, trying to be hopeful, with any luck we ought to see some changes. And sure enough small changes began. On Sunday, he and Kitty went back to Parish Street to collect their things and give in their notice. On Monday, he set off to work whistling, and on Saturday, he brought home some 'specks' that *ol' Manny* had given him for free and Rosie made an apple pie. But the secret change she yearned for still didn't happen. They lay in bed like brother and sister and there were nights when she didn't even get a kiss. He seemed to be stuck in that horrible gloom of his and she didn't know what to do to tease him out of it. Until one sultry night at the beginning of July.

They were lying side by side on their bed with the windows open and only a sheet to cover them, when he turned his head and gave her an odd little smile. It was little more than half a smile really but it encouraged her. She propped herself up on her elbow and leant towards him. 'Give us a kiss, Jim,' she coaxed.

What happened next was so upsetting that at first she didn't know how to respond to it. He turned his head away from her and began to cry.

'I can't, Rosie,' he said. 'It's not . . . I ain't . . . Now when all them fellers are dead an' gone. Good fellers, they was. I been thinkin' about 'em all day long, off an' on, talkin' about 'em with Manny. Poor sods.'

She felt so rejected she spoke without thinking. 'Don't you love me no more?' she asked.

'It ain't that,' he said. 'I mean, yeh, course I do. It's jest . . . Oh Rosie you should ha' seen 'em. They was blown to bits. Hanging on the barbed wire they was, shot to bits. Jest hanging there, as if they was on their knees praying and they was dead.' Tears were rolling down his cheeks but he hardly noticed them. 'It was bleedin' awful.'

She put her hands on either side of his face and tried to wipe his tears away but he shook her off. 'Don't,' he said. 'It's too bleedin' awful.' Now that he'd start talking about the horrors he had to go on. He had to tell her. To make her understand. 'Got knocked off me feet once by some poor bleeder what'd just been hit. He jest fell backwards like a ton weight and knocked me off me feet. Didn't have no face. Shot away it was. He was making a noise like a duck quackin'. Poor sod. Strugglin' fer breath, he was, and makin' this awful noise. It ain't right Rosie to do such things. Them bleedin' generals should ha' been put up against the wall an' shot.' The memory was making him ache but he had to go on. He told her about the wounded men he saw in the ambulance and the dreadful state they were in and how brave they were, and about the men lying out in no-man's-land calling for help and dying on their own in the mud. He was shaking with anger at the things they'd had to endure. And she held him as though he was a child and let him rave. Eventually he wore himself out and fell asleep in the middle of a sentence.

She lifted his head tenderly and pushed his pillow underneath it to support his neck. Then she lay down beside him and tried to make sense of the things he'd been saying. My poor Jim, she thought. He's right. Those stupid generals should ha' been shot. It was monstrous making men suffer like that. I don't think this is ever going to change, she thought miserably, not now.

But the change she wanted did come eventually, when she'd almost given up hoping of it. He came home one balmy August evening with a copy of the *Standard* under his arm and in quite a perky mood. 'What d'yer say we go to the flicks ternight?' he asked. 'They're showin' 'em in the theatres now according to this. Mr Feigenbaum took his ol' lady an' he says they're ever so good.'

'Not ternight,' Kitty said. 'I'm going to a restaurant with Mr Matthews.'

'Are you though?' Jim said and now he was wearing his teasing face. 'Oh well then, Rosie, it'll jest be you an' me. Whatcher think?'

So they went to the pictures and sat in the back row, cuddled together, and very nice it was. Rosie was so happy she hardly paid any attention to the film which was very long and rather confusing and Jim spent more time gazing at her than he did looking at the screen. When they emerged from the relative privacy of the dark back row into the noise and bustle of Leicester Square, they both felt a bit off balance.

'Come on,' Jim said, taking her hand, and he set off at

a brisk pace, despite his limp, but instead of walking south, as she expected, he headed west.

'Where are we going?' she asked.

'Piccadilly Circus,' he said, grinning at her in almost the old way, 'an' then up Piccadilly. I want ter see if our ol' tree's still there.'

That made her laugh. "Course it'll be there,' she said. 'Trees don't walk about.'

And of course it *was* there, as private and magical as they remembered, standing with its sheltering branches spread ready for them. They kissed as if nothing had happened since the last time they were there, and kissed again and again and again until he was groaning and she was trembling.

'I *do* love you, Rosie,' he said, his face taut and pale in the darkness. 'You do know that, don'tcher?'

'Let's go home,' she said and she was thinking, it might be better this time.

It was. But when he was lying blissfully asleep beside her, looking quite leonine again, she lay quiet and wondered. Should it have hurt her like that? Surely not. It hadn't hurt him. She was sure of that even though he'd groaned. Oh, she thought, if only I had a woman friend or a relation I could ask about it. But Ma was dead and the others were too young. Not that Ma would have been much help to her even if she *had* been alive because she never spoke about marriage and what you had to expect from it except to say, 'T'ent a bed of roses, I call tell 'ee that,' which was uninformative then and would have been less than useless now. She turned on her side and sighed. Maybe, she thought, trying to be philosophical, it won't hurt so much next time.

They were late getting up next morning and Kitty was already in the kitchen laying the table by the time they came yawning down. She seemed to be in a very cheerful mood.

'I got sommink to tell yer,' she said, putting their loaf on the breadboard and setting the margarine dish alongside it. 'I couldn't tell yer nothin' yesterday on account of I wasn't sure about it but I can now.'

They looked at her and waited.

'You ain't the only one ter lose yer job, our Jim,' she said. 'Mine's gone an' all now some of the men are back. They told me yesterday.' She seemed perfectly cheerful about it and was grinning at them as if it was a good thing.

'Oh dear,' Rosie said, glancing at Jim.

'It's orl right,' Kitty told her. 'I got another one. That's why I went out with Mr Matthews. He said he'd got plans for me and he'd tell me what they was when we was in the restaurant. Which he done an' it's orl right. I'm to work in the sorting room. On more money.'

'Thank God for that,' Rosie said. 'You had me quite worried.'

'No need ter worry,' Kitty said. 'We've fell on our feet, ain't we Jim.'

'You got any bacon?' her brother asked. 'I could just fancy a rasher a' bacon.'

How odd life is, Rosie thought as she put the bacon in

the frying pan. Two jobs lost and new ones found in no time at all, an' yet me an' Jim only just a proper husband an' wife to one another after all these weeks. It makes me wonder what the next change is going to be.

In fact the next change was predictable but because she was kept so busy in her dual life as waitress and housewife she didn't have the leisure to foresee it. Autumn came and went and her disappointing love life continued until she accepted it as normal: November brought a fog so thick that the trams had to have men walking in front of them with blazing torches to show them the way: and then it was December and Kitty said it was colder than it had any right to be and stoked the kitchen fire halfway up the chimney. The first sprouts appeared in the market alongside delicately wrapped mandarin oranges, and decorated boxes of dates. But Rosie's work never eased up for a minute. There were mornings when she was so rushed she didn't even have time for breakfast or it made her feel so sick she couldn't eat it when she'd cooked it. And she lost count of the afternoons when she felt so tired she wanted to lie down on the floor in the restaurant and go to sleep. In fact there were days when she had to hang on to her control to keep going at all.

'It'll be Christmas 'fore we know it,' Kitty said. 'Are we goin' to midnight mass our Jim?'

Midnight mass, Rosie thought, and her mind was suddenly filled with a vivid memory of sitting in their familiar pew at St Mary's, as the carols were being sung, with Ma and all her babies around, straining her neck to see the babe in the manger and thinking what it must have been like to be born in a stable in the middle of the winter. Babies, she thought, remembering them all, Tess an' Tommy an' Edie an' the Baby Jesus. And her mind suddenly clicked into understanding and she knew why she'd been feeling sick at breakfast time and dropping with exhaustion by mid-afternoon. A baby. That would explain everything. I'll go and find my little diary she thought and see when I made my last mark. Now this very minute. And she left Kitty and Jim planning their Christmas and went upstairs, her heart fluttering with excitement.

The last mark she could find was at the end of August, which was over three months away. If this *is* a baby, she thought, I'm a third of the way there. The thought filled her with awe. I shan't tell Jim yet. It would upset him, having another mouth to feed and nappies to buy and everything and me not working. I'll keep it to myself until I show and then break it to him gently. After all, I can go on working until it's born. So he won't have that worry yet awhile. I can let out my skirts and blouses. That should hide it for a bit. He's bound to notice I'm putting on weight sooner or later but I'll have worked out what to say to him by then.

But as it turned out it wasn't Jim who noticed she was putting on weight, it was the housekeeper at the club.

*

Two weeks before Christmas, the *maître d'* appeared in the restaurant when all the guests had gone and they were clearing the tables and setting them for breakfast. It wasn't like him to return to the restaurant when the meal was over so they paused in their work to see what he wanted. He picked his delicate way between the tables until he reached Rosie, then he inclined his head by way of greeting her and asked if she would be so good as to come to his office. There was a surprised silence. Rosie was aware of questioning faces turned in her direction all around the room. It made her feel a bit uncomfortable but there couldn't be anything wrong, could there? She stuck her chin in the air and followed him, trying to look unconcerned.

His office was a quiet place after the endless coming and going in the club, leather chairs like the ones in the smoking room, an oak desk, rows of important-looking folders on the shelves behind his head, brown velvet curtains gathering dust at the window, a strong smell of cigar smoke.

'Do sit down,' he said, indicating the chair on the other side of his desk. Then he leant his elbows on the desk, folded his hands neatly one on top of the other in front of his mouth, rested his nose on them and pondered. It was some time before he spoke.

'It has been brought to my attention,' he said, giving her a vague smile, 'that it might be possible that you are – how shall I put this? – that you are – um – in the family way.'

'Yes, sir,' she said happily. 'I am.'

'Ah!' he said and pondered again. 'This presents us with

something of a problem,' he said. 'As you will appreciate. It is company policy not to employ any woman who is – um – in the family way.'

She was so appalled she fought back at once without thinking. 'That ent fair,' she said hotly. 'I mean to say, it ent a disease. It ent catching, like consumption or diphtheria. It's natural. Why should I be sacked just because I'm carrying?'

'Quite,' he said, smoothly. 'I take your point. But it's company policy, you see.'

Her answer was hot and instant. 'Then it ought to be changed.'

'Quite possibly,' he said, giving her a fleeting smile. 'However until it is, I'm afraid we have to abide by it. I'm sorry I've had to give you such unwelcome news. We will pay you until the end of the week, of course. Your usual envelope is waiting for you at the desk.'

And that was that. She got her coat and hat and steamed to the front desk, hot with fury, chin in the air, eyes blazing. Which was how Gerard de Silva saw her as he strode into the welcoming warmth of the club with a group of his friends, splendid in his winter cape and his flamboyant muffler and a dramatic black hat.

'Well, well, well,' he said. 'If it's not our Rosie, bigod. What's up?'

'They've give me the sack,' she said, angrily.

'Have they too,' he said, looking at her calculatingly. 'Well if that's the case, you'd better come and work for me. I've

226

just lost my latest model. Off to the Riviera with some silly young idler, more fool her, and you have just the sort of colour I'm looking for.' His friends were teasing and calling out to him but he ignored them. 'What do you think? Would you take it? I pay well.'

She accepted his offer at once, without thinking at all. That'ud show 'em. 'Yes, sir. I'd like to.'

'Good,' he said, smiling at her, brown eyes gleaming, teeth very white in the dark bush of his beard. 'There's my card. Come to that address, nine o'clock Monday morning.' He put the card in her hand and strolled off to join his friends, 'Yes, yes, I'm coming, you dreadful impatient lot!'

She held the card in her hand and read it. '*Gerard de Silva. Portrait painter to the great, the good and the frankly impossible. Member of the Uffizi Society Oxford.*' And then an address in Cheyne Walk, Chelsea. Wait till I show them this at home, she thought.

It was a lovely moment. She waited until she had dished up their supper and they'd all started to eat. Then she told them. 'Got the sack today,' she said, with splendid aplomb, 'so you two ent the only ones.'

Kitty was instantly sympathetic. 'Oh Rosie!' she said. 'That's awful.'

'Got another job though. Straight away. Just like you.'

They both asked, 'Where? What?' their faces eager to know more.

'I'm going to be an artist's model,' she told them. 'What d'you think a' that?'

'My stars!' Kitty said, deeply impressed. 'You *are* comin' up in the world.'

But Jim's face was a study in horror. 'A model?' he said, his voice rising with alarm. 'Oh fer cryin' out loud, Rosie! You can't work as a *model*.'

She fought back at once, chin in the air. 'I can,' she said. 'I'm going to.'

'No,' he said, doggedly. 'You can't. You don't know what them artists are like. Terrible some of 'em are. They paints women in the nu . . .' Then he stopped because he was embarrassed and none too sure of the words he needed to tell her what he meant. 'Wivout . . .' he tried. 'I mean ter say, wiv no clothes on.'

She laughed at him. 'You're such an old Puritan,' she said. 'They don't all paint nudes.'

'But what would you do if he asked yer to?'

'I'd tell him no, I wouldn't do it.'

He was still scowling. 'Leave it fer a day or so,' he urged. 'See if you can find somethin' better. You don't 'ave ter go rushin' into it. Me an' Kitty can manage fer a week or two, can't we, Kit?'

'I ent got a week or two,' Rosie told him crossly. 'An' neither've you. I got to earn as much as I can while I still can.'

'Whatcher mean "still can"?' he asked. 'What's ter stop yer?'

She blurted out the answer before she thought about it. 'I'm carryin',' she said, almost crossly. 'That's why. I got till

May to earn as much as I can, then I shan't be earnin' no more for months.'

The news gave him a shock he couldn't hide. 'Oh my dear good God!' he said.

'Yes,' she said, glad he'd understood her need to work even though she was already regretting the way she'd told him. 'So you see . . .'

He was still digesting the news, caught between a rising delight that he'd fathered a child and the most hideous anxiety that they wouldn't be able to pay the rent. 'Oh my dear good God,' he said again.

'So I shall go to work on Monday morning,' she said. And as he didn't argue, she assumed it was settled.

Chapter Fifteen

Gerard de Silva had lived in Cheyne Walk ever since he'd got his first sizeable commission and had begun to earn substantial fees. That was several years ago but the thrill of owning such an elegant house on such a prestigious street was still as strong as it had been when he first moved in and he enjoyed it every morning, strolling from room to room just for the pleasure of knowing it was his, admiring the Italianate moulding on the ceilings, the elegant fireplaces, the splendid view of the Thames from the high Georgian windows of his studio and his drawing room, relishing the sense of order and comfort. He'd taken the house with two live-in servants already installed in the top floor flat, a married couple called Fenchurch who cared for him in a discreetly attentive way, she as cook/housekeeper, he as butler and general factotum. Add to that a succession of riotous dinner parties with his artistic friends, a cellar stocked with French wine and a library full of books, and there were days when he knew he couldn't possibly want for more. It was true that lovers and models tended to come and go but the urge to paint grew stronger by the day. And now he had a new model and the canvas already stretched and primed ready to welcome her and the portrait was growing so strongly in his brain he couldn't wait to begin. He glanced at his fine clock on the mantelpiece and saw that it was two minutes to nine. And the doorbell rang.

*

Rosie Jackson had dressed very carefully that morning in her best red skirt with the seams let out, her prettiest blouse and a new pair of stockings bought for the occasion, thinking that if she was going to be a model she'd better try and look the part. She regretted it as soon as she reached the tram stop because it was raining and blowing a gale and the cold and damp seeped into her bones. By the time she reached Mr de Silva's fine house, with its important windows and its elaborate door and all that fine brickwork, red against the slate-grey of the sky, she was very cold indeed and aching for the protection of her old thick skirt and her knitted cardigan. But she tried not to be disheartened by the cold – or daunted by the house. Whatever this job required of her, she would do it to the best of her ability, even if it meant feeling chilly now and then. She climbed the stairs to the front door, feeling purposeful and rang the bell boldly.

A nice, comfortable-looking woman opened the door and ushered her in saying, 'Come on in out this wicked cold, my lovely. I got a nice fire a-goin' for 'ee.' And when she'd taken Rosie's hat and coat, she led her up a grand staircase and along the landing into a room that seemed to be full of light. There was very little furniture in it apart from a plain wooden chair set against the wall, a chaise longue with an easy chair to match it, a little round table, a painted screen and an artist's easel, but there were shelves full of books lining the walls and a good fire in the grate. She could feel the warmth of it from where she stood, just inside the door, taking it all in, aware that everything about this house said wealth and comfort. Then Mr de Silva emerged from behind the screen with a paintbrush behind his ear and a beautiful red velvet gown and a pair of long red gloves draped over his arm.

'Ah there you are,' he said. 'Good, good. Just slip behind the screen and put this on, will you?'

'Land's sakes sir,' the comfortable woman said. 'Let the poor gel get her breath. She's mortal cold.' She turned to Rosie and put a restraining hand on her arm. 'You stand by the fire me dear and warm yourself up. That's my advice to 'ee.'

Gerard de Silva grinned at her. 'This is Mrs Fenchurch, Rosie,' he said, 'who is my housekeeper and sees it as her mission in life to tell me what to do, as you will observe. Not that I ever take any notice of her. Do I Mrs F?' And he grinned at Mrs Fenchurch too.

He treats his servants like human beings, Rosie thought, admiring him for it. It made a nice change after the haughty way they'd dealt with their staff at the castle and the arrogant superiority of those two Eden boys.

'Well come and sit by the fire then,' he said. 'I suppose I can spare five minutes for you to thaw out. Don't forget our coffee, Mrs F.'

'As if I would,' Mrs Fenchurch reproved him. Then she smiled at them both and left them to it. Rosie perched on the edge of the chaise longue as close to the fire as she could get and held out her hands to the blaze and, after a few minutes, Mr de Silva walked across to her, laid the gown and the gloves across the other end of the chaise longue, and took hold of one of her hands.

'You *are* cold,' he said.

'Yes sir.'

'Um,' he said, still holding her hand and looking thoughtful. 'Perhaps we should get one or two things straight before we start working together. You don't have to call me 'sir' or 'Mr de Silva'. Just call me Gerry and I will call you Rosie and life will be a great deal easier. When you're warm enough, go and put this gown on. You can do it behind the screen if you're feeling modest. Only be quick. I want to see what you're going to look like.'

She went at once, carrying the gown over her arm very carefully because she felt rather in awe of it and feeling pleased by that nice modest screen, thinking it would be something to tell Jim about. She was shivering by the time she'd taken off her skirt and blouse but the weight of the gown was warming around her body even if it *did* leave her neck bare and it was a good fit, despite the baby. She looked down at the lovely train, swirling about her feet, and the heavy gold thread of the embroidery round the hem and all over the bodice and felt like a queen. The only problem was that it fastened at the back and she could only reach the hooks at her waist. And of course she had quite the wrong shoes on. She emerged from behind the screen, feeling breathless and not at all sure of herself. And was reassured by a happy smile.

'First rate,' Gerry said. 'As I knew it would be. Come here and let me fasten it.'

She stood still in front of him while he hooked her into her finery. 'I've got the wrong sort of shoes on,' she said.

'I will paint you different ones,' he said. 'And jewels at your neck. Just put the gloves on and I'll arrange you and we can get started.' His beard was bristling and his eyes were lustrous with excitement. But he took his time over arranging her, settling the train into a lovely swirling curve and lifting her head so that she was holding it at just the right angle.

'What do you want me to do with my hands?' she asked.

'Hold onto the curtain with one of them and let the other one dangle.'

She did as she was told.

'Now keep perfectly still,' he said. 'Don't move until I give you permission.'

For the first half an hour she stood as still as a statue, looking out of the window at the boats on the Thames and wondering where they were all going. It was so quiet in the room she could hear the lick of the flames in the fire. From time to time this man she was to call Gerry sang to himself in a tuneless way or shifted his feet with a sudden shuffling sound. Soon she had a stiff neck and wanted to move it to ease it – and didn't dare. Then she wanted to sneeze and had to struggle not to and couldn't manage it. And at that, he put his head round the side of the easel and said, 'All right?' but didn't wait for her to answer. She was really quite relieved when Mrs Fenchurch arrived with a coffee tray which she put down on the little table beside the fire. Now perhaps she could stop modelling and move about a bit.

Mrs Fenchurch made up the fire. 'There,' she said, when it was done. 'That'll burn up nicely. Don't let the coffee go cold.'

'You see how she bullies me,' Gerry said, stepping out from behind the easel. His smock was splashed with paint and he was looking extremely pleased with himself.

'You wouldn't eat anything if I didn't,' Mrs Fenchurch told him. 'Now come an' sit by the fire the pair of you an' drink this up while it's hot. Then you'll get the beauty of it.'

The coffee was very welcome to Rosie. She took off her gloves and set them aside so that she wouldn't spoil them and put her hands round the cup to warm them. And Mr de Silva sat in the easy chair with his long legs stretched out in front of him towards the fire and drank his own coffee and scowled, which was a bit disquieting. As soon as his cup was empty, he got up and rushed back to his easel, so she finished her own coffee and took up her pose again. After a few seconds, he appeared beside her to re-arrange her train but he still didn't say anything.

Exactly the same thing happened when they paused for dinner. He ate in silence, apart from scowling now and then, and, as soon as his plate was clean, he went back to work and Rosie returned to her solitary contemplation of the Thames. At four o'clock he emerged again to complain that the light was going. 'We shall have to stop,' he said. 'Damned light. Same time tomorrow.'

'Was it all right?' she asked.

He didn't seem to understand the question. 'What?' he said.

'What I been doin'. The posing.'

'Yes, yes,' he said, almost tetchily. 'Of course. See you tomorrow.'

As she stomped off to the nearest tram stop, glad for the warmth of her coat and hat, and her thick muffler and Jim's nice thick gloves, she felt as tired as though she'd done a full day's work at the club. But she took care to make light of it when she got home and they were eating their supper and talking. Kitty was eager to know what it was like being a model.

'Whatcher 'ave ter do?' she asked.

'It was boring,' Rosie told her. 'All I did was stand still an' look out the window,' and she looked at Jim and added, '*fully clothed.* I had to change into a different dress but there was a screen there so I could do it in private. It was all very proper.' And she was pleased to see that he looked chastened, although he made no comment.

*

She stood still and looked out of the window for the next four days. But as the light fell on the fourth day, Mr de Silva put down his brushes and asked her if she'd like to see how the portrait was progressing. 'It's not finished,' he said. 'Not by a long chalk. But it's shaping.'

She was impressed by it. The gown looked so beautiful it made her blink and she saw that he'd painted the prettiest pair of slippers to match it. But then she moved on to her face and that gave her a shock she didn't expect because he'd made her look so fierce. She was staring at it when she became aware that he was grinning at her and looking devilish.

'Well?' he asked.

She tried to be diplomatic. 'The dress is lovely,' she said.

His grin broadened. 'But?' he teased.

'I don't really look as fierce as that do I?'

He laughed at her. 'You do to me. It's one of the best things about you.'

That was a surprise but she didn't want to pursue it, so she changed the subject. 'Am I to come in tomorrow?'

'No,' he said. 'Tomorrow is Shabbat. I shall expect you at nine o'clock on Monday.'

And that was all. The fierce face he'd given her bothered her all the way home but eventually she decided he was wrong about it. He had to be. She wasn't like that at all. She was expecting a baby and expectant mothers were always serene and beautiful.

*

In the middle of February when she reckoned she must be about five or six months and she could feel her baby moving every day, she went serenely and beautifully to visit the local midwife and was booked in for the third week of May and told everything was coming along lovely and that the baby had a good strong heartbeat. By that time Jim seemed to have come round to the idea of being a father and was actually thinking up names for this baby of theirs. And Gerry was using her to model hands and feet for a couple of wealthy sisters who wanted to appear younger than they were, which meant that all she had to do was sit in a chair and stay fairly still, which suited her very well. It was peaceful and quiet and a lot easier than standing up.

She was so easy she was nearly asleep when his voice spoke to her from behind the easel one darkening afternoon. 'Do tell me,' he said, 'as a matter of interest, why did the club dispense with your services?'

'Because I was "*in the family way*", as the *maître d'* put it,' she said. 'Apparently it's not company policy to employ expectant mothers.'

'Is that right?' he said. 'Rather short-sighted of them.'

'Downright stupid, if you ask me,' she said. 'I mean to say pregnancy ent catching. I *did* tell him but he didn't take no notice. He said it was the system.'

'And what did you say to that?'

'I said if *that* was the system, it was time it was changed.'

He gave a great roar of laughter and put his head round the side of the easel to look at her. 'And you say you're not fierce,' he said. 'You're a blood-red revolutionary, damme if you ain't.' He put down his brush and walked over to the bookshelves, trailing his left hand over the spines until he found the book he wanted. 'Read that,' he said, opening it. 'The bit in italics, by my thumb. It was written in 1776 but I think you'll agree with every word of it. Read it out loud and tell me what you think of it.'

She took the book and did as she was told, stopping to comment whenever something struck her. '*American Declaration of Independence July 4th 1776*,' she read. '*We hold these truths to be self-evident, that all men are created equal* – quite right – *that they are endowed by their Creator with certain unalienable Rights* – what does "un-all-inable" mean?'

Gerry had gone back to his painting but he answered from behind the easel, pronouncing the word correctly. 'Unalienable. Rights that should never be taken away.'

'Ah,' she said. 'I see.' And read on. '. . . *unalienable Rights that among these are Life* – well of course – *Liberty* – yes – *and the pursuit of Happiness* – well that's an extraordinary idea. But why not? The toffs think we're just here to wait on them all the time an' clear up after them an' do as we're told but why shouldn't we have a better life an' be happy? – *That to secure these rights, Governments are instituted among Men, deriving their just powers from the consent of the governed* – that's what the suffragettes say – *That whenever any Form of Government becomes destructive of these ends, it is the Right of the People to alter or to abolish it, and to institute new Government, laying its foundation on such principles and organizing its powers in such form, as to them shall seem most likely to affect their Safety and Happiness.* He's saying ordinary people should have a say in how they're governed, isn't he? And that if we don't like what our rulers are doing we got the right to change it. '*Alter or abolish*' – I like the sound of that. Has anyone ever done it?'

'Twice,' he told her, gratified to see how responsive she was. 'Once in France in 1789, when ordinary men took over the government from the king and his courtiers and chopped their heads off, and once in America in 1776, when ordinary men decided they weren't going to put up with being ruled by us any longer and formed a citizens' army and drove us out.'

'Extraordinary,' she said. 'All that from an idea.'

He echoed her happily. 'All that from an idea.'

'How do you know all this?' she asked, intrigued. 'Was it reading all those books?'

'Some of it was,' he told her, 'but I learnt it at school too.'

'Must have been a different sort a' school from the one I went to then,' she said. 'They learned us how to read an' write an' how to do sums but nothin' like this.'

'I can see I shall have to take your education in hand,' he said happily. Hadn't he always known she was different? There'd been a lot of women in his life, either as models or lovers or both, but none of them had been the slightest bit interested in revolution or literature or poetry. Or art, come to that. In fact he'd often thought that, beautiful though they were, their heads were as empty as thistledown. Whereas this one would be worth teaching. It could be an interesting experiment. 'That's enough work for today,' he said. 'Same time tomorrow.'

From then on Rosie's pregnancy and education continued together and apace. As her body grew steadily more cumbersome and lethargic and modelling less and less possible, her mind leapt into activity, devouring books and newspapers, struggling to make sense of poetry and politics, accepting any challenge that Gerard de Silva threw at her. 'Try this,' he would say, handing her one of Dicken's formidable novels. 'See what you make of that,' giving her an article from a newspaper. He still paid her a weekly wage even though her modelling assignments were few and far between, which was very good of him and troubled her conscience whenever she stopped to think about it, but she went on deciphering books, and was reading voraciously when her pains began.

By that time she'd given up her modelling until after the baby was born and on that particular morning she was on her own in the flat, sitting by the window in the new easy chair she'd bought for Jim with her wages, with Gerry's copy of *Oliver Twist* open on her lap and the busy street below her for company. She was feeling extremely uncomfortable and kept getting a nasty little pain in her belly but she ignored it, thinking that she must have eaten something that disagreed with her, and kept on reading because she'd reached the point when Oliver had been taken to court accused of theft and she was eager to know what happened next. It wasn't until he was happily established in Mr Brownlow's house that she gave her body any attention and then she realised that the pain was a lot stronger and seemed to be coming at regular intervals, which was what the midwife had told her would happen. She watched the clock and sure enough the pains were coming every quarter of an hour. So she waddled downstairs to ask Mrs Rogers if she would send her little lad to fetch the midwife.

It was a gentle birth and very quiet. The midwife padded about in her carpet slippers, murmuring the occasional instruction, the noise of the street was a distant clatter, the pains came and went and, although they were so strong that they made her pant, they didn't worry her. She'd watched her mother panting through her pains too often to be alarmed by them. What she wasn't expecting was the strength of the love she would feel for her baby when she finally slipped into the world, small, damp and slightly bloodstained, with a mop of dark hair and huge dark eyes. She looked up at Rosie at once, her gaze solemn and unwavering as if they'd known one another for years.

'Oh my little darling,' Rosie said. 'I just love you.'

The midwife beamed approval. 'Well nat'rally,' she said. And when the baby began to root around, she said, 'Well will you look at that. She wants feeding al-a-ready, the dear little mite.' And Rosie fed her.

The next ten days passed in a milky haze. The baby was named Grace when she was five hours old, because Jim said she was a Tuesday's child so it was only right an' anyway she looked like a Grace, and Rosie was pleased to see that he and Kitty came home in a rush every day to see her. Four weeks later, Tess and Edie and Johnnie wangled a Sunday off work to travel to London to see her too, bringing a punnet full of raspberries from the garden and a pot of jam from Mrs Taylor and a nice hock of bacon from their Pa. They passed their new niece around to one another all through the visit, handling her very carefully as if she was made of bone china. And Jim had his back slapped until it made him cough and said it was 'a bit of orl right havin' a family'. After the clumsy way she'd broken her news to him, it was a relief to Rosie to see how much he loved this baby. And he hadn't said anything about her lack of wages, although to be fair she *had* saved up quite a lot and was paying into the pot as often as she could.

*

By the time Gracie was three months old, she was a lovely plump baby with the roundest, prettiest face, who smiled at everybody who came within sight. At six months she was sitting up in the high chair her now doting father had bought for her, happily eating rusks. And when Christmas came she was the star of the feast, even though she demanded to be fed in the middle of the meal.

'An' why not?' Kitty said, as Rosie unbuttoned her blouse ready to let her suckle. 'We're all feeding *our* faces, when all's said an' done. Why shouldn't she, pretty dear?'

'I s'pose I ought to go back to work soon,' Rosie said, as the child sucked. 'I haven't written to Mr de Silva or anythin' and I should've really.'

'There's no rush,' Jim said. 'We're doin' all right, our Rosie. Don't worry yer head. If 'e's all that keen to 'ave you work for 'im again, he'll write.' And he was secretly thinking *an' if he ain't, good riddance.*

The letter came in the first week of February.

Chapter Sixteen

It was such a nice letter. Rosie and Kitty read it one after the other and they both thought it was lovely.

'That's what I call a gentleman,' Kitty said, handing it back to Rosie. 'Not like all those toffee-nosed gits what treat you like dirt an' won't give you the vote.' It still rankled with her that only wealthy women over thirty had been enfranchised and everyone else had been ignored.

Rosie read the letter for a second time and it *was* gentlemanly, hoping she'd recovered from the birth and that the baby was thriving and asking, very delicately, when she '*might be*' coming back to work, adding, '*I have received an excellent commission from one of my patrons in the Uffizi Society for four large-scale paintings and would like you to model for all four.*' Yes, she thought. I'd enjoy that.

But when Jim read it, he had other ideas. He didn't hold with her working as a model – never had, if the truth be told – all on her own with another man, dressing up in poncy clothes and getting silly ideas. He should've told her that long since, and he would've done too, if he'd thought she'd listen. Now he could speak his mind with justification. 'Write and tell 'im you can't do it,' he said. 'Not with a baby. I mean ter say, you can't go traipsing about all over London with a baby. It wouldn't be fair to her, 'specially in this weather. We don't want her catchin' cold. And what would you do with her while you're posing? You can't leave her to cry, poor little thing. She needs lookin' after. You write an' tell 'im.'

'Oh come on, Jim,' Rosie said. 'This is a good job. Four large-scale paintings. A year's work. An' don't say we don't need the money.'

He set his jaw and argued on. 'Money ain't everything.'

She was exasperated to hear him say such a stupid thing. 'Oh yes!' she said sarcastically. 'That en't what you said when we first moved in. It was all *how're we gonna manage?* then, an' *we shall be skint.* If you can remember.'

He remembered every word but he was determined not to be out-argued. Now he'd made a stand, he had to go on with it. 'We'll manage all right,' he said, stubbornly. 'You'll see. You just write an' tell 'im it can't be done. I'm off ter work or I'll be late. Don't forget. Write an' tell 'im.' And he left them on very self-righteous feet.

'Oh lor'!' Kitty said, pulling a face. 'What'll you do now, our Rosie?'

'I shall write to Mr de Silva,' Rosie said, calmly. 'That's

what he told me to do. You heard him. So I shall do it. I'll tell him everything Jim's just said, an' see if he's got any answers to it.'

Which she did. And Mr de Silva's careful and lengthy answer arrived by second post the following afternoon.

'*My dear Rosie*,' he wrote.

'*Thank you for letting me know the position. I have given it thought. Let me explain how our problems can be resolved.*

Firstly, there will be no need for you to bring your Gracie out in bad weather nor for you to travel on the tram. I have a car now and I will drive over and collect you both. Secondly I will give you a telephone as part of your wages and have it installed in your house and then I can phone you whenever I need you and we can make the necessary arrangements over the phone. Thirdly, I will hire a nursemaid to look after the baby while you are posing. Fourthly, I shall pay you by the day, weekly, if that is agreeable. Sometimes I shall need you every day, sometimes not. It will depend on how the paintings progress and how quickly I am working. And of course you can borrow books from my library whenever you would like to. That goes without saying. What did you think of Oliver Twist, by the way?

Write back and let me know if this is agreeable to you. If it is, we will start work on Monday morning.

Yours with very kind regards,

Gerry.'

Rosie read it through twice just to be sure of it. It was sensible advice and she knew she would take it. The only problem was that she would have to persuade Jim to agree with her and, given the stubborn mood he was in, that wasn't going to be easy. But she was on her own with Gracie all afternoon and she ought to be able to think of the right way to tell him by the time he got home.

Unfortunately Gracie needed her nappy changed at just the wrong moment and Rosie was down in the bathroom attending to her when Jim came home. By the time they returned to the kitchen he was sitting in his chair with his boots unlaced, a scowl on his face and the letter on the table in front of him.

'Well, what d'you think?' she asked, speaking boldly to disguise how worried she was.

'Well 'e's got all the answers,' he said sourly. 'I'll say that for 'im.'

She was lowering Gracie into her highchair and didn't look at him. 'Then you won't mind me going,' she said.

''Course I mind you goin',' he told her crossly. 'I don't *want* you goin'. I'd ha' thought I'd made that clear. It ain't fittin'. Not now you got a baby.'

'No,' she said, 'but it'll pay and it'll pay well. It's a good offer, Jim, an' I ent turnin' it down.' And she lifted that stubborn chin of hers and looked straight at him.

'What happened to 'onour an' obey?' he said. 'I seem to remember you sayin' somethin' of the sort in some ol' church somewhere. Or did I get it wrong?'

'Obeyin's all very well when it's somethin' that makes sense,' she told him, tying a bib round Gracie's neck. 'It ent when it's somethin' foolish.'

His face darkened. 'Oh, so I'm foolish now, is that it? Is that what you're saying?'

'No,' she said. 'I'm not sayin' you're foolish. It's just you get silly ideas sometimes.'

He was so close to losing his temper, he had to get out of her way. 'I'm off up the pub,' he said, refastening his boot laces.

'What about your supper?'

'Sod supper,' he said. And left her.

If he's goin' on like that, Rosie thought, I shall certainly go, an' he needn't think he's going to stop me. And when she'd fed Gracie her groats and taken her to bed, she sat down at the table and wrote to tell Mr de Silva she would be happy to model for him on his four commissioned portraits and was looking forward to starting work.

*

He arrived on Monday morning almost immediately after Kitty and Jim had gone to work, with a baby's shawl over his arm 'to wrap round her legs for the journey' and his eyes snapping with excitement.

'We've got a pram for her,' he said as he put the car into gear, 'and I've hired an excellent nursemaid. Her name's Joan and she's very willing. I think you'll like her. And we've found some bricks and a teddy bear for Baby to play with.

And some spring dresses for you to wear. Everything's ready. I'll show you the telephone first and then we can get down to work.'

It was standing on the hall table, looking very odd, black as jet and shaped like a frozen daffodil.

'There you are,' he said, grinning at her. 'Allow me to introduce you to the wonder of the age. You pick up this receiver – so – and a voice answers you from several miles away and asks you to whom you wish to be connected. And then you wait for a second or two and the person you want is on the other end of the line and you can speak to them. What do you think of that?'

She said it was amazing, which it was, but wondered how long it would take her to learn how to use it. It couldn't really be as easy as that, could it?

He was blazing with energy. 'Come on!' he said, and led her upstairs to the studio, where he introduced her to the girl called Joan, who couldn't have been more than fourteen but was obviously eager to do the right thing.

'You can look after Baby while she plays, can't you,' Gerry said to her. 'Good. Good. Just ask if there's anything you want to know. Rosie and I have work to do. Sketches for *Spring* today Rosie.' He waved a hand at the *chaise longue* which was heaped with old-fashioned dresses. 'I want to see what you look like in a few of these. It doesn't matter which you start with.'

They were very old-fashioned but very pretty, and all in the most delicate fabrics, which Rosie had seen and lusted over in the stores, but never imagined she would ever wear herself. She decided on a pink muslin with a row of pearl buttons down the bodice because it would be handy if Gracie needed to be fed. There was no sign of the screen but, as there was very little false modesty left in her after giving birth, she simply took off her skirt and blouse and dressed in front of the fire, as Gracie banged the bricks together and Joan sat on her heels on the hearthrug and watched her.

'Hold that shawl in your hand,' Gerry said when she was dressed. 'Bunch it up and pretend it's a bunch of flowers.'

She did as she was told, imagining the flowers hanging, heads down, against her elegant skirt. Then, as he hadn't told her where or how she should look, she watched Gracie banging the bricks. Her expression was so tender it was the first thing Gerry tried to catch. He'd almost managed it when the baby began to cry. Joan was instantly agitated and he was surprised.

'What is it?' he said, emerging from behind the easel. 'What's the matter?'

Rosie was touched by his anxious expression. 'Nothing terrible,' she reassured him, smiling at Joan. 'She wants feeding, that's all. I shall have to stop posing for a few minutes and see to it. Is that all right?'

He said of course and then watched, intrigued, as she took the baby on her lap, undid the buttons on her bodice and let the little thing suck. He'd seen lots of paintings of the Madonna and Child during his training but he'd never

251

seen a nursing mother in the life and the sight was so unexpectedly moving that he went back to his easel at once, put the sketch for the commissioned painting to one side and began a completely new sketch while the emotion of what he was seeing was strong in him. It was a disappointment when the feed was over and the bodice re-buttoned and the baby handed back to her nurse. Luckily he was rescued into the rhythm of his domestic life by the arrival of Mrs Fenchurch with the announcement that lunch was ready to serve. So while he cleaned his brushes, Rosie gave her new nursemaid the shopping bag in which she'd packed a pile of clean nappies and her pot of baby cream, and told her to change Gracie's nappy, and wrap the dirty one up in newspaper, and then put her in the pram and take her out for her afternoon nap. And she and Gerry went down to lunch.

It was a cheerful meal because they were both so happy to be working together again.

'How often do you feed your Gracie?' he asked, when Mrs Fenchurch had served their apple pie.

She was a bit puzzled by his interest but she was getting used to his eccentric ways by then so she told him. 'Three times during the day, usually, sometimes more, and once at night to settle her. She has groats in the morning and for her supper but apart from that . . .'

'Good,' he said. 'Then in that case I shall paint you in action. You'll be my Madonna and Child. Think of it Rosie. I shall out-Renoir Renoir.'

'What about the *Spring* picture?' she asked. 'That's a commission ent it? Don't you have to paint that first?'

'Oh that can wait,' he said airily. 'The sponsor won't mind. He's a good chap. I've got a year for all that. We can leave those dresses for another time too. I didn't think much of that pink one, by the way. It's the wrong colour.' His eyes were shining with a quite wicked delight. 'Eat your pie. We've got work to do.'

It didn't seem like work to Rosie at all, sitting by the fire either languorously suckling her infant or reading *David Copperfield* while Joan took her out for a walk in her pram, but Gerry was painting like a man possessed, singing in his tuneless way and grunting and muttering things to himself. 'No, not quite, not quite,' and once, very triumphantly, 'Yes!'

It took him two weeks to get his Madonna down on canvas. He wasn't satisfied with it. Naturally. He was very rarely satisfied with his work. There was always more to do. But he was happy enough with this one to let his model look at it and delighted to see how much it pleased her.

'Well?' he asked, unnecessarily. 'What do you think of it?'

'It's beautiful,' she told him. 'What a dear little thing my Gracie is. You've got her exactly.'

'I shall need to work on it for a few more days,' he said. 'But on Monday I'm going to change that portrait of you in the red dress. I think it would fill the bill for *Autumn*, with a little alteration. I'll have to look sharp because my patron's coming to see me on Thursday week and I want to have something to show him. They're going to install your telephone on Monday, incidentally, so you'll have to stay in for that but give me a call when it's done and I'll have everything ready for you here and we can get on.'

They got on until late afternoon the following Wednesday and by that time Rosie was tired and the picture was completely changed. Where it had been rather austere with a white sky behind the window and very little colour other than that red dress, it was now a blaze of red and gold and bronze. Autumn leaves swirled beyond the window and a fire leapt in the grate and he'd painted the echoes of firelight in everything in the room, fire-irons, lustres, a bowl of chrysanthemums, the scarlet dress, her hair, even her skin. She still thought she looked too fierce but it was a wonderful painting.

'I shan't need you for a week or two now,' he said, as he drove her home. 'If *Autumn* suits the patron, and I'm pretty sure it will, he'll want me to paint his portrait next. He's just down from Oxford, you see, and standing for Parliament at the next election. He means to be ready for it.'

'All right,' she said. 'I shall miss . . .' She was going to say 'you' but thought better of it. '. . . being driven about. I like cars.'

'So I've noticed.'

'First one I saw, I was twelve years old,' she told him, 'an' on my way to Arundel to start work. I thought it was the most wonderful thing I'd ever seen but Pa said I'd never get to ride in one because it wasn't for the likes of us.'

He grinned at that. 'Well you've proved him wrong,' he

said, turning into Newcomen Street, 'and good for you. Here we are. You're home. I'll give you a call when we can get back to *Spring*.'

*

But spring was long over and so was summer and autumn was half gone and Gracie was a sturdy seventeen months, babbling into speech and toddling about, before the call came. It had been a very long time and often difficult for her and Jim, because without her wage and with her savings long gone, they were hard put to it to pay the rent. In fact she was beginning to think she'd have to find an evening job in one of the local pubs to eke out, when the silent telephone finally rang.

'Tomorrow?' Gerry's voice said, cheerfully. 'Nine o'clock? Joan's ready and waiting.'

To be invited so peremptorily after all that time took her breath away but she answered sensibly. 'All right.'

'Bring your shopping basket. I've got a commission for six townscapes. Could take us some time. Certainly months. Might even run to a year.'

'All right,' she said again. Then there was a pause because, not being able to see his face, she wasn't sure what to say next. She didn't like to ask about *Spring* in case he'd decided not to do it. 'Have you finished painting your patron then?' she tried.

'At last,' he said with obvious relief. 'He was rather pernickety. It's not framed yet so you can see it tomorrow.'

It was the first thing Rosie saw when she walked into the studio with her shopping basket over her arm and Gracie astride her hip. She recognised the sitter at once. 'Heavens,' she said, handing Gracie over to Joan. 'It's Anthony Eden.'

He was surprised and impressed. 'You know him?'

'I worked for him when I was eighteen,' she explained and told him the tale. 'He hasn't changed much,' she said, gazing at the picture. 'You've made him look very learned sitting in front of all those books.'

'He thought it gave him the necessary *gravitas*,' he said and grinned. 'I aim to please.'

'You didn't aim to please me,' she said rather tartly. 'I didn't like my fierce face and you never changed *that*. You said it was the best thing about me.'

'Ah,' he teased, 'but you're not the eldest son of a baronet.'

She gave a wry grin. 'No,' she said. 'I'm the eldest daughter of a dairyman. What do you want me to wear?'

'What you've got on will be perfect,' he said. 'I'm going to paint a picture of a market and you will be one of the shoppers.'

That made her laugh. 'I shop in the Borough Market nearly every day,' she said. 'My Jim works there.'

'Even better,' he said. 'In that case I will paint you both *in situ.*'

'What's that?'

'In the market instead of the studio,' he said, grinning at her. 'Now then. Let's start, shall we. I'll sketch your little one first because she won't want to pose for hours and when she's sick of it she can play or go out in her perambulator with Joan and you can go on posing.'

It was an excellent arrangement.

*

That evening over their supper when Gracie had been fed and settled for the night, she told Jim he was going to have his portrait painted working in the market. 'An' you'll get a fee for it. He said to tell you.'

For a few seconds Jim wasn't sure whether to be flattered or annoyed. 'I hope he won't expect me ter stand around doin' nothin', mind,' he said. 'Not with all the work we got. 'E'll 'ave to put up with a lot a' movin' about. When's 'e thinkin' a' comin'?'

'Tomorrow.'

'That's a bit short notice ain' it?'

Rosie grinned at him. She'd learnt a lot about how to handle his moods in the last few months and she recognised the grumble. He was keeping his end up. 'You're such an old grouch,' she teased. 'You don't have to dress up. You just got to be there doing your work. Cheer up! You might enjoy it.'

Jim made a grimace because he was determined not to do any such thing. Bad enough to have to put up with that damned artist poncing about in the market without having to enjoy it. He didn't like Mr de Silva and that's all there was to it, even though on that particular day the man was at his most charming, telling them what a magical place their market was and what a superb picture it was going to make.

'It's got such style,' he said to Mr Feigenbaum. 'All that wonderful tracery – such a good green – and the trains going past overhead and the *colour* of these stalls and so many *interesting* faces. I could paint here for months.'

He sketched all morning, took them all off to the *Tavern* for beer and sustenance at lunchtime and sketched again all afternoon. It took him a fortnight before he had most of the material he needed and on the last day he worked on the centrepiece, which was a sketch of Rosie holding out her basket for Jim to fill with potatoes and onions and a cabbage and – at his request – a couple of oranges. It was an excellent choice for a centrepiece not just because the colour was so good but also because he'd caught the loving look that passed between them. When Rosie saw the sketch of it in the studio on the following Monday she was quite touched by it and wished Jim could have been with her and seen it too. And what a work it was when it was finished. Christmas was approaching by then and he'd finished it off by adding holly wreaths and branches of mistletoe above Mr Feigenbaum's stall.

'As soon as the weather's good enough I'm going to start on Buckingham Palace,' he said. 'The great queen on her plinth staring sourly into the distance and you below her cuddling your daughter. It will make a good contrast.'

It did and it gave her another two weeks of work but

then he turned his attention to the palace and the guardsmen and didn't need her and money was short again. And to make matters worse she was pretty sure she was carrying again. It was all very difficult. I'll give him another week, she thought, and then I shall have to go round the local boozers. We must have the money for the rent.

His call came two days later, cheerful and peremptory just as it had been the last time. He wanted to start work on the *Spring* picture. 'I've found just the dress for it,' he said. 'Tomorrow at nine? We shall be working in the garden so bring a coat for when you're not posing.'

*

It was pleasant to be at work on *Spring* again, knowing that steady money was going to start coming in, with Joan handy to look after Gracie, and the sun shining and a pretty dress to wear. She stood in the garden, with a huge bunch of daffodils in her arms and a straw hat on her head, completely unburdened, while Gracie was out for her usual afternoon walk, and smiled for the sheer joy of being alive. And Gerry observed her and painted her and fed his dream.

'Penny for 'em,' he said on their third afternoon, as he stood back from the canvas thinking that he might just have caught that happy smile. And when she looked puzzled, 'What are you thinking about?'

She told him, dreamily and without thinking of the proprieties. 'My new baby,' she said. 'I wasn't sure about it. Not at first. I mean a child costs a lot of money. But now . . .'

'When is it due?' he asked, looking at the painting.

She smiled at him lazily and told him that too. They were so easy with one another out there in the sunshine. 'August I think.'

'Then *I* think the time has come for you to have a bit of fun,' he said and put down his brush.

Fun seemed an odd thing to be offering her. Fun was something that happened when you were young and unencumbered. But he was walking towards her across the lawn, looking very handsome, his face full of mischief, his beard bristling, his eyes daring. 'Come on,' he said, and took her by the hand and led her back into the house.

She went with him, almost as though she was mesmerised, intrigued even though she suspected in a deeper and more sensible part of her mind that it wasn't what she ought to be doing. And she *knew* it when they stepped into the house for, as soon as he'd closed the door behind them, he pulled her towards him, lifted her face very tenderly with a gentle finger under her chin and kissed her mouth long and languorously and so pleasurably that she was breathless when he stopped.

She tried to protest, moving away from him. 'We shouldn't,' she said.

'Quite right,' he agreed, putting his arms round her waist and smiling at her. 'But we are and it's fun isn't it? A bit of fun with no strings attached. Just what you need.' And he led her upstairs. She was quite relieved to find that they were walking into the studio and that everything was as it should be, with a fire laid ready in the grate and a canvas waiting on the easel.

'Where do you want me?' she asked, looking round at her usual posing positions.

His answer took her breath away for the second time. 'I want you everywhere in the house,' he said. 'I've wanted you since the first moment I set eyes on you. You're the most beautiful, extraordinary creature I've ever seen in my life. Please don't say no to me now. I couldn't bear it.' He had his arm round her shoulder. He was leading her to the connecting door. They were in his bedroom and she had a brief rather dizzying glimpse of a high bed with a scarlet coverlet and mounds of cream-white pillows. Then he was unfastening her pretty dress and easing it over her head, gently removing her shoes and stockings and everything else until she was naked except for her chemise. 'Lovely, lovely Rosie,' he said kissing her neck.

She was drowning in sensations, knowing she ought to tell him to stop but wanting him to go on. And really, why shouldn't she? He could be right. A bit of fun with no strings attached could be just what she needed. Just what she deserved. Jim could be very hard work sometimes, especially when he was low, and he'd been downright unpleasant about this modelling.

'Yes?' Gerry asked, kissing her throat.

'Yes!' she said.

*

Afterwards, as she lay recovering her breath and trying to control her spinning thoughts, she knew she ought to feel guilty. But she couldn't do it. That amazing explosion of pleasure was still echoing in her mind and her body, powerful, overwhelming and quite unlike anything she'd ever experience before. It had been wrong to let it happen, of course. She knew that now. Terribly wrong and unfair to her poor Jim. It wasn't the way she should have behaved and she must never, ever do it again. But it had been so wonderful that all she wanted to do for the moment was to lie beside him in the sunshine and savour it.

Chapter Seventeen

Strong sunshine was reflecting light from the river yet again, projecting its delicate rippling patterns across the creamy wallpaper. Rosie lay on her back among the pillows, with Gerry drowsy beside her, and gave herself up to the pleasure of enjoying it, as she usually did now that she'd stilled her conscience. After all Jim didn't know what she'd been doing and it *was* fun and very pleasurable. This is such a beautiful room she thought. There ent a thing in it that ent really classy.

Gerry stirred himself, smiled at her lazily and picked up his watch to check the time. 'They'll be back in ten minutes,' he said. 'We'd better make ourselves respectable, I suppose.'

Rosie eased herself from the bed and picked up her clothes.

'That's a very pretty belly,' he said, admiring her.

Nobody else would have noticed it, Rosie thought. That's

what's so interesting about this man. He notices things. Poor old Jim just looks away.

'It don't *feel* partic'ly pretty,' she said, as she began to dress. 'It feels huge.' And in two more months, she thought, I'll be as big as a house, same as I was last time. She wasn't looking forward to it. Big as a house and all these lovely afternoons over – even if *was* only for the time being. She knew she was going to miss them very much. They'd become a private reward for all the times that Gracie had woken her in the night needing a drink or a cuddle or when money had been tight or she'd had a struggle to ease poor Jim out of another bout of miserable despair. Poor old Jim. He looked so drawn and unhappy when he was down and his lovely mane of hair was flattened and dull as if the life had gone out of it. She felt so sorry for him then. It was sometimes quite hard to remember the handsome, daring young man he'd been before that foul war. Marriage might be an honourable institution, she thought as she pulled her smock over her head and I wouldn't be unmarried for the world, but it's darned hard work.

But for the moment, life was good and she meant to make the most of it. They had picnics in the garden and the park, whenever she wasn't posing, and took Gracie to the zoo no fewer than three times in July and gave her rides on the elephant and introduced her to the penguins and the lions and the polar bears, while Gerry made sketches. As he drove home after their third visit, Rosie said he was spoiling them.

'Ah,' he said, smiling at her, 'but then this is a sort of goodbye present. I'm off to the States next week with Augustus. They're running an exhibition of our war pictures and want us there for interviews. And my patron wants me to take *Spring* and *Autumn* over to him at the same time.'

Her heart was suddenly squeezed with misery. It hurt her that he could be speaking so casually about leaving her, even if it *was* only for a few weeks. It made her feel he didn't really care about her at all, despite all the fun they'd been having. But she put on her bold face at once, determined not to let him know. If he could be casual, so could she. 'How long will you be away?' she said.

'I couldn't say,' he said, negotiating a right turn. 'This sort of trip is unpredictable. I know they've got a lot of things planned for us once we're there. I'll phone you as soon as I'm home again.'

And that was that. He helped her out of the car, gave her four day's pay in his usual plain envelope, kissed her on both cheeks in his usual flamboyant way and drove off. The street seemed shabbier for his going, noisier, dustier and much more dull. I *shall* miss him, she thought. But what was the use of even thinking it? There was nothing she could do about it. He was a law unto himself.

*

The hot summer and her rapidly expanding pregnancy made life increasingly difficult for her. In the middle of August when the baby was kicking so much it was hurting her ribs,

Jim took her to the pictures for a treat, leaving Kitty to look after Gracie. It was a Charlie Chaplin and very funny but she couldn't enjoy it much because she was so uncomfortable.

'I shall be glad when this baby comes,' she said to him as they strolled home. Even walking was difficult by then and she did so hate waddling. It made her look like a duck.

He tried to cheer her up. 'Can't be much longer. There ain't much left of August now. Soon be here.'

But the baby stayed where it was until August 31st and then it took nearly eighteen hours to be born. Rosie was exhausted before it even began. She'd spent most of the previous day doing the wash, struggling to put their heavy sheets through the mangle in a steamy, clammy washroom and hanging them out on the clothes line through the kitchen window, with a lot of difficulty. The pulley was stiff and hard to work, the washing dripped all over the place, her back ached and Gracie seemed to be grizzling for attention all day.

'I need my bed,' she said to Kitty as she dished up their supper. And she was only half-joking.

'You look done in, mate,' Kitty said, sympathetically. 'Leave the washing-up. I'll do it.'

But Rosie only slept for a few hours and then she was woken by the first pains. It was half past one in the morning. From then on she tossed and turned and timed the pains until dawn, when Jim woke up and went downstairs to make her a cup of tea and to ask Mr Rogers if he would send his boy to fetch the midwife. Then he and Kitty cooked the breakfast – which Rosie couldn't eat – and washed up and swept the kitchen and went to work.

I wish giving birth wasn't so lonely, Rosie thought. Gracie was sitting on the bed chattering to her but she needed an adult that morning and preferably a knowledgeable one. It was a great relief when the midwife came toiling up the stairs carrying her black bag and with her starched apron all newly washed and clean, ready for action. But action was a long time coming and the baby didn't emerge until supper time. Jim and Kitty were both home from work by then and had carried Gracie's cot into Kitty's room and put her to bed. They were waiting rather anxiously in the kitchen when the new child gave its first complaining cry. Jim took the stairs two at a time without noticing them, which was the first time he'd dared to do such a thing since he was wounded, and the midwife met him at the bedroom door.

'We've got a little lion cub,' Rosie said, lifting the baby up so that they could both see her. 'Look at her. She's the spit an' image a' you, Jim.'

She looked like a scrunched up newly born baby to Jim but he had to admit her hair had a tawny tint to it, what there was of it. 'Least she ain't got my great hooter spread all over her face,' he said. Which made all three of them laugh.

'What are you going to call her?' the midwife asked.

Her parents answered with one voice because that was one thing they were perfectly sure about. 'Mary.'

'Welcome to the world, little Mary,' the midwife said and made a note in her book.

Rosie was stroking the baby's face and breathing in the warm newborn smell of her. 'Was it nasty then, my darlin'?' she crooned. 'All that pushin'. I know. I know. But you're here now an' you shall have some titty presently.'

Kitty sat on the bed beside them and stroked the baby's foot, very gently. 'I wonder what our Gracie'll say,' she said.

She was saying it very plaintively at that moment, from the prison of her cot in the next room, 'Mummeee! Mummeee!' So Kitty went to get her and Jim lifted her up onto the bed so that she could see her new sister.

She wasn't interested in the baby at all but snuggled up to her mother demanding a hug. 'You can't blame her,' Rosie said, cuddling her. 'She must have felt very out of it, stuck out there on her own.'

*

Their lives settled into the familiar and time-consuming routines of looking after a new baby. Kitty phoned Mr Matthews at breakfast time the next morning to tell him the baby was born and to check that it was all right for her to have the next ten days off work to look after Rosie. The midwife called every day until Rosie's lying-in was completed. Gracie got used to having a newcomer in her life although she needed a lot more cuddling than usual and sucked her thumb a lot, especially when Mary was being fed.

Once she was up and about again, Rosie went out and

bought a second-hand pram so that she could put both her babies in it when she went shopping, Mary lying cocooned and snug under the hood and Gracie sitting at the other end, wrapped up warm with an old shawl over her coat and an umbrella beside her in case it rained. Mr Rogers let her keep the pram in the office behind his shop which was very kind of him and saved having to drag it up and down stairs. But even so there were days, especially when she was wearily boiling up nappies in her steaming bathroom and both her babies were fretful, when she felt what she really needed was a second pair of hands to do all the things that had to be done in the course of a day, and she thought longingly of the days when she'd had a nursemaid to take Gracie for a walk while she wallowed in what Gerry called 'sinful idleness'. I wonder where he is now, she thought, pushing the damp hair out of her eyes and straightening her back to ease it, and what he's doing. Not boiling nappies and that's a certainty.

When Mary was seven weeks old and smiling, Edie sent a postcard to say that she and Johnnie and Tess were coming up to London to see them all. '*I got a bit a news of my own for to tell you,*' she wrote, '*what I hopes will please you.*' But she didn't tell them what it was until they'd all taken it in turns to cuddle the new baby and made a fuss of their Gracie. Then she gave a grin like a Cheshire cat and said. 'Now.'

Rosie guessed what was coming. 'Yes?' she said, grinning at her sister.

Edie blushed and ducked her head. 'Me an' Joey Taylor's gettin' married,' she said.

'That's lovely, our Edie,' Rosie said. 'Best a' news. When's the weddin'? You got it planned have you? What does Pa say?' Then her intelligence caught up with her excitement and she realised that although Jim and Johnnie and Kitty were all smiles, Tess was being too quiet and looking down. And she felt sorry for her and knew she was feeling left out of it.

'We thought next summer,' Edie said. 'We'll both be eighteen by then, what's about right, don'ee think? He's a good chap, Rosie. He's got a job as a fireman on the railway an' he says he's going to be a driver one a' these days, what I'm sure he will.' Then she gave Rosie a rather anxious look and said, 'I got sommink to ask you, our Rosie. Well not ask you exactly. I mean for to say, if it ent right you've only to say. I mean for to say, it's a bit of a sauce really. I wouldn't want you to think you got to or anythin'. Only . . .'

Rosie laughed at her. 'Spit it out Edie,' she said. 'Ask away. I won't bite you, whatever it is.'

'It's only . . .' Edie said and then plunged into her request. 'You wouldn't let me have lend a' your weddin' dress would you? I'd look after it. I wouldn't spoil it or nothin'.'

'Course you wouldn't,' Rosie said. 'Come on. Let's go upstairs an' try it on. Jim an' Johnnie'll look after the babies, won't you. What a lark!'

It fitted quite well. 'Just the odd seam here an' there,'

Rosie said, 'what'll need lettin' out. An' you'll need the hem took up. You're shorter'n me. What sort a' length d'you want it?'

'You look a treat,' Tess said, as Edie admired herself in the mirror. 'You'll need a new hat to finish it off. One a' them modern ones with flowers in. Might treat mesself to one an' all.'

They came downstairs pink-cheeked with success.

'About time,' Jim teased. 'We thought you was makin' a new one, didden we Johnnie? Who wants tea? Kettle's on the boil.'

From then on the visit became a long and happy conversation about weddings, Rosie's remembered and Edie's planned. There wasn't a sour note until they were all saying goodbye. And then it was Edie who struck it.

'Two lovely babies in two years,' she said to Rosie. 'You're gonna be just like Ma.' She meant it as a compliment but it made her sister cringe.

And Jim made it worse. Now that that smarmy artist was out of the way, his confidence had tripled. 'Boy next time,' he agreed. 'Eh Rosie?'

'Who knows?' Rosie said, trying to make light of it. But she was thinking, *not if I have anything to do about it.*

She went on thinking about it at odd moments for the next few weeks. She would *have* to do something about it. She couldn't go on churning out babies for the rest of her life. Two were quite enough. But apart from refusing poor Jim – and she couldn't do that – there was nothing else

271

she could think of. If Gerry had been there, she might have asked him, but what was the use of thinking that. He was still gadding about in America. He'd sent her a postcard just after Mary was born, to say he'd won a prize at the Carnegie International Exhibition. But that was no help to her at all because he hadn't put an address on it.

In the end it was the local Tate Library and Gracie's affection for the tale of the three little pigs that gave her the information she needed. She'd bought a rather battered copy of the fairy tale from the second-hand bookstall in the market and she and Gracie had read it every night as a bedtime story until it began to fall to pieces with over-work.

'Tell you what,' she said to Gracie, when the tenth page had fallen out, 'let's go down the library and see if we can borrow somethin' else you'd like.'

And although Gracie insisted on 'more free piggies', that's what they did.

The librarian was very taken with a two-year-old book lover and having given Rosie a form to fill in, provided her with a ticket and suggested that she should borrow '*The Three Billy Goats Gruff*', which she did. Then she asked if there was anything that Rosie was interested in borrowing for herself. 'A novel maybe?'

Rosie squared her shoulders and stuck out her chin. 'Something about marriage and having children maybe?' she said and was annoyed with herself because she knew she was blushing.

'Ah yes,' the librarian said, smiling at her kindly. *'Married Love.* Of course. Wait there and I'll get it for you.'

It was a plain-looking book written by someone called Dr Marie Carmichael Stopes and it started with the bold declaration that, *'Far too often marriage puts an end to a woman's intellectual life.'* From then on, Rosie was hooked and read on avidly, but it wasn't long before she realised that what was being said was so embarrassing and made her blush so much that she could only read it when Jim and Kitty were out of the house. But it was full of useful information. *'When the man tries to enter a woman whom he has not wooed to the point of stimulating her natural physical reaction of preparation,'* the doctor wrote, *'he is trying to force his entry through a dry-walled opening too small for it. He may thus cause the woman actual pain.'* Just like Jim did when we finally got round to having a wedding night, Rosie thought. I wish I'd known all this then. Gerry knows about it. I'm not sure how, but he does. That's what's so good about being with him. He's gentle and takes his time. I must see if I can learn my Jim to do the same. He rushes me somethin' chronic sometimes.

But it wasn't until the end of the book that she found the information she really needed. *'Children,'* the doctor wrote, *'should be planned by means of birth control.'* And she went on to describe how it could be done and gave the address of a clinic in North London where there were midwives who would show you how to do it.

Rosie sat by the fire in her nice warm kitchen, with her children at her feet and wanted to cheer. Now she could take charge of her life. I'll go there first chance I get, she thought. And did. Although it took planning, patience and a downright lie. The first thing she had to do was to find someone who would look after the babies while she was out, and the only person she could think of was Kitty and, as she could hardly tell her what she was really going to do, she had to invent an old friend from the RAC Club who wasn't well and wanted to see her. Kitty was very sympathetic.

'Poor thing!' she said. ''Course you must go. Only thing is, you'll 'ave ter wait till Tuesday now 'cause I've had me day off for this week. Is that orl right?'

So Tuesday it had to be and it felt like a very long wait. It was also rather a difficult journey. Holloway was a good way out of the London that she knew and simply heading north could have taken her well out of her way but, by dint of asking tram drivers and her fellow passengers and several passers-by, she finally arrived at Marlborough Road, out of breath but still determined. Number sixty-one was a small and very ordinary-looking shop with a half curtain masking the window and an explanatory sign on the fascia saying '*The Mothers Clinic*'. She set her shoulders and stuck out her chin to give herself the courage she needed and opened the door. Her heart was beating most uncomfortably.

The room was ringed with wooden chairs, and there were half a dozen women sitting in them, knitting and waiting, and a nurse in her reassuring uniform looking up from her desk and saying, 'Good afternoon. May I help you?' But for a few seconds Rosie felt muddled and unsure of herself. Then she took a deep breath and walked to the desk. She was there. The first step had been taken.

It was very quiet in the waiting room and very little was said. Her fellow patients were shy and only spoke in whispers and, although she smiled at them and they smiled back, she didn't like to press them to talk to her for fear of embarrassing them. She hadn't had the foresight to bring any knitting or even a book to read so time passed slowly. But at last, when three more quiet women had joined the queue, the nurse called her name and led her into the surgery. It was a plain, functional room, green walls, lino on the floor, a white screen like the ones she'd seen in Jim's hospital, a long cupboard, an examination couch with a very strong light suspended above it, and another desk, with two chairs, where a midwife was sitting waiting to greet her. She sat down in the empty chair and the midwife asked her a series of questions, writing the answers on a card as she proceeded, her age, her husband's age and occupation, the date of her marriage, the number of children she'd had and how old they were. Then the midwife took a little round tin out of one of the cupboards and introduced her to the cervical cap.

'It is a simple device,' she said, 'as you see, and it comes in a variety of sizes so that we can fit it exactly to our patients. I will give you an internal examination, rather similar to the ones you had when you were in labour and nothing to be alarmed about, and once we have discovered the size that is right for you, I will show you how to fit it.'

Rosie looked at the rubber circle and wondered how on earth she would do it but the midwife took her through the process very gently, explaining things to her step by step. 'If you cover it with this cream like this, and pinch the sides together like this, you will find it will slide in quite easily. Use it every time and you will soon get used to it. Now if you will go behind the screen and take off your knickers and your stockings I will examine you.'

By the time she left the clinic, Rosie was a fully fledged member of the twentieth century and in charge of her fertility. She felt as if she was walking on air.

Chapter Eighteen

The telephone gave a click like an unexpected hiccup and let out its sudden shrieking call. It had been silent for such a long time that the sound of it made Rosie jump. She was hard at work in the kitchen, sewing a bridesmaid's dress for Mary and concentrating so hard she wasn't paying any attention to anything else. Edie's wedding was a mere matter of weeks away and rushing down on them like a steam train and there was a lot to be done.

'Oh drat!' she said, looking cross. But she put the dress on the table and went to answer it before it woke the girls. She didn't want to have to settle them for the second time that evening on top of everything else.

'Yes,' she said into the mouthpiece.

'Is that Helen of Troy?' Gerry said.

'No,' she told him, tetchily. 'It's me and I'm very busy.'

'Well then Me,' Gerry answered and it sounded as though

he was laughing, 'you've got an invitation to an exhibition.'

She was annoyed to be laughed at. He should be treating her much better than that after leaving her without a word all this long time. 'A what?' she said.

'I've been given an exhibition of my work at the Beaux Arts Gallery,' he said, sounding pleased with himself. 'It opens tomorrow evening and you're the star of the show. I've been there all afternoon and they're raving about you.'

It pleased her to be told she was the star of the show but she was still ruffled. 'Well,' she said. 'I'm not sure about all that.'

'I'll pick you up around five,' he said, 'if that's ok, then we can have a bite to eat beforehand.'

'Well . . .' she said again.

'Go on,' his voice teased. 'I dare you. Wear something pretty. You'll be the cynosure of all eyes.'

She was intrigued, despite her disgruntled mood. 'What's a cynosure?'

'Come with me and you'll see,' he said.

Jim was none too pleased when she told him she wanted to go out that evening, especially when he knew she would be with that artist. 'I can't see the point,' he said, scowling. 'Gallivantin' off ter some party this time a' night. It ain't as if you'll be earnin' or anythin'.'

'You never know what'll happen at a party,' she said, trying to persuade him.

It didn't work. 'That's what I mean,' he said and scowled worse than ever.

But she looked out her prettiest blouse and her red skirt, stuck out her chin and went, no matter what he said. It was *her* life. Why shouldn't she? And it was an amazing party. First of all, the exhibition was in a huge room, very grand and opulent with his pictures hanging everywhere she looked, and secondly there were lots of people there admiring them, all looking important in evening dress, drifting around, drinking champagne and talking to one another in drawling voices. She recognised Augustus John and Anthony Eden straight away and there were several others she'd seen at the RAC Club and, for a few seconds, she felt a bit out of place among so many toffs. Not that she showed any of *them* how she was feeling. That would never have done.

Presently Gerry stopped a boy with a tray full of champagne glasses, took two and handed one to her.

'Sip it,' he advised. 'It's a noble wine and one never gulps nobility.'

She sipped once, and enjoyed it, twice and decided it was the tastiest drink she'd ever tried, three, four, five times and discovered that the exhibition was the best place in the whole world. From then on she drifted through the crowds in a champagne haze, following Gerry wherever he led, half hearing what was being said, glimpsing the paintings, and feeling that it was only right and proper that she should see her own face looking back at her from the walls. When they were joined by a strange man and Gerry introduced him as Mr Alexander Korda, she smiled at him as if he was an old friend. She couldn't see him very well because the champagne seemed to be playing tricks with her eyesight but she had a vague impression of a rather short, dark-haired young man with thick lips and very thick glasses. 'Pleas' 'a meetcher,' she said and smiled again.

He was talking to Gerry, praising his painting and telling him he certainly knew how to pick his models but the conversation was difficult to follow and somebody was holding out another tray covered in glasses full of champagne so she took one and let her attention drift. Oh it was wonderful being here.

Then she noticed that Mr Korda was holding out his hand towards her so she took it, as that seemed to be expected, and he raised it to his lips and kissed it. Heavens! 'If you ever think of changing your occupation, Miss Rosie,' he said, 'it would be worth your while to get in touch with me. Gerry knows where to find me. Your face could be your fortune you know. The camera would love you.' Then he was off into the crowd and there were two other people pushing their way towards them to tell Gerry how wonderful the exhibition was.

The wonderful exhibition went on until it was quite late and by then Rosie had drunk so much champagne she could barely stay awake. Gerry laughed at her all the way home and eased her out of the car when they arrived as though she was made of glass. But when she'd giggled her way up the stairs and staggered into the kitchen, Jim was *not* pleased.

'You're sloshed,' he said crossly. 'Look at the state a' yer. Didn't I warn you? But no, you would go.'

She was flushed and giggly and so ridiculously happy that, for the first time in their marriage, she didn't care what he thought or said. 'You're such an ol' grumps,' she told him gaily. 'I'm goin' 'a bed.' And she lurched out of the door towards the stairs.

'She'll 'ave a thick 'ead in the morning,' Jim growled at Kitty. 'An' serve her right, goin' off with that poncy artist. 'E's no earthly good for 'er, never was, never will be.'

He was right about the headache. When she was woken by her babies the next morning, Rosie felt as if her skull was splitting. She struggled from the bed to lift her howling Mary from the cot and suckle her back to smiling, vowing she would never drink like that again. Ever.

It was a difficult day. Both babies were fretful and needed a lot of attention, and in the middle of the afternoon Gerry rang to ask how she was and to tell her he wanted her to model for him the next day. It didn't please her at all, because modelling was the last thing she wanted to do in her present state. But she said yes, because she was far too proud to tell him how fragile she felt and in any case, she needed the money, and the next morning he turned up in his grand car and drove her and her fractious girls to Chelsea.

It was a disaster. Mary grizzled to be fed and wouldn't take a dummy or be placated with sponge fingers and Gracie refused to go out with the nursemaid, setting her jaw and declaring, 'No. Won't.' until Rosie gave in to her. Then she spent the rest of the day clinging to Rosie's skirt or hanging round her neck. In the end, Gerry flung his paint brush on the floor and erupted into bad temper.

'God damn it!' he roared, stamping about the room. 'How can I work in this racket? It's like being in a farmyard. Squawk, squawk, squawk. I'm just wasting my bloody time and that's a fact. Is it any wonder I won't get married? Look at the state of this damned room. Babies are death to art. If I've said it once, I've said it a thousand times. Absolute bloody death. All right then, I give up. I give up. Absolutely give up! Take 'em away Rosie. I can't bear them another minute.'

She went home feeling like a whipped child, angry with him for being so unkind and angry with herself for letting him do it. It was a struggle to get on and off the trams with one baby in her arms and the other clinging to her hand. By the time she got back to Newcomen Street, she was tired and cross.

'Now see if you can behave yourselves for five minutes while I put the kettle on,' she said to her infants. She was too weary to scold them but her disapproval was clear on her face and, although Mary gave her a rapturous smile, Gracie knew she was in disgrace and put her thumb in her mouth, looking cast down. And that made Rosie feel even worse than she did already. After all, they'd been behaving badly because they were upset and she had a sneaking feeling that they were upset because she'd had a thick head. So when the tea was made she sat in Jim's comfy armchair and took them both on her lap and cuddled them to make amends. But Gracie was still weepy when Jim came breezing

into the kitchen bringing the smell of the market with him
and carrying a large punnet full of fruit.

'Whatcher think, gels?' he said. 'Ol' Manny's give me a
bonus. What say I take you all out fer a treat Sunday?' And
he picked Gracie up and tossed her onto the air until she
squealed. 'I thought we could go down the seaside an'
paddle an' that. They got a charabanc goin' ter Worthin'
Sunday. Whatcher think?'

Rosie was still too down to be enthusiastic but Mary
clapped her hands as if she knew what was being said and
Gracie said, 'Oh yes, Daddy. Let's.' So it was decided.

Later that night when he'd gentled her into an easier
state of mind with the sort of tender lovemaking that was
usual to them now, Jim asked her why they'd all been upset
when he came home – 'You was, wasn'tcher?' – and she
told him what a horrible day it had been. He was delighted
to think that the great Mr de Silva had lost his rag. That'll've
cut him down to size, he thought. And not before time.
But he didn't say anything. Not then.

Rosie didn't say anything either although she too was
thinking a lot. It was really good of him to spend his bonus
on this outing and she didn't want to spoil things by saying
she didn't want to go. But she didn't. She was worried sick
that the row with Gerry might mean that she'd lost her
job. And how would they pay the rent then? It kept her
awake off and on all night. But the next morning she had
a postcard from Edie that changed her mind.

'*Me and Joe have got rooms in a little house in Worthing,*' she wrote, '*what we move in Saterday an what I hope you can come and see soon. Its just what we want. Nice and near the station.*'

She wrote back at once to tell Edie about the outing, ending, '*See you by the pier, one o'clock, your loving sister.*'

So it was a successful expedition after all. The charabanc was crowded and lively, they sat side by side on the long wooden benches and sang songs all the way there, the sun shone on them nearly all day, they made sandcastles and went paddling and met up with Edie as the town clock struck one. Then they all went off for some of Gracie's favourite *fish a ship*. And at the end of the afternoon they walked up to the railway station to admire the house, the women taking it in turn to carry Mary, and Jim giving Gracie a piggyback. It was a small terraced house, rented by a lady called Mrs Kennedy, who wore her hair in curlers and had a half-smoked cigarette attached to her lip and smiled when she opened the door.

'Yes, my lovey,' she said, when Edie asked if it was all right to come in. 'Go on up. You know the way.'

They traipsed up the stairs to inspect the rooms.

'I'll have to give 'em a good scrub through,' Edie said. 'They ent been lived in for quite a while – you can see that can't you – but they're a good size, an' we got the use of the copper of a Tuesday, an' I can cook over the fire, an' we got our bed, an' the table an' chairs, an' a chest a' drawers.' Then she looked anxiously at Rosie.

Rosie kissed her. 'You're goin' to be very happy here,' she said.

All in all, it had been a good day.

And it was followed by an even better one when Edie and her Joey got married, Edie looking very pretty in her borrowed suit and a new cloche hat made of white felt and trimmed with roses to match her bouquet and Joey blushing so much he looked as if his cheeks were on fire. The sun shone on them so brightly when they walked out of the church that their guests cheered; Gracie and Mary were well behaved for once; Pa looked more frail than he used to be but he seemed happy; and Mrs Taylor and Tess had produced their usual feast, spread out on the familiar trestle tables back in the cottage. And then, when the bridal pair had been driven off to the station in Pa's cart and the usual shower of rose petals, the guests had wandered off home, and Jim and Kitty had taken the girls for a walk by the river, Tess sprang a surprise.

'I didn't say nothin' while the weddin' was goin' on,' she said to Rosie, as she poured tea for them both. 'That wouldn't ha' been proper but I can tell you now, I'm gettin' married an' all.'

'Oh Tess,' Rosie said. 'That's lovely. Who to?'

'Sydney,' Tess said.

That was a puzzle. The only Sydney Rosie knew was Mr Turner, the man who kept the piggery, and he was sixty if he was a day. She couldn't mean him, surely.

But she did. 'Yes,' she said, speaking boldly because she'd read Rosie's horrified expression. 'It's the piggery man, an' I know what you're thinking. He *is* gettin' on a bit. But I'll tell you this, Rosie, he's a good man, an' he's been ever so lonely since his wife died, an' he's got a cottage. He'll treat me proper.'

'But he's old enough to be your father,' Rosie said and regretted the words before they were out of her mouth because Tess looked so bleak.

'It's no good saying that Rosie,' she said.' 'He's offered and I've accepted. That's all there is to it. Beggars can't be choosers. There ent the young men around to marry my generation. That's the truth of it. They've all been killed off. An' I don't want to be left on the shelf.'

'Does Pa know?'

'I told him last week.'

'And?'

'He said to go ahead on account of Sydney's a good bloke.'

It's settled, Rosie thought, and turned the conversation to safer ground. 'D'you want a lend a' my dress?' she said.

'No,' Tess said sadly. 'It ent that sort a' weddin'.'

'What rubbish!' Rosie said trenchantly. 'A weddin's a weddin', an' a bride's a bride. If you want to look grand on your weddin' day, you should go ahead an' do it. You'll need a new hat to go with it, mind. Nothing like a new hat to set off an outfit. An' you might need a new pair of shoes to match an' all. We'll go shoppin'. I know some very grand places in Arundel an' your Sydney could afford it, couldn't he?'

To hear her intended called *your Sydney* cheered Tess up

as nothing else could have done. It was a sign of their easy affection and it meant her marriage was approved of. 'Well,' she said. 'Let's get our Edie settled an' we'll see.'

They saw four weeks later and found a pretty hat and a pair of stylish shoes. Then they went off, arm in arm, to have tea and buns at Rosie's favourite tea shop.

'Now all we need is a date to put in our calendars,' Rosie said, licking her fingers. 'You'd better get on with it, especially if I'm going to make pies.' It was doing her good to be involved with this wedding because she was privately feeling rather down. She hadn't heard a word from Gerry since he took exception to her infants and as the weeks and the silence went on, she was beginning to think her job and her affair really *were* over. Losing her job was the more worrying of the two because the rent had to be paid whether she was working or not. If I haven't heard anything by the time this next wedding's over, she thought, I'll have to find myself a job in a local pub or a shop.

It was a good wedding despite everything. Mr Turner wore a suit and was unrecognisably clean which made him look quite different, if a little uncomfortable, and Tess was calm and elegant, in her white silk suit and her splendid hat. Mr Turner's two sons, who were called Dick and John, had come with their wives and their children and they all said how pretty Tess looked and how fond of her they were.

'What comes a' knowin' her all our lives,' Dick said. 'We're a-goin' to call her Tess, on account a' that's what we've always called her, an' we could hardly call her nothing else.' And he smiled across the table at her.

Rosie was heartened by the way they were talking and she felt very proud of Tess, sitting at the centre table with her new husband attentively beside her and wished her well with all her heart. Dear, dear Tess. And towards the end of the meal she was proud of Edie too. She'd been sitting next to Rosie, enjoying the meal and looking plumply pretty, but when it was over and Mrs Taylor had started to clear the dishes, she turned towards her and whispered that she had 'a bit a' news'. Rosie guessed what it was before the words were said and beamed in readiness.

'Me an' Joey are expecting,' Edie said. 'Onny don't say nothing to our Tess, yet awhile. I mean for to say, it's her day an' I wouldn't want to take the limelight.'

Rosie kissed her at once and told her she was a dear little tender-heart and asked when it was due.

'Not till May,' Edie said. 'Plenty a' time to talk about it later. It's just I *did* so want you to know.' And was kissed again.

The tables were nearly clear and Mr Turner had climbed up on a chair. 'Christmas carols,' he called. 'Our Mr Boniface has got his fiddle, ent yer Bert? *God Rest Ye Merry*, if you please.'

*

The new year of 1925 began with a snow storm that kept Rosie and the girls indoors for nearly three days. Jim went to the market with the collar of his greatcoat pulled up round his ears and a thick muffler covering his mouth and Kitty looked out a very old shawl and wore it over her coat and hat 'fer another layer'. They were both glad to be back in the flat by the fire when their work was over.

'Bli, but it's cold,' Kitty said, holding out her hands to the fire. 'We'll all get chilblains if this goes on. I couldn't feel my feet at all comin' home. An' it's that slippy on the pavements it's a wonder we ain't all got broken legs.'

Rosie put hot-water bottles in their beds at night, kept their clothes clean, warm and dry and their socks and stockings neatly darned, made lots of tea and hung on. But it was the middle of January before she could go out job hunting and then it took her several days before she found the sort of work she could do. It had to be in the evenings when Jim and Kitty were around to look after the girls and it had to be fairly nearby so that she didn't have to spend too much time travelling. In the end, she settled on a job pulling pints in a nearby pub.

After the ease of modelling she found it tiring, especially if she'd had a difficult day with the girls, but it paid the rent, which calmed Jim's anxiety, bought an occasional storybook for Gracie, who loved being read to and was beginning to recognise a word or two, and it kept her mind off her altered circumstances. After a week she got used to the routine and began to enjoy it, saucing the customers and keeping the bar in order; after a month she felt as if she'd been doing it all her life. She liked the routine of a steady job and was grateful for the steady pay. If someone had asked her opinion about what she was doing, she would have said, 'Long may it continue.'

And then just as she'd sorted that out, a letter arrived.

It was a mild April morning and Rosie had just filled the copper ready to do the weekly wash, when Mr Rogers called up the stairs to say the postman had been and there were three letters for her. It was a dratted nuisance because it meant she had to dry her hands and take the children downstairs with her, carrying Mary and leading Gracie by the hand, because she couldn't leave them on their own in the flat with the copper on the boil.

'Free letters,' Gracie said as her mother picked them up from the bottom stair. 'One, two, free.'

'They'd better be good,' she said to Gracie as she put them on the kitchen table. 'Now stay there and play with your bricks like good girls till I get the washing started and then we'll see what they're like.'

The one postmarked Worthing was from Edie and more or less what she expected. She was '*going on well enough*' but felt as big as a house, '*what is no surprise being it's so near now.*' The one from Binderton was a surprise. '*I just had to write and tell you,*' Tess began, '*on account of I can't keep it to myself. Me and Sydney are expecting. We're both so happy you wouldn't believe. Mrs Taylor says she reckons it will be in October. I am feeling very fit.*'

'Well, well, well,' Rosie said to her children. 'You're going to have two cousins. Imagine that.'

Mary smiled at her without understanding but Gracie asked. 'What's a cousin?'

'Your aunties are going to have babies,' Rosie said but she was speaking vaguely because she'd noticed that the third letter was postmarked New York and that it had a foreign stamp on it. It had to be Gerry. She didn't know anybody else who'd be writing to her from New York. The thought made her feel cross. He'd left her for ten months without a word and with a telephone that never rang. Damn nearly a year and now I suppose he thinks he can write a letter an' I'll come running back to him. Is that it? Well if that's the case, he's got another think coming.

'Like Mary?' Gracie asked.

Rosie dragged her mind back to the conversation with an effort. 'What?'

'Babies,' Gracie said patiently. 'Like Mary.'

'Yes, yes,' Rosie said. 'Only smaller. Let me read my letter like a good girl and then I'll check the washing's all right and we'll read *Billy Goats Gruff.*' And she opened the envelope.

'*My dear Rosie,*' it said.

'*So much has happened during the last few months* (Few months!) *I hardly know where to begin. Briefly, I was offered a very large commission to come to the States and paint the portraits of all the managing directors of a large oil company. I thought it would take me about six months. Unfortunately it has not turned out in quite the way I envisaged it.* (Well serve you right.) *For a start they wanted far more portraits than they had originally suggested and every single one of the sitters has been difficult in the extreme. As far as I can see, it will be another year before the work is done.* (Then why are you writing to me now?)

In the meantime I am being pressured to complete the four seasons which I would much rather paint, providing you will still model them for me, (Ah! I see) *and I also have other work waiting for me in the UK.*

I trust you and your babies are well.

Yours affectionately, Gerry.'

She put the letter on the table, with *Billy Goats Gruff* beside it and went to the bathroom to check on the washing, her thoughts in turmoil. She was still cross with him for leaving her all that time without a word but those rich Americans had obviously taken him for a ride and that was unfair. He was too good an artist and too conscientious to be treated like a hired hand. By the time she'd hung out the washing, she'd decided that she would model for the *Summer* and *Winter* pictures, even if Jim didn't want her to. Gerry had asked her kindly and she needed the money. And besides, it made her feel special to think she would be the model for all four pictures. But the affair was over. There was no doubt about that. It wasn't fair to her poor Jim to cheat on him, not when he worked so hard and was so good to the kids. It made her feel ashamed now even to remember it.

'*Billy Goats Gruff*?' Gracie asked, when she reappeared in the kitchen.

'Yes,' Rosie said. 'A' course. I promised.' *Billy Goats Gruff* was easy.

Chapter Nineteen

It was a chilly spring that year but it was followed by quite a gentle summer. Jim wangled a day off work for Gracie's fourth birthday and he and Rosie took her to the zoo because she wanted to see the bears again. She and Mary stood as close to the railings as they could get and watched, open-mouthed, as the great beasts padded about on their wide paws and after that they had a ride on an elephant, which Mary said was 'the bestest'. She was tumbling into speech now, just as Gracie had done, and chattered from the moment she woke until she was teased into bed at the end of the day.

At the end of May, Edie had her baby and they all went down to Worthing the next Sunday to see him. He was a long, rather skinny baby and they'd called him Frank. He looked exactly like his father, who was very proud of him and kept telling everyone how marvellous Edie was. 'I thought I loved her when we got wed,' he said to Rosie, 'but now . . .'

They went down to the seaside whenever the money would run to it that summer. Rosie knitted yellow swimming costumes for the girls and treated herself to one of the new swimsuits, which looked very daring. And after their second trip, she had her hair cut short in one of the new bobs, which made it a lot easier to dry when she came out of the water.

And then the autumn blew in to scatter the bright leaves along the pavements and Kitty dropped a bombshell.

They were sitting at their *fish a ship* supper round the kitchen table and Mary was cadging chips from her father in her usual way, when Kitty put down her knife and fork, licked her fingers clean and said, 'I got a bit a' news for yer.' The girls went on eating but Jim and Rosie looked up at her curiously and waited to be told what it was.

'I been writin' to your sister, off an' on, fer quite a long time,' Kitty said. 'Not the young one, though. I mean to say your Tess. She got a lot a' sense in her head, you ask me, your Tess. We been talkin' a lot. Well not talkin' exactly, sort a' writin' things. Not that your Edie ain't sensible. You onny got to see how she's lookin' after that kiddie of hers ter know that. It's jest that me an' Tess . . . Me an' Tess . . . Well we got more in common so ter speak. We both know beggars can't be choosers, fer a start. Not in our generation anyway. We got a lot in common. Ideas an' such. Not right at the moment, I grant yer that. I'm more of a wallflower at the moment ter tell the truth. But we could have.'

It was such a rigmarole that Rosie was baffled and looked it. But Jim laughed.

'Spit it out, our kid,' he said. 'What you on about?'

Kitty gulped and blurted out her news in one breath. 'Mr Matthews has asked me ter marry him an' I've said yes.'

Rosie was so surprised she didn't know what to say. Jim had an immediate answer. 'If that's the case kid, it's about time you brought him home to meet us.'

'He's a good bloke, Jim,' Kitty said, and her voice sounded defensive. 'He's been ever so good ter me. You think about it. Givin' me a job an' all. An' he ain't as old as Mr Turner, not by a long chalk, an' *he's* turned out lovely. Mr Turner I mean. You got to admit. An' he's had a terrible time of it what wiv one thing an' another, his wife walking out on him an' takin' the kiddie an' all. Mr Matthews I mean not Mr Turner, although I suppose he could say the same losin' *his* wife an' all. An' you're gonna need my room soon, the way the kiddies are growin'.'

She's nervous, Rosie thought, watching Kitty's face. She thinks we're going to object to him. Or not like him. 'Bring him over for supper,' she said.

'I'll ask him,' Kitty said. 'He's ever such a good bloke Rosie. Really. An' I can't stay on the shelf fer ever.'

Later that night, when they were on their own together and in bed, Jim and Rosie had a long whispered conversation about it. They were both upset, he because he didn't want his little sis to feel they were pushing her out – 'an' you heard what she said about the kiddies growin'' – she because of something Kitty *hadn't* said. 'Not one word about how much he loved her or how she loved him an' that's usually the first thing they say. Look at us an' Edie.' In the end they gave up trying to make sense of what they'd heard and decided to reserve judgement until they'd met this Mr Matthews and seen him for themselves.

'We might be pleasantly surprised,' Rosie hoped.

They weren't.

For a start, Mr Matthews wouldn't come to supper in Newcomen Street but insisted on taking them to dinner in a London restaurant, which meant that Rosie had to find someone to look after the kids for the evening and although Mrs Rogers offered at once and said she didn't mind at all, it was still worrying to leave them. Then he assured Kitty that the restaurant was a top-hole place and it turned out to be no such thing. It was a long narrow room, and very poorly lit, although not dark enough to hide the stains on the tablecloths. After the luxury and good service she'd been used to at the RAC Club, Rosie was decidedly unimpressed. Then, instead of letting them chose their meal for themselves, he ordered for them and that didn't please her either. And he spent the entire evening talking about himself.

'Although I say it myself, I think I can claim to be a good judge of character,' he told them. 'Kitty will make an excellent wife. She has all the attributes.'

Then he revealed that he'd already arranged the wedding for the third Saturday in October, 'and seen to such catering as we shall require', that it would be in a registry office because he didn't hold with churches and that he was house hunting because 'as a married man I need a good house'. By the end of the evening Rosie loathed him.

'He's a bully,' she whispered to Jim when they were alone in their bedroom that night. 'An' it ent as if he's anything to look at, with that nasty mean little mouth turned down all the time and those nasty piggy little eyes. An' he's hardly got any hair.' She was hot with anger that Kitty could be making such a mistake. 'I can't think what she sees in him.'

'A meal ticket,' Jim said, 'an' a house of her own, an' a weddin' ring on her finger. Lots a' gels'ud settle fer that these days. It's what comes a' killin' off all the young men in the war.'

'We've got to stop her, Jim,' Rosie said, so urgently she was hissing. 'We can't just stand back an' let her marry him. I mean, he's just vile. We got to do something.'

'There ain't nothing we *can* do,' he said, sadly.

'We should tell her what we think of him for a start.'

'That'ud only make her more determined to do it. She's much too pig-headed to be told what ter do. We'll just have to leave well alone an' hope she sees sense for herself.'

'That's stupid,' Rosie said. 'We ought to put up a fight. She's a dear kind woman, an' helpful an' lovin' an' hard-workin', an' he's a bully. We can't hand her over to a man like that. We should tell her what's what.'

'We ain't handin' her over,' Jim said. 'She's goin' willin'. Don't you understand? Of her own free will. She's not gonna listen to us. She wants ter do it.'

'It's madness,' Rosie hissed. 'An' I think we ought to stop it.'

Jim made a resigned grimace. 'We got no option,' he said and turned on his side to sleep.

Rosie was so angry she couldn't sleep for a long time. And worse was to follow. She had to stand by and watch the preparations for this wedding and do nothing and say nothing, which was very difficult for her. Kitty came home from work more excited than they'd seen her in a long while, to report that Mr Matthews had bought a lovely new house in a road called Totterdown Street, 'what's jest round the corner from where you was in hospital in Tooting Jim. Imagine that!' and she was going to see it on Sunday.

She came back after her visit, wonderfully happy and bubbling with information. 'It's got a proper kitchen wiv a sink an' a copper, an' one a' them cookers, an' a larder what you can walk right in an' everythin'. An' a livin' room, an' a parlour wiv great big winders. An' a bathroom upstairs, wiv a lovely white bath, all new an' clean, an' a washbasin, an' a WC. An' there's a garden out the back. I'm gonna have me own garden Rosie, jest like you done in the country. Imagine that. I can grow all sorts out there. You'll need to come over an' show me how. But you will, won'tcher? Ain't it jest grand?'

How could they disagree with her?

She was in such a happy mood, that Rosie felt she could

talk about the wedding without showing her how she was feeling. 'D'you want to have a lend of my weddin' suit?' she offered.

But Kitty wasn't sure about that and her face changed even thinking about it. 'I shall have to ask Mr Matthews,' she said. 'He's a bit partic'lar about what I wear.'

'Well let me know if you do,' Rosie said and changed the subject. 'Tell me about the garden. Do you want to make a vegetable patch?' But she was thinking, she'll marry him now, poor Kitty. And hard on the heels of that, came another equally unpleasant thought. How are we going manage the rent? And then she was flooded with shame to be mercenary. That ol' gad-about de Silva had just better come home quick, that's all.

But that old gad-about was still obdurately in America. And in the meantime, family life was rushing her along.

At the start of October, Rosie had a postcard from Tess to say her baby had been born and it was a dear little girl and they were going to call her Anna, so they all went down to Binderton the next Sunday to see her. She was a very ordinary baby but both her parents were completely enamoured of her, which made Rosie admire old Sydney more than ever.

'He's so like Pa,' she said to Jim as they walked through the fields to her old home. 'Only not so pale.' Poor Pa grew paler and more fragile with every visit although he was always pleased to see them and maintained that he and young Johnnie were *'managin' all right, all things considered'*.

And then it was the third Saturday in October and she and Jim were standing in the registry office to watch their poor Kitty marry Mr Matthews who turned out to be 'I, Herbert' and looked stiff and pompous in a new blue suit and a high starched collar and didn't smile once the whole time they were there. Rosie said, 'Oh dear, oh dear!' all the way home and was touched when her daughters held her hands and gave her their most loving looks to comfort her, because they sensed something was wrong even though they didn't know what it was.

And there was still the rent to pay and the gad-about was still gadding.

*

Christmas was a very lean time. Rosie made a Christmas pudding from the cheapest ingredients she could find in the market and bought two little Bakelite dolls there, marked '*made in Hong Kong*' and knitted clothes for them on the quiet out of scraps of wool so that at least she had a present for her girls, but the meal was scanty. In January, funds were so low she took her wedding suit and shoes back to Petticoat Lane, and sold them for as much as she could get, which was disappointingly little. And then, just before Easter, the phone rang. At last. She was so relieved she ran to answer it.

'Yes?' she said hopefully.

'Hello,' Kitty's voice said.

'Kitty? How are you?'

'Not so bad,' Kitty said. 'I'm gettin' the hang a' this marriage lark now. How'd'yer like ter come an' 'ave tea wiv us Easter Sunday?'

'Yes. 'Course,' Rosie said, although she didn't like the idea of having to endure another meal with the Monster. 'What time d'you want us there?'

So the arrangement was made and when Jim got home that evening Gracie rushed at him to tell him they were going to have tea with Aunty Kitty. 'Wiv or without the Monster?' he asked Rosie.

'With, I suppose.' Rosie said, and when he grunted. 'Maybe he's mellowed.'

'What monster?' Gracie wanted to know.

'I bought current buns fer our tea,' he told her, waving a paper bag at her to deflect her question. 'Who wants one?'

'What monster?' Gracie said.

'The one in the fairy story,' Rosie said. 'Let's set the table shall we.'

Gracie persisted. 'What fairy story?'

'We'll read it after tea. Come an' get the plates.'

That evening, when his daughters were safely asleep, Jim was able to laugh at the mistake he'd nearly made. 'That kid's a darn sight too cute,' he said, as he got into bed.

''Course she's cute,' Rosie said, brushing her hair. 'She don't miss a trick now. She'll be five in May, don't forget, an' off to school come September.'

'Just as long as she behaves 'erself when we're wiv the Monster. That's all I want.'

'You worry too much,' Rosie said, grinning at him. 'They'll be fine.'

'You comin' ter bed?' Jim said, making eyes at her. 'Or are you gonna sit there all night whackin' yer barnet with that brush?' One of the few good things about Kitty leaving home was that they got a bit more privacy at night.

*

The tea party started easily enough because it was nice to follow Kitty on a tour of the house and admire it and tell her what a fine place it was, but once they were at table it was a sticky party in every sense of the words. Both the girls ate a slice of Kitty's simnel cake and got their fingers in such a mess she had to rescue them with a flannel, while her husband pursed his lips and looked disapproving, and from then on, he dominated the conversation, bragging about the new car he was thinking of buying and going into exhaustive detail about what a demanding job he had and how well he was doing it. They were very glad when it was finally over and they could escape and catch their tram home.

'Come an' see me durin' the week,' Rosie suggested as she kissed poor Kitty goodbye. 'Thursday maybe. We can walk down the market an' see Jim and then you could have tea with *us*. Be like old times.'

'I'll try,' Kitty said. 'I'll 'ave ter make sure I'm back in time fer his supper though. He's a bit partic'lar about his supper.'

He's a bit partic'lar about a sight too much, Rosie thought. He could be partic'lar about this an' stop you coming. But she didn't say so. 'You won't be late,' she promised. 'We'll watch the clock. An' if anything comes up and you can't get here you can always phone an' tell me, can't you?'

She wasn't a bit surprised when the phone rang on Wednesday morning. 'There you are,' she said to Jim, putting down the teapot. 'He's stopped her. What did I tell you?'

But it wasn't Kitty. The voice on the line was male and asking if he could speak to Helen of Troy. 'Good heavens,' she said. 'It's you. When did you get back?'

'If I asked you sweetly,' Gerry said, 'would you lend your lissom body to an old biddy who has need of it?'

He's been away all this time and he hasn't changed a bit, Rosie thought. He's still talking in riddles. 'What are you on about now?' she asked.

Her brusque tone made him laugh. 'It's my latest commission,' he explained. 'A doting husband who wants a portrait of his wife as she was when they met. Your body, her face. It will be a peculiar portrait but I aim to please and he'll pay well. Will you do it?'

'When?'

'I'll be with you in half an hour.'

'I shall have to bring the girls,' she warned.

'Not to worry,' he said, expansively. 'I've got young Joan ready and waiting.'

'That was Mr de Silva,' she said to Jim as she hung the receiver back on its hook.

'Yeh. So I gathered,' he said. He'd enjoyed the rather dismissive way she'd said, 'Good heavens. It's you.'

'Now we can pay the rent,' she said, realising it as she spoke. 'Oh Jim! We can pay the rent.'

*

It was pleasant to be back in the luxury of Gerry's Chelsea house, being admired. The girls played with the toys laid out for them and behaved themselves, the sun shone through the long windows, and she and Gerry had their usual disjointed conversation while she posed and he painted.

Once he said, 'Head up just a trifle.'

And she answered, 'Like that?'

Ten minutes later he said, 'Drop your shoulders. You're hunching them.'

And she obeyed that too, smiling at her daughters.

But when Joan had taken them off for a walk by the river, the talk got more personal.

'I'm quite surprised at you, you know,' he teased, peering at her round the side of the easel. And when she scowled at him, he gave her his most winning smile and went on, 'I thought you'd have had another baby while I was away. Or two even.'

'I'm not a breeding machine,' she told him sternly. 'My poor old Ma might have been, well she was, poor woman, but I'm not. I've had enough babies for one lifetime. Don't misunderstand me. These two are lovely. I wouldn't be without 'em. But I ent gonna have any more.'

He grinned at that. 'You sound very sure of it.'

'I *am* sure of it,' she said trenchantly. 'I've taken steps.'

'An emancipated woman bigod,' he said. 'Well in that case we must use our time to advantage. What do you think?'

'And that's another thing,' she said, keeping her pose but making her intentions clear by her tone. 'All that is over. You can't walk away and leave me without a word and then expect to come back and pick up where we left off.'

'Ah!' he said, thinking he would have to play this extremely carefully. 'Would it make any difference if I said I was sorry?'

'No,' she said. 'It wouldn't. It's all gone much too far for that. I'll model for you whenever you like but nothing more.' She spoke so firmly he knew he had to accept her decision, at least for the moment, though he would do whatever he could to make her change it.

'Very good,' he said, lightly and picked up his brush again.

The next day he was careful to keep the conversation as light as his brushstrokes. If he was going to win her back he needed delicacy. He even offered to let her go with the children when the nursemaid took them out for their morning walk, 'as it's such a lovely day. I've got plenty to keep me occupied.' And when they came back and she took up her pose again, his conversation was deliberately fitful.

'I like the new haircut,' he said at one point.

'It's easier to dry when I've been swimming,' she told him. 'We go swimming quite a lot now, don't we girls?'

There was a long pause. 'So you've got a swimming costume?' he said.

''Course,' she told him, laughing. 'I could hardly go swimming in my clothes.'

Another long pause. 'You've given me an idea for the *Summer* picture,' he said. 'That's the next thing I've got to do. I can't put it off for ever. How about you and the kids on the beach? You wet from the sea, sitting on a breakwater, them making sandcastles. What do you think?'

'In Worthing?' she asked.

'If it's got a good beach.'

So Worthing it was, and that summer she and her girls spent more days than she could count out in the sunshine playing, while he sketched and painted. Edie came down to the beach to join them on their third trip bringing her little Frankie. He was fifteen months old by then and had grown into a sturdy little boy, a little in awe of his older cousins but a dab hand with a spade. On their fourth trip Tess turned up too with Anna, who was a plump ten-month-old in a frilly sunhat, which she removed at regular intervals and flung as far away from her head as she could so that Tess had to spend most of the day retrieving it. The group at play in the painting got more complicated with every trip, but it was Rosie who was at the heart of it, sitting on the breakwater with her long brown legs stretched out before her, the sun glinting on her bobbed hair and her face turned up to the sky. The sight of her made Gerry more determined than ever to get her back although he was careful not to say anything. But really she was altogether too beautiful to go to waste.

For Rosie, her days on the beach were a glimpse of paradise. She enjoyed everything about them, the amazing blue of that huge sky over her head, the long, slow days when she was absolutely idle, the beautiful expanse of sand at low tide shimmering like mother-of-pearl and ridged under her bare feet, even the shock of cold when she waded into that green sea. She had sisters to gossip with and ice cream to refresh her and on her seventh visit she learnt to swim.

September came as a shock to the system for all of them. The sisters missed their days together by the sea. Gracie and Mary missed the sandcastles and paddling and Sno-frutes and Uncle Gerry's picnic basket. In fact the only one pleased to see the season change was Jim and he was secretly cheering because he'd got his life back to normal and could walk home from the market every evening knowing they would all be in the flat waiting for him and not gallivanting about with that poncy artist. There *were* changes of course but they were the kind of things he was used to. Like the arrival of the first blackberries and a new Charlie Chaplin film coming out, and his little Gracie starting at Lant Street school.

Rosie was far more concerned about that than he was. It seemed such a formidable building to swallow up a child so small, all that soot-blackened brick and those dominating windows rising above their heads. But Gracie wasn't deterred by it at all and walked boldly through the gate on her first morning as if she'd been doing it all her life. By the end of the week she was an old-timer, reporting that they were 'learning us our letters', adding with easy confidence, 'I know mine already,' which was perfectly true.

'She's took to it like a duck to water,' her father said happily.

'Well naturally,' Rosie said. Whatever else I've done, she thought, pushing away the knowledge that she should never have started her affair with Gerry and she really ought to have stopped Kitty from marrying the Monster, I've made a good job of bringing up these girls.

Gracie's first year of school progressed in a steady, easy rhythm and she was soon learning to read. Rosie modelled for a series of pictures purporting to be studies of Gypsy life and Gerard taught her to drive which she found remarkably easy and rather thrilling. Mary grew out of her boots twice in twelve months and started to learn her letters too. Kitty visited every week. That Christmas they had roast chicken with all the trimmings and Rosie bought books and colouring pencils for her daughters.

Change, when it came, arrived in a storm.

Chapter Twenty

Rosie woke with a start in the middle of the night. It was the beginning of January and bitterly cold; rain was pattering against the windows like grit, a banshee wind screamed down the chimney and she could hear her babies crying for her. She got out of bed at once, calling, 'I'm coming!' and went to comfort them. They were sitting up in bed huddled together and wide eyed with alarm.

'Shove over,' she said and got into bed with them, one on either side of her so that she could cuddle them both because they were very cold.

'Is it the monster?' Gracie said, fearfully, as the wind roared again.

'No, my lovey,' Rosie said, stroking her hair. 'It's just that ol' wind making a row. That's all. It's a storm. All be over by morning. Snuggle down and get warm.'

But although the storm subsided just as she predicted,

when seven o'clock struck and they woke for the second time, the news of the night was alarming. Jim went down to get his paper, just as Mr Rogers was tuning the wireless in, so the two of them stood on either side of it and listened to the news together, as they often did. What they heard gave them a shock. The Thames had flooded its banks during the night and seventy-five feet of the embankment near the Tate Gallery had collapsed and been swept away. The Houses of Parliament were flooded and so was the Tower of London. There was, as the announcer said in his lugubrious voice, 'considerable damage throughout the city. Some streets are under four foot of water. Rescue teams are at work along the north bank.'

'That'll be all them little houses up Marsham Street, I'll bet,' Jim said. 'Jerry built, they are. Wouldn't stand an earthly in a flood. If ol' Manny's agreeable, I shall go down an' lend a hand.'

'I would an' all,' Mr Rogers said, 'only someone's got to keep shop.'

Jim picked up his paper. 'Give us a shout if there's any more news,' he said. And went upstairs to tell Rosie. It took a bit of doing because Gracie was still very alarmed and asked anxious questions at every stage of the story. 'What's the Tate?', 'What's a gallery?', 'How big are four foots?' and finally, 'Can I stay at home today Mummy?'

'I wouldn't send you out in all this,' Rosie said, frying the last egg. 'Anyway the school's closed. You'll have to come with me to Uncle Gerry's if he wants me to model but you won't mind that, will you.' She slid the egg onto Jim's plate alongside his bacon and sausages and urged them all to eat up. 'We'll need a good inner lining on a day like this,' she said. It wasn't even half-light outside the window and the yard was shrouded by river mist and looked icy.

'Goin' in car?' Mary hoped.

'Yes,' Rosie said. 'Providing he wants us and providing you're a good girl and eat up your nice egg.'

Jim was mopping up the last trace of her fried egg with a piece of bread and posting it in her mouth, when the phone rang.

It was Gerry, sounding very excited to tell her the roads were two feet deep in water round his way and that the Tate was flooded. 'I heard it on the wireless,' he said. 'They're trying to get the pictures out. I shall don my wellington boots and my sou'wester and go and give them a hand. We can't have the Turners ruined. They were his bequest to the nation.' Then almost as an afterthought. 'You're all right, are you?'

'We seem to be,' she said.

'Good,' he said. 'Well look after yourself.'

'Right,' Jim said when she came back to the kitchen. 'I'm off. Are you going to de Silva's?'

'No,' she said and explained as she poured herself another cup of tea.

'Good,' he said, heading for the door. 'I'm glad to hear it. See you tonight then. Keep in the warm.' And he was gone.

Gracie and Mary were rummaging in the battered cardboard box where they kept their toys. 'Shall we have *Billy Goats Gruff*?' Gracie said, waving it aloft.

*

It was bitterly cold out on the streets that morning and there was a powerful stink of river water that grew more foetid the nearer Jim got to it. The market smelt exactly the same as it always did, of sweat and naphtha, fish, sawdust and potatoes but Mr Feigenbaum's stall was poorly stocked because the vans hadn't been able to deliver his order.

'I can't see much doin' in the vay a' trade,' he said when Jim asked him if he could go and help out. 'Go, my son. They need all the help they can get, poor souls. Vat times ve live in! Some food you vill take?'

'I'll come back fer food,' Jim promised.

But he didn't, for when he reached Lambeth Bridge and saw what was happening on the other side of the river, the sight put all thought of food, his job and even his family right out of his head. The Thames was running swiftly and so high it was still slopping over the embankment and pouring along the street. It looked muddy and oily and extremely threatening, and Millbank was completely under water. A bit further west, past the Houses of Parliament, Grosvenor Road had become a torrent, rushing inland at every turning. The railings were still visible, protruding out of the dark water to mark where the river edge had been and there was an incongruous line of city workers in waterproofs and trilbies struggling eastward along what used to be the road, holding onto them to keep their footing. The whole area was dark, dangerous and evil smelling and there was something ominously familiar about it.

Jim took a breath to steady himself and waded into the extended river, pushing through the icy water until he reached the corner of Marsham Street. At that point the onrush had slowed and it was moving sluggishly because it was full of debris, broken planks and lathes, chunks of filthy plaster, old rags, downtrodden shoes, broken bottles and crushed tins, all being tossed about and flung against the walls, which were crumbling and falling as he watched. He could hear voices calling out to one another and saw that there was a gaping hole just ahead of him where several ramshackle buildings had fallen down, so he pushed on and scrambled over the wreckage to see what was happening on the other side of it. He found himself in one of the tenement backyards. It looked as though it had been hit by an earthquake. The roof of the building had collapsed and lay in a misshapen heap, shedding tiles. Two doors had been ripped off their hinges and flung aside like so much cardboard and standing in the mud and muddle of the debris were four women looking stunned and a little girl, who made him think of Gracie. They were calling for Peggy.

'Hang on!' he called. 'I'm coming.' And as he got nearer, 'D'you know where she is?'

'Could be anywhere mate,' one of the woman said. "Idden away, I 'spect. We never saw the goin' of 'er. Bleedin' river!' And she called again. 'Peggy! Peggy-peggy-peggy. Come on! Where are yer?'

'How old is she?' Jim asked. If he had some idea of the size of the child he'd have a better chance of finding her.

'No idea,' the woman said. 'Used ter belong to my neighbour, you see. I took her in when she left on account a' she'd got a flat an' they wouldn't allow cats.'

Jim readjusted his thoughts. 'What colour is she?'

'Tabby,' the woman said. 'Not that that's gonna help us. She'll be drowned-rat colour be now. Look at the state a' this place.'

There was a clatter of falling bricks behind them and Jim turned to look, instantly alert and ready to pull them all to safety. But it was a fireman clambering over the debris into the yard.

'Let's have you out of here,' he called as he approached. 'I'll carry the kiddie.' And he picked her up and settled her against his shoulder.

'We can't go till we've found our Peggy,' the woman said, looking stubborn.

The fireman was patient and reasonable. 'You can't stay here,' he said. 'It's too dangerous. We don't want to have to dig you out the rubble. This lot'll come down if you sneeze.'

'I'll find the cat,' Jim said to her and explained to the fireman. 'I don't live 'ere. I come to help out.'

'Watch out fer the mud, then,' the fireman said.

Jim laughed. 'I'm used ter mud,' he said. 'I was in the trenches.'

'Ah well then,' the fireman grinned, 'you're just the sort a' bloke we need. See if there's anyone up that alley, will you. Some of 'em are in shock an' don't move.'

Jim never found the cat but he worked long and hard that day, persuading people out of the remains of their houses, supporting them when they were too hurt or shocked to walk, comforting them when they wept, slipping off to buy fags and handing them out to anyone who needed them. It was as if he was back in the trenches, mud caked to his knees and with the stink of the wreckage in his nostrils, and in an odd sort of way he almost enjoyed it, partly because he was helping people who needed his help and partly because he felt so at home there. By the time it grew dark and he limped back to Newcomen Street, he was worn out and filthy from head to foot but undeniably pleased with himself.

Rosie and the girls had been cooking all afternoon and the kitchen was warm and welcoming, with a good fire going and the smell of a hotpot rising succulently from the oven. All three of them rushed at him as soon as he got in.

'That smells good,' he said, fending them off. He wanted to hug them all but he was much too dirty for that. 'Must jest nip an' have a bit of a wash first.'

'I'll run a bath for you,' Rosie said, 'an' you can tell me

all about it.' Which, once she'd settled the girls with the gruff billy goats, she did, while he sat on the bathroom chair and told her what a terrible mess the flood had made.

'Put your clothes straight in the copper,' she said, when the bath was ready. 'I'll bring you in some clean ones presently.'

He did as he was told, throwing his wet jersey on the floor, unbuttoning his mud-stained shirt and dropping that too, stripping off his sweaty vest where he stood, glad to be rid of them. And she watched as if she was mesmerised. For here was her own dear lion again, mane bristling, tawny eyes shining, muscled and powerful, his hands looking so strong and competent and loving, she simply had to put her arms round him. He was such a good honest man, even if he did get depressed and grumpy now and then. He hadn't spent his day rescuing silly paintings, he'd been looking after people. 'Oh Jim,' she said. 'I do love you.'

'Likewise,' he said, grinning at her. 'I'd show you if I wasn't so filthy-dirty.'

'Later,' she said happily.

And later it was, most pleasurably. Well who'd have thought *that* after such a day?

*

The next morning the papers told the full story of the flood, horrors, pictures and all. Fourteen people had been drowned, most of them in their cellars before they could escape, six thousand had lost their homes and a great swathe of central London had been completely destroyed. Later in the day, firemen began the long job of pumping the water out of the tube and clearing the debris from the Embankment, where the cobbles had been ripped out of the road and thrown about like children's bricks. The next day the schools opened, Mr Feigenbaum's supplies got through, the trams ran again and life in the Borough began to return to normal. Not that Jim and Rosie noticed very much of it for they were in love again and so happy they could hardly believe it.

Even the first snow of winter was something to enjoy. On that first whitened Sunday, when it was so cold there were frost ferns halfway up the bedroom windows every morning, they bundled their daughters into every bit of warm clothing they possessed – jerseys, coats, thick skirts, two pairs of socks, boots, mufflers and knitted hats, and took them off to Hyde Park, like two tightly wrapped parcels, to play snowballs, which Gracie said was 'the bestest game ever'. On their second visit, the Serpentine was frozen over and there were people skating on it. Gracie was enthralled. 'Can we do that, Mum?' she asked.

'If we had skates we could,' Rosie said, wondering where she could get some and how much they'd cost. 'I'll have to see.'

But the person who saw wasn't Rosie, it was Gerard de Silva, who rang early the next morning to say he'd got the perfect idea for the *Winter* painting. 'You and the kiddies skating on the Serpentine,' he said. 'It'll be an absolute winner. Your Gracie is off school isn't she? Yes. I've got the perfect outfit for you and the light couldn't be better. Have you got any skates?'

It riled her to be given her orders so peremptorily, even though she was used to it, and she told him quite crossly that she didn't possess such a thing. Why should she? It didn't quell his excitement in the least. 'Just tell me your shoe sizes,' he said, 'and I'll get some for you.' And when she'd told him, he said, 'Right-ho! I'll be with you as soon as I can. Wear lots of warm clothes.' And rang off.

He was outside the flat in less than an hour with his usual picnic basket, three expensive-looking shoeboxes and a lady's coat and hat made of thick blue velvet trimmed with white fur. It made Rosie's mouth water even to look at it.

'Try the boots on,' he said as he drove off. 'I want to know if they fit.'

It wasn't the easiest thing to do in the confines of the car and the girls made a better job of it than Rosie but all three pairs were a good fit when they were on and laced, their fine white leather very grand against their dark winter clothes and the skates shining like silver. And then, after an impatient drive, they were in the park and on the ice among all the other skaters, slipping and slithering and falling over as they tried to find their balance and enjoying themselves so much that Rosie could actually feel her spirits expanding with the sheer joy of it all.

It took them all morning before they could move about with any ease and Gerry skated with them, holding their hands and laughing at them and hoisting them up when they tumbled. But in the afternoon, when they'd had bowls of steaming hot soup poured from a huge Thermos flask and lots of bread rolls and eaten every crumb of Mrs Fenchurch's seed cake, he decided the time had come to start sketching and produced his folding stool, a sketch pad and his new Agfa camera and worked by the edge of the lake while they played. From time to time he waved his arms to show that they were to join hands and skate towards him but for the rest of the afternoon they simply skated, making a better and better job of it until they were flying like birds, fairly skimming across the ice as the wind bit their cheeks and the crowds swirled around them.

'Shall we come back tomorrow, Uncle Gerry?' Gracie asked as they drove home in the dusk.

'And tomorrow and tomorrow and tomorrow,' he promised her, 'providing the weather holds and my hands don't fall off with the cold.'

She was thrilled by the idea. 'Will they?' she asked, her eyes wide.

He turned his head to grin at her. 'You never know,' he said.

The next morning it was snowing but they skated on, their coats patterned with snowflakes. At the start of the next week, Gracie had to go back to school but Rosie and Mary went skating again, which Gracie said was very unfair particularly when her sister was being smug about it. It was more than three weeks before the picture began to take shape and by then all hope of any more skating was over because the ice was melting. But it was a very good picture. Rosie thought it was the best thing she'd ever seen, with all those dark figures swirling and dancing and making patterns in the background and she and her daughters skimming together right in the middle of it all. The girls looked so pretty and that blue coat was the most handsome garment she'd ever worn. She was really quite sad to have to hand it back.

'I wonder what'll happen next,' she said to Jim as she packed the skates away at the top of the cupboard.

'Somethin' will,' Jim said. 'It always does. You ever comin' ter bed?'

*

Once the weather improved, Kitty went back to visiting them every week, usually on a Wednesday because it was half-day closing and usually with a cake of some kind for 'the littl'uns'. In the middle of March she arrived with a chocolate sponge that Gracie and Mary said was their 'very favouritest'.

As soon as Jim got home from work, they sat around the table in the kitchen with the windows open to let in the nice fresh air and Kitty opened the tin. 'They do like their cake,' she said, watching the girls as they ate.

'That's kids for yer,' Jim told her, grinning at her.

Kitty grinned back. 'As I shall find out mesself in a month or two,' she said, 'accordin' ter the midwife.'

Rosie's eyebrows rose so far into her hair they all but disappeared. 'Midwife?' she said. 'Are you . . .?'

'Yep!' Kitty said with wonderful aplomb. 'Comin' August, so she says. Whatcher think a' that?'

Then what squeals and cuddles and kisses there were. 'Fancy my kid sister expecting,' Jim said, giving her a bear hug.

'Not so much a' the kid, if you don't mind,' Kitty said beaming at him. 'I'll be thirty come October. That's old fer havin' babies.'

'You're gonna have another cousin, our Gracie,' Jim said. 'Whatcher think a' that?'

Gracie wasn't impressed. 'I'd rather have a cat,' she said.

Later that night as they were undressing, Jim began to giggle. 'Who'd ha' thought the ol' Monster would've had it in him?' he said. 'It beats cock-fightin'.'

'Well I hope he treats 'em right, that's all,' Rosie said. 'I wouldn't trust him an inch with anybody, newborn or not.'

'I shall watch him,' Jim said, suddenly serious and frowning.

'Good,' Rosie said. 'You do. An' I'll take her to the seaside, an' give her a breath a' fresh air. Day trip from Balham. That'ud do her no end a' good. As soon as we've got the weather for it. An' the money.'

The weather arrived with a flourish of roses at the end of May. By that time Kitty had reached the cumbersome stage of her pregnancy and thought a trip to the sea would be just the thing. 'I'd like to see your sisters again,' she said.

So Rosie looked out their swimming costumes, sent post-cards to Tess and Edie to say they'd be down on Saturday, and off they went.

They had a lovely idle day. Rosie and her sisters sunbathed and went for a swim to cool off; Kitty took the little'uns paddling and fell asleep in her deckchair afterwards; they had *fish a ship*, to Gracie's delight, and a steady supply of ice creams; and the cousins played in the pools and built a sandcastle under Gracie's bossy supervision, while their mothers reminisced about what it was like when they were little and played in the fields.

'It seems such a long time ago,' Rosie said, gazing out to sea. 'And now here we are with kids of our own.'

'An' three more coming,' Edie said, grinning at her.

That was news. 'Three?' Rosie said.

'Me an' Tess,' Edie told her happily. 'I'm due November and she's a month later. We're gonna be waddlin' about like elephants together, ent we Tess?'

'My stars,' Rosie said. 'That'll be seven cousins. Think a' that. There won't be room for us all on the beach.'

'I always thought it'ud be you havin' all the babies,' Tess said, flicking a fly away from her face. 'Like Ma.'

'Well you were wrong.' Rosie said.

'If they come, they come,' Kitty said, shifting her bulk uncomfortably in her deckchair. 'An' that's the truth of it. You jest have ter grin an' bear it.'

'Not in the twentieth century you don't,' Rosie said, turning her face to the sun.

She'd spoken carelessly, feeling pleased by how much she knew and without thinking of the impact of what she was saying, but she regretted it as soon as the words were out of her mouth because the others were instantly intrigued and staring at her so hard she could feel their eyes on her face. 'What d'yer mean, you don't?' Kitty said.

Oh God! Rosie thought. I shall have to tell them. I can't backtrack now. 'There are things you can do,' she said vaguely. 'I mean, you don't *have* to get pregnant.' She could feel her cheeks reddening with embarrassment and ducked her head to hide them.

'What sort a' things?' Kitty said. Her voice didn't sound disapproving, simply very interested.

'I'll tell you later, if you like,' Rosie said. 'I mean it's a bit sort a' private. Not the sort a' thing to talk about on a beach.'

'No nat'rally,' Kitty said, rubbing her belly. 'That's understood. I shall hold you to it though. I don't want a baby a year neither.'

Gracie was running up the beach towards them, trailing a long strand of brown seaweed behind her and calling, 'Look what I got!' so her mother was rescued. But only temporarily. As they were travelling home on their crowded train Kitty came back to the topic, in a round-about way.

'You know what we was talkin' about on the beach,' she said. 'I been thinkin'. When I've had this baby will you tell me about it? It might be . . .'

'Yes,' Rosie said. "Course. It ent a secret. It's just most women don't know.'

'Secret's the size of it fer me though,' Kitty said, looking anxious. 'I wouldn't have ter tell Herbert would I? He wouldn't like it an' there might be ructions. I mean, he's a tricky chap at the best a' times. I sort a' live round the edges with him. If you see what I mean.'

'No,' Rosie reassured her. 'He wouldn't need to know a thing.'

'Good,' Kitty said, and grinned. 'In that case, I'll ask you when the time comes.'

They were rattling into London by then and Mary was looking out of the window at the long lines of identical houses. 'Are we goin' to the beach again?' she said.

'Soon,' Kitty said. 'I'll give you a ring an' we'll fix it.'

She rang them the next Tuesday but it wasn't to fix a trip to the seaside. She was bubbling with excitement. 'We've got the vote, our Jim,' she said. 'At last. It's jest been on the news. Everybody over twenty-one, men *and* women. We've done it. Whatcher think a' that?'

'Not before time,' Jim said. And told Rosie.

'I shall wear my sash to the polling booth,' Kitty said when Rosie took the phone. 'I can't wait. After all these years an' all them marches, an' all them brave women bein' sent to prison an' force-fed, an' Emily Davison dyin' an' everythin' an' our Sylvia fightin' so hard, we done it. It's a triumph.'

'Yes,' Rosie said, swelling with pride for her. 'It is. You've made history. When's the next election?'

'Next year, probably,' Kitty said and squealed. 'I can't wait. We'll see some changes now.'

Two days later she rang again, sounding even more excited than she had in her last call. 'Guess what?' she said.

'You know when the election's going to be?' Rosie said.

'Better than that,' Kitty whooped. 'I'm expecting twins. Whatcher think a' that?'

Rosie wasn't altogether surprised given how big Kitty was but she didn't say so. 'Two for the price a' one,' she said.

Chapter Twenty-One

Gracie wasn't impressed with Kitty's babies. 'They're very small,' she said, looking at the two pale heads, lying against the pillows in their identical cots. They'd been born the previous afternoon, each of them weighing in at less than five pounds, and for once, and because they knew the Monster would be at work, the entire family had come to Tooting on the tram to see them.

Mary didn't even bother to look at them. She was far more interested in her new boots. 'When September comes,' she confided to Kitty, 'I'm goin' to school. Mummy's bought me new boots. They're ever so nice. I can't wear them till I go school, or you could see them.'

'Fancy,' Kitty said vaguely, stroking the nearest baby's head. 'This one's Robert,' she said to Rosie, 'and the other one's George.'

'I've got new socks an' all,' Mary said.

'Take them out in the garden and show them the bird-bath,' Rosie said to Jim. 'You'd like that, wouldn't you girls? Me an' your Aunty Kitty want to talk.'

So they were taken, chatting all the way downstairs, and the two women were left alone to get on with the serious business of discussing the birth, which they did, happily. Then Kitty turned the conversation in a different direction.

'You know what we was talkin' about in Worthin' that time,' she said, and when Rosie nodded, 'Well, when d'you reckon I ought ter do what I got ter do, if you know what I mean? I don't want to get caught out a second time. These two are enough of a family to be goin' on with.'

'I've got to go back to the clinic myself in November,' Rosie told her. 'You can come with me if you like. That'ud be about the right time.'

'Is it far?'

'Couple a' trams. Quite a distance.'

'Only, I'd have ter take the babies wiv me, you see.'

'That's all right,' Rosie said. 'Mary'll be at school by then, so we can take a baby each. It *is* a bit of a trek, but they're ever so nice an' really helpful. They'll explain it all to you and show you what to do an' everything.'

'An' I can keep it a secret from Herbert?'

'Easily,' Rosie said. 'All you got to do is find a nice safe hiding place for a little, round tin, about that size. Somewhere where he won't look.'

So it was agreed. And Rosie assured her that it would

be all right, once she got the hang of it. 'All you got to do now is fend him off for a few weeks.'

'Easier said than done,' Kitty said. ''E's very demanding, when 'e's in the mood. 'E can go weeks without a peep out of 'im and then wallop. Can't stand bein' denied. That's his trouble.'

'Try changing a couple a' nappies under his nose,' Rosie grinned. 'That's enough to put anyone off.'

That made Kitty laugh. 'You're a wicked woman, our Rosie,' she said.

'I know,' Rosie said.

The girls were coming back. They could hear their piping voices rising towards them, as they climbed the stairs. 'We'll have to be off presently,' Rosie said, looking at the clock.

''Course,' Kitty said. 'See you again soon.'

*

Now that her boots and socks had been bought, Mary couldn't wait to get to school. 'I'm going to be like our Gracie,' she said.

'You're not like me,' Gracie told her scornfully. 'You're going to be an infant and I'm going to be in the juniors.'

Rosie was short with her. 'If you know what's good for you, young woman,' she said, 'you'll look after her and stop showing off.'

'If she's old enough to go to school,' Gracie said, truculently, 'she's old enough to look after herself. Nobody looked after *me* when I started school.'

But, as Rosie was quick to notice, she took hold of Mary's hand as they walked to Lant Street that first morning and held it all the way.

'I'll be here waiting for you when you come out,' Rosie promised, because she didn't want her baby to feel lost in this great building, but Mary kissed her and walked straight through the gates, exactly as her sister had done before her and didn't look back.

She'll be all right, Rosie told herself as she walked home.

And she was. After three weeks she came home to report she'd got a reading book and by half term she was full of the news that she was doing sums.

'That's nothing,' Gracie said. 'We're doing fractions.'

'You're both of you very clever little gels,' Jim told them.

And so they are, Rosie thought, watching them. In fact there was only one fly in the ointment at the moment and that was her lack of work. If I don't get a phone call soon, she thought, I'll ring *him*. It's silly to sit at home with nothing to do except the housework when I could be earning. If he doesn't want me I ought to get another job.

Gerry's phone call came the next day. 'I've got two days to put the finishing touches to *Winter*,' he said. 'I'll be with you in a few minutes.'

'I've got a commission to paint Bernard Shaw,' he told her as he drove back to Chelsea. 'Something of an honour actually. He doesn't sit for anyone. The only trouble is, that he wants to start on Wednesday. Hence the rush.'

Rosie wasn't terribly interested in Bernard Shaw

whoever he was. Her aim was to earn enough money to buy the girls some clothes. She'd let Gracie's skirt down as far as it would go and now that November was coming, they both needed new winter coats. Mary had worn Gracie's hand-me-down, until it was threadbare. And if she could earn enough, she wanted to buy a little rattle for Edie's new baby, who was a plump little girl called Dorothy, because she knew how easy it was for the second-born to be neglected. But two days' pay was all she got and then it was time for her visit to the clinic. I must go job hunting once I've got that out of the way, she thought.

It was quite a to-do to take two babes-in-arms on a tram and their presence there caused a stir, which made Kitty bridle with pleasure. She didn't seem to be unduly worried about what was going to happen and when they were walking the last few yards to the clinic and Rosie asked her if she was all right, she said she was fine.

'I'm a tough ol' thing,' she said. 'I been shoved around by the police enough times.'

That was a shock to Rosie. 'Have you?'

'Yeh! 'Course,' Kitty said. 'That's what they done to us. Very rough they was. This couldn't be worse than that.'

'They're nurses,' Rosie told her, 'an' they're very gentle. They'll ask you lots a' questions. That's the only thing.'

'Like what?'

'Like, have you been on queer since you had the babies, an' if you have, when was the last time. That sort a' thing.'

330

'First time was last week,' Kitty told her easily. 'And no, he ain't been near me since. Well he ain't been near me for more'n a month, to tell the truth. He says I put him off, always feeding 'em. So I'm not up the spout again. That's what they want to know, ain't it?'

She's going to be all right, Rosie thought, with some relief. She can handle it. The only trouble was there was a long queue waiting when they got there and working through it took even longer than usual. Both the babies needed feeding during the course of it. So what with that and travelling all the way to Tooting and back afterwards, she was very late getting home. The girls had been home from school for nearly two hours, so it was just as well she'd asked Mrs Rogers to look out for them, and Jim was home too, sitting in his chair with a child on each knee, reading a fairy story to them.

'We was thinkin' a dishin' up,' he said, 'wasn't we gels?'

'You could ha' done,' she said, heading for the oven. 'I left it all cooking.'

'Yeh! We could smell that. Was the twins all right?'

She'd almost forgotten the diplomatic lie she'd told that morning, it seemed such a long time ago. 'Yes,' she said. 'They're fine. Still a bit on the small side, but that's to be expected with twins. Now then you two go an' wash your hands, an' I'll dish up.'

She noticed that Jim was giving her rather an odd look, which was a bit disquieting but he didn't say anything else.

Until they were in bed. They were lying snuggled together, warm and satisfied after their lovemaking, he on his back and she with her head on his shoulder.

'Now tell me,' he said into her hair. 'Where did you really go? I know them twins go to a clinic, pretty reg'lar, Kitty told me, but that's in Tooting and it wouldn't ha' took so long. So where was yer?'

He knows, she thought. Or he's guessed. 'Holloway,' she said. 'Marlborough Road. In the women's clinic.' And then she stopped because she didn't have the words to tell him anything else. Finally she said. 'It's where you go when you don't want to have any more babies.'

'Ah!' he said. 'Thought as much. You went there after our Mary was born, didn't yer?'

'Yes,' she said, looking bold but feeling miserable.

'I knew somethin' was up at the time,' he said, 'but I didn't know what it was. You used to go off for a pee and come back to bed, smellin' sort a' different. Made me think of hospitals first off. An' then a lot later on, I was lookin' for a fresh towel, an' I found a pink tin, so . . . Well after that, I knew what it was.'

This time it was her turn to say, 'Ah!'

He kissed her hair. 'Why didn'tcher tell me?' he said. He didn't sound angry. Just puzzled.

'I thought it'ud upset you.'

'It did.'

'Well then.'

'I thought it was *me* you'd took against, d'you see, not

more babies. Only fer a while mind. I mean we sort a' got into the swing a' things, an' then it was all right.'

She was limp with relief. 'Yes,' she said. 'It was.' And she lifted her head to kiss him.

'Tell me next time there's anythin' you're thinkin' a doin',' he said. 'It ain't a lot a' fun bein' left in the dark.' And after a pause he said, 'You was right though. We couldn't've afforded more than two kids. Takes every penny we got to look after them two, never mind havin' any more.'

And that's true, she thought, as she settled to sleep. Tomorrow I shall go out and see if they'll take me on at the pub again.

*

Despite rather miserable weather, December was a good month that year. Rosie got her job at the pub, although the landlord warned her it might not go on for very long, 'things bein' what they are', Mary and Gracie enjoyed being at school, Edie's little girl put on weight, Tess had a new baby boy and called him Richard, and even the twins were doing well and growing fairly steadily. There was a lot to celebrate when Christmas came. And as Kitty said, 'Next year we shall have our election.'

It was held in May and true to her promise, Kitty looked out her Suffragette sash and washed it and ironed all the creases out of it, so that it would look good at the polling station. Unfortunately she left it hanging in the doorway of the twins' room and Herbert saw it when he went upstairs for a pee. He came downstairs holding it in front of him, his face wrinkled with disgust, as though it had a bad smell.

'And what's this?' he said, dangling it into the kitchen.

Kitty was cooking his chop. 'That's my Suffragette sash,' she told him calmly, 'what I'm gonna wear when I goes out to vote.'

He dropped in onto the floor like some old rag. 'Excuse me,' he said, furiously, 'you are not going to do any such thing. I absolutely forbid it. You are not to wear this ridiculous sash and you are not to vote. It isn't seemly.'

'It's legal,' she said, sliding the chop onto a plate and defying him for once. 'It's legal an' I got the right to wear it. We fought fer this a long time, me an' the others.'

His face was turning an ugly red, he was so angry. 'I absolutely forbid it,' he shouted, glaring at her. 'Do you understand? I absolutely forbid it. No wife of mine would be seen dead wearing such a thing. And no wife of mine, would demean herself to vote. It's unnatural.'

She looked at him for a long second, estimating whether to defy him again or to let it slide the way she usually did. After all, she could go to the polling station wearing her sash and cast her vote for the first time while he was at work and he'd never be any the wiser.

'Have it yer own way,' she said at last, pleased to think she was being so calm. 'I'll bring yer supper through to you, shall I?'

He glared at her for quite a long time, almost as if he'd

read her thoughts, but then he turned on his heel, kicked the sash and strode off to the dining room.

Good riddance to bad rubbish, she thought.

*

On polling day, she pushed her new twin pram to the polling station, wearing her suffragette sash and feeling very proud of herself. She was much admired for it, for now that women had been given the vote, the popular view of suffragettes had changed. Even the police were smiling at them and the newspapers were writing about them as '*hero-ines*'.

'Things *have* changed,' she said, during her phone call to Rosie that Saturday afternoon. 'After all the rubbish they wrote about us when we was campaigning.'

'Never mind,' Rosie said. 'You got your own way in the end, an' that's what counts.'

'Yeh. It is,' Kitty said happily. Then her voice altered. 'Got ter go. Bobbie's roarin'.'

It was a disappointment to both of them, that, although Ramsay MacDonald's Labour party got more seats than either of the others, it was too small a majority for an outright victory.

'Hung Parliament,' Kitty said knowledgeably to Rosie, when she came visiting on Thursday. 'They'll have to hope Lloyd George's lot'll vote with 'em.'

'Will they?'

'Not always,' Kitty said, 'an' there's so much to be done.

Still at least the rich man's party didn't get in, an' that's one good thing. Be interestin' to see who he puts in his cabinet. He'd better have a woman or I shall have sommink ter say.'

She knows so much, Rosie thought, admiring her. I suppose it's being in the suffragettes all those years.

And she got her wish. On June 7th when MacDonald announced his cabinet, sure enough, there was a woman in it. Her name was Margaret Bondfield and she was appointed as Minister of Labour. Kitty told Rosie she was a trade unionist and stood up for women's rights and was just the sort of person to do the right thing. But Herbert was apoplectic with rage.

'For crying out loud!' he said, rattling his copy of the *Daily Mail* that evening, as if he wanted to shake the news right away from him. 'Bad enough the fools have elected a Labour government, without having a woman in cabinet. A woman! I ask you! What use will *she* be? I never heard of such a thing. This is what comes of letting a lot of stupid fool women go out and vote. I knew it was a mistake. I said so all along, didn't I?'

Kitty said yes, because that's what he seemed to want and then shut her ears as he treated her to a long diatribe. She was so used to shutting her ears these days, she did it automatically. I wonder what our Rosie would say if she knew the way he goes on, she thought. Not that she could tell her. That wouldn't have been fair or sensible.

Apart from being glad that she had the right to vote and that the Labour party had got in, Rosie wasn't terribly concerned about politics those days. She knew there were far too many men out of work. You only had to walk a few yards along the street to see them, standing miserably in the kerb with a tray full of matchboxes or shoelaces round their necks, or trailing along the road looking dejected and carrying a handwritten sandwich board, that said things like, '*Brickie. Needs work. Wife and two kids.*' Or '*chippie*', or '*willing worker*'. She felt sorry for them. Who wouldn't? But there was nothing she could do to help them. The government would have to do that. Not that 'government' meant very much to her either. It was just a vague word, with very little meaning, something incomprehensible that went on in some grand building, a long way away from her. She had far too much to do, to give much thought to it. And when she wasn't busy, she was happily watching the changes in her daughters.

They were growing up fast now. Gracie had turned eight in May and Mary would be six come August and they were both so self-assured, it was a joy to watch them setting out to school in the morning, all neat and clean, like the seasoned scholars they were, heading off to the library together every week and coming back with their arms full of books, reading by the fire and absorbed in the story, their heads bent over the page, playing out with their friends and returning, scruffy and happy, to supper. Hardly a day went by, when there wasn't something to notice and be pleased about. She remembered how weary she'd been as a child, carrying one or other of her siblings about and cleaning them up when they got filthy and coping with them when they cried. My Gracie never had *that* to put up with, she thought, and she won't go out to work when she's twelve either. She might not go to work even when she's fourteen. She's clever enough to get a place at a grammar school. And so's my Mary. But that was a wonderful, private dream that she kept to herself. She'd heard quite a lot about the grammar schools from Mrs Rogers, whose cousin had a clever boy, who'd passed what she called 'the scholarship' and was in his first year at the local boys' grammar. But she kept her new knowledge hidden under a smile and didn't say anything to anybody, not even Jim. It was a hope and a dream in a dark world.

*

On October 29th that year the world got even darker, although neither Jim nor Rosie paid much attention to it. The papers were full of it, calling it 'Black Tuesday'. But it was over in America somewhere, in a place called Wall Street, where there had been a crash of some kind. It was something to do with stocks and shares, as far as they could make out, and as neither of them had ever owned shares, and were never likely to, they didn't feel it concerned them. They were shocked to read that hordes of people had been queueing to get into the bank, in some street in New York because their shares had 'collapsed' and they'd lost all their money, but they didn't understand what it was all about even then. The term 'Wall Street Crash' entered into their vocabulary because they saw it so often in the papers, but it didn't make much sense.

'I always thought a bank was supposed to be a safe place to put your money in,' Rosie said, as she and Jim were reading the evening paper. 'If you had any to spare.'

'Safe as the Bank of England,' Jim said. 'So they say.'

'Banks in America can't be much cop,' Rosie said. 'Just as well we've got different ones.'

'I got a star for my sums today,' Mary said.

'So did I, too,' Gracie said, not to be outdone. 'I always get a star. I'm the best in the class.'

'Pride comes 'fore a fall, young lady,' Jim said, but he was grinning at her, so she didn't take any notice of what he was saying. He approved and that was what mattered.

Rosie watched them, lovingly, and her dream stirred in her mind to warm her.

*

She needed warming that winter and so did Jim for, although they still thought the Wall Street Crash was nothing to do with them, they felt its consequences no matter what they believed. Rosie lost her job at the pub and couldn't get another one and Jim had to take a cut in pay, which was even more worrying. Kitty was determined to look on the bright side and helped to organise a New Year's Eve tea party for the kiddies, to celebrate the new decade, at which she arrived with her two toddling infants and a tin full of cakes. The twins had reached the grand old age of sixteen months and seemed to be walking about all the time, even with their mouths full of cake, which made rather a mess of the kitchen. Rosie didn't complain because Kitty said it was the only time they had so much freedom 'on account a' Herbert's such a stickler fer manners' but when the tea party was over and the twins had gone home with their empty cake tin, and her father had gone downstairs to get some fags, Gracie complained bitterly.

'Look at the mess they've made,' she said. 'They ought to sit up to the table like the rest of us.'

'You sit up properly because you're big girls,' Rosie told her. 'They're only babies. Anyway, if anyone's going to complain about the mess it's going to be me, not you, because it's my kitchen.' She felt sorry for the twins, poor little things, having to put up with the Monster. It couldn't be much fun for any of them, living with a man like that, especially when times were so tough.

Thanks to the Wall Street Crash, times were getting tougher by the week. There was less and less work to be had and what there was of it was poorly paid. By the middle of March, unemployment had grown to more than one and a half million, no matter what the government was trying to do about it. By August, it was more than two million and rising.

'It's a vicious circle, seems to me,' Jim said, sadly. 'The more businesses close down, the more people out a' work, the more people out a' work, the less they have to spend, the less they have to spend, the more shops an' businesses'll close, an' then there's even more people out a' work. It jest goes on an' on. Manny says he'll have to cut my wages again, next Sat'day if things don't pick up.'

Which they won't, Rosie thought, but she didn't say so. 'Maybe I can get a job at another pub,' she said.

But there were no jobs available. 'I could fill any job, ten times over,' one landlord told her, 'if I had the cash to offer one, which I don't. Times are hard.'

'You can say that again,' Rosie told him sadly. And she was thinking, we'll just have to cut back, until I can get some modelling, that's all. But no modelling jobs were available either, now that Gerry was taking on so many commissions for portraits of the rich and famous. And things went from bad to worse, with unemployment figures climbing month by month all over the world. Germany had over ten million out of work and in America a quarter of the population had no job to go to. There were days, as the first two years of the thirties inched further into poverty and misery, when she wondered what on earth was going to happen next.

What happened was a letter dated September 1931, addressed to Mr and Mrs Jackson, from the headmaster of Lant Street School. It was pleased to inform them that their daughter Gracie was one of a small group of pupils, who had been selected to sit the L.C.C. Common Entrance Examination in January 1932 and ended, '*If she continues to work as well and as hard as she is presently doing, we have every expectation of her success.*'

Rosie was on her own when it was delivered and she read it twice, because she couldn't believe her eyes the first time. Then she burst into tears. Hadn't she always known her Gracie would do well? Dear, earnest, hard-working little thing. She couldn't wait for Jim to get home from work and read it too.

He read it carefully, in his usual way, concentrating hard while his family waited with happy anticipation to hear what he would say. Then he read it to Gracie. 'You're a clever gel,' he said. 'Me an' your mum are proud of you.'

Gracie smiled her impish smile. 'I know,' she said.

Our little girl going to a grammar school, Rosie thought, proudly. It was one of the happiest moments of her life.

Chapter Twenty-Two

Young Gracie Jackson sat the scholarship exam the next January with perfect aplomb, heading off to school in the morning, as if it were just another day. Rosie wished her luck and watched her go but then there was nothing she could do but wait, and waiting was very difficult. She got on with her housework in a desultory way, but her mind was spinning with anxiety all day.

Her clever daughter returned that afternoon to report that the exam was easy and to ask whether there was any plum jam left. 'I could just fancy a slice a' bread and jam.'

'You can have the top brick off the chimney,' Rosie said, admiring her.

Gracie grinned at that. 'I'd rather have jam,' she said.

Then they all had to wait again until the results arrived and they weren't expected until the end of the term, which seemed ages away. Rosie tried to keep everything as normal as she could and deliberately didn't talk about it, just in case Gracie hadn't passed, but she needn't have worried. When the plain brown envelope finally arrived, the news it contained was everything she could have asked for. Gracie had passed the exam and won a state scholarship to attend whichever grammar school her parents chose. There was a list of possible schools enclosed and among them was their nearest one, St Saviour's and St Olave's in Southwark.

'That's the one,' Rosie said. 'I'll write an' tell 'em.' And did. It was a very proud moment.

And it was followed by an even better one. The school wrote back within a week, to tell her that they had accepted Gracie's application and had arranged a time when she could visit the school and meet the headmistress. Gracie took it calmly, but Rosie was so excited she could barely breathe. Then what washing, ironing, polishing and general titivation there was. Gracie had to be shining clean and on her best behaviour because, as Rosie kept telling her, this was a very special day.

And despite her over-attentiveness, it was. The grand school building impressed them both and, once they were inside, there were so many wonderful things to see – hundreds of girls in gym tunics and scarlet blouses, a library where they were quietly reading, a gym where they were climbing up ropes, a huge empty hall, a field for games, science labs, a music room, an art room. Gracie's eyes grew rounder with every step she took and by the time they were ushered into the head's study she was almost speechless.

But she listened dutifully as the headmistress told her she had been given a wonderful opportunity and that they hoped she would make the very most of it and, when she was asked if there was anything she'd particularly enjoyed on her tour, spoke up quite confidently to say it was the science lab and the music room. Then they were given an envelope containing what the secretary called 'some more information about our uniform' and went home, starry eyed.

'I can't wait to see you in your uniform,' Rosie said, giving her daughter a hug. 'Just wait till we tell your dad.'

Jim took one look at their glowing faces and laughed out loud. 'I can see I'm gonna get my ear bent this evenin',' he said and he settled himself in his armchair, grinning at them. 'Fire away!'

They fired all through the evening, not even stopping when Rosie dished up the supper. At one point he took Mary on his lap, because he could see she was feeling out of it. 'Listen to this kid,' he said, cuddling her. 'It'll be your turn next.' They were still telling him things when it was time for bed. But at last, and half an hour later than it should have been, Mary and Gracie were upstairs and tucked into their beds and Rosie could show him the list.

And then everything changed.

He read it through very carefully, while Rosie sat opposite him and waited. Then he put it on the table and scowled. 'Good God alive,' he said. 'Do they think we're made a' money? Eight an' eleven fer a tie an' a hatband? It's ridiculous.'

'It'ud only be the once,' she said reasonably.

'An' blazers, an' gym tunic, an' blouses, an' sports equipment. There's no end to it. You tot that all up, it's more'n I earn in a year.'

'We don't have to buy it all at once,' Rosie urged. He was beginning to alarm her. 'We can do it bit by bit. We might find some of it second-hand.'

'You ain't listenin' to me Rosie,' he said. 'We ain't got this sort a' money. Never 'ave 'ad, never will 'ave. 'Specially now. Never mind do it bit by bit. We can't do it at all.'

'We can't not do it,' Rosie said, fighting back. 'It's an opportunity for her to better herself, an' it'll only come the once. If she doesn't go, she'll leave school at fourteen an' go to work in Woolworths for a pittance or end up a skivvy. Is that what you want for her? Because I know I don't. She's worth more than that. A lot more.'

Jim sighed and ran his fingers through his mop of hair. 'You ain't listenin' to me,' he said. 'We ain't got the money, an' that's all there is to it. I spend every penny I earn on rent, an' food, an' bills, an' ordin'ry clothes. I can't run to all this as well. Eight an' eleven fer a tie, fer cryin' out loud. It ain't possible.'

'We can make it possible,' Rosie said, passionately. 'I'll get a job an' pay for the uniform. We *can* do it. Truly.'

But his mind and his jaw were set. 'It ain't possible,' he said. 'We got three million unemployed in this country. There ain't no jobs fer no one. You know that. Not no more. It can't be done. How many times I got to tell you?'

She wouldn't give up. Couldn't give up. It was far too important. There had to be something she could say to make him change his mind. But although they argued until it was past two in the morning and they were both exhausted, they were no nearer agreement than they'd been at the start.

'I'm fer my bed,' he said wearily. 'We shan't agree, an' that's all there is to it.'

She made one last despairing plea. 'Don't tell her yet,' she begged. 'It'ud break her heart. Give me a few days an' see what I can come up with.'

'A week then,' he conceded.

'I'll do it,' she said. 'I'm damned if I'm going to let anyone take this away from her. Not now she's come so far. I'll think of something.'

But he was already on his way to the stairs and she was making her vow to the air.

*

The next day, when he'd left for work and the girls had gone cheerfully off to school, she walked into the front room, sat down in front of the phone, squared her shoulders, lifted her chin and asked for Gerry's number. She couldn't think of anyone else who would employ her now but, with luck, he might have something he wanted her to do, providing he wasn't still painting the rich and famous. Fingers crossed.

It was Mrs Fenchurch who answered the phone and she

was plainly pleased to hear her. 'Wait there, my lovely,' she said, 'an' I'll go an' get him for you. Shan't be a tick.' Then she was gone for what seemed to be a very long time.

But there he was, eventually, a surprised question in his voice. 'Rosie?'

'Ah!' she said, feeling a bit discouraged, and told him quickly before she could lose her nerve. 'I just phoned to see if you had any work for me.'

''Fraid not,' he said, lightly. 'I've just got a commission to paint a full length portrait of Lawrence of Arabia. Imagine that. The great T E Lawrence. It's a real honour. But I don't have to tell you that, do I? A real honour. The Uffizi Club broke open the champagne when they heard and I've been dining out on it for weeks, ever since I got the letter. Augustus is spitting feathers. Bernard Shaw recommended me, of course. I thought he would, because that was a damned good portrait I did of him. Made headlines, though I sez it as shouldn't.'

She could feel her heart falling and shrinking. The rich and famous were getting in her way, just as she'd feared they might. 'Ah,' she said again, her voice small and apologetic. 'I hope you didn't mind me asking.'

Even in his present euphoric state, he still felt enough affection for her to recognise that she was disappointed and that something was obviously wrong. 'What's up?' he said, gently. 'Are you short of cash?'

The sympathy in his voice gave her a little hope, so she told him about Gracie's scholarship and explained how

348

desperately she needed a job that would pay her enough to buy all that expensive uniform. 'I couldn't bear to have to turn it down,' she said. 'Not now. It wouldn't be fair after all the work she's done.'

He was thinking about it as she talked, wanting to help her. 'Tell you what,' he said, when she'd finished. 'Why don't you go and see if Alexander Korda could use you? He was very taken with you at my exhibition, if you remember. He'd have offered you a job there and then. He might have something for you. You never know.'

She remembered in an instant, a short, dark man wearing thick glasses, and a voice saying, '*Your face is your fortune. The camera would love you. If you ever need a job come and see me.*'

'Where would I find him?' she asked.

'He's got a studio in Borehamwood,' Gerry told her. 'Elstree. Just starting on a new film, so he's been telling me. If I were you, I'd go and see him. I'll send you a map and instructions.'

He was as good as his word. The map arrived in the afternoon post the next day, with a note written on the back. 'It's a huge place. You can't miss it. Take the train from King's Cross to Elstree and Borehamwood. Good luck.'

She went the following morning, without telling Jim, just in case nothing came of it. It was a long journey and it ended with a long walk, but Gerry's map was easy to read and he was right about the size of the building. It was absolutely enormous and stood incongruously in the fields with a line of cars parked beside it, looking like six giant beach huts, stuck together side by side. It had a bold sign right across the front of it saying '*British International Pictures*', so there was no doubt that she'd come to the right place, and the entrance seemed to be through another, smaller hut. She squared her shoulders, took a deep breath and walked in.

There was a pimply youth in a yellow Holland overall sitting watching the door, with his very large feet propped up on the desk in front of him. He didn't put them down or smile. He just said, 'Yerss?' in a questioning sort of way.

Bull by the horns, Rosie thought. 'Rosie Jackson, come to see Mr Korda,' she said, glaring at him.

'He's doin' auditions.'

What a bit of luck, Rosie thought. 'I know,' she lied. 'That's why I've come.'

The youth looked at a long piece of paper that was lying on the desk in front of him. 'You're not on here,' he said and gave her a look, heavy with suspicion.

The connecting door was being opened and another young man was walking in. Slightly older than Pimples and infinitely better looking. 'Hello,' he said. 'What can I do for you?'

'I've come to see Mr Korda,' she told him. 'For an audition.' She noticed that Pimples was sitting up and had put his feet on the floor, so this one had authority.

'Where's the time sheet?' he said, looking at Pimples and the youth handed a piece of paper across the desk to him and oiled an answer. 'All ready an' waiting, Mr Gordon, sir.'

'They're all on set,' Mr Gordon said. 'If you'll just follow me.' And he led her through the door into the studio.

It was a huge place and very confusing, being a series of long corridors lined with identical doors, each with its own printed sign, *'Make-up'*, *'Costume'*, and endless dressing rooms all numbered, and there were so many people rushing about, pushing tea trolleys and long rails full of costumes or carrying little boards with papers clipped to them, that it made her head spin to be walking through the melee but, in the end, they arrived at a door labelled *'Studio 4'* and walked through into a different world. It was just a huge space, but it had the brightest lights she'd ever seen, all shining like suns, and standing quite still in the middle of the room, a woman in a full-skirted dress and a cap and apron. There were cameras on stilts grouped in a half circle all round her and several men with those odd boards and, standing to one side watching it all, Alexander Korda, looking exactly the same as he'd done at that party and obviously in command. It was remarkably quiet for such a large space and so many people, so she stood very still and watched and waited. And after a few seconds Mr Korda called, 'Action!' and the cameras began to buzz like mosquitos and the woman walked about until she reached a table where she stopped and said, 'Will that be all, sir?' in the oddest of voices, high pitched and wobbly, as if she was going to burst into tears. And Mr Korda called, 'Cut!' and everybody began talking and moving again.

Now, Rosie thought, and she set her chin and walked through the room until she was standing beside the great man himself. 'Mr Korda,' she said. 'You won't remember me . . .'

But he was smiling at her. 'Gerry's model,' he said. 'I remember you very well. I can't remember your name, but I never forget a face.'

'Rosie Jackson,' she said. 'You told me if I ever needed a job I was to come and find you. So I've come.'

He considered her for so long she began to feel anxious. Then he shouted, 'Hamish!' and the young man called Mr Gordon ran towards him, saying, 'Sir?'

'Screen test for this young lady,' Mr Korda said. 'Rosie Jackson. Cook. See to it will you.' And Mr Gordon led her through the door and out into the corridor again.

From then on the day became peculiarly disjointed. She was dressed in a servant's costume like the other girl had worn, was given a card with her lines printed on it, and had her face plastered with make-up, which the make-up girl assured her was so that she would be seen under the lights, and after that she just sat about with a group of other costumed women, drank tea, ate sandwiches, gossiped and waited – endlessly. It seemed hours before Hamish appeared to call her to the studio. But then when she got there, it was as if she'd never been away. It was all exactly the same, except that she was the girl under the lights and Mr Korda was calling, 'Action!' for her.

She walked boldly across to the empty table and spoke

to it as though she was saucing a customer in the RAC Club. 'Will that be all, sir? Or was there something else?' And Mr Korda called, 'Cut!' and roared with laughter, and at that, the intense quiet in the studio was broken and everybody else laughed too.

'Yes,' Mr Korda said, grinning at her. 'We'll run it again and this time stick to the script, if you please. Action.'

She did it four times, which she found very boring, but, at the end of the fourth attempt, the great man came over and told her that was all he needed for the moment. 'Come back on Wednesday, when we've seen the rushes. We'll send a car to pick you up at the station at 8.30. Right?' And that was that. She wiped off her make-up, hung up her costume, put on her own clothes and went home. She had no idea whether she'd got a job or not.

It wasn't until Wednesday morning that she discovered that she'd been cast as the cook and would be required in crowd scenes and was to work on the film for the next six months. There was a contract waiting for her to sign and, among many other things, it gave her details of the salary she would be given. It was three times as much as she'd ever earned with Gerry and it would be paid monthly. It made her feel weak at the knees. The only drawback was that she was only going to earn it for six months. I'll work really hard, she thought, and do my very, very best and then he might hire me for another picture when this one's finished. For the moment, the knowledge that she could earn this sort of money was dizzyingly enough.

'There you are,' she said to Jim that evening. 'I've got a job.' And she handed her copy of the contract across the table, feeling pleased with herself. 'Read that.'

He read with growing and obvious amazement. 'Good God alive!' he said, and turned to grin at the girls. 'Yer Mum's gonna be a film star,' he told them. 'Whatcher think a' that?'

They were very impressed. 'Seriously?' Gracie said. 'Are you really?'

'Well, I've got a part in a film. Yes,' Rosie said, being strictly truthful. 'But I'm not going to be the star. It's just a small part, an' I'll have a lot to learn.'

But her daughters didn't care whether she was going to be the star or not. Having a part in a film was excitement enough. 'Wait till I tell them at school,' Gracie said.

*

During the next two weeks, Rosie worked hard and learnt fast. She discovered that the film she was working on was called *The Private Life of Henry VIII*, that a film progresses at the director's speed, that Mr Korda was a perfectionist and that the way to please him, was to work out exactly what he wanted and give it to him. It wasn't long before she recognised the actors who were playing the main parts and were *really* stars. Sometimes she sneaked in to watch Mr Korda directing them and was impressed by the way they could stop being themselves and become someone else between one breath and the next. Two of them were people she'd seen on screen and her first sight of them was a revelation. The handsome heart-throb, Robert Donat had asthma and could sometimes be tetchy because of it and he often looked downright ill, while the beautiful, smooth-skinned Merle Oberon, who played Anne Boleyn, had a really wicked grin when she was off-screen and talking to her friends. But it was Charles Laughton who intrigued her the most. He was a big, rather wobbly looking man who played Henry VIII and he was mesmerising. When he began to act, she found it impossible to look at anybody else and stood in the shadows watching him and marvelling. He looked so huge and bulky in that padded costume and much larger than life in every way, as if he had become the king and wasn't just pretending.

After a month, she was completely accustomed to her work in the studio and had adapted to living in three completely different worlds, the world of cinema, that was entirely fantasy and full of passions that sounded fierce but were actually quite harmless, her life at home, that got better and better now she was earning well, and the life out in the wider world, where all sorts of terrible things were happening, that were hard to understand and that no one seemed able to control. The newspapers were full of them and so were the newsreels.

When she wasn't needed on set, she sat on a deck chair, costumed and in full make-up, and read the papers, checking the unemployment figures, that just went on rising and rising, and wincing at pictures of weary-looking men, loafing around in the streets because they couldn't find work. After a while she noticed other pictures too, of a horrible-looking Italian, like a toad in a tight uniform who was called Mussolini and a German called Adolf Hitler, who was the German Chancellor and always seemed to be bellowing with his mouth open. And she wondered why anyone in their right mind would vote for such people and was horrified that they did. And she remembered Keir Hardie, who'd been such a strong, gentle man and had spoken to people so directly and honestly, without all that roaring and shouting.

Sometimes there were pictures of Hitler's supporters marching through the streets in their black uniforms, with their legs all kicking in unison and their right arms sticking up in the air like robots. At the end of April, there was news that he'd opened a place called a concentration camp where he was going to imprison everybody who opposed him, which she didn't like the sound of at all. And in May his followers built a huge bonfire in a street in Berlin and burnt hundreds of books he didn't agree with. And she remembered Gerry's library and shuddered.

Work on *The Private Life* continued until November and by then Gracie was well into her first term at St Saviour's, Jim had stopped worrying about money and Rosie had earned so much she'd even managed to put away some savings in her bank account. Which was just as well, because Mr Korda decided that his next project was to make a series of what he called 'shorts', which only required two or three actors, so there was no more work for her in the studios. It worried her a lot but she kept her worries to herself, hoping that there would be another big picture after the shorts and that she could audition for a part in that. But after Christmas, her savings had dwindled so far she was seriously worried. Maybe I'll write to Gerry, she thought, and thank him for his help, which I ought to have done long since, and tell him how I got on with *Private Life*. He might be able to think of something else I could do.

*

Although she couldn't have known it, her letter arrived in Cheyne Walk, at a peculiarly opportune moment. Gerry had been puzzling over an offer for a new and very different commission that he'd received three days previously. It had come from one of the big chocolate manufacturers, who were offering an exorbitant sum of money for a set of ten rural pictures to use on their chocolate boxes. He'd been talking it over with his friends at a party only the night before, and with one exception – a young artist who said he'd give his eye teeth for such an offer – they'd all been horrified at the idea, saying it would devalue the currency and telling him to put the idea right out of his mind. Even Augustus John had spoken to him in his avuncular way to remind him, that he was worth far, far more than any 'chocolate box painter' and he really shouldn't consider it. So, to receive a nice, easy letter from his lovely Helen of Troy after all that, was quite a relief. Now if they'd asked me for ten portraits of *her*, he thought, I'd have done it like a shot. And that put an idea into his mind. He wasn't really a landscape painter, but he could offer them a series of portraits of country girls, milkmaids, harvesters, gypsies even, and she could model for all of them. She needed the work and, if he earned the sort of money they were offering, he could pay her well. He might even win her back and that was something he'd never stopped wanting, no matter how many other women had drifted in and out of his life. He phoned that afternoon to ask his putative sponsor what he thought of the idea.

The putative sponsor was receptive to any idea this much-admired artist could offer him and, after half an hour's satisfactory discussion, it was agreed that Mr de Silva would paint ten portraits of gypsy girls in country settings and that a contract would be drawn up the next day to that effect and sent to him for signature. The deal was almost done. Then he only had to ring Alexander Korda and find out if he could hire some costumes from the studio.

He found out a great deal more in that conversation too, for naturally they talked about Rosie as well as costumes.

'An excellent worker,' Mr Korda said, 'and the camera loves her, just as I knew it would. Unfortunately she can't act.'

'Will you be using her again?' Gerry asked.

'Possibly,' his friend said. 'Quite possibly. But only for bit parts and not for a year or two.'

It was just what Gerry wanted to hear. Now he could

write to his lovely Helen of Troy and offer her the gypsies. Which he did, telling her he would be working on them for about a year, and that he would pay her the same rate as she'd earned at Elstree, and ending his letter with the words, *'If you are happy with the idea, give me a ring.'*

She was so relieved, she rang as soon as she'd read the letter. And the following Monday she was back in Cheyne Walk.

*

The studio was reassuringly the same as it had been the last time she modelled there, except that the dresses that lay in tumbled profusion all over the chaise longue were gypsy costumes, headbands, scarves, castanets, gaudy jewellery and all. She and Gerry enjoyed themselves picking out the first one and he watched very happily while she changed into it and stood ready to be arranged and to take up her pose. It was as if they'd stepped back in time. The same old river flowed peacefully beyond the window, the fire shone warmly in the grate, the books stood in their usual order, there were various canvases standing against the wall. It was all exactly as it used to be.

On her third day, they began to talk in a desultory way about some of the other times she'd modelled for him, remembering the red dress and the way he'd changed that picture to turn it into *Autumn*.

'Glad you're back now?' he asked, from behind the easel.

'Very,' she told him. 'I like this sort a' work.'

'You do it well.'

'To tell you the truth,' she confessed, 'I thought I might be getting a bit too old for it. I mean, it's a long time . . .'

'Age, my dear Helen, has nothing to do with it,' he said. 'It's the beauty of the model that counts and you are more beautiful than ever.'

It was such a pretty compliment it made her glow. 'Well thank you, kind sir,' she said.

He emerged from behind the easel, his intentions clear on his face and in his eyes. 'It's nothing but the truth,' he said, walking towards her. 'You're still the most beautiful woman I've ever seen. I still love you to distraction. You don't know how good it is to have you back in the house.' And he put his arms round her and kissed her, just as he'd done in the old days. And, despite her good intentions, she kissed him back. She simply couldn't help it. She was enjoying it too much. Somewhere in the back of her mind, she knew she ought to tell him to stop, but she couldn't do it, any more than she'd been able to on that first dizzy time. He was already turning towards the bedroom, his arm round her waist, leading her. And why not? she thought. He'd given her a job when she needed it most, he was paying her well, he was the best friend she'd ever had, there was no harm in it, and Jim would never know. She'd make sure of that. There was only one worry and even that seemed small, given the pleasure of the moment.

'I haven't got my Dutch cap,' she warned him.

'Never mind,' he said. 'You can bring it next time. I'll take care of you today.'

So their love affair resumed, under the same unspoken rules and in the same pleasurable way. It was almost as if nothing had happened to either of them since those early days of – what was it he used to call it? – sinful idleness. She was back living in her three worlds again.

*

It took more than a month to complete a picture, small though they were, so Gerry estimated they would be working together for more than a year, which pleased them both. In March he sent his first two gypsies to the sponsor, who wrote back at once to say they were all delighted with them and to promise that they would go into production by the end of April. And sure enough, at the beginning of May, they sent him two chocolate boxes, beautifully packed, one for him and one for Rosie, to show him how well they looked. Rosie took hers home to share with Jim and the girls and Jim said he'd never known such extravagance. It worried him that she'd gone back to work with that artist feller and, even though the picture of her was very pretty, he wasn't sure it was the right thing to let her do. Not that he could have stopped her. That was one thing he *did* know.

In June there were two more boxes and in August another pair arrived. The girls said they'd all get fat, gobbling up chocolates at that rate. But when September began and they had a letter from Lant Street School to tell them that

Mary was being put in the scholarship class, they not only had enough spare cash to celebrate with a tea party and an iced cake, but bought another box of chocolates too.

Their family life continued to provide them with treats. In October when Gracie had been at St Saviour's for over a year, they all went up to Leicester Square Theatre, dressed in their best clothes to attend the premier of *The Private Life of Henry VIII*.

It was a very grand occasion, with photographers taking pictures as they walked in and people serving champagne in the foyer and everybody bright-eyed and excited. It was a revelation to Jim that a party could actually be enjoyable; and quite a thrill to Rosie to be part of such a prestigious crowd and to know so many people there, and to think that her daughters were going to see her on screen. She wondered what they would say when they did and hoped they would like it. She wasn't disappointed. They were both very impressed, although Mary said it didn't look like her.

'Not really,' she said. 'You're still my mum but you look different up there.'

'It's all the make-up they put on you,' Rosie explained.

'Um,' Mary said. 'Well I wish they wouldn't. I like you as you are.'

'Nothin'll ever change that,' Jim told her. 'She'll always be yer mum, no matter what. You can depend on it.'

'It's all make-believe, this film lark,' Rosie said. 'None of it's real. It's like modelling. That's all make-believe too. You put on a costume and you become somebody else. It's all a game. It don't mean anything.' She was talking to Jim now, looking up into his face, trying to convince herself, as much as she was trying to convince him. 'What's real is at home. That's what's important.'

'Glad to hear it,' he said and made a joke of it. 'I wouldn't like ter think I'd married a gypsy.'

And then, just before Christmas, Edie wrote to Rosie in great excitement to say that Frank and Dotty had both been given parts in the school nativity play and wasn't that good. 'It's on the last day of term,' she wrote. 'Do say you'll come.'

So they all went down to Worthing, as Gracie and Mary had already broken up, and Jim took the afternoon off to join them – with Mr Feigenbaum's permission of course. As it turned out, it was just as well he did.

Chapter Twenty-Three

The nativity play was plainly staged and elaborately costumed in the usual motley collection of gowns made of old curtains and threadbare blankets, of gauze wings, paper crowns and a variety of tea-towel headdresses kept in place with pyjama cords. Frank played Joseph and remembered his lines with an obvious and scowling effort and Dotty was one of the six self-conscious angels, who got their wings entangled and didn't smile until they were urged forward to take a bow at the end. Afterwards they all went back to Station Road for tea and rock cakes, and Mary and Gracie told the kids they were wonderful and they didn't stop talking until the clock struck five.

Then Jim said they'd better be going because they'd got a train to catch. And they kissed one another goodbye, bundled into their thick coats and hats, wound scarves round their necks and headed out into the cold. And Mary looked at her father and changed their direction.

'Are we going to the beach?' she asked. And when he looked puzzled, she put her hand on his arm and wheedled, 'You *did* promise.'

'It's much too late for beaches,' Rosie said. 'You won't see anything. It'll be dark before we get there. *And* cold.'

But Gracie waded in to support her sister. 'I'd like to see the sea too. And you *did* promise Dad. I remember.'

Jim looked at Rosie with a question on his face and Rosie shrugged. 'If you ask me,' she said, 'it's a damned silly idea. But if you want to do it, you'll do it. Don't blame me if you all catch cold.'

So Jim and his daughters walked down to the sea, arm in arm and singing carols all the way, and Rosie trudged beside them thinking how stupid it was. They'll be frozen down there in the dark, she thought, and there'll be nothing to see.

Sure enough, by the time they reached Marine Parade it was bitterly cold and so dark that the street lights had been lit. They stood looking down at the rapidly blackening sea, as it rolled monotonously toward the shore, each long wave tipped with a froth of foam that shone silver-white under the street lamps and fell on the shingle with a long hiss. The shops were all shut, the streets were virtually empty and there was nothing else to see or do.

Rosie put up with it until she began to shiver. Then she asked if they had had enough. But even as she spoke, everything changed. The doors of the domed Pavilion at the end of the pier were flung open, letting out a strong beam of light and the noise of a crowd. Within seconds, the pier was filled with a long column of marching men. They were dressed in uniform black, from the military caps on their heads to the jackboots on their feet, and they all had their right arms sticking up in the air, the way those awful Germans did, and were chanting and bellowing. At first Rosie couldn't hear what they were saying but, as they grew nearer to the road, their words became clearer and she realised that it was 'England for the English! Mosley! Mosley!' And she saw that the column was being led by a tall man in the same black uniform. He walked with a limp and had a moustache like Hitler's and the most arrogant face she'd ever seen. The sight of him made her feel suddenly and terribly afraid. There was something sinister about these men, something alien, inhuman. She glanced to her left to see if the girls were all right and noticed that they were clinging to their father's hands.

'I don't like this,' she said to Jim. 'Let's get out of here.'

'We'll have a job,' he said, looking towards Marine Parade. It was crowded with people, hundreds of them and mostly men, all in ordinary working clothes and all standing still and looking towards the pier with determined expressions on their faces.

'My God!' she said. 'Where did *they* come from?'

Jim didn't know. But it was obvious *why* they'd come. As soon as the head of the marching column left the pier, the crowd surged forward, mocking their chant with one of their own, 'Mos-lee! Mos-lee! Chuck the blighter in the sea!' and completely blocking their way. Several of the boys in the crowd produced peashooters and fired them and for a few minutes there was a lot of pushing and shoving as the two sides faced each other. Then half a dozen policemen arrived, brandishing truncheons, and by dint of pushing and threatening they made a way for Mosley and his henchmen to walk through. But as soon as they'd gone the gap closed up again and the rest of the marchers were left to fight their own way through, which they did with ugly ferocity, punching and kicking. Rosie saw a woman thrown to the pavement and one man being attacked by four of Mosley's men, two of them pinioning his arms while the others punched him.

'Hang about!' Jim said suddenly. 'That's my sarge! God damn it all! I'm not 'aving this!' And he was off into the crowd before Rosie could stop him, using his shoulders to force a way through, quick-footed as a lion, his mane tawny in the street lights, his spine determined.

She watched as he reached the punching gang and saw him pick the largest of them and fell him, just as he'd done in Trafalgar Square all those years ago. Then there was a confusion of shouts and punches and she saw that he'd taken on a second assailant and hurled him to the ground too and that the man they'd been using as a punchbag had shaken himself free and was fighting alongside him. It all happened so quickly he was back beside her almost before she could take it all in and the punchbag man was with him, bleeding from a cut over his eyebrow but beaming all over his face.

'You're never gonna believe this,' Jim said happily to his family, 'but this is my sarge from the war. Best man in the army. Never knew yer name, Sarge or I'd introduce yer.'

'Jack,' the sergeant said, shaking Rosie's hand. 'Jack Johnson. Pleased ter meetcher.'

'My sarge from the war' stayed with Jim and Rosie until they were satisfied that his cut had stopped bleeding, while the noise of the street fight roared to the north of them and Mary and Gracie watched him round-eyed. Then he said he ought to be getting back, 'or they'll think I'm desertin' of 'em, poor beggars.' But he didn't go until Jim had torn two pages out of Rosie's pocket diary so that they could exchange addresses and had discovered that his old wartime mate lived in Hackney.

'Jest up the road,' he said, his face delighted. 'That's no distance. Come an' see us. 'Ave supper. Bring the missus.'

So having sorted that out, the two men grinned at one another and parted. Jim talked about it all the way home. 'What a turn-up fer the books,' he said. 'Fancy findin' my ol' sarge. I can't believe it.'

Rosie was pleased to see him so happy but the other things she'd witnessed that evening worried her too much to share his feelings. She'd never seen a street fight before and it shocked her to think that grown men could behave so violently. They should have had enough fighting being in the war, she thought. She had to remind herself that the war had been over for fifteen years, so a lot of them would have been children when it was going on and wouldn't have known what it was like. Our poor Tommy would ha' been thirty-two this year if he'd lived, she thought. And that made her feel uncomfortably old and for several miserable moments pitched her back into her terrible yearning grief again.

That night she had a searing nightmare in which the robot men were pulling her children apart, limb from limb, and she was tied to a wheel and couldn't stop them. She woke weeping and in a muck-sweat and it took Jim nearly an hour to comfort her calm again. 'They're such dreadful men,' she wept. 'They look as if they'd be capable of anything. All those kickin' feet and their horrible arms stuck up in the air like that, what ent natural, and their horrible cruel faces. And when you think what Hitler's doing.'

'Don't cry,' Jim said, cuddling her. 'I'll look after you. I looked after my ol' sarge, now didn't I?'

'Yes,' she said, sniffing and trying to smile. 'You did.'

'Well there you are then.'

But the images were still toxic in her mind and she couldn't shake them away, although she tried to keep cheerful so as not to upset the girls, who were busy cooking mince pies now that school was over and Christmas was so close. It wasn't until the afternoon post arrived that she recovered her balance.

The third letter she opened was from Edie who was

bubbling about the success of the play and said she was *'ever so glad you got off in good time last night'* explaining, *'there was a fight here in Worthing after you'd gone. Ever so bad it was. There was hundreds in it so they say all over South St and the Arcade and everywhere. Some of them got up on the roof of the Arcade and pulled off a great chunk of stone and threw it down. Imagine that. They could've killed someone. It's a real mess. I went down this morning and had a look and there was stones and all sorts everywhere.'*

'Tell her we were there,' Gracie said, 'and we saw it all.'

'Tell her Dad saved his sergeant's life,' Mary said.

'That's a bit of an exaggeration,' Rosie said, feeling they had to be accurate.

But Mary wasn't having that. 'No it's not,' she said, sticking up her chin. 'It was four onto one. They could have killed him. And our dad rescued him.'

They wrote the letter between them, passing it from one to the other, and the tale was told in all its heroic and fully embellished detail. When it was finished Rosie added a postscript. *'The sergeant is coming to have supper with us soon, so we shall hear more about it then.'* Then they made up the kitchen fire so that they'd have a warm house to come home to and walked it down to the postbox together.

It was a good Christmas with such stirring tales to be told. Kitty came over on Boxing Day with her two boys and without the Monster and listened to every detail. ''E allus was a firebrand,' she said, 'even when 'e was a nipper, stickin' up fer me an' poor ol' Ma. D'you remember him in Trafalgar Square that time Rosie? You never saw nothink so quick.'

So naturally *that* story had to be told too, even though Jim tried to put her off. His daughters were thrilled and George and Bobby listened with their mouths open.

'You ought to have a medal,' Mary said.

But he said he'd rather have another slice of ham, and held up his plate.

*

Christmas eased them into January which was dark, dank and drizzly and in the middle of the month Sergeant Johnson wrote to Jim as he'd promised and a date was set for his visit. Jim was fidgety with excitement, wondering if they could run to a Sunday joint and coming home from the market with a tin of pineapple to make 'somethin' special fer afters'. And when their guests arrived, he and his sarge spent the first five minutes grinning at one another like loonies and hitting one another's arms the way they'd done before, until Rosie begged them to stop before they did one another a mischief.

'It's always the same with him, when he meets up with his old mates,' Mrs Johnson said. 'I'm Minnie, by the way, which he'd ha' told you if he hadn't been so busy thumpin' your feller.'

At which the two men subsided somewhat and Jim remembered his duties as a host and took their coats and hats and hung them on the landing and they all went into the kitchen for their supper. It was a lively meal. The conversation never stopped, because although Jim and Jack didn't say anything about their time in the trenches, which she'd expected, they had a lot to tell one another about their families and their jobs.

Jack read gas meters. 'I wouldn't say it was a barrel a' laughs,' he said, 'but it pays the rent.'

'Which is all you can say for most jobs,' Jim told him, cheerfully. ''Cept fer Rosie's. She's an artist's model.'

Jack and Minnie were very impressed. 'Straight up?' he said.

So Rosie told them about it, in entertaining detail, which impressed them even more. Their admiration made her feel so swollen-headed she was quite relieved when the meal came to an end, and the girls had been sent to bed, and she could take her guests to the front room to sit round the fire on her nice new settee and roast chestnuts and change the subject. But naturally, now that the girls were out of earshot, the conversation moved on to the punch-up in Worthing.

'Who *were* those awful people?' Jim wanted to know. 'Where did they all come from?'

'British Union of Fascists,' Jack told him, 'an' a right load a' blighters they are.'

'I can't stand the sight of 'em,' Minnie said. 'Give me the creeps they do. Wouldn't touch 'em with a bargepole.'

'They put the wind up me,' Rosie confessed. 'I don't mind telling you. All that marching about an' shouting. It's like the Germans. I can't see any difference between 'em. I hope they don't start burning books. Or building concentration camps.'

'I reckon it's play-actin',' Jim said, hoping it was true. 'That's all. Dressin' up in uniforms an' poncin' about, feelin' important. They was off PDQ when we stood up to 'em.'

'Only wish it *was* a play, ol' son,' Jack told him, peeling a chestnut. 'Trouble is, it ain't. They means business. That Mosley bloke reckons we're all gonna turn Fascist same as the Jerries an' the Eyeties, an' he's gonna be another Hitler. Turn Fascist an' beat up the Jews. That's the size of it. You should see the sort a' things they do in the East End. That's why we was there, tryin' to stop the beggar.'

'He couldn't do it though, could he?' Rosie said. 'I mean surely nobody'd vote for him here.'

'Wouldn't put it past 'em,' Jack said. 'He's got the *Daily Mail* behind 'im, yer see. That Lord Rothermere's all for 'im. There's articles about how wonderful he is nearly every day a' the week. An' 'e funds the beggar so 'e's not short of a few bob. More's the pity. They vote for 'is lot in Worthing. 'E's got a man called Budd elected to the council. The *Mail* was cock-a-whoop. They said Worthing was the Munich a' the South.'

It was an intriguing and informative conversation and it went on until past eleven o'clock, when Minnie gave her husband a nudge and said they'd have to be going.

'He's a good bloke,' she said to Rosie, 'but he'll talk till the cows come home. Never knew such an ol' jaw-me-dead.'

'You can always come again,' Rosie told her, 'now you know where we are.'

'Wild horses wouldn't keep us away,' Jack said, and grinned at her.

'Maybe we could invite 'em next week,' Jim said, when they'd gone.

'I'd rather you didn't,' Rosie said. 'It's Mary's exam an' I think she's worried about it.'

He made a grimace. 'Never,' he said, disbelievingly. 'She's a tough little thing. Like her sister.'

But Rosie had doubts and, when the morning of the examination arrived, she knew she was right, because Mary looked so pale and ate so little. She said goodbye to her father when he went to work and kissed Gracie goodbye when she left for school, but she didn't smile. She just sat looking at the food congealing on her plate.

'You've lost your appetite,' Rosie said as she took the plate away.

Mary nodded. 'I don't feel much like eating this morning,' she admitted.

Rosie sat down beside her daughter and put an arm round her shoulders. 'What's up?' she said. 'You worried about this scholarship?'

Mary kept her eyes down and her face looked so drawn it tugged Rosie's heart. 'You won't be cross with me if I fail, will you?' she said.

'Cross?' Rosie said. 'The idea! 'Course I won't. If you

did fail, which I very much doubt, I'd give you twice the cuddles and twice the treats to make up for it.'

And at that Mary threw her arms round her mother's neck and burst into tears. 'I'll do my very, very best,' she wept. 'I promise. My very, very, very best.'

Rosie kissed her hair and hugged her while she cried. Then she got a flannel and cleaned the tears from her poor girl's face.

'Now,' she said, 'I'm going to walk down the road with you an' keep you company. Not to the school. Don't worry. Just to the main road or until you meet up with your friends. All right?'

And it *was* all right. Mary seemed quite glad she was there and Rosie was comforted to be able to look after her. Not that it stopped her worrying. She fretted all morning, picking things up and putting them down, unable to settle to anything. It was as bad as it had been when Gracie took the exam. But she just had to bite her nails until Mary came home. It was a great relief to hear her footstep on the stairs.

'How did you get on?' she asked, speaking before she'd thought whether it was sensible or not.

Mary smiled at her, looking almost like her old self. 'It was all right,' she said. 'Some of it was easy. Can I play out when I've had tea?'

And that was that. Then there was nothing to do but wait for the results like they'd done before. There was the last gypsy to be painted, which kept her occupied for a week or two, but for most of the time she did her house-work mechanically, tried not to worry too much and worried all the time. When the end of term arrived bringing the familiar brown envelope, she was in such a state her hands were shaking as she opened it and she had to read it twice before her brain could take it in.

Mary had passed the examination with distinction, just like her sister, and had won a scholarship to attend an LCC grammar school. A list of schools was enclosed.

*

Once her worry had lifted, Rosie could see that spring was beckoning to them from the parks and gardens. The sky above her head was richly blue, the daffodils danced, they had enough money for rent, school uniforms, new shoes, even the occasional trip to the seaside. All was well with their world. Out in the wider world the news was nowhere near so good but she didn't take any notice of it. Let that horrible Hitler rant and roar. It was nothing to do with her. Let Mussolini scream that Italy needed an empire. It was nothing to do with her. Even when the *Daily Mail* shouted that the BUF was holding a rally at Olympia on the seventh of June and that it was going to be the biggest and most important political event of the year, she took no notice. It was nothing to do with her.

But she was wrong. There was a member of her family in the audience that night and one she might have expected to be there if she'd given it any thought.

Chapter Twenty-Four

Mr Herbert Matthews had a seat in the stalls for the
Fascist rally at Olympia that night and, from the moment
he entered the arena, he'd been thrilled and uplifted by
the implacable pounding power of it all. It was exactly as
a political meeting ought to be. The whole place was hung
with flags, Union Jacks alternating with the bold black
and yellow of the Fascist banner; there were powerful
amplifiers all around the hall blasting out the most
wonderful patriotic music, and thousands of blackshirts
lining the aisles, standing to attention, neat and well
groomed and detached, like soldiers on parade, and in the
middle of it all, a huge, high stage heavily draped in apricot
drugget and spotlit by a row of huge arc lamps, waiting
for the Leader. And what a wonderful thing it was when
he arrived, looking so tall and noble, as he strode through
the crowd. This is the man who will save us, Herbert

thought. A great man. And he settled down to absorb every word he said.

'This meeting,' Mosley said, his voice wonderfully clear, 'the largest indoor meeting ever held under one roof in Britain, is the culmination of a great national campaign, in which audiences in every city of this land have gathered to hear the fascist case. The slow, soft days are behind us, perhaps forever. Hard days and nights lie ahead. There will be no relaxing of the mind and will. The tents of ease are struck, and the soul of man is on the march.'

He was given such a loud cheer that it made Herbert's ears ring. But then some fool in the gallery started shouting. 'Fascism means murder!' over and over again. How uncalled for! Didn't do him any good though. The great arc lamps swung round and fastened on him like a searchlight and then the blackshirts moved in and punched him to the ground and dragged him out. Serve him right, the dirty Red, Herbert thought. And he turned round to enjoy the speech again. But now there were other people jumping to their feet and shouting, three more in another gallery and some in the stalls. The lights swung from one to the other and the whole place seemed to be on the move with black-shirts running in to deal with them and jumping over the seats to do it and men shouting and women screaming. It was absolutely disgraceful. But the leader took it calmly and, when the last of the Reds had been dragged away with blood pouring from his head, he spoke out boldly and said just the right thing. 'We shall not be deterred. You are not hurting us. We are hurting you.' Oh he was wonderful! Wonderful!

At the end of the evening, Herbert went home feeling twice the man he'd been when he entered the hall and more than twice as powerful. By the end of the week, he had joined the BUF. And the next Saturday, he went on a march in full uniform all through the East End. It was absolutely thrilling. The pavements were lined with sturdy-looking policemen there to make sure the Yids were kept in their place – and quite right too – and they had the street to themselves nearly all the way and marched along chanting and shouting. At one point a gang of yobs tried to push into the march, shouting their silly slogans – Reds and Yids of course, the usual sort of rabble – but they soon had them sorted out. The boys had their knuckle dusters on in seconds and laid about them right and left and the police were absolutely splendid, wading in with their truncheons. He felt so powerful it was as if he'd doubled in size. This is the way to go on, he thought. We'll show 'em.

When they finally disbanded, he and another blackshirt called Henry travelled on the Tooting tram together and they had the most splendid conversation. Henry was a fine chap. Worked in the City so he knew what he was talking about and he said the only way out of the country's problems was to get rid of the Jews.

'They're like tapeworms in the body politic,' he said. He had a wonderful voice, very confident and loud. Everyone on the tram was looking at him. 'They eat our life's blood, filthy things. They need sorting out for good and all. That's what they need. Well I tell you I won't have anything in my house that's been *touched* by a Jew and I certainly wouldn't buy anything from one of them, ever. It's a matter of principle.'

'Quite right,' Herbert agreed. 'Neither would I. It's a matter of principle with me too.'

They talked all the way to the Broadway, where Herbert got off, and by the time they parted they were firm friends and promised to meet up again at the next demonstration. Herbert strode back to Totterdown Street feeling cock-a-whoop. If he'd been a vulgar sort of man, he'd have been whistling.

He hung up his hat in his usual neat way and strode into the dining room, ready for his dinner. His two weedy little boys were playing one of their stupid card games.

'Clear this rubbish off the table,' he said to them, speaking sharply because the sight of them annoyed him so much. He should have had two fine manly boys, not a pair of weeds like them. 'Look sharp or I'll take the cane to you.' It pleased him to see how quickly they scrambled the cards together and ran out of the room. That was the way to deal with weeds. Keep them on their toes. Kitty had better dish up his dinner PDQ or he'd have something to say to her. In fact he'd got quite a lot he wanted to say to her right now. She needed telling she wasn't to buy anything from any Jewish shops. He straightened his tie and smoothed his hair and called for her.

Kitty was in the kitchen carefully peeling the potatoes. He was so particular about his food and she didn't want to provoke him by leaving any eyes in. She'd been talking to the twins, who'd run out of the dining room in a bit of a state, poor little things. But when she heard his bellow, she put the potatoes aside, dried her hands, told the boys to stay where they were and went to see what he wanted.

'Ah,' he said. 'There you are. Now listen carefully. This is important.'

She took up her listening-carefully position and waited.

'Now,' he said in his pompous way, 'we've got some serious thinking to do. I've been speaking with some of the senior officers in the party and they are seriously of the opinion that the difficulties this country is presently experiencing could be ameliorated if more of us were to make a conscious decision not to have anything of Jewish origin in our homes and not to buy anything from any Jewish shops. That being so, from today, we will be following his instructions to the letter.' How well that sounded and how inescapably true.

Kitty gazed at him in disbelief, thinking how objection-able he was and wondering how he could possibly be so ridiculous and not realise it. Then he was talking again.

'So tomorrow, I want you to sort out all the things in this house that were produced or sold by Jews and get rid of them. Is that understood?'

She laughed at him. She really couldn't help it. He was

so ridiculous. 'If I was to do that,' she said, 'I'd be walking about stark naked.'

She was in danger of making him lose his temper. 'Try not to be coarse,' he said, sneering at her.

'It ain't coarse,' she said, laughing again. 'It's the gospel truth. I ain't got a stitch a' clothin' I ain't bought from Petticoat Lane, either from ol' Mr Segal or Mr Levy. An' while we're on about it, you couldn't find a kinder pair a' men than them two.'

'They're Jews!' he shouted at her. 'Dirty filthy Jews. They're tapeworms in the body politic. That's what they are. Tapeworms in the body politic. They need putting down, every last one of them.' He was into his stride now and enjoying himself immensely. This was the way to talk. 'Well you listen to me. You're not to have anything more to do with them. I forbid it. And you must take all that Jewish trash right back where it belongs.'

She stood in front of him, pale with the horror of what he was saying, her mind full of remembered words and images, old Mr Levy saying, '*Pretty Kitty Jackson, as I live an' breathe,*'; Mr Segal holding out Rosie's wedding suit so gently and offering to throw in the shoes to match; Manny Feigenbaum losing his son in that awful war and taking Jim on; all of them good, kind, gentle, loving men. How dare he say they should be put down! It was obscene. 'Now look here,' she said, her cheeks flushed, 'they're some a' the cleanest men I ever come across an' the kindest an' the nicest. You stand there callin' 'em names, an' saying they ought ter be killed, an' you don't know nothin' about 'em.' She knew she was fighting him and that it was dangerous, but now she'd begun she couldn't stop.

His face was distorted with anger. He stood up and walked round the table until they were standing toe to toe. 'Don't you *dare* speak to me like that,' he said and punched her in the face.

It was such a powerful blow, it knocked her off her feet and while she was lying on the carpet, he kicked her with those awful jackboots. The pain of it was so sharp and terrible it made her scream. She put up an arm to protect her face and tried to roll away from him.

'Get up!' he roared at her. 'Get up! You're like an animal. Rolling about like that. Get up! Get up!'

But she could barely move, and simply lay where she was and went on screaming.

By then he was beginning to feel afraid of what he'd done but that only made him frantically angry. 'Stop it!' he yelled. 'Stop that noise! You'll have the neighbours in. Have I got to take the cane to you?'

She was stunned and in so much pain she could barely think, but she made an enormous effort and managed to pick herself up and stumble to the door. She was aware that the side of her face was throbbing and that there was a sharp pain in her chest, and she saw that the boys were sitting on the stairs, looking sweaty, pale and very frightened. We must get out, she thought, now, this minute, we can't stay here, not now. She staggered into the kitchen to find her handbag and had to lean on the table for a little while to get her breath, noticing, in a vague and almost detached way, that there was blood dripping from her face and falling onto her hands. She picked up the tea towel automatically, to staunch the flow. Then she grabbed hold of Bobby's hand, told Georgie to follow her, opened the front door as quietly as she could and they all ran.

*

Rosie had had a rather worrying letter from her brother Johnnie that afternoon. She was sitting in the kitchen, reading it through for the second time and waiting for the kettle to boil, when the phone rang. She was still pondering the problem the letter had set her and for a few seconds she couldn't make out who it was on the end of the line. It was the oddest voice, and it seemed to be bubbling and gulping. 'Hello?' she said. 'Who's that?'

'Is Jim . . . there?' the voice said. 'Is . . . my Jim . . . there?'

'Kitty?' Rosie said. 'What's up?'

'Is my Jim . . . there?' Kitty said, struggling to speak clearly. 'I got ter . . . Thing is . . . Can't breathe. Is my Jim . . .?'

She's hurt, Rosie thought. She's been hurt. Or she's ill. 'He's just coming upstairs now,' she said. 'I can hear him. Hang on. I'll get him.' And did.

He took the phone from her calmly. 'Hello, our kid,' he said. But then his expression changed. 'Where are you?' he said. 'Speak slow. It's a bit hard to hear yer.'

Kitty was gasping but she managed to tell him. 'In the . . . phone box. End . . . a' the road. Common end.'

'Stay there,' he said. 'I'll be with you as soon as I can.'

'She's hurt,' he said to Rosie. 'Sounds serious. I'm gonna go an' get her.'

'Shall I come with you?'

'Where are the girls?'

'Pictures. I could leave 'em a note.'

'No,' he said. 'You wait here. I'll be as quick as I can.' And he was off.

Rosie's brain slid into gear. I'll bet that bloody monster's hit her, she thought, and if she's hurt bad, she'll need a doctor and it's Saturday. They don't all shut down of a weekend though. There must be one open. Or a hospital somewhere. I'll go down and see if Mrs Rogers knows. She turned the kettle off and headed for the stairs.

And the phone rang again. What's happened now? she thought and she ran back, feeling alarmed and moving so quickly she was breathless when she picked up the receiver. 'Yes,' she said, 'what is it?'

'Delectable creature,' Gerry's voice said. 'I've got a favour to ask.'

'Oh,' she said. 'It's you. I'm sorry I can't talk, something's come up. Can I ring you back?'

'Of course,' he said. 'I hope it's not anything serious . . .' but she had already hung up and was halfway down the stairs.

Mrs Rogers was shocked to hear that their nice Kitty

had been hurt, but she knew exactly where to find a doctor and got the address at once. 'She's a lady doctor,' she said, 'and ever so kind. I been to see her twice. Newington Causeway by the Borough Tube station. Big brass plaque on the door. You can't miss it. Poor Kitty. What a business. An' here's your girls come home. Well that's one good thing. Evening Gracie. Evening Mary.'

'Why is it a good thing we've come home?' Gracie asked as she followed her mother upstairs. 'What's up?'

'Let's get in the flat,' Rosie said, 'an' I'll tell you.'

*

Jim's second tram seemed to take an eternity to get to Tooting, and by the time he was there, he was so anxious, he ignored his gammy leg and ran to the phone box. Kitty was sitting on the kerb with her twins on either side of her and she looked so awful it gave him a shock, even though he'd tried to prepare himself for what he would find. Her face was puffy and swollen, her nose clogged with congealed blood and she had the beginnings of a black eye. Even worse she was leaning over sideways and plainly finding it difficult to breathe.

'Oh my good God,' he said. 'What happened to you?'

"E lost . . . 'is rag,' Kitty panted.

'I should think he bloody did,' Jim said.

'He was . . . worked up,' Kitty tried to explain. 'He's . . . joined the Fascist party . . . you see . . . an' they gets 'im . . . in a lather.'

'I don't care what they gets him in,' Jim said furiously. 'He's got no right to use you as a punchbag. Come on. I'm taking you home. Grab hold a' me hand.'

Kitty found the walk to the tram stop extremely difficult but Bobbie carried her handbag and Georgie held her hand and she clung onto Jim's arm and took it slowly. They were all very glad when the tram arrived and she'd climbed aboard. And, although she found the motion of the tram very painful and her face was stiff and sore, she didn't complain or cry and even managed to smile at Jim now and then to reassure him.

Rosie was waiting for them at the tram stop, calm and in complete command. 'You boys go back to the flat,' she said. 'The girls are waiting for you. Get the table set and rustle up a few more chairs, an' we'll have supper when we get back. I got you an appointment at the doctor's, Kitty. It's not far. Hold on to our arms. We'll soon have you there, won't we Jim?'

Kitty struggled valiantly, but it was a difficult walk, especially after the buffeting she'd taken on the tram. But the doctor, who was small, elderly and thorough, was every bit as kind as Mrs Rogers had promised. She examined her patient very gently and told her that she had a cracked rib that was going to be very painful for quite a few days, but she would bind it up and it would heal in its own time and that, as well as that, her nose was broken. 'It isn't blocking your air passages,' she said. 'When the swelling subsides, you'll be able to breathe a great deal more easily than you can now.' Then she asked, 'How did it happen?' And Kitty told her, haltingly and painfully.

'I will write you a full report of what I have found in this examination,' the doctor said, after she'd bound Kitty's chest. 'You might need to take this further.' And when Kitty looked confused, she added, 'That is entirely up to you of course. But if you *do* decide to take action, you will need medical evidence of your injuries. My advice for the moment, is for you to take things easy for a week or two, until your bruises have cleared, and if you don't feel quite a lot better by then, which you ought to do, come back and see me again.'

'She's going to stay with me an' her brother,' Rosie said. 'He's waiting for us in your waiting room. We'll look after her.'

The doctor smiled and said that was a very good idea and Rosie paid the fee and thanked her and then she and Jim held Kitty up as she staggered back to the flat. She was totally exhausted by the time she got there and sank into Jim's armchair as if she never wanted to get up again. The girls and the twins had laid the table ready for supper and gathered chairs from the bedrooms so that there were enough for all seven of them.

'Now then,' Rosie said when they were all comfortably seated. 'First things first and then we'll have some supper. You three are *not* going back to Tooting tonight, or ever if you don't want to. But certainly not tonight. I can make you up a bed on the sofa, Kitty, and the boys can sleep in

Mary's bed and the girls'll double up in Gracie's. We've sorted it all out, haven't we girls?'

'Really an' truly?' Bobby asked. 'Don't we have to go home then?'

'No,' Rosie told him. 'You can stay here with us, until your mummy's decided what to do. You don't have to go anywhere.'

'What about school?' Georgie asked, nervously. 'Daddy's ever so particular about us going to school. He gives us the cane something awful if we don't go to school.'

Rosie was shocked to hear it, but she didn't comment. There'd be time for that later. 'Daddy won't know *what* you're doing if you're here with us.' she said. 'He can be particular all he likes.'

But Kitty was looking anxious and finding it extremely hard to breathe. "E'll come . . . after us . . . our Rosie,' she panted. "E might be . . . on 'is way . . . this minute.'

'Shop'll be shut in ten minutes,' Jim said, looking at the clock. 'So if 'e's comin' 'e'll 'ave ter look sharp or 'e'll 'ave a wasted journey. I'll nip down, an' warn Mr Rogers not to let him in, if that'll make you any easier.'

"E'll make . . . a scene,' Kitty worried. "E's a . . . tartar . . . when 'e makes . . . a scene.'

'So I've noticed,' Jim said grimly. 'Don't you worry yer 'ead, kid. I'll sort 'im out.'

'We can't . . . stay here, Jim. 'E'll find us . . . sure as fate.'

'Put the kettle on girls and go and get a tin of condensed

milk, an' a straw for your Aunty,' Rosie said, 'an' we'll make a pot a' tea. It'll have to be condensed milk till the milkman comes tomorrow, but you won't mind that, will you? Then I'll tell you what I think you ought to do.'

The tea was made, the straw found and when they were settled, she told them her plan.

'Now then,' she said, taking Johnnie's letter out of the oddments drawer, 'I'm going to read you a letter I had from my Johnnie this afternoon. I was reading it when you phoned me Kitty. Right?' And she read. '*Dear Rosie, I got a bit of news what I thought you might like for to here. Me and Connie Taylor is walking out. We hopes for to get wed in the autumn when the harvest is in, tho it might take longer. Onny the thing is Pa ent too well. He is a bit frail like and it is a bit of a worry to us. The truth is he needs more looking after now being frail and he needs more than just me to look after him so Connie will help out once the autumn comes. I am hoping Tess will help out till then to tide us over.*' Then she looked up at Kitty and grinned. 'How would it be if I was to take you and the boys down to Binderton first thing tomorrow morning, an' tell 'em you'd come to help 'em. What d'you think? You'd be right out a' harm's way and Johnnie'd have someone to look after Pa while he's at work. I think it'ud suit all of us, all round.'

It took Kitty a few seconds to digest the idea, while the others watched her and waited, the twins in awe, Gracie and Mary swelling with pride because their mum was so wonderfully in command, Jim remembering that night in St James' Park, when she'd been so determined to send *him* to Binderton to save him from the call up, and they'd had their first row. She was wrong then, he thought, admiring her, but she's bang to rights now.

Eventually Kitty swallowed and spoke. 'Yes . . .' she said. 'Tha's a . . . good idea. Providin' . . . they don't mind.'

'Mind?' Rosie said. 'They'll be glad to see you, you daft happorth. You're just the sort a' person they need. That's settled then. Now let's have supper.'

They had fish and chips, naturally, except for Kitty who could barely manage to open her mouth by then, but sucked up some tomato soup through a straw and was applauded for it. Then they tried to settle for the night and Kitty pulled at Rosie's sleeve and whispered to her that she'd have to put a wad of towels in the boys' bed. 'They . . .has . . . little accidents . . . sometimes.'

Rosie understood at once. 'You mean they wet the bed? Is that it?' she said cheerfully. 'Don't worry. We'll pad it all up for 'em. An' I'll bet Pa's still got a rubber sheet you could use when you're down there. He had to have one for Ma when she was so ill. Leave it to me. We'll get you settled first, 'cause you need a good night's sleep. We've got a long day ahead of us tomorrow.'

And a long day it was, because they caught the first train out of Victoria. Rosie and Gracie got up at dawn to strip the single beds and make them up again all fresh and clean and put the dirty sheets and the wet towels to steep in the copper. 'So as not to leave any evidence behind in case *he* comes here,' Rosie said to Jim. At breakfast Gracie explained that she and Mary were going to Binderton too, 'then Mum can look after Aunty Kitty and we can take a twin apiece.' So there were six of them travelling which worked out very well, because it meant that they had a compartment to themselves and that gave Kitty a chance to tell Rosie what had happened to her the previous day. She'd been thinking about it off and on all night and now it was necessary to spill it all out and weep it through, even though crying took away what little breath she had left.

"E's such a tartar,' she said. 'We 'ave ter . . . give 'im . . . 'is own way in . . . everything . . . or you never heard such ructions. 'E was all on an' on . . . about the Jews . . . an' how they was filthy dirty . . . an' they ought to be . . . got rid of, an' I couldn't . . . stand it . . . no more. An' the way he . . . lays into my . . . poor boys . . . you'd never believe.'

'Well you've left him now, ent you?' Rosie said. 'You don't have to see him ever again. Not if you don't want to. It's all over. Dry your eyes. We're nearly at Chichester.'

When they reached the halt at Lavant, Rosie and Gracie walked on either side of their poor Kitty so that she could lean on their arms all the way to the cottage and Mary followed behind them, holding the twins' hands. It seemed odd to them to be walking through the fields in such a sombre procession. But once they reached the cottage, they had such a loving welcome that the day was completely changed.

'My stars!' Johnnie said when he opened the door. 'What's happened to *you*?'

'She's been beat up by that horrible husband of hers,' Rosie told him.

'My stars!' Johnnie said again. 'Come in. I got a leg a' lamb in the oven. I was just givin' it a bastin'. Look who's come, Pa. It's our Rosie, an' Kitty an' the kiddies.'

They crowded into the cottage and were kissed and hugged and the tale was told again, this time in rather easier detail.

'Just as well we got a joint,' Pa said, grinning at his son. 'He's turned out ever such a good cook. Ent you, Johnnie?'

'We'll need a few more vegetables though,' Johnnie said. 'I've only got enough for the two of us. There's lots in the garden. The beans 'ave come along lovely this year.'

'The kids'll pick 'em,' Rosie said. 'Where's your tayties? I'll do *them.*'

So the meal was prepared and more chairs borrowed from the neighbours and they sat round Pa's familiar table and made what he called 'a plan of action'.

'We can't have our Kitty knocked about,' he said. 'That'ud never do.'

'I thought . . . he'd come back . . . after me, today,' Kitty told him. 'That's why Rosie brought me . . . here.'

'Quite right,' Pa said. 'You'll be safe here. You can sit out in the sun. Get a spot a' fresh air. Have you right in no time.' He was taking command and quite his old self, frail though he looked. Dear Pa, Rosie thought. Hadn't she known this was the best place to come to?

By the time they'd done justice to the roast, everything

was settled. Kitty and the boys would have the girls' old room and there *was* a rubber sheet. Kids who wet the bed were no problem in that house.

'Have we got to go to school?' Bobby asked.

'Not till September,' Pa told him. 'There's no rush. Have a nice long summer in the fields eh? Put some roses in your cheeks. That's the style.'

'You can go to the village school,' Rosie told them. 'That's where me, an' Johnnie, an' Tess, an' Edie went. You'll like it there.'

'I'll take you down the river, arter dinner,' Johnnie said. 'Might find some tiddlers. That 'ud be a lark.'

'An' me an' the girls'll make a bit of a cake,' Rosie said. 'How would that be?'

'You can take some back to your Jim,' Pa said. 'Left on his own, poor critter.'

'He's holding the fort, Pa,' Rosie explained. 'In case Kitty's husband comes after her.'

'Won't do him no good if Jim's there,' Pa said and chuckled.

Chapter Twenty-Five

Herbert Matthews got up late that morning, feeling irritable and annoyed. He'd waited for his dinner for over an hour the previous evening. Over an hour mark you. It wasn't as if he'd been impatient. And then, when he'd gone out to chivvy her up a bit, he'd found an empty house and nothing to eat except a chunk of sweaty cheese and some stale bread, which was most unsatisfactory. It was an absolute disgrace. He couldn't think what she was playing at.

Oh well, he told himself as he got ready for bed, she'll come back when it's dark. She's bound to. She won't want to stay out there all on her own in the dark. And neither will those two stupid boys. On which satisfactory thought he settled to sleep. But the house was still empty the next morning and there was no one to cook him his breakfast and, by then, her absence was making him angry.

She's run off to that brother of hers, he thought, telling

tales. That's what she's done. The idea brought a spasm of fear because Jim was a big bloke and he remembered that he'd been a docker before the war – as Kitty was constantly telling him – and everybody knew what yobs *they* were, but he recovered himself resolutely. I'm not having any nonsense, he thought. I shall go straight there and bring her back home where she belongs. Then we'll see who's boss.

He dressed himself very carefully in his second-best suit and a clean white shirt with a stiff collar, and applied plenty of Brylcreem to his hair so that it would lie flat even if he got into a temper, and set off. It took him quite a time to find the right place. He'd assumed that Jim and Rosie would live in a house of some kind, the way most respectable people did, so to discover that it was a flat above a news-agents – and one that opened on a Sunday, what's more – gave him a distinct sense of superiority. If they're hiding her up there, I shall soon have her out, he thought, and strode into the shop.

'Mr Matthews,' he announced to the shopkeeper. 'Come to see Mr and Mrs Jackson.'

'Oh yes,' Mr Rogers said, giving him a long look and he went through the door and called up the stairs, 'Visitor fer you Jim,' the way he and Jim had arranged.

'Send 'im up,' Jim called back.

So Mr Rogers did, saying. 'Top a' the stairs turn right.'

How common, Herbert thought. But they'd be easy to handle in a place like this.

Jim was waiting at the top of the stairs and led him into

the kitchen without saying a word. Then he sat down in his chair and left his visitor standing.

There's no call for rudeness, Herbert thought, but he decided to ignore it for the moment. 'Nice to see you Jim,' he said smoothly. 'You don't happen to know where Kitty is, do you?'

'No, I don't,' Jim said. 'An' if I did I wouldn't tell you.'

Herbert was ruffled. 'There's no need to take that tone, I'm sure,' he said. 'I asked you a civil question. I expect a civil answer.'

'What you expect an' what you'll get, are two different things,' Jim said, 'as you'll find out.'

'I expect my brother-in-law to help me to find my wife,' Herbert said stiffly, adding sarcastically, 'if that's not too much to ask. I know she's here.'

Jim got out of his chair. 'She ain't 'ere,' he said. 'There's no one here but me. But I'll give you a guided tour an' you can see fer yerself.' He led Herbert round the flat from one unoccupied room to the next and when they were back on the landing again he said, 'See?'

'Well she's not here now,' Herbert admitted. 'I'll grant you that. But she can't just go running off because we have a little argument.'

Jim's face darkened alarmingly. 'Argument?' he said. 'You beat the shit out of her.'

'So you *have* seen her,' Herbert sneered. 'She *has* been here.'

Before the words were out of his mouth, Jim had seized him by throat and thrust him bodily against the wall. 'Yeh.

I've seen her,' he said, 'so you listen an' you listen good. If you ever lay so much as a finger on my sister ever again, I'll punch your stinkin' teeth right down your stinkin' throat.'

Herbert struggled to fight back but he was held too firmly to move. 'You can't talk to me like that,' he squeaked. 'I'll call the police. I'll have the law on you.'

'You call the police, Sunshine,' Jim growled, holding him against the wall. 'You go ahead an' do it, an' I'll show 'em the way you've treated my sister an' then I'll have the law on *you*. You can't go round punchin' women whenever you feel like it an' think you're gonna get away with it.'

'She's my wife,' Herbert protested. 'I can do what I like with my wife. And you can't stop me.'

'You wanna bet?' Jim said, banging him against the wall again. 'I'll smash you ter pulp.' His anger was so powerful it was shaking him.

Herbert was afraid to look at him. 'Now look,' he spluttered. 'Look here! I mean to say!'

'You're a stinkin' little toerag,' Jim said and let him fall on the floor. 'Piss off out of it! I don't have wife-beaters in my house.'

'I'll be back,' Herbert shouted, as he staggered down the stairs. 'You needn't think you can beat me. I know my rights. She's my wife. You tell her that.'

But Jim was already on his way back to the kitchen, flexing his knuckles, and took no notice of him.

*

Later that day, when Pa and the others were sitting round the cottage table again, eating her cake, Rosie told them all what she was going to do next.

'We shall have to catch the train presently,' she said, 'on account a' getting the girls home for school, but first thing tomorrow morning I shall go out and hire a furniture van. I'll send you a postcard when I've done it, Kitty, and then you can come up to Tooting on Tuesday an' we'll collect your things. You got your return ticket, ent you? Right. Don't go in the house till I'm there, in case he's at home. Just wait for me at the corner a' Church Lane. All right?'

It was a well-planned operation. Kitty met the van as she was told and was very impressed by the size of it and the nice kind man who was driving it, and when they went to the house, it was empty.

'Just take whatever's yours,' Rosie told her, 'an' anythin' else you fancy that's small enough for him not to notice. I've got some boxes for your clothes an' the china.'

It took them the entire morning to pack even the few things Kitty decided to take and by the time the van had been driven to Binderton it was past teatime.

'Your gels'll be home from school be now,' Kitty worried. 'Will they be all right?'

'They'll be fine,' Rosie said. 'They're very grown up. I'll be back in time to kiss 'em goodnight.'

In fact they were so grown up, they'd cooked the supper and made a very good job of it.

'You had a phone call from that artist feller a' yours,' Jim said, as she dished up.

She'd forgotten all about poor Gerry and now she felt a bit guilty. 'He rang before, while all this was going on an' I promised to ring him back,' she remembered. 'An' then so many things happened it went clean out a' my head. I'll ring him in the morning.'

Which she did and was rather chastened when he said, 'I thought you'd forgotten all about me.'

'How can I help you?' she said, trying to make amends. 'You said there was something you wanted.'

'I've got a commission for a small portrait of an ancient roman,' he said. 'I'd like you to sit for it.'

She agreed at once, saying of course she would, providing he didn't make her look too ancient. And when he asked whether she could start that morning, she agreed with that too.

*

After all the drama of the last four days it was peaceful in his house in Cheyne Walk. Everything was so blessedly unchanged. It took him ages to prepare her for the portrait just as it always did. The long tunic had to be carefully draped and her hair had to be pinned up to look like a chignon and tied with plaited ribbon, but she found it comforting because it was what she expected. However, when she was posed in exactly the position he wanted, he stood back, took a long look at her and said something she didn't expect. 'This could be the last time you pose for me.'

'Are you going away?' she said.

'Yes, my dear beautiful Helen,' he told her. 'I'm going to America.'

'What for?' she asked. 'Is it another exhibition?'

'No,' he said sadly. 'The truth is, I'm running away.'

To hear him say such a thing made her shiver. 'That doesn't sound like you,' she said. 'What are you running from?'

That answer gave her a shock. 'The war.'

'What war?'

'The one that's coming. Sooner or later people will have to stand up to Herr Hitler.' And when she looked puzzled. 'Haven't you heard about the concentration camps? You must have done. It's been in all the newspapers.'

Now that he'd reminded her, she remembered there'd been something about a new concentration camp only the other week. 'Dachau,' she said, pronouncing it Datch-or. 'That's it, isn't it? It's where Hitler's going to lock a lot more people up. Gypsies, it said in my paper.'

'*Gypsies, Jews and other subnormals,*' he quoted and he retreated behind the easel and started to paint. It was some time before he spoke again and then it was with a controlled anger that was so unlike him she was shaken by it. 'They call us *untermensch,*' he said. 'Subhuman. If Hitler gets his way – and I can't see anyone stopping him now – not without a war – we shall be exterminated like so much vermin. That's what these camps are for. To kill Jews. And gypsies and anyone else he hates. He's unleashing the most terrible cruelty.'

She wanted to say it couldn't be true but she was

remembering the twisted faces of the blackshirts in Worthing as they rushed in to beat people up and the awful way Herbert had beaten poor Kitty. So she just said, 'Yes,' very sadly, and went on posing, gazing at the peaceful river the way she usually did.

'The artists are leaving Germany in droves,' he said after a while. 'Berthold Brecht and Kurt Weill have gone already. I can't say I blame them. He really hates them. And Kandinsky and Paul Klee are planning to go.'

The names meant nothing to her so she didn't answer him. It was easier to pose when she wasn't talking and he was talking enough for both of them, telling her what a twisted megalomaniac Hitler was and how he'd been vilifying the German Jews for years and blaming them for the ten million unemployed and everything else that was wrong in the country. 'You should see some of the dreadful cartoons the papers are printing,' he said. 'They're caricatures, of course – Jews with huge hooked noses and rapacious expressions – and they're being used to stir up hatred. Once you believe the cartoons, Jews become the easiest people to hate and blame. And once you start blaming people, the next step is to kick them out of the country or kill them. Nobody believes it in this country.'

'I do,' she said. 'It's what my ghastly brother-in-law says.' And she told him how Herbert had joined the BUF and how he'd beaten poor Kitty.

'That's horrible,' he said. 'But it doesn't surprise me. It's all of a piece with what's going on in Germany. These are ugly times. I tell you Rosie, if Hitler has his way, in a year or two there won't be a Jew left alive in the whole of Germany. And God help the Polish Jews if he invades Poland. Or any of us if he comes here.'

'Will he?' she asked.

'Very likely. He wants an empire, you see. All the big boys want empires these days. The smaller the ego the more they want to grab an empire. I think he'll invade a lot of places, Poland, Czechoslovakia, Russia even. His ambition is boundless. He says he's going to build a "Third Reich" and it's going to last for a thousand years. So yes. He could well come here and I don't want to be around if he does.'

'I don't think I'd want to be either, if I were a Jew,' she said, 'if that's what's going to happen.'

There was a very long pause while he painted and she thought about what he'd been saying. Then he spoke again, almost tentatively. 'I suppose you wouldn't like to come with me, would you?' he asked.

The question buzzed in the air between them, growing more significant by the second. It was an unfair temptation and they were both aware of it, he shaken by his uncharacteristic daring, she flattered to be asked and undeniably tempted. The thought of living in America, being spoilt and pampered, with nothing to do but model, right away from housework and family worries and all the cruel things that were happening because of those hideous Fascists, was enough to tempt a saint. If he'd asked her when their affair was just beginning and Jim was being such hard work, poor man, she might well have agreed to it. Now, so much had changed in their lives and so much had happened, it was impossible even to think about it. But impossible not to.

'I couldn't do that,' she said, eventually. 'You know that, don't you. Even if I wanted to. I couldn't leave Jim and my girls.'

'No,' he agreed from behind the easel. 'Of course. You *couldn't* do it. It was just a thought.' And he continued to paint in silence while she went on posing.

Their odd exchange cast a chill over the rest of the day and kept them both rather quiet. When he was driving her home, he asked, almost tentatively, if she would model for him again the next day. 'I'd like to get this finished before I go,' he said, 'so I've only got tomorrow.'

'When are you going then?' she asked.

'First thing Monday morning,' he said. And sighed.

The sigh made her suddenly and miserably aware that she really *was* going to lose him. 'If that's the case,' she said, 'I'll model for you whenever you need me.'

She posed for him all through the next day until the little picture was completed, more or less to his satisfaction, and was touched to notice that he was careful to talk about his famous sitters and tell her stories that wouldn't upset either of them. But he didn't suggest any 'sinful idleness' either and when he finally stopped painting and was cleaning his brushes, he said, 'Well that's that then,' and looked so downcast that she walked across the room and kissed him on both cheeks, the way he kissed her when they parted.

'War is a terrible thing,' he said. 'Some of the things I saw out there in France you would never believe.'

'I would,' she told him. 'My Jim was in the trenches.'

'Ah yes,' he said. 'I'd forgotten that.' Then he shook his head as if he was shaking away bad thoughts and smiled at her. 'I've got a little present for you and your Jim,' he said and walked across the room to pick up a canvas carefully wrapped in brown paper. 'I think you'll like it. Open it when you get home. Now we'd better get going or your family will be wondering where you are.'

It was a quiet journey back to Newcomen Street but when he'd opened the door for her and eased her out of the car with her present under her arm, he kissed her on both cheeks in his usual way.

'I don't know when we shall meet again,' he said. 'How can anyone tell? Look after yourself.'

'You too,' she said. 'I shall miss you.'

He looked at her for quite a long time and then bent his head to kiss her mouth, gently and sadly. 'My beautiful Helen,' he said. Then he got into his car and drove away without looking back.

She put her key into the lock and opened the front door, trying to be sensible about their parting – and failing.

Jim was waiting for her at the top of the stairs and he didn't look at all happy. 'You're late,' he said, frowning at her. 'I thought you was never comin' home. The gels 'ave gone to bed long since. What was all that kissin' about?'

She walked through into the kitchen and put the kettle

on. 'He's going to America,' she said. 'We were kissing goodbye.'

'So I noticed,' he said sourly. 'I was watchin' you out the winder.'

Her throat filled with a sudden panic. We're not going to argue about this now, she thought. Surely to goodness. Not when it's been over an' done with.

But it appeared that they were. 'If you ask me,' Jim said, settling into his chair, 'it's just as well he *is* goin' to America. If you ask me, I hope he'll stay there a good long time an' give us a bit a' peace. He was bein' a darn sight too familiar out there on the pavement.'

Bull by the horns, Rosie thought. 'He could be gone years, if you want to know,' she said. 'He's runnin' away from the Nazis on account of they're killing off all the Jews in Germany and he thinks they'll come over here an' kill him.'

'Well that just shows how stupid he can be,' Jim said. 'They won't come over 'ere. An' I'll tell you fer why. They won't come over 'ere on account of we won't let 'em.'

'He thinks there's going to be a war,' Rosie said, measuring the tea into the teapot. 'An' you can't say you don't, because that's exactly what your sarge was tellin' us the last time he was here and you were agreeing with him. If I remember rightly, he said Hitler was gearing up for it.'

'Well, it's on the cards,' Jim admitted. 'I'll grant you that. Depends if he invades Poland or Czechoslovakia. Just as well we're not runnin' away an all.'

'We're not Jewish,' she said, filling the teapot.

'Well, I s'pose not,' Jim admitted. 'You got a point there. Anyway I'm glad he's goin'.'

'He gave us a present,' Rosie said, remembering. She'd been so worried by the way Jim had been frowning, she'd left it on the landing. 'I'll just let this stand an' go an' get it.'

Jim wasn't impressed. 'It's a painting,' he said. 'Why does he imagine I'd want one of his paintings?'

Rosie was removing the paper, carefully. The painting was facing the wall but she was feeling too down to wonder what it was. She folded the paper and put it away in the oddments drawer. Then, without very much interest, she turned the canvas round. It was one of the first sketches he'd done in the Borough Market all those years ago. And there they were, she and Jim and little Gracie, standing round Mr Feigenbaum's stall, pretending to do the shopping. 'Oh my dear heart alive,' she said. 'Will you look at that?'

The sight of it had stopped Jim in mid rant. 'Don't we look *young!*' he said, staring at it.

'Gracie wasn't two. I was carryin' our Mary.'

'It's ever so good of you. I've seen that look on your face so many times, you wouldn't believe. An' 'e's caught the look of our Gracie too. Pretty little thing.'

'I've seen your look an' all,' Rosie said, gazing at it. She'd forgotten what a wonderful picture it was and how loving they'd been with one another. It was as if their younger selves were in the room with them, smiling their love at one another to remind them. 'Oh Jim!'

He left his chair and came to stand behind her, kissing her hair. 'That's a very good picture,' he said. The sight of it was making him change his opinion of Mr de Silva. Only slightly, of course, but it *was* changing. He could've painted us with any expression he liked, he thought, an' yet he painted us looking like *that*. Maybe there was some good in the man after all.

'I do love you,' she said, still gazing at the picture. 'You *do* know that don't you.'

'Couldn't be off knowing with that in the room,' he said and kissed her hair again.

She turned and put her arms round his neck, encouraged by the change in him. 'We've come through a lot together, you an' me,' she said.

'Yes,' he agreed. 'We 'ave. Couple of ol' war horses. That's us.'

A couple of old war horses sounded about right, although the word 'war' gave her pause and she crossed her fingers behind her back just to be on the safe side. One war in a lifetime was quite enough. 'Let's have our tea,' she said, 'an' we can decide where we're goin' to hang it.'

'Over the mantelpiece,' he said at once. 'Where else? In the middle a' the room where we can see it every day. After all, it's part of our lives.'

ENDEAVOURINK

Endeavour Ink is an imprint of Endeavour Press.

If you enjoyed *Everybody's Somebody* check out
Endeavour Press's eBooks here:
www.endeavourpress.com

For weekly updates on our free and discounted eBooks sign up
to our newsletter:
www.endeavourpress.com

Follow us on Twitter:
@EndeavourPress